1784

11/6/91 21.73 *

DARK OF THE MOON

G·K
Hall
&Co.

Also by Karen Robards
in Large Print:

Heartbreaker
Nobody's Angel
Walking after Midnight
Morning Song

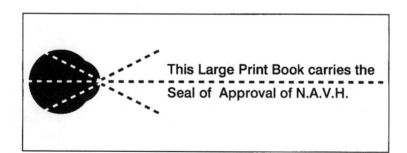

This Large Print Book carries the
Seal of Approval of N.A.V.H.

DARK OF THE MOON

KAREN ROBARDS

G.K. Hall & Co.
Thorndike, Maine

Library of Congress Cataloging in Publication Data

Robards, Karen.
   Dark of the moon / Karen Robards.
     p.   cm.
   ISBN 0-7838-8228-9 (lg. print : hc : alk. paper)
   1. Large type books.   I. Title.
   [PS3568.O196D37 1997]
   813′.54—dc21   97-14533

This book is dedicated with love to
the memories of my maternal grandparents,
Kate Laha Skaggs and Albert Leslie Skaggs.
And, as always, to Doug and Peter.

I

❈ ❈ ❈ ❈ ❈ ❈ ❈ ❈ ❈ ❈ ❈ ❈ ❈ ❈ ❈

Caitlyn O'Malley was a lass, but none would have
known it who saw her swaggering along Dublin's
narrow cobbled laneways on that misty April afternoon in 1784. For the last eight of her fifteen
years of life, she had aped the role of a male. So
successful was she at it that she herself forgot her
true sex for days at a time. Her unkempt black
hair was cropped into a ragged bob that just
touched her shoulders. A constant layer of grime
obscured delicate features. Thick-lashed kerry
blue eyes, big as agates in her hunger-pinched
face, passed almost unnoticed amidst all her dirt.
With her spindly frame clad in shabby, castoff
coat and breeches that were two sizes too large,
she looked as much like a ragged twelve-year-old
boy as her companion, who could lay claim to
the condition in truth.

"B'God, O'Malley, would ye take a whiff o'
that, now?" Willie Laha stopped to sniff enviously
at the tray of meat pastries that the vendor was
setting out on the counter of his cart. They were
so fresh steam was rising from them. Staring at
the golden-brown crusts, sniffing their delicious
aroma, Caitlyn felt her mouth water. Pangs of
hunger twisted her stomach. Neither she nor Willie had eaten the night before nor all that day,

7

and it was nigh onto evening again. Pickings for supper were likely to be slim. The gangs of urchins and beggars that haunted the mews intersecting O'Connell Street had become so notorious that the merchants were going about armed. It was worth a lad's life to pinch so much as an apple. With the street fair in progress and the workers from the quays crowding the street every night, pickings should have been plentiful. But revelers were guarding their purses, and merchants were watching eagle-eyed over their wares. Only a week ago, Tim O'Flynn, one of the loose gang of boys that was the closest Caitlyn had to family since her mother died, had been hanged for stealing two plums and a chunk of bread. With that example fresh in mind, Caitlyn was more cautious than was her wont, although hunger was beginning to override her unaccustomed prudence. If she did not steal, she would not eat.

"You there! Move along or I'll be takin' me stick to your hides!" The growl came from the red-faced merchant, who had noticed their interest and was glaring ferociously at them, stout stick in hand. Caitlyn made a rude gesture in return but did not resist as Willie pulled her along the street, which was lined on both sides by vendors' carts displaying everything from meat pasties to leather shoes.

"We'd best hold off until Doyle and the rest come up to us. Two alone's not good odds."

Caitlyn scowled at Willie's caution. O'Flynn's fate was making women out of the lot of them.

They had to shake the specter of it if they were to eat on anything approaching a regular basis. It was foolishness pure and simple to think — as Willie and some of the others did — that they were cursed by bad luck. O'Flynn just hadn't been careful enough or fast enough. The lesson to be learned there was not to stop stealing, but to make certain sure not to be caught. And she wouldn't be. She'd always been careful, and she was fleet of foot, the fastest of them all. No fat merchant would catch her, like had happened to O'Flynn. And Jamie McFinnian, who'd been taken the month before O'Flynn, had always been clumsy. That he'd escaped capture as long as he had was a miracle, nothing less. No, it was not bad luck dogging them at all, at all. It was bad judgment, pure and simple.

"Look there." With a nudge she directed Willie's attention farther down the street. A tall, lean man in a froth of lace and finery was making his way with fine unconcern through the dirty, bare-armed quay workers who with their doxies were beginning to fill the street. As they watched, he pulled a gleaming gold watch from his pocket, flipped it open with a polished thumbnail, and looked at it for a brief moment before carelessly replacing it. Scorn twisted Caitlyn's mouth into a sneer. Obviously the gentleman was new-come from bloody England, one of the hated Ascendancy, and none had thought to warn him not to venture into the city's dangerous Irish quarters. He strolled along as though he hadn't a care in the world, completely oblivious to the sullen looks he was receiving from the shabby tides of the oppressed surrounding him.

"A right lamb for the fleecin', Willie, me lad." Caitlyn's eyes gleamed with a combination of avarice and hatred as they fixed on the gentleman. The hatred had nothing to do with him personally. The Irish hated the English from birth onward. It was bred in blood and bone. "Sent straight from the Holy Mother to brighten our path. These boyos'll have every stitch off him before he goes much further, so we'd best be gettin' the cream off the top."

Willie looked around uneasily. He was redheaded and freckle-faced under the layers of grime, but instead of being bold and hot-tempered, as redheads were supposed to be, he was both cautious and easygoing by nature. O'Flynn's fate had merely aggravated unfortunate qualities that he already possessed. "Whisht, now, O'Malley, there's too many witnesses about. It's caught we'll be for certain sure."

"Don't be daft, Willie, there's naught that's different from always." She was impatient. "We hit him and run, just like we've done more times than you can count. We'll have his pockets cleaned and be off before he even knows something's amiss."

"He's bloody tall." Willie both sounded and looked dubious.

"Holy Mary, Willie, and here's you wantin' to ride with the Dark Horseman. He'd never take such a wee coward." Caitlyn conjured up the name of Ireland's boldest highwayman deliberately. Becoming a member of his gang had long been a dream of Willie's, a dream with about as much substance as one of Ireland's mists. The man was practically a national hero, after all. What accounted for his astounding popularity was that he robbed only the rich Anglicans of the hated Ascendancy and was rumored to share his largesse with his starving countrymen. His identifying mark was the Cross of Ireland, which he always wore in the form of a silver pendant hanging from a chain about his neck. That was how the people knew that the Dark Horseman was as Irish as they. Although the Horseman was highly revered and much talked about in the Irish quarters, and regarded with universal fear among the Anglicans, no one could lay claim to have ridden with him, or knew his true identity, or even if he truly existed. But his name could galvanize Willie, without fail.

"I'm no coward! And the Horseman would take me sure! Just you watch this!" Willie was already starting toward the gentleman. Caitlyn followed a little way behind him, a small grin curving her lips. invoking the Dark Horseman was better than flaying Willie with a whip.

"Please yer lordship, c'n ye spare a copper? For a starvin' boyo?" Willie had reached the gentleman and was bowing and scraping in front of him, whining his beggar's whine. The purpose was to focus the victim's attention on Willie to the exclusion of all else. While the gentleman was distracted, Caitlyn, walking past, would supposedly stumble and fall against him, muttering a pardon as she deftly relieved him of his purse and the gleaming gold watch that was tucked into a waistcoat pocket, its chain glinting across the fine white cloth covering his middle.

"Don't beg, lad," the mark said gruffly, scowling down at Willie, who continued to grovel and whine before him. "You shame yourself."

Here was a fine gentleman in truth, Caitlyn sneered silently as she approached, worried about a starving lad shaming himself. She'd like to see him forced to steal and beg and do anything and everything for a crust of bread. From the prosperous look of him, he'd never so much as missed a meal in his life. His hair, black as her own but curly and so clean it shone with blue lights, was secured by a fine black bow into a little tail at the nape of his neck. His face was narrow and his features were not unhandsome, but his skin was whitened by an application of rice powder, making it look as soft and smooth as any female's. His frock coat, a deep bottle green in color, was of fine wool cloth. The waistcoat beneath it was blinding white, as was the frilled jabot at his neck. A ceremonial sword in a jeweled scabbard hung from his waist. His breeches were a light tan, very tight over the long muscles of his thighs, and his clocked stockings appeared to be made of silk. They were white, and spotless, which told much about how he had passed the hours of this day. His black leather shoes sported, of all things, two-inch-high red heels. This, then, was the secret of his intimidating height.

"Please, sor. . . ." Willie continued to whine and scrape, blocking the gentleman's way. Caitlyn, passing by on the outside, pretended to stumble over a loose cobblestone. She fell heavily against the gentleman, her hands moving with practiced speed even as she mumbled an apology. Swift as a snake, her right hand slid into the pocket of his coat and emerged with a satisfyingly heavy purse. Then she reeled against him again as though she had not quite recovered her balance, while her fingers closed over his watch. A small smile curved her lips as she withdrew her hand. The English were ever as stupid as they were evil.

"Hold, now." The voice was quiet but steely enough to send shivers down her spine. It unnerved her more than the hard hand that closed like an iron band around her wrist. Holy Mary, she'd been nabbed!

"Run, Willie!" she shrieked. Willie's eyes widened as he took in her plight. He stared at her for a single wild instant, horror plain on his face. Then, with a high-pitched wail, he turned tail. Caitlyn's last sight of him was a pair of kicked-up heels as he disappeared into the stream of quay workers.

"Let go!" Pulling frantically against the hard hand that imprisoned her, Caitlyn heard her heart pound out loud rhythms of terror. If she

13

didn't get loose she'd hang. . . .

In a final, desperate bid for freedom she flew at her captor like an enraged gamecock, kicking his shins with the hard edge of her square-toed shoes and launching a mighty blow upward with her free fist that, had it connected with his nose, would likely have broken it. But he was tall and he jerked his head out of range, so that her fist only caught him a glancing blow on the neck. Still, it was enough to make him cough — and to tighten that imprisoning hand until the watch dropped from her numb fingers to clatter against the cobblestones and she was forced to her knees. It was all she could do not to whimper as he scooped up his watch and restored it to his pocket without easing that bone-crushing grip. Kneeling, white-faced with pain and burgeoning panic, she was nevertheless defiant as she stared up into that soft-no-longer face. Caitlyn O'Malley asked for no quarter, ever.

"Call the constabulary, then, ye bloody Sassenach!" she hissed, defeated but still proud. His eyes narrowed at her. She saw that beneath thick black brows they were a strange combination of blue and green, almost aqua, with a circle of black around the irises. Shivering, she thought: Devil's eyes, and barely managed to refrain from making the horned sign with her fingers that warded off the evil eye. The only thing that stopped her was a refusal to let him see her fear.

"Don't fash yerself, lad; we'll not be turning our own over to a bloody Orangeman!" That low-timbred rumble came from the huskiest man in the small crowd of quay workers and their women that had gathered around them. Caitlyn, still on her knees, looked at the angry faces with renewed hope. Had she robbed one of them, they'd have shown her no mercy. But a Sassenach . . . ! She might cheat the hangman yet.

Her captor pulled her to her feet, his eyes moving swiftly around the surrounding circle of the angry oppressed. He had to know fear, this Orangeman who could see the hatred the Irish felt for his kind in every eye focused on him; but if he did, not a flicker of it showed. He faced them with cool unconcern while their expressions turned uglier by the second.

Taking advantage of his predicament, Caitlyn jerked at her hand, which he still held imprisoned. The answering pressure on her wrist made her go weak at the knees. At the wince she could not control, a growl arose from the crowd. The man who had spoken earlier took a step forward. Almost casually, her captor transferred her wrist to his left hand and placed his right hand on the dress scabbard at his waist. Then, with a lightning movement, he pulled free a weapon that was no ceremonial sword good only for show, but a glistening-sharp rapier.

"Willing to die for the lad, are you?" The question was addressed to the crowd in general, but her captor's eyes held the eyes of the man who had spoken, the crowd's ringleader. Caitlyn knew that besting the ringleader was the swiftest and surest way to preserve oneself when faced with a hostile group. She had done it herself more than once, by whatever means it had taken. But now that her captor's attention was distracted . . . She was just drawing her foot back to kick the vulnerable back of his knee when another voice interrupted.

"What's amiss here?" A pair of burly constables shouldered their way through the shifting, muttering throng. Caitlyn felt her heart sink as she saw their blue uniforms. O'Flynn's fate would surely be hers now.

"A slight disagreement only. Nothing that can't be handled privately." To Caitlyn's astonishment, her captor was not handing her over. His hand was as tight as ever about her wrist, but he was not denouncing her to the constables. Why? She looked at him with wary suspicion but said naught.

"You'd best stay out of this part of the city, sirra," one of the constables warned her captor. The crowd from whom Caitlyn had hoped for so much was drifting away. Taking on a single foolish Englishman was one thing; bringing the full wrath of the hated Orangemen down on the heads of kith and kin was something else again. Caitlyn could understand and even shared their reasoning. The English were butchers, and their wrath if their constables should come to harm would be terrible. Irishmen throughout the city would be made to pay, some most likely with their lives.

"I will in future. Thank you for your assistance." Her captor slid that deadly-looking rapier back into its deceptively fancy scabbard, nodded in a friendly fashion to the constables, and moved away, dragging Caitlyn behind him. With the constables looking after them suspiciously, she had no choice but to go with him without a fight. Nothing he could do to her would be worse than her fate if they took her up. Not even if he were the devil himself. . . . Caitlyn shivered, remembering those strange light eyes. Where no one could see, she formed her fingers into the sign that warded off evil and immediately felt a little better.

In moments, the gentleman had pulled her around the corner onto the Bachelor's Walk, which ran alongside the River Liffey. The passersby here were very different from those in O'Connell Street. These well-dressed pedestrians were of the Protestant Ascendancy, the hated ruling class brought over from England and set firmly into place by the bloody butchery of Oliver Cromwell (curse the name) some hundred years before. To them, the Irish were heathen peasants of inferior culture and intellect, barely above the beasts in the fields. They were the enactors of the hated Penal Laws, which denied Irish Catholics virtually every human right. Under their rule, an Irishman in his own land was forbidden to own land, receive an education, vote, hold public office, practice his religion — and, worse yet, was forced to pay a yearly tithe to the Anglican

Church. They were colonizers of a once-free land, butchers, oppressors. Any Irishman worth his salt hated each and every one from birth to death. Caitlyn was no exception.

Once the constables were out of sight, Caitlyn jerked violently against the hand that still shackled her, hoping that the surprise of it might make her captor's grip loosen so that she could escape. His grip remained as unbreakable as ever, but he did slacken his pace and look around at her. The sheer size of the man was intimidating, it was true, but if Caitlyn O'Malley had ever feared man or beast, none had known it. She glared at him. Despite the fact that he had not turned her over to the constables, her hatred for him had not lessened. If anything, it had grown. She hated to be bested, and this powdered and primped Englishman had undeniably gotten the best of her.

"Bloody Sassenach," she hissed at him. Those devil's eyes narrowed on her face. He was easily double her weight, and head and shoulders above her in height, but discretion had never been one of her virtues.

"I'll thank you for my purse," he said, stopping and turning back to face her, holding out his free hand. Passersby on either side of them looked on curiously. He paid them no mind.

"Take it, then! I've little doubt 'tis filled with coins stolen from the Irish, just like your bleedin' countrymen have stolen our land!" Flushed with outrage and chagrin, shamed at her public downfall, knowing that angering him was the stupidest thing she could possibly do under the circumstances, she tried to do it anyway. She could no more stop the fierce flow of her Irish temper than she could hold back the fog that was beginning to thicken along the river.

He said nothing, just held out that narrow, long-fingered hand implacably. Glaring at him, teeth bared, she had no choice but to dig into the capacious pocket of her overlarge coat and produce his purse. She passed it to him ungraciously. He accepted it from her with a cool nod, then dropped it back into his own pocket with scarcely a glance. Without speaking, he considered her. She stared back at him defiantly, forcing herself to meet those strange light eyes without cringing. It would not do to think of devils and conjurers while she was concentrating on standing her ground. . . . His eyes narrowed as they ran over her dirty, hunger-pinched face and scrawny, shabbily dressed form.

"So I've caught myself an Irish thief." His drawling words flicked her to the raw. She glared at him.

"Lowest of all steals from the Irish!" It was a rash retort, but her blood was up. Her pride had been badly flayed, she was frightened and off balance, and to top it off she was at the mercy of a bloody painted Sassenach with an iron grip and evil eyes.

He shook his head at her. "Hotheaded like all the Irish, I see," he said placidly. "That trait will get you killed faster than pinching purses, my lad. At the rate you're going, you won't live to shave your first whisker. Or bed your first colleen."

"And what in bloody hell would you be knowin' about it? Damned lily-livered English dog!"

"Mind your mouth, now. I've taken about all the sass I care to from a half-pint stripling who tried to rob me blind." His brows came together in a fierce V as he scowled at her. Glaring ferociously back at him, both pleased and alarmed by the anger she had at last managed to incite, Caitlyn was quickly reduced to mortification by the loud rumble that came without warning from her insides.

"Hungry, are you?" His frown cleared. "Do you suppose if I feed you, you can keep a civil tongue in your head?"

"I wouldn't break bread with the likes of you if I was starvin', which I ain't. I just ate," she lied, pride stung again. "Fresh bread and butter boiled potatoes and fish. . . ."

"And I'm St. Patrick," he answered amiably. She blinked, frowning in surprise at the unexpectedness of his answer. Before she could respond he set off down the street again with her in unwilling tow. Just past the stone arches of Christchurch, he stopped and cocked his head in the direction of a public house across the way. A sign above it, creaking in the slight breeze, proclaimed it The Silent Woman.

"I'm for supper," he said. "You're welcome to

join me in a bite. It occurs to me that if I buy you a square meal, you might stay off the gibbet for one more day." With that he dropped her wrist, and with a nod at her as if to say the choice was hers, he crossed the street and disappeared into the pub. Caitlyn was left standing stock-still in the crowded street, thoughts awhirl as she stared after him. The bloody English dog had let her go. She was free to take to her heels, to chase after Willie and take up where they had left off. To find some other, hopefully less wide awake mark and prig his purse. . . . The thought sent a shiver down her spine. Maybe they were cursed by bad luck, as Willie thought. She didn't want to go the way of O'Flynn, face turning blue as she swung, choking, in the wind. But she was so hungry she was nigh sick with it.

The bloody Sassenach had offered to buy her supper.

Pride warred with hunger. Curiosity warred with wariness. Generations of racial hatred screamed at her to deny the empty aching in her belly. But, Sassenach or no, her stomach needed filling. As she thought about it, it seemed only just that a Sassenach should fill her emptiness. Were not he and his kind the cause of it, after all?

II

Still pondering, she crossed the street, in her distraction almost getting run down by a farmer with a cart. At the public house, a popular gathering place judging by the number of patrons going in and out, she hesitated just outside the carved oak door. All her instincts warned her to turn tail and run. Everyone knew that Sassenachs were not to be trusted. But what could he do to her in such a place, after all? If he'd wanted to turn her over to the authorities, he would already have done so. And whatever else he had in mind — be he devil or mortal, banshee or solid flesh — would probably wait until after she'd eaten. After that, she could vanish like the mist. But if she didn't let him feed her, she would have to feed herself or go without. And after the debacle of her attempt on his purse, her confidence in her abilities was severely shaken.

Hesitant but increasingly hungry, she pushed open the door and looked into a welcoming room well lit with tallow candles. The hated English were everywhere, their funny, mincing voices filling the room with talk and laughter. The place even smelled funny, sort of like a whore's cologne. She'd never been inside a pub outside the Irish quarters.

"And what do the likes of you think you're doing in here? Get on out of here!" A plump woman in a huge mobcap with a white apron over her dark gown came bustling out from behind the bar, flourishing a broom at Caitlyn. "The gall of you heathen Papists! Get, now — get out!"

Caitlyn's eyes flared, and her hands balled into fists. Wisdom dictated a hasty retreat. She was only one person, and a small one at that. The woman descending on her was large and plump and carried a broom. The room was filled with the hated Sassenach.

"Hold, mistress. The lad's with me."

He walked easily around the woman and caught Caitlyn by the arm, compelling her to abandon her imminent attack.

"I won't be eatin' in a room full of bloody Orangemen!"

"We don't want no Irish trash in here!"

If it had not been for the gentleman's iron hold on her arm, Caitlyn would have fallen on the woman and rent her limb from limb there and then. As it was, she was pulled protesting from the pub with the serving woman following after them, brandishing the broom like a weapon and calling curses down on the heads of the Papists. Caitlyn's answering abuse was vulgar and explicit.

"Enough, bantling." His voice was quiet, but there was in it that steely authority that silenced her continued fuming. She glared up at him,

23

trying to wrest her arm from his grip as he dragged her down the street.

"Bloody Sassenach!" The woman's insults had brought all her hatred of the race, forced into abeyance by the needs of her stomach, flooding back.

Those strange light eyes glinted at her. "I'm tired, I'm hungry, and I'm growing weary of listening to your insults, my lad. Now get yourself in here and keep your bloody mouth shut. Or I'll be likely to shut it for you with the back of my hand."

Caitlyn found herself seated inside another pub before she had a chance to sneer at its lily-white English patrons. Unlike the first place, this one was small, dark, and filled with smoke. No one was paying the least bit of attention to her, she discovered as she cast a belligerent look around. Her eyes caught the narrowed ones across the table from hers, and something about that look from those devil's eyes caused her to keep her unruly tongue under a semblance of control as the barmaid came over to their table. Under the gentleman's continuing impaling gaze, she sat in silence as he ordered a meal for both of them, firing up only briefly when the serving maid's eyes raked her with contempt. But the girl left before aught was said. Caitlyn was left glaring suspiciously at the man seated across the scrubbed pine table. In the dim light of the candle on the wall, it was hard to make out his expression. But she thought she detected a brief glint of amusement behind the warning look in his eyes. She bristled, but he spoke before she could put tongue to her feelings.

"Have you a name, halfling?"

"What bloody business is it of yours?"

He grinned suddenly, unexpectedly, white teeth gleaming at her through the darkness. "Charming lad, aren't you? You can thank your patron saint that I have a fondness for scrawny gamecocks. I could have handed you over to the authorities back there, you know. Most would."

"So why didn't you?"

"As I said, I have a fondness for scrawny game-cocks." The meal arrived then, thick bowls of beefy stew with hearty slabs of fresh bread and foaming glasses of ale. Caitlyn's traitorous stomach rumbled loudly again. Her cheeks flushed with embarrassment even as her mouth watered at the succulent aroma. Her eyes lifted from the chunks of tender meat and potatoes floating in the rich brown gravy to stare suspiciously at the man. He appeared not to have heard the latest insubordination from her insides.

"I'll not be payin' for this. Not in any way, if you catch my meaning."

He had just put the first forkful of stew in his mouth. Before he answered, he chewed it judiciously, swallowed, and washed the whole down with a mouthful of ale. Then he looked at her. Caitlyn shivered at the impact of those eyes. The sudden spurt of apprehension ignited her temper anew. Feeling better now that she was armed with comforting anger, she glared at him. She would not let herself think of the meal until all was straight between them.

"Eat, lad. There're no strings to the food. I know what it's like to be hungry." Despite those unsettling eyes, his voice was gentle.

"You?" She stared at him with disbelief. Then pride reared its head. "Anyways, I ain't *that* hungry. Like I said before, me pals and me, we just had tea. Boiled potatoes and . . ."

"I'm sure you can manage something. Just so as not to be rude."

She looked at him for a long, wary moment. But the aroma of that stew was not to be denied.

"All right. I guess I owe you something, seein' as how you didn't hand me over back there."

"Indeed." If there was just the faintest touch of dryness to his voice, his face was perfectly bland. There was no offense to be taken there.

Afier one final, suspicious look at her companion, Caitlyn picked up her fork and dug in. The first hot, cooked meal she'd had in weeks was so delicious that, after the first bite, she quite forgot the Sassenach who had provided it and wolfed it down like the starving child she was. When she had finished, the last crust of bread used to sop up the last drop of gravy, she sat back, replete, to find him watching her. The look on his face told her nothing, but she felt herself flushing. She'd made a right pig of herself, despite her fine words. And before a Sassenach.

"You keep pinching purses, you're going to

hang. You're not that good at it." His tone was one of impersonal warning.

Stung, her eyes widened with indignation. "I'm bloody good! I've been doing it for years and never been nabbled! Afore, I mean! You . . ."

"You're slow, and I felt your hand in my pocket like a lead weight. If you haven't been caught before, it's sheer good luck."

"What the bloody hell do you know about it?"

"I know a poor thief when I'm robbed by one. A poor, stupid thief. Because you're not going to quit until you're caught, are you? You'll hang higher than Christchurch's steeple." He sounded disgusted.

"Then you can come cheer at the hangin', can't you, you bloody pious Orangeman?" Her voice rose on the last word. Buoyed by a sudden surge of rage, she jumped to her feet. Men turned from the bar and swiveled in their seats to look. The gentleman sat back in his seat, his eyes narrowed as he took in her anger for a long moment with no reaction whatsoever. Then, reaching across the table without a word, he twisted his hand in her coat front and yanked so hard that she abruptly found herself sitting on the wood bench again. Her first reaction was to rub her tender behind, which had just suffered a severe bruising. She managed to control the impulse while she blinked at him.

"You'll curb that temper with me, my lad, or I'll curb it for you, understand? I've had some considerable experience with hotheaded bantlings." He paused, his eyes glinting at her. Then he said abruptly, "You know aught about sheep?"

"What's to know about sheep?" Her response was surly, but she remained seated.

"Answer the question!"

Caitlyn's eyes narrowed. "I love the little beggars like they was kin." It was a lie, and a brazen one at that. The closest she'd ever been to a sheep was to sleep in a barn with one once. But his arrogance deserved a lie.

"Think you can cut peat and muck out a stall?"

"Depends on why it needs doing."

He chose to ignore her insolence. "I've got a sheep farm in County Meath. I can use another lad about the place, if he's willing to work hard and behave himself. Of course, I was picturing someone a little meatier, stronger . . ."

"I'm strong as an ox, I am!"

"Three hot meals a day, a bed in the barn, lots of fresh air, and hard work is what I'm offering. Unless I'm mistaken, it's more than you have here."

"You offerin' me a job? Why? I just prigged your purse — almost." Honesty forced her to add that last, while suspicion shone out of her eyes as she looked at him. His expression was unreadable.

"Because I used to know a lad who was a lot like you. A hotheaded, ready-for-anything gamecock. I had a fondness for him."

The look he gave her seemed honest enough. But she had seen a lot of honest looks in her time, and most of them came from the biggest liars around.

"I'm no' interested."

He shrugged, standing up. "Suit yourself. I'll be at the Brazen Head in Lower Bridge Street. I'm leaving at first light tomorrow. If you want honest employment and a safe berth, be there. If not, good luck to you."

He laid some coins for the meal on the table, nodded at her, and walked out of the pub. Caitlyn chewed her lip as she watched him go. A job — he was offering her a job? She'd never had a job as such before. And, he'd said, a safe berth. A loud burst of laughter from the bar distracted her from her thoughts. She was an Irishman in a bloody Sassenach pub, which was not at all a good thing to be.

As she got to her feet her eyes chanced to fall on the table. Hesitating, she looked around to find herself unobserved. Then with a lightning movement she scooped the coins he had left from the table and into her pocket and swaggered out the door.

III

"O'Malley! And here was I thinkin' you were hanged for certain sure!" Willie stood up to greet Caitlyn as she ducked into the tumbledown shanty that served as home to a fluid group of eight or so lads. Made by their own hands of discarded lumber and tin, it leaned against the back wall of the Royal Hospital. Dozens of such tiny structures had been erected along the stone walls of the building. They were regularly torn down by dragoons and just as regularly built up again by the residents. It was a way of life.

"Ah, you know I've the luck of the Irish, Willie." Caitlyn basked in Willie's amazement at her escape as she crouched to warm herself at the tiny peat fire. The smoke the fire gave off was malodorous, but she scarcely noticed. From birth she had been exposed to the awful stink of Dublin's slums. Sewage ran raw in the gutters, at least in the Irish quarters. Garbage rotted in the streets, breeding enormous rats and cockroaches the size of fat mice. After a pair of hours spent in the Protestant sections of the city, Caitlyn felt even more keenly than usual what the interlopers were robbing them of. Protestant Dublin had wide streets, beautiful brick homes and shops, and a semblance at least of law and order. Catholic Dublin was menaced by roving gangs of beggars and thieves. The pinkindindies, as they were called, roamed about the mews after nightfall, slashing and robbing their victims, raping women in the streets, breaking into shops and homes almost at will. Homelessness, hunger, and brutality of the worst sort were part of daily life. Liffey fever was rampant. People died of it every day, their corpses dumped into the gutter with the sewage and garbage if they had no kin to arrange a burial for them. Surviving was the sole employment of thousands, and it made them as vicious as wild dogs.

"Doyle and the others've gone to the pub for a dram. I didn't feel like going with 'em. I — I thought never to see you again, O'Malley."

"Holy Mary, Willie, don't start blubberin' like a babe. You should've known a bloody Sassenach couldn't hold me."

Willie gave a watery grin. "Aye, I should've known it. How'd you get away, O'Malley?"

Caitlyn stood up, her hand going to her pocket where the Sassenach's money was tucked well down into the farthest corner. She'd meant to tell no one of her windfall. If word got out, the coins would be taken off her before she could say bloody England and her throat likely slit for their trouble. But Willie was her friend. When her mother had died in childbed, after having been turned off from her position as maidservant at Dublin Castle because she was increasing (through no fault of her own; she'd been forced by a drunken lord), young Willie, orphaned like Caitlyn, had been the first to stand her friend. Although he was younger than she, he'd been on the streets all his life and was wise in their ways. It was he who'd shown her the ropes. For a long time Caitlyn had been haunted by memories of her beloved mother, shamed and with nowhere to go but the streets, racked with coughing spells that had left her so pale and thin that the sunlight had almost shone through her except for the increasingly swollen mound of her belly. The end had come some eight years ago at the self-same Royal Hospital against which Caitlyn's shanty now leaned. Kate O'Malley had died in the charity ward, frightened and in pain, without so much as a pillow on which to rest her head. Caitlyn, with her until the end, had been left with her mother's blessing and naught else. It was while she lay dying that Kate O'Malley had insisted that her daughter begin to dress as a lad to protect her from the predators that were men. Caitlyn, with a horror of suffering her mother's fate, had not resisted, and by the time she had met Willie sheltering under a bridge she'd almost forgotten that she'd been born a lass. Willie and the others had no inkling of it.

In those early weeks, Caitlyn had cried at night, frightened and missing her mother. Willie had comforted her then when the others had laughed, his thin young arm hugging the shoulders of the lad he'd thought her to be. Remembering, Caitlyn looked at Willie, who was the closest thing to family she possessed. Her mother's thin face seemed to float before her.

"Take a chance, Caitie. 'Tis likely the only one you'll get." The words were as clear as if they'd actually been spoken. Caitlyn blinked, crossing herself reflexively. The vision had been so real, only Willie's tear-marked face convinced her that she'd imagined it. Earlier that day she'd come face to face with the evil eye, and now she was seeing banshees. It was unsettling.

"Come, Willie, I've a wee surprise for you," she said, draping an arm around Willie's shoulder in an unusual gesture of affection and leading him from the shelter. "I've somethin' to talk over with you . . ."

IV

� � � � � � � � � � � � � �

Caitlyn stood uneasily outside the Brazen Head
in Lower Bridge Street the next morning. Only a
few people were up and about, servants mostly,
stoking up fires and seeing to animals. The day
was dawning sluggishly, the sun seeming reluctant to poke its head through the floating curtain
of gray mist. Rain threatened. The clouds overhead were so low that they looked ready to settle
on the rooftops. The smell of dampness was in
the air.

A shaggy Connemara pony pulling a well-laden
farm cart plodded around the corner and was
pulled up at the hitching post not far from where
she stood. The scrawny ostler she'd seen earlier
jumped down from the seat and walked stiff-
legged to hitch the animal to the post. That done,
he straightened and looked her over with glum
disapproval.

"You got business hereabouts, lad?"

"As much as you."

"That so? Well, I got to go back and get another horse. If aught on this cart is disturbed
while I'm gone, I'll know where to look."

Caitlyn's reply was crude, and the gesture that
accompanied it was cruder. The ostler spat in
her direction, glared, and stumped off toward

the stable behind the pub. Caitlyn eyed the pony and cart with some interest. Making off with them wouldn't have occurred to her if the ostler hadn't put the idea in her head. But since he had, she calculated that the pony itself would be worth a good bit of change, to say nothing of the cart and its contents. Perhaps she could just put aside the idea of taking the Sassenach up on his offer and prig the pony and cart instead. She could live on the proceeds for a goodly while, and handsomely too. If she didn't swing for it. . . .

The Sassenach walked out of the Brazen Head. His linen was as snowy as it had been the day before. Despite the just-hatched gloom of the morning, the white shirt and frilly jabot seemed to glow. This morning the rolled collar of his frock coat was black, and his breeches were black too. He'd changed the red-heeled shoes for kneelength black boots meant for riding, and he'd evidently left off the face powder, for his skin was no longer softly white; but he was still as foreign to her kind as a Hottentot. A sneer curled Caitlyn's mouth as she looked at him. Despite the physical strength she knew he possessed, and the kindness that had prompted him to feed her and offer her a job and a home, he was still bloody English. A bloody English popinjay.

He was looking up and down the street, a slight frown creasing his forehead and bringing those thick black brows together over his devil's eyes. Clearly he hadn't noticed her, standing as she was in the structure's shadow. Or if he had, he had forgotten who she was. Sudden anxiety beset her. She had not realized how much she had counted on his offer. To be quit of the hellhole that was Dublin, to eat regularly and not have to worry about hanging for it, seemed suddenly infinitely desirable.

"Eh, yer lordship, here I be." The scrawny ostler came back around the corner leading a great black horse, saw the Sassenach, and hurried toward him. "Fharannain here wasn't inclined to wear a saddle today at all, at all."

"He never is." The Sassenach accepted the horse's reins and rubbed an absent hand down the beast's nose. Casting a narrowed eye at the ominous-looking sky, he said, "We'd best be on our way, Mickeen. Maybe we can ride out of this before it hits."

"Aye." The ostler came around to the hitching post and untied the pony, casting a darkling look in Caitlyn's direction as he did so. Clearly the time had come to make her presence known, if she meant to do so. An unaccustomed attack of nerves hit her. The bloody Sassenach hadn't meant his offer, had forgotten it already, she knew. Caitlyn O'Malley had never asked anybody for anything in her life. Her pride wouldn't even let her be the one to do the mock begging in their scams. She couldn't ask for a crust if she was starving. But he had offered her honest employment, as he had called it, and she was here to take him up on it. She wouldn't let the bloody

36

Sassenach go back on his given word without a fight.

"Eh, you. Remember me?" She came out of the shadow and walked boldly toward where the Sassenach stood with his horse. He turned and looked at her, frowning. Then a slow smile curved his lips.

"I do indeed. You taking up sheep farming?"

"Aye. Leastways, I'll give it a try."

"Fair enough. Climb up there in the cart with Mickeen. We've got a ways to go, and I'd be getting on with it."

The ostler looked at his master. "You know we don't need no more help at Donoughmore. You've got as many as you can take care of now."

"Close your mouth, Mickeen, and get in the cart. The sheep've been getting away from you and Rory lately, and *that* I can't afford. Who knows, another hand with the sheep might make all the difference. Maybe three can do the work of two."

Mickeen looked from the Sassenach to Caitlyn again and spat very deliberately on the cobbled street. "You'll do what you've a mind to, as always. Get up, then, lad, and be behavin' yerself, mind."

Caitlyn picked up the small bundle that held her few worldly possessions. Then, swallowing hard, she looked over at the man who represented all in the world she had been taught to hate. Asking for favors came hard to her, especially from a bloody Sassenach, but a pair of hopeful eyes gleaming at her from the shadowed laneway at the side of the pub spurred her on.

"Er — there's something I got to tell you." The Sassenach had just put a foot in the stirrup. He paused in the act of swinging aboard his horse to look at her as she spoke. "I got a friend." It came out sounding belligerent, and she looked belligerent too, standing there with her head cocked to the side and her eyes bright and challenging. The Sassenach narrowed his eyes at her and swung into the saddle. Then he said, a resigned note in his voice, "Where is he?"

"Come on out, Willie."

Willie sidled out from the shadows and stood on the cobblestones beside Caitlyn, looking fearfully up at the imposing figure of the Sassenach, who grimaced.

"Ah, the little beggar. Of course. You want to try sheep farming too, I gather?"

"Aye, sor. If you please." Willie nodded nervously.

Caitlyn said, "Him and me, we're a team." The words were a challenge to him to disagree. The Sassenach shifted his eyes to her, their aqua depths unreadable. Then he nodded once.

"So be it, then. Get up, the pair of you, and let's be on our way before we're drowned." He made a sound to his horse, which began moving off down the street. Caitlyn and Willie both stared after him. Did he mean to make no more protest than that at the inclusion of another mouth to feed?

"Heaven and the Saints preserve us, he'll be runnin' a bloody orphanage before we know where we're at. And him with more'n enough worries as it is." As their attention swiveled back to the little ostler, Mickeen scowled at the pair of them, then spat again and gestured at the cart with his hand. "You heard 'im: get up."

Willie made an excited sound, a wide grin wreathing his face as he scrambled up into the cart. Caitlyn followed more slowly. Her fists had been clenched tight with tension. Slowly her fingers relaxed as she realized that she wouldn't have to have a showdown with the bloody Sassenach after all. She would have fought for Willie; his scared delight since she had told him that they were going to live on a farm with plenty to eat and no more thieving had touched her heart as nothing had since her mother's death. But the Sassenach had agreed to take both of them with scarcely a pause. It was not possible that a bloody Orangeman could possess a kind heart, but it seemed this one did.

Pondering the alternatives, she settled herself on the rough plank seat. Her bundle she put in the back, carefully tucking it beneath the oilcloth that covered the cart's contents. Mickeen, still muttering under his breath, climbed up beside Willie and took up the reins. In silence except for Mickeen's indecipherable grumbles, they rumbled past St. Patrick's, past the feeding deer and gray stone walls of Phoenix Park, past derelict monasteries and water mills and windmills at the city's edge, to finally turn onto the road north.

It began to rain. Shivering, Caitlyn and Willie huddled together, tugging their coats up over their heads and watching the tall figure on the horse ahead of them that seemed now and again to vanish into the misty squalls. Beside them, Mickeen pulled his hat down lower over his eyes and swore steadily under his breath. In that way they passed through Clonee and Dunshaughlin, and rode until the rain stopped in the early afternoon. Caitlyn came cautiously out from under her coat as the sun peeped through the clouds, with Willie soon following suit. Though Mickeen's disgruntled silence discouraged conversation between his seatmates, they still looked about with fascination. Caitlyn had never been outside the confines of Dublin before, and to her knowledge Willie had not either. The largest expanse of green she had ever seen was the groomed acres of Phoenix Park. The sight of emerald hills undulating toward the blue horizon in every direction, broken only occasionally by a gray stone wall or a scattered flock of sheep or a little cluster of thatch-roofed huts that represented a town, was as remarkable to her as a three-headed cow would have been. She gazed with wonder. Willie looked equally awed. But as time passed, physical discomfort began to get the better of Caitlyn's appreciation of the beauties of nature. Her arse hurt. The wooden seat had made unforgiving contact with it too many times, and it felt bruised all over. Ahead of them, the Sassenach rode on without pause, Fharannain's great hooves seeming unimpeded by the thick mud. The cart, on the other hand, lurched about like a ship at sea, its wooden wheels making squishing noises as the hill-bred pony pulled them steadily through the quagmire. Gritting her teeth, Caitlyn set herself to endure. Never would it be said that Caitlyn O'Malley asked for quarter.

When finally the Sassenach stopped in the lee of a large grassy hill midway through the afternoon, she could barely stand to climb out of the cart. Shafts of pain shot through the tender part of her anatomy down to her feet and up her spine. Willie let out the groan that she suppressed. Annoyed at him for betraying his weakness, she practically shoved him from the cart.

"Awwk, what'd you do that for, O'Malley?" Willie turned injured eyes on her as he recovered his balance.

"Hush, ye looby," she hissed at him in annoyance, climbing down to stand beside him. Then, unable to help herself, she rubbed her aching bottom. Willie did the same.

Some dozen feet away, Mickeen was conferring with the Sassenach, who had dismounted and was holding Fharannain's rein as the great beast cropped grass. Caitlyn and Willie stayed near the cart, eyeing the other two while Caitlyn at least fought the urge to rub her posterior again (Willie showed no such discretion). The Sassenach unrolled something from Fharannain's saddle and tossed it to Mickeen, who looked sour as he caught it. Then the Sassenach remounted and, with a nod in the lads' direction, headed off down the road. Mickeen, clutching the bundle, came back to them, scowling.

"We're to eat a bite here and rest the pony, then ride on."

"What about him?" Caitlyn couldn't resist asking, nodding her head in the direction the Sassenach had taken.

"If you mean his lordship, he'll be waitin' for his meal till he gets home. He left the good nuncheon the cook at the Brazen Head packed for him for you two lads. He said you needed it more than he did, but I'll be takin' issue with that. 'Tis a fine man, is his lordship, while you be naught but a pair o' little beggars."

"Who're you callin' beggars? You get your bread from the bloody Sassenach same as we!" Caitlyn doubled her fists, bristling at the little man, but before she could attack, Willie grabbed her arms, holding her back.

"For Chrissake, O'Malley, don't do it!" he groaned in her ear. "He'll be leavin' us out here in the middle of nowhere!"

Caitlyn, incensed, tried to shake Willie off. Mickeen picked up a stout stick and brandished it at her.

"Don't you be tryin' none o' that now," he warned. "Or I'll have to split your skull for ya."

"C'mon, O'Malley. Pay the old gremlin no mind and let's eat. It's wantin' to leave us, he

42

is," Willie whispered, giving her a shake. Caitlyn had to admit the probable truth of that. Mickeen probably would love an excuse to leave them behind. Considering the source, she decided she could ignore a few ill-tempered words. She shook off Willie's hold, stalked over to a soft tussock of grass, and sank down upon it. Willie followed, holding the bundle of food Mickeen had given him. Mickeen watched with obvious disgruntlement, still balancing the stick in his hand. Ignoring him, the two youths fell like hungry dogs on the bread and meat and cheese they found wrapped in the cloth. After a few moments, Mickeen grudgingly put the stick down. Unwrapping his own package, he stood a little way apart and ate his meal with only an occasional sour look in their direction.

"I'm for home." Licking the last crumb from his lips, Mickeen wiped his mouth on his sleeve and eyed his two unwelcome journeymates with disfavor. Willie and Caitlyn had finished eating a short while before. At Mickeen's words, they got slowly to their feet. Exchanging pregnant glances, they crawled back into the cart, Willie groaning and Caitlyn fighting the urge to. Mickeen climbed up after them. Unhitching the reins, he released the brake and clucked to the pony. Caitlyn winced as her bottom made its first jolting reacquaintance with the plank seat.

"Where we headin', anyhows?" Willie, quicker to forgive and forget than Caitlyn, asked the question of Mickeen. The ostler moved his eyes over the redheaded boy looking up at him with eager curiosity, then shifted his gaze to the black-haired one scowling at the redhead. Turning his head, the little man spat over the side.

"Donoughmore," he said.

"Is it a town?"

He grunted. Then, grudgingly, "Was a castle. Now it's naught but a sheep farm."

"Does he own it?"

"Who?"

"The Sassenach." The words were Caitlyn's. They had slipped out of their own accord despite her wish to appear disinterested in the conversation.

Mickeen looked at her with acute disfavor. "If you're meanin' himself up there, you're talkin' about Connor d'Arcy, his lordship the Earl o' Iveagh, and you show him some respect. Himself's no more a Sassenach than I be, or you. He's as Irish as the good green earth, descended from Brian Boru himself on his father's side and Owen Roe O'Neill on his mother's."

"He's Irish?" Caitlyn's eyes widened. "But —"

"Don't be believin' everything your eyes and ears tell you. His lordship was educated at Trinity College with the bloody Protestants at the wish of his father. He can ape their ways well enough when he needs."

"But why . . . ?"

"Argh, that's enough out o' you, boyo. It's not for a beggar-boy to be questioning the activities of his lordship."

44

Caitlyn's eyes flashed at the description of her as a beggar-boy, but Willie nudged her in the ribs with enough force to keep her silent. She turned angry eyes on him. He urgently shook his head. Choking back her temper, Caitlyn conceded that Willie was in the right of it again. No purpose would be served by taking a swing at such an old bag of bones as Mickeen. All she would get for her pains would be to get thrown off the cart and left up to her arse in mud.

V

It was near sunset when Caitlyn got her first glimpse of Donoughmore Castle. Mickeen had been forced to halt the cart where the road turned upward to wend its way over another in a series of rolling hillocks. The little man sat swearing at the errant members of a flock of sheep taking their own sweet time to cross the road. Grinning to herself at Mickeen's ire, Caitlyn looked up and saw the Castle. Situated at the top of an emerald hill some three hillocks over, it looked down toward the steep banks and swift-flowing waters of the River Boyne. Its four round stone towers rose in majestic silhouette against the orange-streaked sky. As the cart began to move again and they slogged inexorably closer, Caitlyn could not drag her eyes from its centuries-old grandeur. Clearly the Castle had been designed as a fighting fortress. Round battlements with slits in the stone through which arrows could be fired upon besiegers below crowned the towers. The windows, small and close together, were set higher than three men standing on one another's shoulders could reach. The peaked roof was of slate to repel fire. It was every bit as tall as Christchurch in Dublin, and Christchurch was the most magnificent building Caitlyn had ever seen.

"Cor!" Willie said, as awed as she.

"He lives here?" Caitlyn could not hold back the question.

"His lordship, to the likes o' you," Mickeen muttered, casting Caitlyn a nasty look. Then he added, "Nah. The farm. Though his lordship and his brothers were birthed at the Castle, and their mother died here. As did the old lord, from the Fuinneog an Mhurdair, at the time the Castle was set ablaze."

"The — the what? Fuen . . . og?" Fascinated, Caitlyn could not respond to Mickeen's surliness with silence as she would have liked. The look the ostler turned on her was disparaging.

"So you've not the Gaelic," he said, in a tone that implied he had suspected as much. "The Fuinneog an Mhurdair. Murder Window. So called because the old lord was pushed from it to his death."

"He was murdered?" Willie breathed, his eyes huge as they fastened on Mickeen.

"Aye, for the land. The thrice-damned Penal Laws hold that a follower of the True Church cannot inherit. The old Earl was of the true religion, as was his wife by conversion, but his wife's mother was Anglican, niece of the Viceroy. Lady Ferman she was, and she used her influence at Court to prevent Donoughmore's seizure under the Penal Laws as long as she was alive. She died only days before the old Earl was murdered. Doubtless they thought wresting Donoughmore from the d'Arcys would be easier when it belonged to a lad instead of a tough old devil like the old Earl, but there they miscalculated. The old Earl, always being one to hedge his bets and foreseeing that Anglos would try to take Donoughmore from the d'Arcy family who has held the land from the time of Brian Boru, took steps. He had his lordship the present Earl schooled in the Protestant religion and registered him as such, though it fair broke his heart to do so. Aye, the old Earl loved his land more than his God, and is certain paying for it now. But Donoughmore is still in the hands of the d'Arcys as it rightfully should be, so it's my guess the old Earl would say that the torments of Purgatory are a small price to pay. But then, there's Protestants and there's Protestants, and I'm sure the good Lord is knowin' the difference."

This last cryptic comment sailed over the heads of his audience. "Who murdered the old Earl?" Caitlyn was as fascinated as Willie.

"Ah, now *that* we don't know, though there are some . . . But if his lordship knew for certain, you can be sure he'd have been avengin' his da afore now. Aye, and would probably have swung for it. So it's as well we dinna know."

"But who set the Castle afire?"

"We'll not be knowin' that for sure either. It was night, and the Castle was beset by a band of Volunteers, disguised to conceal their true identities, the Anglo cowards! They tried to burn us out, they did, howling 'Death to the Papists!' like bloody banshees while they looted and killed.

48

We was taken asleep, you see, and afore we knew what was about they were upon us. They murdered the old lord, and many there were who saw it too, but not afore he was able to send his sons to safety. Likely they meant to kill the lads too, but there their evil plan went awry. His lordship was but a lad of twelve, but he took charge of his wee brothers that night and has had charge of them ever since. For thirteen years he's been father and mother both to 'em, and bonny lads they've grown to be, though they've known their share of troubles. Aye, and I'd like to see the man who could take Connor d'Arcy's land from his hold now!" This last was said under Mickeen's breath, with an air of almost gloating.

"But . . ."

"Eech, the pair of you chatter like squirrels. It's tired I be of answerin' your questions." It was a measure of the fury that Mickeen had worked himself up to in the telling that the snarl he sent Caitlyn's way was not meant for her. The expression of sheer hatred on his weathered face was directed at the anonymous Volunteers, the secret organization of Anglo bloodmongers who rode out at night, hooded and cloaked, in huge gangs to wreak bloody havoc upon the Irish Catholics. The Irish in turn had their own Straw Boys, so called because, since they were poorer, their disguises from hoods to cloaks were made of straw and they resembled nothing so much as walking haystacks. Caitlyn had seen an assembly of them just once, when they had marched on

Dublin Castle. She had been no more than a wee bairn, but they had left an indelible impression on her. Like the city, the countryside was rife with violence, it seemed, as sectarian gangs warred on one another and the innocent.

Mickeen's rebuke left Caitlyn and Willie silenced. As the cart slogged through the mud, taking a meandering path that led finally around the Castle's outer wall, Caitlyn saw that the structure was indeed no more than a burned out shell. Sheep grazed in the overgrown bawn, the keep inside what was left of the fortifications. As she watched, one of the flock outside leaped baa-ing through a hole in the tumbledown wall to join its brethren feasting within. Three of the round towers were intact, but the fourth was crumbling, leaving a gaping wound in its side. Caitlyn stared at the high-set windows, shivering as she wondered which one was the Fuinneog an Mhurdair. Black streaks scorched into the gray stone gave mute testimony to the conflagration that had once raged within. The cart rounded the far side of the Castle, and Caitlyn saw that dozens of timber shacks leaned against its charred masonry. Living quarters for the peasants who worked the farm, she deduced from the presence of the women who sat in open doorways watching their young children playing nearby. Sheep grazed apparently at will on the green velvet slope leading to the Boyne. Rough-clothed peasants, both male and female, walked among the sheep. On the other side of the stone wall that bisected the grassy meadow, a group of peasants labored together with the scythe and slane, cutting turf.

"Is this the farm, then?" Willie's question was subdued. Mickeen's harsh recital and the devastation they had just passed had obviously shaken him as they had Caitlyn.

Mickeen snorted, bitterness twisting his face as he stared at what lay before them. "Aye. The farm. Connor d'Arcy, descendant of the first King of Ireland, true son of Tara, Lord Earl of Iveagh, a sheep farmer! His da would spin in his grave did he know. But as they say, needs must when the devil drives. And the devil drives his lordship for certain sure."

Caitlyn shivered upon hearing that, remembering those devil's eyes. Sure, and if his lordship were possessed of the devil she and Willie were in the soup, and no mistake. They'd likely escaped the hangman only to fall prey to Hellfire. With a sideways look at her companions, who were paying her no mind, she crossed herself and prayed that as protection that would suffice.

A magnificent view of the Boyne lay before them. It slashed like a silver whip deep into the valley separating the d'Arcy family holdings from the woodlands across the way. The hiss of the water as it rushed past rocky banks formed a muted background to the plaintive bleating of the sheep and the rhythmic thud of falling scythes. As the cart creaked downward toward the river, Caitlyn became aware of the manor house nestled in a grove of mighty oaks. Com-

51

pared with the Castle, the house was small and poor, but as they approached she saw that, taken on its own, it was a neat residence, two story and solid, made of stone with a corralled roof. Behind the house lay two barns and a smaller shed. Chickens scratched in the yards of both barns. A calico cat washed herself on the front steps of the house, while what appeared to be a very old dog sunned itself in a side yard. There was a well-cared-for air about the place that Caitlyn immediately liked.

As the cart approached, the dog got stiffly to its feet and began to bark, tail wagging. The cat looked up and then disappeared into the bushes at the side of the porch. Two men standing in a walled patch of fresh-tilled land midway between the house and the first barn looked up, squinting. With an air of disgust one threw down the staff with which he had been prodding an unresponsive sheep and headed toward them. The other shook his head and, abandoning the straggler, waded in among a tight-bunched group, flapping his arms in an attempt to herd them as they milled about, clearly paying his antics no mind. A dozen or so of the baa-ing creatures had apparently wandered into what was almost certainly the kitchen garden, and the men had been trying to get them out with what appeared to be little success. As the first man strode toward the cart, Caitlyn got the impression that he was glad for an interruption to their task.

"Mickeen, thank the lord you're back! Mayhap you can get the blatherin' sheep out of the bloody garden! Rory and I are havin' no luck at all, and Connor's sure to come out of the stable any minute and chew the hide off the pair of us. You know he thinks we're all natural-born sheep farmers, as he is, if we'd just try a little harder."

"And right he probably is too. I ain't noticed either you nor your brothers givin' tending sheep the care it deserves. If sheep farmin' is good enough for his lordship, it should sure be good enough for the likes of you, Cormac d'Arcy."

Given Mickeen's recent comments on the awfulness of an Earl of Iveagh's having sunk so low as to become a sheep farmer, Caitlyn could not repress a grin at this lecture. The young man who had greeted them so frenziedly turned his attention to her and Willie as Mickeen stepped laboriously down from the cart.

"And what have we here?" He was taller than Mickeen by half a head. His loose linen shirt and breeches could not conceal that he was gangly in the way of lads who have not yet achieved their full growth. His black curly hair, carelessly tied, dubbed him unmistakably as one of his lordship's brothers. But the narrow, even-featured face was not so striking, and as Caitlyn pondered the difference she realized it lay in the eyes. Those devil's eyes of his lordship's were dominating, unforgettable. This lad's eyes were a laughing hazel.

Mickeen looked back at them, his expression

as sour as Caitlyn was coming to believe was habitual to him.

"I know not their names. Your brother took pity on 'em in Dublin, and here they be. Runnin' a bloody orphanage, we are, it seems."

"I'm Willie Laha." Willie jumped down from the cart, his freckled face apprehensive as he looked up at Cormac d'Arcy. "We're to be farm-hands, his lordship said."

Caitlyn climbed down more slowly, giving Willie a censorious look as she did so. He was practically slavering his gratitude already. She didn't trust these people, any of them, his lordship included, despite Mickeen's sad tale.

They were strangers, with no reason to feel kindly toward Willie or herself. After all, why should these d'Arcys and their hangers-on share even a meager part of what was theirs with anyone else? In her experience, a body hung on to what he had. In their place, that's what she would do.

"What's your name, then?" Cormac turned his measuring gaze from Willie to Caitlyn. A grin lurked around the corners of his mouth, and his eyes looked as if he were always laughing. Caitlyn estimated his age at perhaps two years more than her own, which would make him around seventeen. She stood mute, contemplating him with a scowl. Such open friendliness made her warier than ever.

"He's O'Malley. A bit of a temper he has, but a good lad." Willie poked her in the ribs with his elbow as he spoke. Caitlyn shot Willie a look that should have silenced his tongue forevermore.

"I can speak for meself," she said, her eyes meeting Cormac's with more than a trace of belligerence. He lifted his eyebrows at her expression and whistled comically. She scowled at him.

"His lordship must have been all about in his head, is all I can tell ya. This one's a real hothead," Mickeen muttered, spitting. Then, to Cormac, "Let's go get them sheep out o' the garden afore his lordship sees where you've let them get." He moved off with Cormac following, adding over his shoulder to Willie and Caitlyn, "You may as well come along and make yourselves useful. No point in just hangin' about."

Willie loped off after them. Caitlyn followed more slowly. With all of her other worries, another had just lifted its ugly head. She had a sneaking suspicion that she was not going to like sheep. . . .

By the time she reached the walled garden, the others had managed to get the sheep rounded up into a tight little group and were herding them toward the open back gate, which led to the velvety meadow where sheep were apparently intended to be. A renegade cut and ran as Willie, following Cormac's example, flapped his arms at it. Baa-ing wildly, it headed straight for Caitlyn, who had just stepped through the front gate, its sharp little hooves churning the manure-rich, rain-wet furrows into thick black mud as it went.

"You! O'Malley! Stop 'em! Turn 'em!" They were all shouting at her as three other sheep whirled and pounded after the ringleader. Sure enough, the stupid creature in the lead was still heading at a gallop straight toward where Caitlyn stood transfixed just inside the whitewashed pickets of the closed front gate. But this was not a fleecy little white lambkin. It looked enormous, and furious, and it had horns.

Enough was enough. She was not risking life and limb to herd some murderous sheep. As it bore down on her, head lowered and baa-ing louder than Gabriel's horn, she scrambled to get out of the way. Her foot slipped in the mud where the sheep had already apparently churned up the moist earth, and she slid face first into thick ooze. The shock of it as she lay facedown in muck took her breath for a moment. Then what felt like a thousand-ton weight slammed into her left shoulder, and she realized that the bloody stupid sheep had run right over her. Her mouth opened at the pain of it. Black mud immediately filled her mouth.

When she surfaced, spitting mud, it was to find the four would-be sheepherders bent double with laughter. She glared, feeling fury start to heat in her toes before boiling up toward her head. They were laughing at *her*, Caitlyn O'Malley. Even the bloody sheep, bunched now with its three followers in the bloody corner, seemed to be laughing as it shook its horned head at her.

"So you think to make sport of me, do you?"

She got to her feet, shaking her hands to send mud flinging from them, wiping her fingers down her face with no more success than to spread the mud around. From head to toe she was covered with malodorous black ooze. Inside, her temper was raging. She was filled with a desire to kill the guffawing foursome on the other side of the garden plot. Roaring inarticulately, she charged, fists clenched and murder in her eyes.

"Look out! Beware!" Still laughing, they scattered before her assault, the one whom Cormac had called Rory leaping straight up to balance on top of the gray stone wall. Making sounds of inarticulate rage, Caitlyn charged after Cormac, who was laughing the loudest. He ran, zagging this way and that as laughter shook him. Launching herself off the ground, she tackled him, catching him around the waist and knocking him on his side in the ooze. Laughing so that he was almost helpless, he rolled onto his belly, lifting both arms to shield his head as she straddled him, battering his head and back and whatever else of him she could reach with her fists.

"Here now, O'Malley, stop!" Cormac managed to get out between gusts of laughter. Lean as he was, he was still far bigger than she. But the laughter he could not seem to control weakened him, and Caitlyn's years on the street had made her tough. Add to that the fact that she was ragingly angry, and the blows she landed were damaging. Still, all he did to defend himself was block the blows aimed at his head, and laugh.

Which only fueled her fury to greater heights.

Mickeen was scurrying toward them, stick in hand. "You there! O'Malley! Stop! Stop now, do you ken?"

Caitlyn knew she was in for a thrashing when he reached her, but she didn't care. The urge to kill burned strong inside her. From his place up on the wall, Rory was laughing even harder at his brother's comeuppance, while Willie, in the far corner of the garden across from the sheep, looked suddenly scared. His eyes went wide.

"What in the name of all the Saints is going on here?" The roar made even Caitlyn start and look around. There, on the other side of the gate which Caitlyn had recently abandoned to escape the charging sheep, stood Connor d'Arcy, Earl of Iveagh, giving off anger like a peat fire gives off heat.

VI

"You!" he bellowed, pointing at Caitlyn. "Get off my numbskull brother. And you . . . and you . . ." He pointed at Cormac, who was no longer laughing but merely grinning as he lay under Caitlyn, his arms still shielding his head even as he looked at his older brother; and at Rory, who was already jumping down from the fence. "Get over here and explain to me how you've come to make such a bloody mess of a garden that was just planted a week since!"

"Get off, you little monkey!" Cormac hissed, bucking Caitlyn off his back into the mud again as he got to his feet. He was as muddy as she, and wiped himself down with as much success as she'd had as he approached his brother. Rory, black-haired and thin like Cormac but a year or so older, squished through the mud at the same time, reaching the gate just before Cormac. Caitlyn, struggling to her feet, watched the three d'Arcys with hate-filled eyes.

"Well?"

The two younger d'Arcys attempted to explain, until Connor silenced them with a growl.

"I don't want to hear it. I want the garden replanted by tomorrow. Tonight we've got supplies to get in, but that'll have to wait until the gang of you has a bath. You smell like sheep dung, and I can tell you now Mrs. McFee won't have it brought in the house. You can use the horse trough to bathe. If you want to eat, you'll move fast."

"But, Connor, we —"

"Move!" he roared. "And take those two bairns with you!"

Connor turned on his heel and strode toward the house. Cormac and Rory turned back to the trio in the garden, their expressions wry.

"We'd best get this muck off," Rory said. "Connor's right. Mrs. McFee won't let us in the house like this."

Mickeen looked at the pair of them gloomily as they came toward where he stood with Caitlyn and Willie, the one fuming and covered with mud, the other white and scared-looking. "His lordship's proper fashed with the lot of us, and no mistake."

"He'll be over it by the time supper's on the table," Rory said philosophically. "You know Connor."

"We never wanted to be sheep farmers anyhow," Cormac added. "I hate bloody sheep. But there's no talking to Connor about it. He says impoverished Irish nobility should be glad to have sheep to tend to."

"Farming's a good, respectable occupation," both brothers chimed together as if repeating something they'd heard many times, and grinned. Caitlyn scowled at them. Though they appeared to have put the contretemps from their minds, she was not quite so willing to let bygones be bygones. But with Connor still within probable hearing range, she was loath to take up where she and Cormac had left off. There'd be time and more to get back at him.

"That's enough sass out of the two of you. His lordship'll be wroth indeed if you're late for the meal on top of this." Mickeen urged them in the direction of the barn. Gesturing to Caitlyn and Willie to fall in, he trudged after Rory and Cormac. Once they were out of the garden, the ground was firm beneath their feet, but they squished anyway. They even had mud in their shoes.

Rory stopped in front of a wide wooden watering trough, climbed in, and sat down, clothes and all. Though he was not near as filthy as his brother or Caitlyn, still he was liberally spattered with mud. Like Cormac, he was dressed in a loose shirt and breeches, with wool stockings and sturdy buckled shoes. He didn't even bother to remove the shoes.

"Hey, brother, who said you could go first? You'll get the water dirty!" Cormac jumped in after him, and a good-natured wrestling match sloshed most of the water out of the trough. What was left was brown with mud.

"They're a pair, they are," Mickeen grunted to no one in particular, though Caitlyn and Willie listened avidly. Even Caitlyn, grudgingly, was beginning to find the d'Arcys fascinating. Never in her life had she met anyone like them. She didn't know what to make of them, and she guessed Willie did not either. "Always sportin' around and plaguing his lordship. It's a wonder he don't knock their heads together sometimes. But he's real patient."

"Conn, patient?" Cormac hooted, overhearing this remark as Rory briefly released his head from under the water. "Go on with you, Mickeen!"

"More patient than you deserve, idiot. Seed's expensive, and so's the time spent putting in a garden. Though if you and Rory are to replant it, we'll save on that, at least. Your time sure won't be missed with the sheep." A voice behind them made Caitlyn look around. The young man who stood there was auburn-haired, blue-eyed, and perhaps twenty years old. Unlike the two in the trough, he looked as if he were serious-natured. But there was something about his tall, rangy build and narrow face that made Caitlyn think he might be the remaining d'Arcy. The whoops with which the two in the water greeted the newcomer confirmed her guess.

"Hey, Liam! Look what Conn brought home! Some help for us!" Barely checked hilarity was in Cormac's voice as he climbed dripping wet from the trough. A wide grin split his face as he indicated Caitlyn and Willie, who looked very small, very young, and very bedraggled as they stood beside Mickeen awaiting their turn in the trough. Liam turned to look at them, disapproval and resignation mixed on his face.

"A fine pair of shepherds, I see. Soaking wet they might weigh four stone between them. Connor thinks he can save the world," Liam said as if the two he discussed were deaf and dumb. Caitlyn bristled. Like the other d'Arcys, this one was too arrogant by half. Then, to Caitlyn, he added, "Come on, get in and wash the mud off. Supper's nigh on the table, and there's chores to do before it gets dark."

"Conn got his temper back yet?" Rory had climbed out of the trough and stood sopping wet beside Cormac. Caitlyn saw that they were enough alike to be twins, although Rory was a little taller and more muscular. Like Cormac, Rory had twinkling hazel eyes and a perpetual grin tugging at his mouth. Liam shook his head at him, frowning.

"Come on, you two. What are you waiting for? The water's grand!" Cormac presented the trough to Caitlyn and Willie with a bow. Willie started to climb in, but Caitlyn stopped him with a hand on his arm. She wasn't going to get soaked to the skin in front of all these males if she could help it. Even with her coat to wrap around her, there was always the chance that the wet clothes might reveal too much. She hit on the first excuse to come to mind, and uttered it with fierce conviction.

" 'Tis accustomed I am to clean water for my bath, if 'tis all the same to you."

Liam stared at her as if he couldn't believe his ears. Rory snorted, and Cormac laughed outright.

"You've likely never had a bath in your life before, much less in clean water."

"Aye, I have. And I'll have clean water now too. What's in there looks like it's left over from some pig sty. Might as well keep the mud I have as sit in someone else's dirt."

"Impertinent little jackanapes, ain't he?" Cormac said to Rory, who rolled his eyes skyward.

"Ah, let him have his clean water. You fetch it," Liam added to Caitlyn, handing her a bucket and nodding at the well nearby. "When you get done, come on up to the house. Supper's waiting."

The d'Arcys walked away toward the house. Watching them go, Caitlyn was struck by how much the three brothers resembled one another from the rear. She had already deduced that no more than three or four years separated them, with Liam clearly the oldest of the three. Connor, who from Mickeen's words Caitlyn had calculated to be twenty-five, was some five years older than Liam, though Connor's calm assumption of almost parental authority over his brothers made him seem even older than that. Rory was the tallest of the three presently under her eyes by perhaps an inch, and Liam the most muscular. They were all arrogant, Connor worst of all, and if they weren't Sassenachs they were the next worst thing. Caitlyn glared after them. Willie shoved her in the back so hard she staggered.

"What the hell's the matter with you, O'Malley? You're going to cost us our place."

"I'll not be taking a bath in their dirt. They're no better than you or me."

"Aye, they are! They're the brothers of an earl. You don't even know who your da is!"

"I do! Anyways, neither do you." But Caitlyn couldn't sustain her anger at Willie. She sighed. "Come on, help me dump this. Then we'd best fill the trough and wash up fast if we want to get something to eat."

"Now you're talking sense!" He grabbed one side of the trough, Caitlyn the other, and between the two of them they managed to heave it on its side so that the muddy water ran out. Working together, they soon had enough clean water in the trough to bathe in. Willie clambered in, splashing vigorously as he scrubbed mud from his person.

Caitlyn approached the trough cautiously. With only Willie as her audience, she hadn't much to fear, but she worried for all that. Her breasts were small, but they were definitely there, and a wet shirt without a coat pulled in front of it would reveal all. And she couldn't be sure of keeping her coat snugly in place until the shirt dried. She wasn't certain, but she thought that might take quite a while. The obvious solution was to wash as much mud as possible from her face, hands, coat, and bottom half, while leaving the voluminous folds of her shirt dry. The mud on that could be brushed away when it had stiffened sufficiently. As Cormac had guessed, she'd rarely bathed, but she thought this could be accomplished without undue difficulty. She climbed into the trough, sitting gingerly in the water which Willie had already thoroughly muddied, and scrubbed with care. The worst of the mud gone, she climbed out with the vital area of her shirt still dry as a bone and no one the wiser as to her sex.

"Ready?"

"Aye."

Trailing a small rainstorm of droplets, soaked to the skin but for that one exception, she and Willie sloshed toward the back of the house.

A heavyset woman with a round, red face made even redder by the whiteness of the crisp mobcap above it stood on the stoop, berating the three younger d'Arcys as Caitlyn and Willie approached. Her arms were folded over her ample bosom, and the expression on her face was clearly one of displeasure. A shapeless black dress covered her from neck to ankles. Her features were as large and heavy as a man's, with deep wrinkles creasing her cheeks. Strands of iron-gray hair showed around the edges of her cap.

"I'd take shame on meself, ye rapscallions, makin' his lordship wait on his supper. Get some dry clothes on now, and get inside. 'Tis on the table." She looked up and saw Caitlyn and Willie. "You two new lads, I'm thinkin' you can wear some old clothes of Cormac's. They're here." She indicated two of the small piles of clothes she evidently had just brought to the stoop. "They might be somewhat large, but you'll have

66

to make do. You'll eat in the house tonight. Tomorrow you start supping with the O'Learys. Mrs. O'Leary feeds the bachelor men for a coin or two."

"Yes'm," Willie said, clearly awed by the large, bossy woman.

Caitlyn frowned. She saw a terrible dilemma facing her. She couldn't don dry clothes here and now. . . .

The woman turned and went back inside the house.

"That was Mrs. McFee," Liam explained. "Anything that upsets Connor upsets her twice as much."

Cormac and Rory were already shucking off their wet clothes. Willie followed suit more slowly, not used to taking off his clothes down to his skin. Caitlyn turned her eyes from the sight of the three naked and near naked males, and sat down plop on the lower step.

"What're you waiting on, O'Malley?" Liam addressed her impatiently.

"I'll not be changing. These clothes'll dry." She said it without looking at him. She couldn't be quite sure, but she didn't think his brothers had yet put on their breeches. As she had discovered in her years of imposture, the bare male arse was not a pretty sight. She had no desire to see Cormac's, or Rory's, or anyone else's.

"Hey, Rory, did you hear that? He's shy!" Cormac chortled. Despite her fears, he already had his breeches on and was pulling on his shirt.

Caitlyn knew, because the sound of him laughing at her again had swiveled her head on her shoulders to fix him with a ferocious glare before she considered the ramifications. Fortunately, there were not any. All four males were at least minimally decent.

Rory looked up from buttoning the last button on his breeches. A grin split his face. "Shy, is he? You got something we've not seen before, O'Malley?"

"Maybe he's got two!"

"Or maybe it's so small that he's ashamed to let it out!"

"You can't eat in wet clothes, O'Malley. Mrs. McFee won't let you into the house." Liam's voice was reasonable.

"The clothes ain't bad, O'Malley, truly. Look at me." Willie had pulled on a pair of Cormac's too-big breeches and shirt. He was rolling up the legs of the breeches as he spoke. All of the younger d'Arcy brothers topped both Willie and Caitlyn by more than a head, but Cormac was the shortest and slightest of the three. Nevertheless, his breeches and shirt were still miles too big for Willie, who was about the same height and weight as Caitlyn.

"I'll not be changing." Her eyes were as uncompromising as her voice as she fixed the gang of them with a challenging stare.

Liam shrugged. "Suit yourself. You'll miss supper, but that's your loss, not ours."

"I'll not be changing."

"Fair enough. The rest of you, come on in and let's eat. There's work to do after the meal. O'Malley, since you're not hungry, you can start unloading the cart. Most of it's for the sheep barn, feed and such. The sheep barn's the one furthest from the house. The saddle and brushes go in the stable, which is where you just came from. The things that go in the house, like salt and honey, just leave by the stoop. We'll sort everything out after supper."

With chortles and jests being exchanged between Rory and Cormac pertaining to O'Malley's equipment or lack of it, the gang trooped into the house. Caitlyn, soaked to the bone except for her shoulders and shirt front, was left outside. She was hungry, but not for anything was she going to strip off in front of them. If she was to preserve her secret, she couldn't.

Fifteen minutes later she had hauled two huge sacks of seed into the barn and had just rolled a big barrel of salt to within about a foot of the back stoop. Straightening, she wiped the perspiration off her brow. The unaccustomed physical labor had made her hot despite the increasing cool of the night and her wet clothes.

The back door opened. Cormac and Rory stepped out on the stoop together. She looked up at them warily. As they saw her, identical devilish twinkles came into both pairs of hazel eyes.

"You missed a good meal, O'Malley. Mrs. McFee's cooking's enough to make the angels sing in heaven."

"You often go around missing meals for no good reason? No wonder you're so little. You'll never be much of a man at the rate you're going. A leprechaun, maybe."

"I'm man enough already to take you on, Cormac d'Arcy. I already took you down in the garden there, and I'm ready to do it again anytime."

Rory whistled, still grinning. "Pretty big talk for a scrawny monkey, wouldn't you say, brother?"

"I would indeed, brother. So you think you can best me in a fight, monkey?"

"Quicker'n I can spit." Caitlyn spat on the grass at her feet to illustrate. She was small, but she was tough and wiry and possessed of a fiery temper that was enough to make many a lad bigger than she back down. The reputation that temper had earned her had saved her from many a fight. But of course these d'Arcys had no notion of her legendary rages, so her reputation would not help her now.

"That quick, eh?"

"You can't fight that halfling, Cormac. Connor won't like it." Rory was speaking seriously now.

"I know it. But maybe I can tan his backside for him. He's a smart-mouthed little cockerel."

Outrage heated Caitlyn's cheeks. Tan her backside . . . ! Rory and Cormac jumped down from the stoop in a single movement. Caitlyn felt a combination of fury and panic as they closed in on her, laughter curling their mouths. They were two together, and they were far bigger than she. Faced with such a situation in Dublin, she'd have cut and run. But here there was nowhere to go, and anyway, she couldn't back down now. They'd bully her forever. Her only chance of surviving with a relatively whole skin and her pride intact was to launch a surprise attack.

She charged Cormac, punching him lightning fast in the nose and then butting him in the stomach with her head. Grunting with pain, he staggered backward, his hand clapped over his nose. Blood was already beginning to gush from beneath his sheltering hand.

"You little bastard!" Cormac took his hand away from his nose to see blood all over it. The grin left his face, to be replaced by scowling anger. Caitlyn, fuming herself, stood facing him in a crouch, fists doubled. She would stand her ground or die in the attempt.

"Look out, little brother, the bantam has already bloodied your nose! No telling what kind of damage he might do to the rest of you," Rory chortled, standing back. Cormac's mouth tightened at the teasing. Caitlyn could see that what had started out as a joke was no longer amusing — anger glittered in Cormac's eyes. Blood still ran from his nose. For all his gangly build, he looked a formidable opponent. He was near a foot taller and stones heavier than she. But for Caitlyn fury was fast banishing caution. She could feel it building up inside her, familiar and comforting.

"Still think you can tan my backside, d'Arcy?" Caitlyn sneered. "It'd take a better man than you or your bloody brothers!"

"We'll see about that, you insolent little beggar!" Cormac charged, his arms closing about Caitlyn's waist, lifting her off the ground. She fought wildly as he turned her over in midair, landing some well-placed kicks and blows that made him grunt with pain and dance to keep the most vulnerable parts of his body away from her. She managed to grab his crotch on the way down and twisted that vulnerable area as hard as she could. He yelped, cursing. Caitlyn went flying through the air to land with the force of a cannonball on her belly in the thick grass. All the wind was knocked out of her. She could only lay stunned as Cormac straddled her back. He lifted the tails of her coat, giving several hard slaps to the soggy backside of her breeches. She didn't have enough wind to curse him, though the blows stung badly. Gasping for air, she swung wildly at him as he turned her over onto her back. Taking no chances with those flying fists, Cormac pinned her wrists to the ground. If looks could have killed he would have died on the spot, but he was grinning in the face of her spitting rage instead, his good humor restored by the success of his revenge.

"Ah, he's naught but a lad, Cormac. Let him up." Rory walked over and looked down at Caitlyn. Heaving her body in an attempt to dislodge Cormac proved useless. He was far too heavy for her to buck off. She lay stiff with fury, spewing out a stream of curses that should have shamed the devil himself. Cormac merely chuckled.

"He's soggy as day-old cake, Rory. My breeches are all wet from sitting on him."

"Well, he wouldn't change."

"Do you suppose he's shy? Or does he have some sort of deformity he can't bear anyone to see?" Devilishness sparkled out of Cormac's eyes. Catching the spirit of the thing, Rory grinned back at his brother.

"We should find out. We'd be doing Conn a favor if this lad turned out to be a freak. Or maybe he's got the mark of the devil on him somewhere. On his backside, say."

"That's a possibility. Or, wet as he is, he could catch the fever and die. We'd be doin' him a favor too."

"Aye, that we would." They nodded solemnly at each other. Caitlyn, catching the drift of this, began to struggle violently, calling them every filthy name she had ever learned on Dublin's streets. They were laughing as Rory squatted to keep her wrists pinned while Cormac straddled her ankles. Caitlyn shrieked imprecations at Cormac's head as he reached up to untie the lacing of her breeches. She writhed wildly but couldn't evade his hands. The worst panic she had ever known in her life seized her.

"No! You bastards, you bloody buggers, no! What are you, the kind that likes boys? I'll kill you! I'll kill you!" But all her screaming, cursing, and fighting were in vain. She managed to get one ankle loose just as Cormac jerked her breeches and her drawers with them down to her knees. Viciously she kicked him, sending him toppling backward while she squirmed over onto her front. Rory's grip on her wrists went curiously slack. She pulled free, then flung her coat over her bare bottom as she grabbed at her breeches and drawers. She was uncovered for no more than a moment.

Cormac was lying on his back on the grass, still in the position in which he had landed when she had kicked him, a stunned look on his face as he swiveled his head to stare at her. Rory, still crouching behind her, was regarding her with an equally stunned expression.

"What the bloody hell is going on now?" The voice was Connor's. A shaft of pure terror shot through Caitlyn as she lifted her eyes to meet that devil's gaze. She was exposed, naked, although her feminine parts were covered as well as they had ever been. But Cormac and Rory had seen. She could no longer rely on the protection of claiming the male sex. As a female, she was hideously vulnerable. . . .

"Conn." Rory spoke in a strangled voice. Caitlyn tensed, her eyes never leaving Connor's face.

"Well, what is it? I warn you, I've had a bloody long day, and I'm getting a wee bit tired of your high jinks."

"Connor." But Rory couldn't seem to say any more than his brother's name. Connor frowned as he looked Rory over closely.

"What ails you, Rory? Can't you speak?"

"Connor, he's a bloody lass!" Cormac blurted, looking accusingly at Caitlyn.

VII

❋ ❋ ❋ ❋ ❋ ❋ ❋ ❋ ❋ ❋ ❋ ❋ ❋ ❋ ❋

"What?" Those devil's eyes swiveled to stare at Cormac.

"He's a lass, I tell you. O'Malley. He — she's a lass."

"What nonsense are you spouting now, Cormac?"

"It's no nonsense." Rory got to his feet, his eyes still fastened on Caitlyn with a kind of horror. "That's a lass."

Connor's eyes turned back to rake Caitlyn, who lay huddled on the grass in a state of what almost amounted to shock, her eyes huge on Connor's face. "He looks like no lass I ever saw. Your brain's getting soft, the pair of you."

Drawing a quick, shaky breath, Caitlyn mustered all her courage and scrambled to her feet. Maybe, just maybe, there was a chance the younger d'Arcys wouldn't be able to convince their brother. Maybe she could even make them doubt what they'd seen. Desperate, she realized that a bluff was her only chance.

" 'Tis naught but a pack of lies! I'm as much a man as any of you! Aye, and more than you, Cormac d'Arcy. I bloodied your nose right proper, did I not?"

The three d'Arcys stared at her. None seemed

76

about to rise to the bait. Connor's eyes in particular unsettled her as he ran them slowly from the very top of her head down the length of her body to her wet shoes and back up again, stopping to frown at strategic spots in between.

"We were sporting around and Cormac yanked his — her breeches to his knees. He — she was as bare as a babe, Connor. And she's a lass. There's no doubt at all, Connor." Rory's voice was hoarsely earnest.

"A lass!" Connor looked as dumbfounded as the others.

"Nay!" Caitlyn yelled, backing away as Connor took a step toward her. Flight was her objective. She would not stay to be abused by men who knew her true sex. Her mother's fate flashed like a horrible warning before her. Although her body had never been used by a man, she was no innocent. She knew the violence that men for their own pleasure perpetrated on helpless females. Her mother had dressed her in male attire to prevent just such a thing from happening to her. She would run, hide in the countryside, make her way back to Dublin . . .

"Catch him — her — oh, hell, just do it, Rory!" Connor gave the clipped instruction just as Caitlyn turned to flee. Rory was already behind her. His hands closed over her upper arms, stopping her in mid-step with her back to him.

"Let me go! Let me go!" Terror gave her strength as she struggled wildly. Her first crazed thought was that she would be thrown on the ground and used by the three of them there and then. Men were beasts about their pleasure. Rory's grip on her arms was unbreakable, so she picked up her foot and kicked backward as hard as she could, catching him in the kneecap.

"Arghh! Sweet Brian, she's a little hellcat! Here, give me a hand, Cormac, quick!"

Caitlyn screamed as Cormac grabbed her around the waist, lifting her clear off the ground with one arm tight around her knees to try to still her kicking while Rory held her flailing fists. Writhing in desperate fear and anger, she shrieked curses at the top of her lungs.

"Watch her feet! Hold 'em, Cormac!"

"Hell, you hold her hands! She nigh tore off my privates earlier! She's vicious as a trapped badger!"

Rory and Cormac barely managed to hold her in a position in which she could do relatively little damage to either of them. They eyed their older brother desperately, but he was watching Caitlyn's frantic struggles, a frown on his face.

"Here, now. No one's going to hurt you. So just give over, lass, do." Connor was speaking to her, his voice gentle, soothing. Caitlyn called him a name that would have made a whore blush and spat in his direction. She had the satisfaction of watching him jump back so that the spittle just missed his boots. His frown darkened as he stared at her.

"Watch it, Conn. She's already bloodied Cormac's nose." A note of humor was beginning to return to Rory's voice. "And tweaked his privates. No telling what she might do to you."

"Be silent, idiot. Can't you see the wee lass is frightened?" Connor said. Then, to Caitlyn in the same gentle voice he had used before: "O'Malley, quit your thrashing and we'll just talk, I swear. No one will lay a finger on you. We mean you no harm at all, at all."

"Burn in hell, you bloody bastard!" With that she writhed so violently that she managed to bring her head down to the level of Cormac's shoulder. With a growl like an animal's, she bit him until she tasted blood.

"Oww! Oh! Jaysus, she's bit me! The little hellcat's bit me!" Cormac danced backward, his grip on Caitlyn slipping, so that her feet touched the ground.

"Hold her, Cormac, damn it!" Kicking violently, she also managed to make Rory leap back. She was nearly free —

"Enough!" The brusque word was accompanied by a hand on the neck of her coat jerking her off balance. As she stumbled backward, she felt an arm slide under her knees. The hand that had been in her coat caught both her wrists, imprisoning them. She was being lifted. . . . Screaming, fighting for her life, Caitlyn found herself slung around Connor's shoulders like a dead deer, her head and arms imprisoned on one side of his chest, her legs trapped on the other. His hold was like iron; her violent struggles availed her nothing. But still she kicked and screamed and cursed as he swung around and carried her into the house.

"Your lordship, what in the name of heaven — ?" Attracted by the bloodcurdling screams, Mrs. McFee came hurrying from the kitchen to stare stunned as Connor headed with his burden toward the stairs.

"What're you doin' to O'Malley?" Willie, his mouth rimmed by some kind of red sauce, had followed Mrs. McFee into the hall. Caitlyn got just a glimpse of them, accompanied by a surprised but grimly satisfied-looking Mickeen, as she was borne off up the stairs.

"You let me go! I'll tear you limb from limb, I will, you — !" Caitlyn was beside herself with fear and rage as Connor gained the upper landing and took her into a small, sparsely furnished room that from the desk and papers strewn about she surmised was used as an office. He bent and, ducking his head, lifted her up and deposited her in a hard straight chair while still retaining his grip on her wrists. Keeping his legs deftly out of reach of her kicks, he leaned forward until his eyes were on the level of hers. The glint in those aqua eyes gave her pause. For just a minute her screaming, kicking struggles were suspended as she stared back at him. If she'd had her hands free, she would have once again made the sign that warded off the evil eye. Then she got hold of herself. Evil eye or no, this was a mortal man who would harm her as a mortal man harms a female. To save herself, she had to fight.

"Lay a hand on me and I'll kill you, I swear I will," she said through her teeth. The fierceness of the threat made his eyebrows lift, and then a corner of his mouth quirked up just a fraction in the suggestion of an unwary smile. Caitlyn, knowing in the part of her mind that was still thinking rationally how absurd it was that she, who wasn't even half his size, should threaten dire bodily harm to him, saw no humor in the situation at all. She might be small, but she would inflict some damage on him if he didn't leave her be. She would!

"Nobody's going to hurt you," he said soothingly. "I just want some straight answers, if you please. First, and most important, are you lad or lass?"

"Lad!"

He looked at her in a considering way. His face was very close, close enough so that she could see that, without the rice powder, his skin was a light golden bronze. The blue-black of his hair and brows was matched by the color of the thick stubby lashes that framed those aqua eyes. His nose was long and straight in his narrow face, his cheekbones high and his jaw strong and lean. A day's growth of whiskers stubbled his cheeks. His mouth was wide and well shaped, and now it quirked maddeningly at her. As she gave him back look for look, her impulse was to spit at him, which she just managed to control for dire fear of the consequences.

"The truth, mind!"

"Lad!"

Connor sighed. "It would be very easy to check, you know, if you make it necessary. Now, I will ask this just once more, and the consequences of a falsehood lie on your own head: are you lad or lass?"

Caitlyn glared at him. She was in a terrible quandary. Every instinct urged her to deny the truth, but as he had said, it would be very easy to check. He would probably enjoy doing so. It might even lead to the very thing of which she had lived in dread for so long.

"Lass," she spat, hating him. Her eyes met his with angry, proud defiance. If he thought she would now cringe before him, he was very mistaken.

"Ahh!" he said. Then, "If I were to let you go, would you find it necessary to rend me limb from limb, do you suppose? Or could you sit there peacefully, knowing yourself in no danger at all, while we exchange a few words of harmless conversation?"

She said nothing, just glowered at him.

"Will you sit?" he asked, his hands tightening only a fraction on the wrists he still imprisoned. Remembering the power those hands could exert from the day before, she nodded jerkily.

"Aye."

"Very well." He straightened, releasing her, his hands on his hips as he regarded her as one would an extremely problematic object. Caitlyn lifted her chin and met him stare for stare. Inwardly she was quaking with fear. But if she had learned nothing else in her years on the streets, she had learned never to show that she was afraid of anyone or anything. "So you're a lassie, are you? What are we to do with you now, I wonder?"

The softness of his voice told her that he was speaking mainly to himself. The answer would occur to him before long, if it hadn't already, she felt sure. What else would a man do with a female who was helpless and in his power but use her for his pleasure? Maybe they all would. At the thought, sweat broke out on her upper lip. She had to escape — she had to! Despair brought the glimmer of a plan.

"I'm sore hungry," she said humbly, dropping her eyes so that he wouldn't see the gleam of desperation in them and be put on guard. "Would there be a chance that you could get me something to eat before we talk further?"

She felt his eyes on the top of her bent head. Daring a peep up at him, she saw that the frown once again creased his brow. Afraid that her very meekness might make him suspect her motives, she took a quick breath for courage. Lifting her chin, she met those aqua eyes head-on. "Or is it that you're planning to starve me?"

The belligerence of her tone sounded entirely natural, she decided. Not a hint of panic or resolve was to be heard. He even smiled a little.

"Nah, we've no plans to starve you, lad or lass. Mrs. McFee has some supper left, I'm sure. But you'll stay in this room while I fetch it. And I'll be locking the door behind me. We still have some talking to do."

With that warning, he turned and left the room, closing and locking the door behind him as he had threatened. Caitlyn could barely contain her relief. It was what she had been aiming for, to be left alone. There was a window in the room. It was small, but then so was she. She would be out it in a trice.

Moving swiftly but as silently as possible across the room, wary of creaking boards, she grasped the latch and pulled. With a loud creak that brought her heart flying into her throat, one side of the casement opened inward. Then she saw why he had been so willing to leave her alone. The window was firmly shuttered. Opening the other half of the casement, she shoved against the shutters with all her might, but to no avail. They were solid wood, firmly latched. Then, through the tiny crack that separated the two panels, she saw a narrow dark line. The latch! If she could just find something thin enough to fit through that narrow space, and strong enough to pry up the hook . . .

Knowing that Connor could return at any instant, she quickly searched the room, and at last found what she sought on the littered surface of the mahogany desk: an elegant silver letter opener! Grasping her prize, she ran back to the window. Its blade was just a trifle too wide, but she managed to wedge it into the opening by holding it in her left hand and using the heel of her right hand as a hammer. Finally she had it positioned, its point just below the latch. Holding her breath, she forced the letter opener upward. After much maneuvering, the point of the letter opener caught the center of the latch. The latch slid up, then with a faint clatter fell back against the shutter outside. She pushed at the shutters, and they opened with a creak of rusty hinges. She found herself looking over the side of the house toward the way she had come. On the horizon Donoughmore Castle was silhouetted against the nearly dark sky, black and huge as it brooded high above. Caitlyn looked down, saw that the yard around the house was shadowy and deserted, and swung her leg over the sill. It was a goodly drop, but she had survived worse. Hanging by her hands from the sill, she let herself fall to the ground. Hitting on the balls of her feet, she staggered forward, caught herself, then dropped into a low crouch. After satisfying herself that she was unobserved, she was off and running. Toward what she didn't know; she only knew that she had to get away.

VIII

✳ ✳ ✳ ✳ ✳ ✳ ✳ ✳ ✳ ✳ ✳ ✳ ✳ ✳ ✳

For two days Caitlyn was forced to lie low. The d'Arcys had bands of peasants scouring the countryside for her. Connor himself rode with Mickeen and Cormac back down the road they had traveled the very night she disappeared, and twice a day thereafter. Caitlyn had hidden in the ruined Castle the first night, and as one day and then the next passed with no apparent letup in the search, she was afraid to leave it, afraid that she would be taken up by Connor along the road or by his minions in the fields. She thought it was best to let the pursuit die down a little before making her way back to Dublin and the life she had always known.

Her one regret was that she would have to leave Willie behind. First, it would be foolhardy in the extreme for her to try to contact him; the d'Arcys weren't stupid. It was likely that they would be expecting that. Second, Willie had undoubtedly learned her true sex by now. She could not count on him to keep her secret indefinitely if he returned with her to Dublin. Willie was a guileless lad. Sooner or later he was bound to let the cat out of the bag. And then she would be in trouble indeed. But she would be lonely when she went back, and that was the truth.

Hunger and boredom were her worst problems as she whiled away the hours until she considered it safe to leave. Fortunately, a trio of hens had also chosen the Castle as a likely roosting spot, so she was able to steal their eggs, which kept her from total starvation. Raw eggs were not the tastiest meal she had ever had, but they were not the worst either. Water was not a problem. It rained for several hours each day, and big puddles lay everywhere.

During the daylight hours she stayed high up in the ruined tower. That first night, frantic to find a hiding place while Connor's bellowed curses rang in her ear (he had missed her almost at once, and his rage at her escape had echoed from the hills), she had scrambled up the hillside toward the Castle without ever really even thinking about it. She had just reached the crumbling walls when Mickeen had run up almost directly on her heels to summon the peasants from their shacks to aid in the search. Leaping over the rubble of stones as nimbly as the sheep had earlier, she had crouched in the shadow of the wall, peering over it as dozens of torches massed at the manor house and then scattered out over the countryside. For some reason, she had not expected Connor to go to so much effort to find her. He must have been furious at the thwarting of his evil plans for her.

As a group of the searchers had drawn near the Castle, she had stumbled away from the wall in a panic, scattering the tight little knot of sheep that had decided to sleep inside the barn. They surged away from her with loud bleats. For a horrible few moments Caitlyn had feared discovery. She had run for the first hidey-hole to meet her frightened eyes. The bite out of the side of the ruined tower showed steps winding up. Heart pounding as the searchers came over the wall, she climbed, keeping close to the wall so that she would be less likely to be exposed by their torches. Safe in the round parapet at the top of the tower, she watched over the side as they searched the keep. It seemed like hours before they went away, their torches straggling back down over the hillside to finally bob along the banks of the Boyne.

Left alone, she shivered as she realized where she was. In the battlement she was safe from the searchers, yes, but was she safe from the banshees that might very well haunt the Castle? The shade of the old Earl, for one, and that of his wife, who had drawn her last breath on this pile of stones, and all those who had come before them. Everyone knew that ghosties walked the earth at the place where they had died a violent or early death. Gray clouds rushing past the tiny sliver of moon overhead caused the moonlight to constantly shift, making it look from the tower as if legions of silvery beings were on the move in the barn. Crossing herself with a shudder, Caitlyn curled up into a tiny ball, hoping to make herself invisible to the things that walked in the night. Finally, as dawn began to streak the sky, she felt safe enough to close her eyes.

By the time she awoke, it was broad daylight. She sat up, stretching and rubbing her eyes, and wondered how long it would take her to walk to Dublin. Not more than two days, she calculated. Standing, she glanced toward the farmhouse, certain that Connor would have lost interest in pursuing a stray lass by this time. Instead she saw him leading a mounted party along the river, while Rory emerged with some men from the sheep barn, shouting something to the effect that she was not there. More men were spread out over the countryside, combing the peat fields in a systematic fashion that alarmed her all over again. Connor was truly serious about finding her, then. Her opinion of his intentions had obviously been right on target. No one would take so much trouble for an orphaned runaway who was clearly of no use to anyone — except as an object for a man's pleasure. That was why he wanted her, no doubt. What other reason could there be?

By evening of the third day, the search had pretty much died down. That afternoon the peasants had returned to cutting peat, and Rory and Mickeen had herded several groups of sheep into the sheep barn and stayed inside with them for over an hour. Connor she had seen just once, as he had ridden off on Fharannain. By sunset he had not returned.

If she had been certain of Connor's whereabouts, she would have set out for Dublin there and then. But there was too much risk of running into him along the road. Of course, she could always hide if she heard his approach, but what if she didn't hear it? Or what if he found her anyway? Those devil's eyes of his probably signified that he possessed the second sight. No, Caitlyn told herself, it was better to remain safely hidden until just before dawn. Then she could slip away and no one would be the wiser.

Later on, she began to wish that she had not chosen to remain in the Castle for a final few hours. The night grew so dark that she could barely see ten feet in front of her face. There was no moon, and the wind whipped wildly through the slits in the battlement, whistling as it went. Before morning she predicted there would be a storm. In the barn, the sheep were unnaturally quiet. Caitlyn thought she could hear whispering voices and muffled footsteps floating on the air. At first she convinced herself that it was strictly her imagination. But as the sounds grew more distinct, with creaks and a single strangled shriek added to the repertoire, she was forced to conclude to her horror that the ghoulies were up and about. Huddling on the cold stone floor of the parapet, she prayed for the quick coming of dawn. As if in sneering answer, the heavens opened and sheets of rain deluged her and the countryside.

The battlement afforded no shelter from the nonstop downpour. Achingly cold, wet to the bone, and thoroughly miserable, Caitlyn vowed to sit out the storm where she was rather than seek shelter inside the Castle, where the ghosties rattled and moaned. But then a great bolt of lightning shot from the sky, illuminating the countryside as it shivered and crashed its way to earth. Within minutes it was followed by another, then another. Staying where she was, perched on the very top of a tall tower in an open plain, was foolhardy. But oh, she did not want to go below where the ghosties could get her! Another sword of lightning, this one crashing to ground alarmingly close, made up her mind. Feeling her way carefully over the rain-slick steps, hugging close to the tower wall so as not to be blown from her perch by the shrieking wind, she began her descent. She would shelter among the sheep in the barn. How could a ghostie find the one human among so many living creatures?

Caitlyn had just ventured out of the tower when a muffled drumming sound caught her attention. Holy Mary, was an entire army of ghosties coming for her? Straining to see through the lashing rain, she shielded her eyes with her hands, staring toward the tumbledown place in the wall from beyond which the sound seemed to be coming. The thudding grew louder, as if a legion of horses were being run straight at the Castle wall. But what horsemen would be abroad on such a night? Even as she thought that, lightning crashed again. At the exact same instant an enormous black beast flew over the wall, followed by another and another and another and another.

Horses! Huge black shapes in the dark night, ridden by faceless riders in billowing hooded capes. Horrified, Caitlyn stared because she could not tear her eyes away. The horses thudded down not ten feet from where she stood, their riders not seeing her as, terror-stricken, she pressed up against the stone tower. Soundless except for the drumming hooves, the ghostly horses galloped straight toward a stone archway and disappeared into the Castle itself. For a moment Caitlyn distinctly heard the clatter of hooves on stone. Then there was a shriek and . . . silence. Nothing at all.

Holding her breath, feeling as though her heart would pound right through the walls of her chest, Caitlyn continued to stare toward the place where the riders had disappeared. It was some time before she realized that they had literally vanished. They weren't coming back out, and they weren't inside the Castle either. They had faded into the air. Barely containing a scream of horror, she turned and scurried back up into her parapet, to huddle shivering against cold stone as she recited the Hail Mary over and over again. Ghosts were abroad this night, and she wanted nothing more to do with them. Better, far better, that she take her chances with the lightning and the rain.

After that sleep was impossible. She kept fearing to see another apparition, to hear more unearthly sounds. The rain kept on until just before dawn. Caitlyn was already making her way down the winding tower steps as the sky started to lighten. Not for anything would she spend another night in Donoughmore Castle. She was convinced that what she had seen last night were specters straight from Hell.

As she climbed over the piles of rubble on the side of the Castle facing away from the farm, she heard voices. For an awful moment she thought the ghoulies had risen up even in daylight to chase her. Then she recognized words and voices, and panic of a different sort assailed her.

"Search everywhere. The dungeons, towers, everywhere. If she's here, I want her found. Though I doubt she is." Caitlyn shivered as she identified that voice: it belonged to Connor. He said the last more quietly than the rest, as though to a speaker nearer to him.

"I tell you, she is here! She's probably been hiding here all along!" That was Cormac.

"I doubt it, Cormac. 'Twas probably a peasant seeking shelter from the storm. The little lass is long gone by now, though how she eluded us confounds me."

"She didn't elude us, don't you see? She hid, here in the Castle!"

"The men will search it thoroughly this time, don't worry. But I still think —"

"There she is!" That bellow from Cormac brought Caitlyn's head swinging around. There they were, rounding the corner of the wall, Connor on Fharannain and Cormac on a shiny bay mare. In that quick, horrified glimpse, Caitlyn saw that a small band of peasants was spreading out inside the Castle walls, obviously beginning a renewed search. Which was unnecessary now that the d'Arcys had seen . . .

As they spurred their horses toward her, Caitlyn started to run. Slipping and sliding on the rain-wet grass, knowing it was useless, that it would be impossible to outrun the horses, still she tried, fleeing like a fox before the hounds. Behind her, hooves thundered. She dared a quick look over her shoulder to find Fharannain almost upon her. It seemed as though Connor meant to run her down. Screaming, she veered to the left. The horse flashed by, brushing her. Then she was caught by a hard arm, lifted, and deposited facedown across the saddle in front of Connor. The shock of it kept her silent for a moment. But only for a moment.

"Let me go!" she shrieked, kicking and hitting out in a blind panic. Her toes thudded into Fharannain's sleek sides; her fists thumped his ribs. Whinnying in surprise at such treatment, the horse reared, hooves pawing the air. Caitlyn was almost thrown to the ground.

"Damnation!" Connor managed to control the beast, bringing it back to earth after a few moments' wild ride. Then he set the animal at a gallop toward the farm. Caitlyn had to wrap both arms around Connor's hard-muscled leg to keep from falling off, straight beneath Fharannain's hooves. The ride took only a few minutes. Then Connor was reining in, jumping down from the horse as he tossed the reins to Cormac, who had followed. Caitlyn found herself hauled from the saddle and slung over Connor's shoulder like a sack of grain. She shrieked a protest, beating his back with her fists. She would have kicked him, but he held her legs securely still.

"Let me go! Do you hear? Let me go!" He was striding through the back door with her. Caitlyn screamed curses at all and sundry as he bore her through the kitchen, past Mrs. McFee in her apron and Mickeen, who was squatted by the great fireplace, apparently stoking up the fire. They both turned to gawk. Caitlyn spat in their general direction as she was carried into the hall.

"Mickeen, bring hot water to fill the bath in my room. Mrs. McFee, we'll be needing some dry clothes. Female clothes. Whatever a female needs to be decent from the skin out!" With these instructions shouted over his shoulder as he moved out the kitchen door, Connor took the stairs two at a time. The gaping pair of servants followed their master as far as the hallway, watching wide-eyed as he disappeared with a shrieking, cursing Caitlyn around the bend in the stairs. Mrs. McFee's face reddened at the curses, and she and Mickeen exchanged a significant look before turning to fulfill their master's bidding. Caitlyn's protests rose to such a volume that they fair shook the rafters.

"You put me down!" Frantic with desperation, her blows seeming to bother him not at all, she pressed her face into Connor's lean-muscled back and bit him in the fleshy area over his ribs. He was coatless, clad only in a shirt, breeches, and black riding boots. With so little resistance, her teeth nearly met in his flesh before she let him go.

"Hellfire and damnation!" Even as he bellowed in rage and pain, Caitlyn went flying through the air. Instinctively she raised her arms to protect her head from the anticipated impact when she slammed into the hard wooden floor. Instead she landed bouncing on a soft feather bed. That knowledge was worse than hitting the floor would have been. She barely touched the mattress before she was scrambling to the other side of the bed and leaping from it.

"I'll kill you if you touch me!" Terror sent her heartbeat drumming in her ears as she stood poised to run. Connor, standing on the opposite side of the large four-poster, scowled and rubbed his wounded side.

"Bite me again and I'll flay the skin from your bones! As God is my witness, I will!"

They glared at each other. Caitlyn looked beyond Connor to the door, which was open behind him. Perhaps she could dash for freedom. But Connor was in the way, tall and strong and threatening. With that grim look on his face and those devil's eyes flaring at her, he in no way resembled the soft-faced Sassenach she had at first thought him. Without his coat, she could see the broad shoulders and hard muscles of his chest and arms, the narrow hips, the long, hard-muscled legs. He was a powerful man. Getting by him would not be easy.

"You son of the serpent!" Casting wild eyes behind her, she spied a silver brush and comb set on his dressing table. Reaching for the brush, she let it fly. He ducked, cursing, and the brush thudded into the wall behind his head. Before he had recovered, she threw the comb after it. He ducked that too, growling as he straightened. As she had hoped, he came around the bed toward her, fury emanating from his every pore. Quick as a cat, she scrambled across the bed and toward the door. Her feet touched the floor, and then a hand closed over her upper arm, yanking her back onto the bed. She sprawled on her back, her wet clothes making damp marks on the coverlet. He loomed over her, eyes snapping, mouth contorted into a snarl. Caitlyn screamed, fearing that she would be ravished there and then. As her scream blasted into his face he snatched her up in his arms.

Thrusting his long legs over the edge of the bed, he turned her over in midair and deposited her facedown across his knee. While she screamed and cursed and flailed, he administered a blistering spanking to the back-side of her breeches. Her soft flesh burned and smarted with each blow. Her pride ached more.

"You can't do this to me! I'll kill you! You bastard!"

"I've had enough of your filthy mouth! And enough of your temper! You will behave yourself in this house, is that understood?"

A hard whack on her behind emphasized his words. Caitlyn screamed, kicked, and cursed.

"Is that understood?" The question was roared.

"No!"

Whack! Whack! Whack!

"Understood?"

"No! Stop it! Bloody bastard!"

Whack! Whack!

"All right!" She was sobbing now, as much from humiliation as from pain. In all her life, Caitlyn O'Malley had never been forced to knuckle under. But she was knuckling now, to this devil-eyed son of Satan who would break her if she didn't. And she hated him for it. How she hated him!

"Very well." He let her slide off his lap. She crumpled to the floor, lying there for a moment, shamed to the core of her being by her surrender. Her bottom ached with a vengeance, but the humiliation she felt was the worst pain of all. Then temper reared its face-saving head, and a red-hot rage flooded her veins.

"You spawn of Satan!" Springing to her feet before he had any inkling of her intention, she slammed her doubled fist into his right eye with every ounce of her strength. The blow was so hard that it knocked him backward on the bed. He bellowed with fury and pain. Caitlyn darted for the door. Before she could make it he was upon her in a flying tackle. This time she did hit the hard wood planks of the floor. His great weight landed on top of her with a *whompf!* Stunned, she lay still for a moment while he lay on top of her, panting.

"Ah, do you need any help, Conn?"

Caitlyn looked up to see Liam, his boots planted just a few feet from her face, staring down at the two of them as they lay panting on the floor, half inside the bedroom and half in the hallway. Behind Liam was Rory, grinning widely, with Cormac, also grinning, behind him. Mrs. McFee stood on the stairs, a bundle of clothes in her hand and a scandalized expression on her face. Mickeen was coming up, puffing as he carried two brimming buckets of water.

"Don't you have chores to do? The lot of you?" Connor growled in response as he got to his feet, dragging Caitlyn up with him. For the time being she was spent, but he dragged her arm behind her back and held it there for insurance, as he pulled her inside his bedroom.

"Aye." Liam hurriedly shooed his brothers back down the stairs, while Mickeen brushed by them to pour water into the tin bath concealed behind a screen in a corner of Connor's bedroom. Mrs. McFee, muttering dire things punctuated with "Sinful!" and "Ungodly!", followed Mickeen into the room and placed the assortment of clothes on the bed. Turning around, she folded her hands in front of her and eyed Connor severely as he stood holding a gasping Caitlyn captive just inside the door.

"I'll have you know, your lordship, that I won't be a party to any shameful goings on in this house! The idea, a lass dressing like that and carrying on in the company of men! And her cursing! It's sinful, it is, and full of sin she is! The ungodly thing should be sent straight back whence she came! Take care that she doesn't lead you down her hellbound path!"

"She's naught but a child, Mrs. McFee, with I doubt any more notion of sin than a babe. And I believe I am still master here?" Connor's voice was soft, but even Caitlyn shivered at the tone of it. Mrs. McFee reddened, then bowed her head, leaving the room without another word.

"Do you need more water, your lordship? The tub's perhaps a quarter full."

"That should be enough, Mickeen. Thank you. You can get on about your work now."

"Aye, your lordship." His disapproving expression as he eyed Caitlyn, standing limply now in Connor's hold, said volumes that he didn't quite dare, after Mrs. McFee's setdown, to express in words. Connor merely jerked his head in the direction of the door. Mickeen left, closing it behind him. Connor dragged Caitlyn over to the door, turned the key in the lock, and slipped it into his pocket.

"I'm going to let you go, but I want no more of your temper, understand?"

Caitlyn nodded once, jerkily. Connor released her. Immediately she moved to the center of the room and turned, eyeing him warily. He sighed.

"Suppose you bathe, then dress yourself in clothes befitting your sex. Then we can have that talk."

"I've already had a bath this week. I'll not be needing another."

Connor's eyes narrowed. "You're soaked to the bone and so cold you feel like a block of ice. I doubt you've been dry since you came to Donoughmore. Now, I don't care to have your death from pneumonia on my conscience, so I am telling you to get in that bath. Or, lass or no, I'll put you there myself!"

"I'm no lass!"

"Hell and the devil confound it! I've had enough of your arguments! I've said you're to bathe, and you will do so! And if you want to do it in privacy, then you'll give me no more sass!" He looked on the verge of an apoplexy. Caitlyn's eyes widened as the full import of his threat registered.

"All right." She conceded immediately, secretly elated that he meant to leave her alone for the task. It was almost inconceivable that he would be foolish enough to make the same mistake twice, but she wasn't about to look a gift horse in the mouth. While he was gone, she would climb out one of the two narrow-paned windows and escape again. It was all she could do to prevent a triumphant grin from curling her lips.

His eyes narrowed at her. She was glad to see that the flesh around the right one was beginning to swell where she had struck him. She hoped he had a black eye to remember her by.

"I'll give you fifteen minutes. If you're not decent by then . . ." He left the threat hanging. Caitlyn nodded in reply. With one more narrow-eyed look at her, he let himself out of the room. Caitlyn heard the lock click shut behind him. For a long moment she stood clasping and unclasping her hands in front of her, afraid that he meant to stand outside and listen at the door. He would likely hear her open the window. But then she heard his booted feet clomping down the hall. Holding her breath until she heard him on the stairs, she ran at once to the nearest window. It opened with difficulty, but using all her strength she managed to force a wide enough space for her body to fit through. Swinging one leg over the sill, she was frozen by a shrill whistle. Heart in mouth, she looked down to see Cormac grinning up at her.

"Ah-ah," he said, waggling a finger at her. Caitlyn cursed and spat at him. He laughed as he jumped back. Climbing back inside, she cursed again, knowing she was defeated. There was no escape this time. To relieve her feelings, she picked up the squat white pitcher that stood in the bowl for washing and hurled it against the door. The ensuing crash of splintering glass was immensely satisfying. She had just picked up the bowl to send it the way of its fellow when she heard the key turn in the lock. As Connor burst through the door, eyes flashing, she hurled the bowl at his head.

This time she hit him. The bowl glanced off his shoulder instead of his head only because he ducked. With a furious roar he dived across the room toward her. Caitlyn turned to flee, but he was upon her in an instant, his hard hands on her shoulders shaking the daylights out of her.

"Damn it, I'll have no more of your tantrums! You break one more thing in this house and I'll take it out of your scrawny hide! Understand?" he roared. His fury was terrifying. It even frightened Caitlyn.

"Aye! I understand!" His eyes were pools of liquid fire.

"Since you won't bathe yourself, I'll do it for you! You'll learn that I'm the master here, and I will be obeyed! Aye, you'll learn, however much you suffer for the lessons!"

His anger was so fierce it had a life of its own. Caitlyn, still being shaken to a fare-thee-well, could only cry out in protest when he wrapped a hand in the worn fabric at the neck of her shirt and jerked down. As the material ripped to the waist, he stopped shaking her abruptly, his eyes on her chest widening with a dawning shock. Looking down at herself, Caitlyn saw her two small but unmistakably female breasts thrusting out at him. There was a moment of deafening silence. Then, for the first time since she was a wee bairn, she burst into tears.

IX

❋ ❋ ❋ ❋ ❋ ❋ ❋ ❋ ❋ ❋ ❋ ❋ ❋ ❋ ❋

"Ah, now, don't cry. 'Tis sorry I am to have done such a thing. I thought you were no more than a bairn. I see that you're not such a wee one as I supposed."

Now that the dam had burst, Caitlyn put her hands over her face and sobbed as though her heart would break. She had not cried this way since the terrible dark days after she had seen her mother borne away to be buried in a pauper's grave. In all the years since, she had not allowed herself the luxury of tears. For a child alone, the world was a hard, cruel place, and she had to be just as hard to survive in it. But the tensions and terrors of the past few days, combined with her very real fear of the man before her and what he meant to do, broke the iron hold she had kept on her emotions and set them free. It disgusted her, but she could not seem to stop crying.

"Hush, now, lassie. There's no need for such grief. None of us means you any harm." He was sounding more Irish by the moment. Caitlyn, overwrought, sobbed louder. She felt his hand brush her body, a featherlight touch on the side of her right breast, and leaped backward.

"Don't you touch me! I'll kill you if you touch me!" She hissed the words at him through her tears, her hands dropping to her sides and clenching into fists as she spoke. Female though she might be, she could still defend herself. If he thought to take her body, he would pay dearly for the privilege.

"I was just trying to make you decent, is all. You've naught to fear, I swear it." His tone was gentle as he gestured at her chest.

A frown lodged between his brows, while those devil's eyes flicked quickly back up to her face. If she hadn't known better, she would have sworn he was embarrassed. Looking belatedly down at her chest, Caitlyn saw that the small, pink-tipped mounds of her breasts were still exposed, and heaving with the force of her sobs. In her overwrought state, she had neglected to cover herself. Feeling unaccustomed heat creep up her neck and over her face to her hairline at the thought of his eyes on her, she pulled the torn ends of the shirt together and glared at him. Though she didn't know it, she looked pathetic, small and dirty and defiant, with huge tears trembling on her lashes and making paths through the dirt on her cheeks as she clutched her torn shirt and scowled like a small creature at bay.

"Trust me, child. I mean you no harm. Neither I nor my brothers would hurt a wee lassie." He crossed his arms over his chest and looked at her compassionately.

"I'm no wee lassie!" flared Caitlyn. Then, at the knowledge that he had every reason to disbelieve that blatant untruth, she burst into tears again. Sobs shook her thin body. She could not let go of her shirt without exposing her breasts to him again, so he was treated to the sight of tears coursing down her cheeks like rain while her mouth trembled and her nose reddened.

"Sweet Jesus." Connor sighed the words under his breath. Then, taking a step forward, he picked her up in his arms as though she weighed no more than a babe. Caitlyn shrieked, flailing. He pinned her arms and legs with ease. " 'Tis all right, child. I told you, I mean you no harm."

"Put me down, damn you! Put me down!" She was choking on sobs even as she fought for her freedom. Ignoring her struggles, he took two strides, then sank down into a large horsehair chair in a corner of the room with her on his lap.

"Cry it out, then, child. 'Tis doubtless what you need."

Caitlyn fought frantically for a moment, sure he meant to do more than merely hold her on his lap as one would a bairn. But he contained her flailing limbs so that she could not hurt him. After a while she gave up and went limp, resting tiredly back against the solid warmth of his chest and closing her eyes. Tears poured down her face, and sobs shook her slight frame. Before she knew it, she was curled sobbing against his chest.

"That's right, lassie. That's the way." His hold gentled as she ceased to fight him. His arms were loose around her, stroking her hair, patting her back. There was a kind of awkwardness about his actions that told her that he wasn't entirely at ease with the situation, that it was one in which he had not found himself many times before. As she thought of him comforting one of his brothers in such a fashion, a small watery hiccup of amusement tried to escape. When they had been hurting as children, Connor more than likely had cuffed them on the shoulder and told them to be men. But she was a female, which made all the difference. For whatever reason, he was being kind. She had never had anyone to comfort her since her mother died, and the luxury of being held in someone's arms while she sobbed and gulped and gasped encouraged her to cry out the fear and loneliness and despair that had been her constant companions for years. With her face pressed against his shoulder, she cried until there were no more tears left inside her. Then at last she lay quietly against him, gulping and sniffing like a tired child. Her fingers had curled unconsciously in his shirt front, which was damp from her tears.

When her snifflings were reduced to no more than an occasional shuddering breath, he spoke very quietly to the top of her head, which still rested against his chest. "Now you see I haven't harmed you, and I will not. You have no need to fear anyone at Donoughmore."

Caitlyn stiffened, sitting upright in his lap. With her tears behind her, her wariness of him returned, not as strong as before but still warning her that he was a man and she a defenseless female. Her eyes flew to meet his, huge blue pools in a tear-drenched little face. Her mouth trembled. With a conscious effort she stilled the trembling, gathering up the shreds of her pride as best she could. Then she remembered her torn shirt, which in the face of all her unaccustomed emotion she had forgotten, and looked down to find her breasts exposed again.

Gasping, she scrabbled for the ends of her shirt and clutched them together, her eyes flying to his. He met her wary look with a slight, reassuring smile. Caitlyn was not reassured. As she had bolted erect, his hold had loosened, his arms slipping from around her so that they rested now on the arms of the chair. There was nothing compelling her to stay in such close proximity to him. She scrambled off his lap and whirled to face him, glaring down at him as she held the front of her shirt together. He looked very big and very strong sitting there at his ease, his shoulders as broad as the back of the chair against which they rested and his legs in their black breeches and boots stretched out before him. His curly black head lay back against the rose-colored horsehair, and those light eyes fixed on her face. Her eyes touched on the cradle of his thighs. Momentarily she pictured herself curled up there. A vivid scarlet blush stained her cheeks. To compensate for her embarrassment, she glowered at him. Like a man in the presence of a frightened young animal, he made no sudden moves but stayed seated, smiling wryly up at her.

"Back to yourself already, I see," he said.

"I'll not be staying here." It was a challenge. Gripping her shirt together with one hand, she swiped the back of the other over her still-wet eyes. Connor sighed and got to his feet with slow, careful movements. Caitlyn took a quick step backward, eyes widening as they fixed on him. He shook his head at her. Then he crossed his arms over his chest and leaned one shoulder against the wall, regarding her as if she were a problem the likes of which he had not faced before.

"I offered you a home, child, and employment. The offer is not withdrawn simply because you are a lass."

"Still, I'll not be staying." Caitlyn was bristling at him, desperate to get back to her lost sense of self after the demeaning weakness of tears. With the revelation of her sex, she felt as if her soul had been stripped bare. As a female, she felt vulnerable, and she hated the feeling. She longed to step back into the skin of the cocky, self-sufficient lad she had been for so long.

"So you would go back to Dublin, back to being O'Malley the thief." The words were slow, drawn out, and he studied her as he spoke.

"Aye!"

"What do you suppose would happen to you if your sex were discovered in Dublin, as it inevitably would be? 'Tis not something a lass can conceal forever. You've been lucky so far because you're not much more than a child. As you mature, the secret is bound to come out. What then?"

"No one will find out. No one ever has."

"We found out, just because my nitwit brothers were joking around with you. If we can discover your secret, so can others. Others who might not scruple to hurt a wee lassie. What if you were taken up for thieving? Do you not think that they would find out you were a lass as soon as you were put into the gaol? Not that it would keep them from hanging you, but they'd have fun disporting themselves upon you first. You do know what I'm talking about? Ah, I see you do. I guessed as much, from your fear of men."

Caitlyn stared at him, chewing on her lower lip with a kind of desperation. There was sense in what he said, but she didn't want to see it. With every fiber of her being, she longed to go back to being the lad she had been.

"We won't harm you, child, but others might. You should thank your patron saint that you landed in a safe berth. You can make your home with us and be a lassie without fear of aught." He paused for a moment, taking a long look at her. Then he added, almost indifferently, "But if you truly wish to go back to Dublin, back to being O'Malley the thief, I'll not stand in your way. The decision is yours, but I'd be having your answer now."

Caitlyn swallowed, her eyes huge and uncertain as they searched his face. In the short time she had known him, those lean dark planes had become almost as familiar to her as her own features. It struck her suddenly, irrelevantly, that he was a very handsome man. The question was, did she trust him? Her heart drummed wildly. She was afraid to abandon the lad she had been, afraid to be a female for all to see. But if he had wanted to take his pleasure of her, he could already have done so and she could not have prevented him. Instead he had been kind. Against everything she had ever learned in her life, she almost felt she could trust him. Licking her lips, drawing a deep shuddering breath as anxiety over the decision squeezed her chest like an iron band, she said, barely above a whisper, "I'll stay."

He smiled at her, his eyes warming. The last flicker of distrust Caitlyn had been harboring wavered. If it did not fall entirely, it crumpled a little. She did not quite smile back at him, but she came close.

"A wise decision." He was as crisp as if he were addressing the lad she had been. Dropping his arms, he moved toward her. Caitlyn, instinctively alarmed, backed away. He raised his eyebrows at her as he walked past where she hugged the wall and headed toward the door. With his hand on the knob, he turned back to face her.

"I know it will be difficult for you to get accustomed to garbing yourself as a female, but 'tis necessary. Mrs. McFee, to say nothing of the rest of the folk around here, will be scandalized if you continue to wear male clothing. So you will oblige me by soaking in the hot water there and then dressing yourself in the things Mrs. McFee found for you. When you're dressed, come down to the kitchen. From the smell of it, breakfast is nigh ready. After you have some food inside you, we'll see what more there is to be done."

"I don't want to wear female clothes." She wrapped her arms around herself protectively. But she was damp, and cold, and the thought of getting into dry clothes of whatever persuasion was tempting.

"I know. But as I said, 'tis necessary. You are a lass, after all, and now that everyone knows it, you could not wear breeches. It would not be proper."

Caitlyn scowled. Connor d'Arcy was bloody accustomed to giving orders, that much was clear. What he would have to learn was that she was not accustomed to taking them.

From his position by the door, he looked at her speculatively. "It would please me greatly if you would don skirts, child." He smiled at her, a lovely coaxing smile that could have charmed a bee out of its hive.

Caitlyn wavered. Put like that . . . She was conscious of a sudden strong desire to please him.

"Very well, I'll try the clothes," she said ungraciously.

"Thank you." He turned the key in the lock and opened the door. Then, bethinking himself of something, he turned back to her. "Have you a name besides O'Malley?"

"O'Malley'll do." She was loath to surrender so much so fast.

Connor smiled serenely at her. His eyes were as placid as summer pools in that dark face. "If you have none of your own, we'll call you Bridget. I've always had a fondness for that name."

Caitlyn's scowl deepened as he started out the door.

"Caitlyn," she said abruptly. "Me ma called me Caitlyn."

He sent a quick glimmering look over his shoulder at her. There was laughter in the aqua eyes, but they were also kind.

"Ah, Caitlyn," he said as if weighing the name. "Yes, that will do. Come down to the kitchen when you're dressed, Caitlyn."

And then he took himself off, leaving Caitlyn to glare at the closed door. It was some five minutes later before she reluctantly turned her attention to the bath.

X

Three weeks later, Caitlyn was rebelliously peeling potatoes under the disapproving eye of Mrs. McFee. In attire she was a miniature copy of that good lady, clad in a sleeveless linen dress of green and yellow stripes that left the long white sleeves of her shift on view. It had been inexpertly cut down from an old one of Mrs. McFee's. While it was cooler than the other dress she now possessed — long-sleeved, solid blue kerseymere, courtesy of the same source — it still seemed hellishly hot in the sweatshop atmosphere of the kitchen, where mutton roasted on a turnspit in the immense stone fireplace and various vegetables and fruits for a pie bubbled in iron pots suspended over the fire. The too-large white mobcap she wore kept slipping down over one eye, driving Caitlyn mad as she had to swipe it back with one hand. Her apron, which was so large she had it wrapped twice about her middle, had started out white but now bore numerous multicolored splotches from all the things she had spilled on herself that afternoon alone. (She had changed the one she had worn during the morning; Mrs. McFee was a stickler for cleanliness.)

Despite the sweat that beaded her brow and upper lip as she worked, Caitlyn herself was cleaner than she had ever been in her life. She feared that her skin would rub clear off her bones if she scoured herself any more. Her hair had been scrubbed by Mrs. McFee personally (who made no secret of the fact that she feared finding lice) until her scalp was raw. Clean, it was soft, shiny, and inky black. Caitlyn wore it gathered into a skimpy, straggly bun at her nape, with the mobcap over the whole as Mrs. McFee informed her was proper. From her hairline to her toes inside the sturdy leather shoes she had been allowed to keep, since they were not much different from women's footgear and anyway there were no shoes at Donoughmore to fit her small feet, her skin was as white as the belly of a whale. Straight, inky-black brows and lashes framing kerry blue eyes and the faint pink of her mouth were the only touches of color in her face. Small nicks from the knife she was using covered her hands, and her blood was mixed liberally into the bowl of misshapen peeled potatoes at her left hand. Piles of potato peelings covered the scrubbed tabletop and littered the flagstone floor. The most disheartening thing about it was that, after she had finished the monumental job of peeling enough potatoes to feed five hungry men (Mickeen joined the d'Arcys at supper), herself, and Mrs. McFee, she would then have to clean up the mess she had made. Just thinking about it made her exhausted.

It was near suppertime. Caitlyn had been working in the kitchen most of the afternoon, learning with a complete absence of enthusiasm how to cook. The truth was, she was inept, just as she was at all the women's work Mrs. McFee had set her to. She hated being a female, she did, and all that went with it!

"All done," she announced finally with an awful sigh. Mrs. McFee looked around from kneading dough to frown at her.

"Aye, and it looks like you've left more on the floor than you've got in the bowl! Ah, well, if his lordship says you're to help me, then I guess you will. Bring the bowl over here, then, lass, and get on with cleaning up the mess."

Making a face at Mrs. McFee's broad back, Caitlyn picked up the bowl and awkwardly carried it to the work table against the far wall where the woman labored. Holding her skirt carefully clear of her feet with one hand (walking without tripping over the voluminous skirt was an art), she made it to the table with nary a mishap and set the bowl down. Mrs. McFee took one glance at the contents, then shook her head.

"It's a mystery to me how two dozen big, firm potatoes can be reduced to so little. You've peeled off so much meat that there's scarce anything left! Well, what's done can't be helped, I suppose, and as his lordship says, you're bound to get better at it."

Caitlyn shrank a little under this disheartening speech. She hated being a female! She hated Mrs. McFee, with her disapproval and bossy ways! And she hated the d'Arcys, every one of them, from Cormac to Connor. Aye, even Connor, though she had to admit to a grudging admiration for him that was the sole reason that she labored so meekly under Mrs. McFee's iron direction. She wanted to please Connor, it was that simple. He loomed large in her life, did Connor, a wondrous being who could boom with rage enough to send his grown brothers scurrying and yet be unfailingly kind to her, a little scrap of nothing who had fallen by accident into his life.

"Sweep up now, do!" With those impatient words, Mrs. McFee put her back to work. Carefully tucking up her skirt into the waistband of her apron, Caitlyn found broom and pan. Then with a quick look at Mrs. McFee to be sure that the lady was not watching, she swept the broom over the table so that the peelings fell to the floor. From there it was a simple matter to sweep all the peelings together and into the pan. Feeling smug that she had at last done something right, she picked up the pan and started for the bucket in which such scraps were put. And promptly tripped over the hem of her skirt, which had worked its way loose from its temporary mooring. With a surprised oath, she went sprawling.

"Devil take it to hell and back!" As oaths went, that was not so bad. Certainly not as bad as the one she'd uttered as she'd hit the flagstone floor. Mrs. McFee, who would have to be deaf not to have heard, launched into a scandalized tirade while Caitlyn lay spent on the flagstones, too dispirited to move. Potato peelings were everywhere. It would take an hour to clean them all up again. Plus Mrs. McFee was going off, as she did half a dozen times a day. Caitlyn lay there with her chin on her hands for a moment, thinking. Then she got determinedly to her feet, pulled off her mobcap, and threw it on the floor. Her apron was next. Mrs. McFee stopped berating her to watch with widening eyes as Caitlyn tossed its starched whiteness deliberately to the floor.

"I'll not be learning any more woman's work," Caitlyn pronounced to the older woman with a lift of her chin. Then, turning on her heel, she stalked from the kitchen, remembering in the nick of time to lift the hem of her dress. Determination growing by the moment, she marched up the stairs and into Cormac's bedroom, one of the four on the second floor. Each of the d'Arcys had his own room, which was an unbelievable luxury when Caitlyn considered that in Dublin's Irish quarters most families of six or seven shared a single small room and thought themselves lucky. Their bedrooms plus the small office and hall made up the second floor. Downstairs there were two sitting rooms, the kitchen, pantries, a small stone washroom, a brewery for the brewing of beer and ale, and the dining room, which was separate from the kitchen so that, as they ate, the members of the family should not be forced to endure the heat of the huge stone fireplace that dominated the kitchen, where most of the cooking was done in iron pots. In the attic were four smaller rooms clearly meant for servants, one of which Caitlyn had been given for her own. She was the only one to sleep in the attic. Mrs. McFee lived with her daughter and son-in-law in a cottage in the village and came in each day to do for his lordship. She was the only household help.

Opening the wardrobe which stood against the far wall, Caitlyn rummaged around until she found drawers, breeches, stockings, and shirt. She was too hot to bother with a coat, and anyway the voluminous folds of the too-big shirt would conceal femininity as budding as hers. With some difficulty she pulled off the cut-down dress, untied the tapes of the two petticoats and stepped out of them, and drew the shift over her head. That left her buck naked, as females did not wear drawers (being bare-arsed under those loose-fitting skirts seemed to her more indecent than wearing breeches, though so far no one had asked for her opinion), and she had taken off her stockings earlier in a futile attempt to feel cooler in the kitchen. Pulling on Cormac's clothes, she felt better than she had in ages. They were miles too big, and she had to tie a string around the waist and roll up the breeches at the ankles and the shirtsleeves to get anything resembling a reasonable fit, but that didn't matter. Taking the pins out of her hair, she tied it back in a neat tail at her neck and looked in the cheval glass in the corner. She still did not look precisely like her old self — she was far too clean for that — but she was closer than she had been since she had exchanged O'Malley for Caitlyn.

Humming a little under her breath, Caitlyn went back down the stairs and out of the house. She chose the front door instead of the back, which went through the kitchen, not because she feared Mrs. McFee but because she simply didn't care to listen to anything the woman had to say.

Once outside, Caitlyn breathed deeply of the fresh air and looked around with pleasure at the verdant beauty of the countryside. It was a gorgeous afternoon, the morning's mist having blown away to leave the weather clear and sunny. Walking around the side of the house, where the old dog rose to greet her (his name was Boru, and he had belonged to the d'Arcy brothers since they had lived in the Castle), she looked toward the fields. The peasants were cutting peat two hillocks away, their scythes making bright flashes as they lifted and fell rhythmically. She saw Connor on Fharannain over by the peasants, both arms resting on the front of the saddle as he talked to one of the men. Closer at hand, Mickeen and Rory were doing something to the ears of a dozen recalcitrant sheep. Cormac and Liam were nowhere in sight. Near the stable, which was closer to the house than the sheep barn, Willie labored, scrubbing down a dappled gray mare. Grinning, Caitlyn went to join him.

"Hey, Willie, you're getting more water on you than you are on the bleedin' horse." Willie was, indeed, very wet. He looked up with a start at this greeting, then grinned all over himself as he saw who addressed him.

"O'Malley!" The name was uttered with transparent delight. Then Willie remembered, and his smile faded, to be replaced by an uncertain look. He turned back to the horse, which he began scrubbing with quite unnecessary vigor. The animal, protesting, nickered and sidled, glancing around at its groomer with a reproving expression. "What're you doin' dressed like that? You're a bleedin' lass!" The last word was accusatory.

Caitlyn walked up beside him, took another sopping brush out of the bucket, and started to wash the animal's neck. She had never been around horses much, but she was not afraid of them, or of any animal. Casting a sideways look at her erstwhile friend, she said, "Ah, Willie, I'm just O'Malley, like I've always been. There's no difference."

"There's a big bloody difference! You're a lass!" He stopped scrubbing to glare at her. His round freckled face was hostile.

Caitlyn rested her brush on the horse's neck and returned Willie's look. "I was a lass then too. You just didn't know it."

"I know it now. I thought his lordship had got you in skirts." Willie was almost sneering.

Caitlyn laughed, the sound rueful. "Aye, he did. But I tell you somethin', Willie, skirts and me just don't mix. I keep falling down!"

A slight grin tugged at the corners of Willie's mouth. "I can't picture it," he admitted.

"It's a sight," Caitlyn assured him, and the two grinned at each other in sudden affinity.

"Where'd you come from . . . good Lord!" The speaker was Liam, who'd just stepped out of the stable, presumably to check on Willie's progress. The ejaculation came as Caitlyn automatically looked over her shoulder at him and he recognized her.

"Connor'll have a fit!" Liam said with certainty.

"I'll not being doing woman's work again," Caitlyn said firmly, going to work with a will on the horse's neck. "I'll do whatever you or Willie or the others do, but I'm not doing woman's work!"

"Tell that to Connor," Liam said with gloomy relish. "It's his say-so, not mine. For now, you go on up to the house and change back into a dress. It's not decent, having a lass in breeches."

"Oh, get along with you!" She was in no mood to listen to Liam's strictures. And she would worry about Connor when she saw him.

Willie rolled his eyes at Caitlyn out of Liam's sight and ducked under the horse's neck to work on its other side, effectively distancing himself from the discussion. Caitlyn dipped her brush back into the bucket and joined him.

"Listen here, Caitlyn, you heard what I said!" Liam ducked under the horse's neck too and confronted Caitlyn, catching her wrist so that she had to stop what she was doing. She turned to face him, her eyes sparking, the wet brush in her hand. Great droplets of soapy water flew to splatter on Liam's shirt front. He brushed the drops away, looking disgusted. An unholy grin lit up Caitlyn's face. Liam scowled at her, his blue eyes fierce.

"You're a lass, and you'll wear a skirt!"

"I will not!"

"You will!"

"Not!"

The sound of carriage wheels interrupted the increasingly heated confrontation. Both Liam and Caitlyn looked around to see a handsome gig with a piebald mare between the shafts roll into the barnyard. Driving it was an exquisite lady. Caitlyn goggled at her. What would such a beauty be doing here at Donoughmore?

"Confound it, it's Mrs. Congreve! Now the fat's in the fire, and no mistake! She'll likely swoon if she finds out you're a female dressed like that, so you keep quiet, do you hear me?" With this fierce whisper, Liam let go of Caitlyn's wrist and walked forward to greet the newcomer with a smile.

"Good afternoon, Mrs. Congreve! If it's Connor you're wanting to see, he's in the fields."

"Hello, Liam! Hard at work as usual, I see! And yes, I do want to see Connor! Could he be sent for, do you think?"

"Well . . ." Liam hesitated, clearly not liking to say no but not wanting to do as she asked either. Mrs. Congreve laughed, a sound like the tinkle of little bells. Caitlyn wondered with a little pang what such a lady could want with Connor. Mrs. Congreve was a beauty, and no mistake. Her elaborately arranged coiffure was white with powder, and her skin was powdered too, with a tiny black patch set beside one pale blue eye to show it off. Her form and features were fragile, her long, slender nose and tiny rosebud mouth the height of fashionable beauty. Her dress was of blue brocade, daringly shortened to show several inches of white stocking at the ankle. All in all, she was dressed as elaborately as any lady Caitlyn had ever glimpsed along the fashionable thoroughfares of Dublin. Caitlyn wondered why she had risked such finery on the dirt roads that crisscrossed the countryside. If that elegant skirt was not ruined past saving with mud, it would be a miracle, nothing less.

"Perhaps you could send one of the lads there for him. They seem to have plenty of time to stand about."

Liam looked over his shoulder at Caitlyn and Willie, who had indeed stopped work, brushes suspended, to gape at the visitor. Meeting Caitlyn's eyes, Liam glared fiercely; then his expression smoothed out as he turned back to Mrs. Congreve.

" 'Tis sorry I am, but —"

The clatter of hooves interrupted him. Connor rode up on Fharannain, drawing rein beside his guest and smiling down at her. Mrs. Congreve dimpled up at him from her seat in the gig. Watching them, Caitlyn suddenly knew the reason Mrs. Congreve had risked her beautiful dress. Caitlyn clearly wasn't the only one who had noticed that Connor d'Arcy was an extremely handsome man.

"Well, Meredith, to what do I owe the honor?" Connor asked cheerfully. Tall, leanly muscled, and dark, mounted on Fharannain, who was as black as the ace of spades, he was a perfect foil to Mrs. Congreve's tinsel-angel femininity. Left out of the conversation now that his older brother was at hand, Liam retreated to stand beside Caitlyn and Willie. Three pairs of eyes fixed on the breathtaking twosome.

"I've come to invite you to dinner," Mrs. Congreve said with a beguiling smile. "I haven't seen you this age."

"We've been busy."

"Who is she?" Caitlyn whispered to Liam. He answered from the side of his mouth.

"She married old man Congreve three years ago. He owned the property abutting Donoughmore to the south. When he died last year, she became a wealthy widow. And she's got her eye on Connor."

"She's beautiful," Willie breathed.

"Aye, but beauty is as beauty does," Liam said darkly. "None of us is wanting her for a sister-in-law."

"Connor seems to like her." Caitlyn was conscious of a faint stirring of unease deep within her breast as she watched Connor flirting with the lady. For some reason, she did not like the vivacious interplay at all, at all.

"Aye, he does," Liam said gloomily, then added, "But who wouldn't? I suppose I'd like her too if she shook her bosom at me like she does at him." Then, apparently just remembering whom he was talking to, Liam cast Caitlyn a quick, furious look and colored up to his ears. "And that's another reason you can't go around in breeches! I completely forgot you were a lass! I'd beg your pardon, but 'tis your own fault entirely!"

"Liam!" Connor called him before Caitlyn could dispute any of the points in that speech with which she felt obliged to take issue. Liam cast a quelling look at Caitlyn, then walked forward to join his brother and the guest.

"Aye?"

"Would you please escort Meredith home? I've things to attend to here, and she's frightened she won't reach home before nightfall."

"Oh, yes, Sir Edward Dunne told me that the Dark Horseman and his gang robbed three carriages near Navan just a few weeks ago! In a single night, mind! I'm sure I wouldn't care to be one of his victims!"

"And I'm sure he'd never harm one so lovely as you," Connor soothed. Mrs. Congreve smiled and fluttered her eyelashes at him. He smiled back at her. Caitlyn felt her unease deepen until it was practically a tangible thing inside her.

"Did you hear that, O'Malley?" Willie whispered excitedly, poking Caitlyn in the ribs with his elbow. Apparently he had forgotten his grievance with her again. "The Dark Horseman's been seen near here! Wouldn't it be grand if we could find out where he is and ask him if we could join his band?"

"Aye, and it would be grand too if we was to discover a pot o' gold at the end of the rainbow, but we won't," Caitlyn rejoined tartly, glad to be distracted.

Willie gave her an indignant look. Caitlyn wasn't in the mood to further his obsession with the Dark Horseman. She felt cross without reason.

"You, Willie, fetch Liam's horse, if you please." Connor rode over to where Willie and Caitlyn stood together and dismounted. "And you can take Fharannain . . ." he began, turning to hand the reins to Caitlyn. Then unaware aqua eyes met apprehensive kerry blue ones and widened. For a pregnant instant, their glances held; then Connor's eyes swept over her. His lips had tightened when he met her gaze again.

"I . . ." Caitlyn started to say, only to be silenced by a hard look and a wave of his hand.

"Take Fharannain," he said brusquely and handed the great horse's reins to her. Caitlyn accepted them with a nervous swallow, then stood watching as he strode back to where his lady friend waited in the gig. As he smiled at Mrs. Congreve, Connor was absolutely charming. Only Caitlyn, who had been the recipient of his previous sizzling look, knew that beneath the lighthearted banter he was furious.

Glumly Caitlyn led Fharannain into the barn, passing Willie, who was leading out Thunderer, the chestnut gelding that Liam habitually rode. Willie had once labored in a stable, so he was familiar with horses, though he was not a proficient rider due to lack of practice. Caitlyn could not ride at all. Growing up in the city, she had never had the chance to learn. As she stroked Fharannain's silky nose while the horse nuzzled her, it occurred to her that here was the perfect opportunity. The thought of Connor's face as she galloped by him on his own horse was irresistible. He would be dumbfounded — and enraged. But then, he was angry with her already on account of the breeches. Might as well be hung for a sheep as a lamb. . . .

Getting aboard was not as easy as it appeared. Fharannain was a tall horse. The stirrup dangled maddeningly just higher than she could hoist her leg, and Fharannain kept cocking his ears and rolling his eyes at her as she hopped about, trying to snag the stirrup with her foot. Finally she stood on both legs again and led him over to a stall door. Climbing up to balance precariously on the narrow boards at the top, she leaped for the saddle. Fharannain sidestepped. Caitlyn fell, sprawling on her hands and knees between him and the stall. Gritting her teeth, she hauled him back into position and tried again. This time she deliberately overshot the mark, anticipating his move. She landed facedown across his back, half on the saddle and half on his rump, clutching the saddle with both hands to keep from sliding off. The horse headed toward the door in nervous two-steps as she hauled herself into the saddle and picked up the reins.

"O'Malley!" Willie barely had time to jump out of the way when Fharannain leaped through the stable door. Caitlyn clung to his back like a bur and yanked uselessly on the reins, uttering a shaky "Who-oa!" She felt a horrible frisson of pure fright as the beast got the bit between his teeth, lowered his head, and streaked for the open meadow at a flat-out gallop. Belatedly it occurred to her that, even to annoy Connor, trying to ride a huge, spirited animal like Fharannain when she had never even sat on a horse's back before was not the smartest thing she had ever done. But there was no undoing it now. . . .

Connor was walking toward the stable, having just seen off Mrs. Congreve and Liam, who were clipping away over the track in her gig with Liam's horse tied behind. Fharannain thundered past him, and he blinked as though he couldn't believe his eyes. Caitlyn summoned a weak smile as the animal flew past, then, throwing pride to the winds, managed to squeak, "H-help!"

"What the bloody hell — !" The ejaculation was cut short as Fharannain pounded into the meadow. Sheep scattered before him, and their bleating seemed to drive him to greater frenzies. He was moving in leaps and bounds instead of at a smooth gallop, obviously intent on ridding himself of this strange rider. Caitlyn hauled manfully on the reins one more time before abandoning them and clinging to the animal's mane. He was heading straight for the stone wall that bisected the hillside. Caitlyn shut her eyes.

Moments later, she was somersaulting through the air, hands and body abruptly losing contact with the horse. Her eyes flew open to see Fharannain sailing over the fence without her just before she hit the ground with enough force to make her see stars.

"May the devil and all the Saints confound it!"

Caitlyn must have blacked out for an instant. She opened her eyes to discover Connor leaning over her, curses falling from his grim mouth seemingly of their own accord and real concern crowding out anger from his eyes. Seeing her eyelashes flutter and then her eyes meet his, he frowned. His face was pale with anxiety.

"Are you hurt?" The question was sharp.

Caitlyn thought about this for a second. She certainly hurt, from head to toe. Cautiously she wiggled her toes, moved her legs, then her fingers and arms. Everything seemed to be in one piece.

"N-no. I don't think so," she said finally.

"Then by God you should be!" he exploded, surging to his feet and jerking her up beside him, his hands tight on her shoulders as he shook her until her hair escaped the ribbon confining it at her nape and the black strands whipped into a cloud around her face.

"Stop!" She tried to jerk away, but his grip

was too strong. His eyes were livid.

"You're lucky you're alive to be shaken! No one, *no one,* has ever ridden that horse but me! It's a bloody miracle he didn't kill you! What maggot got into your brain to make you try such a thing?" He was still shaking her, his words practically hissed through taut lips.

"Would you stop! Oh! I just wanted to learn to ride!" The words tumbled out between shakes.

"You just wanted to learn to ride . . ." His voice broke off as though words failed him, and he closed his eyes. The shaking ceased also, although he retained his grip on her shoulders. When he opened his eyes again, those devil's eyes were no longer furious, but merely grim.

"The Lord looks after fools and children, it seems, and fortunately for your hide you're both! Are you determined to get yourself killed? It's a miracle you've survived unharmed so long!"

"There's blood on her leg, Conn." Rory and Mickeen had come panting up just as Connor had hauled her to her feet. Now Rory spoke, his voice concerned. Looking down at herself, Caitlyn saw that there was indeed a spreading bloodstain on the inside of her right thigh.

"She likely cut it on a stone." Sharp-edged stones littered the ground near the wall. Caitlyn glanced at them, then back down at herself. The sight of her own blood spreading on her thigh, combined with the shock of the fall, made her feel suddenly lightheaded. She swayed.

"Look out, she's going to faint!"

Caitlyn shook her head, trying to clear it. She had never fainted in her life. But before she could regain her equilibrium, Connor, with an explosive, heartfelt curse, swept her up in his arms and stalked back toward the house. Holding her securely against his chest, he told her in no uncertain terms what a nuisance she was. Caitlyn listened with unaccustomed meekness, feeling comforted just to be held in that strong grasp. It was almost worth it. . . .

As he entered the house, Mrs. McFee came to greet him, surprise turning to condemnation when she recognized who it was he held in his arms.

"What's that evil lass done now?" she demanded. "First she leaves a mess in my clean kitchen for me to sweep up, then she —"

"Enough!" Connor silenced her sharply, striding past her. "I'll need bandages and a bowl of warm water. Bring them up, please!"

Mrs. McFee was silenced. Connor climbed the stairs easily, carrying Caitlyn all the way up to her attic bedroom without once seeming short of breath. She twined her arms around his neck for balance, rested her head against the warmth of his chest, and listened contentedly to the beating of his heart. It felt good to know that he was worried about her.

Connor put Caitlyn down on her narrow iron bedstead and reached for the laces at her waist, seemingly intent on removing her breeches himself to inspect the damage. Alarmed at the sudden movement, she widened her eyes and her hands flew to close over his.

"N-no!" she stuttered. As he met her eyes, frowning impatiently, Mrs. McFee entered, huffing and puffing at the climb, the requested water and bandages in her hands.

"Mrs. McFee can help you, then," he said abruptly, apparently remembering that Caitlyn was a female.

"I can do it myself," Caitlyn said, getting shakily to her feet and retiring behind the screen that shielded one small corner. Mrs. McFee sniffed and took herself off. Connor waited, sitting on the edge of her bed.

"Well?" he said finally, when she didn't say anything.

"I seem to be hurt — inside. That's where the blood is coming from." Caitlyn had removed her breeches and drawers and inspected both her thighs and then her stomach and rear as well as she could, but nary a cut had she found. At the thought of how terrible an internal injury she must have suffered to be bleeding so, she felt lightheaded again.

"Inside? Inside where?"

"The blood's coming from my — my privates." The words were tremulous. There was a long silence. His reply, when it came, was oddly gentle.

"Caitlyn, lass, could it be your time?"

"My time?" She didn't understand.

"Your woman's time."

"My woman's . . ." Her voice failed her. Vaguely she remembered that her mother had bled with clockwork regularity until she had gotten with child. But Caitlyn had never associated such with herself. Hot color stole up her cheeks. She felt hideously embarrassed and also at a loss. What happened now? There was so much blood — how did one make it go away? She had been too young when her mother died to have ever discussed the subject.

Her long silence must have told Connor all he needed to know. She heard a deep, long-suffering kind of sigh, then, "Make yourself decent and come out here."

"No!" Never as long as she lived could she look him in the face again. That he should know such an intimate thing about her was mortifying. She felt shamed, unclean.

"Either you make yourself decent and come out, or I'll haul you out just as you are. I want to talk to you. There's no one else to do so except Mrs. McFee. And you don't seem to care for her overmuch. But if you wish I'll fetch her."

"No!" Caitlyn's denial was as emphatic as it was instinctive. Mrs. McFee detested her enough already.

"Then make yourself decent and come out. Now."

Connor was perfectly capable of doing as he threatened, she knew. She had no clothes behind the screen except the bloodstained breeches she had removed. Still wearing Cormac's long-tailed shirt, which by itself covered her to her knees, she reached out an arm, pulled her quilt from the quilt rack where she folded it neatly every morning, wrapped it around herself, and came hesitantly out from behind the screen. Meeting Connor's eyes, she blushed from her toes to her hairline. Then she dropped her gaze to the floor.

"You've no need to be shamed, lass. 'Tis perfectly natural and normal." When she didn't respond to that except to continue to stare at the floor, he sighed again and told her to sit. Caitlyn dared a fleeting look at him, and he indicated the opposite end of the narrow bed from where he perched at its foot. Caitlyn reluctantly sat, face averted and pink as she resolutely studied the bedknobs instead of his face.

"Such a thing has never happened to you before?"

Dumb with embarrassment at the thought of discussing such a thing with him, she shook her head. She still could not meet his eyes.

"You're thirteen, or thereabouts?"

"Fifteen. Almost sixteen, I think." Her voice was muffled.

"Then you're late getting started. Most lasses start a little earlier than that, I'm thinking." His tone was easy, as though he conversed on such intimate subjects all the time. "Still, not having enough to eat during your growing years will account for it, most likely. But whatever the reason for it, you've just become a woman grown. Congratulations."

"Congratulations . . . !" That word so dumb-founded her that her eyes flew to his. He smiled at her.

" 'Tis no very terrible thing after all, you know. In many cultures, we'd be planning a celebration tonight."

"A celebration . . . !" It seemed all she could do was echo his words. A twinkle lighted his eyes.

"I wouldn't go so far as that, either, because most lasses are sensitive about the subject, as you are. That's as it should be, because it's a private thing. But it's naught to be ashamed of. Just as lads are proud, not shamed, when they shave their first whiskers. 'Tis a sign of growing up."

"I hate it." The words were near whispered, and they were from the soul.

"Be that as it may, it's a fact of a woman's life." And in short, succinct sentences he told her all she needed to know to deal with what had occurred. When he had finished, Caitlyn's face was as red as a tomato and a tinge of pink just tinted his cheekbones. Caitlyn could hardly look at him as he got to his feet, his height overpow-ering in the small room, but she did manage a quick upward glance.

"Thank you," she said, her voice barely audi-ble. He stood looking down at her for a moment.

"You have something more to be thankful for, you know." His arms crossed over his chest. She dared another look at him to discover that the pink tinge had faded from his cheeks. He ap-peared as composed as ever, if anything a little stern, and that helped her recover her own composure.

"What?"

"You've been saved a good hiding. One that was richly deserved, I might add."

"Oh." In her embarrassment, she'd nearly forgotten about her foolishness over Fharannain. He'd been furious, and she had no doubt that she would have felt his hand on her backside again if fate had not intervened. Which was something to be thankful for, at that.

"I'm sorry," she offered. " 'Twas a mistake to try to ride Fharannain, I know. I won't do such a thing again."

"Well." The handsome apology took the wind from his sails. He stood eyeing her, his arms still crossed over his chest, his booted feet planted slightly apart on the bare plank floor. With his head tilted a little to one side, he looked very handsome and very male. Caitlyn could quite understand why Mrs. Congreve should drive herself clear from the next county to call on him. "And no more breeches, mind," he added, clearly determined to be admonishing.

Caitlyn suddenly looked him full in the eyes, a mischievous smile lighting her face.

"I'll make a bargain with you," she said, her embarrassment forgotten in the excitement of her idea.

"A bargain?" He sounded wary. Those aqua eyes narrowed on her face.

"I'll stick to dratted skirts if you'll teach me to

ride. A deal?" Hope sparkled in her eyes. Connor grinned slowly as he gazed down at her, shaking his head.

"You've the gall of the devil about you, Caitlyn O'Malley. Very well. 'Tis a deal."

XI

True to his word, Connor taught her to ride. He had no lady's saddle, which forced her to learn to ride astride, but he vowed to rectify the omission on his next trip to Dublin. In the meantime, she was allowed to wear breeches for that one short session a day. Even though they might spend as long as an hour at it, the time seemed short to her. Caitlyn found she loved being on horseback. And she loved Connor's undivided attention even more.

"You're a natural," Connor said with admiration as he watched her circle the meadow alone at the end of her very first lesson. For her efforts, he had chosen a rotund pinto mare named Belinda. Caitlyn soon mastered the essentials, and after that it was just a matter of refining her technique. Connor assumed an advisory capacity merely, riding along with her at a sedate pace as she explored the countryside. If he was not available, one of the three younger d'Arcys would keep an eye on her, although there was much bickering, particularly when Cormac accompanied her on the rides. She did not bicker with Connor, whose company she much preferred. She had developed a respect for him that verged on hero worship, and her rides with him were the highlight of her days.

She had, reluctantly and at Connor's insistence, agreed to help Mrs. McFee in the house in the morning in exchange for being allowed to do outdoor chores in the afternoon. Working under the supervision of Rory or Mickeen, who were in charge of the daily care of the sheep, she became a better than adequate shepherd after learning that the silly creatures feared her more than she feared them. Sometimes she went with Cormac when he oversaw the peasants cutting the peat that fueled the fires and fed the animals come winter, and when Cormac picked up a scythe to help out, so did she. She was strong. for her size and acquitted herself quite creditably in their cutting forays. Or, if the weather was bad, she would retire to the office with Liam or Connor, where she learned to keep the farm's books. What she disliked most was helping at the slaughtering, which was necessary from time to time if they were to have meat for the table and to cull the herd. But fair was fair, and if all the d'Arcys took a hand according to whoever was available, then she would not shirk. After a time, her stomach stopped threatening to disgrace her, and she was able to be as businesslike about it as they.

Connor traveled to Dublin about once every two months to pick up supplies, mail, and whatever else was needed, sometimes loading a sheep or two on the cart to sell. As he had threatened, on his first trip since Caitlyn learned to ride he returned with a lady's saddle. She wanted to protest but thought better of it. Connor had said she must learn to ride sidesaddle if she wished to ride, and she had no wish to quarrel with him over a matter that he would certainly not concede. So she had to transfer all she had learned to the sidesaddle, draping her legs over the horn as best she could and thinking that being a female was nothing but botheration. Skirts were the very devil, and she was likely to break her neck in them one way or another! But soon she could ride sidesaddle as well as astride, and Connor began allowing her to accompany him as he went about his business on the farm.

Some four months after Connor had first offered her "honest employment," she was riding with him along the stone walls that bounded the property, checking to see where repairs were needed. It was just past noon on a lovely August day, and lush rhododendrons bloomed in riotous color along the stone wall. Connor had dismounted to repair a tumbledown place in the wall, replacing the stones himself rather than send workers to do it another day. Caitlyn had tried to help him, only to be told brusquely that she was more hindrance than help. She smiled to herself; if she had been one of his brothers or another of the men he would have put her to work with a vengeance, but Connor rarely lost sight of the fact that she was a lass, although the others often did and she did most of the time herself.

Caitlyn strolled along the wall, admiring the crimson and bright pink and white of the massed flowers and pausing occasionally to inhale their heady fragrance. There was a tinkling stream in a grove of scrub pine at the bottom of the meadow. Heading for that — she was hot and wanted a drink — Caitlyn again smiled to herself. Her life had certainly undergone a drastic change in the past few months. Not only had she acquired a home and security, but the d'Arcys seemed almost like family to her now. They had certainly been far kinder to her than she had ever expected that first day when Connor had carried her kicking and screaming up the stairs to throw her on the bed. While Cormac and Rory might tease, Liam might scold, and Connor was subject to the occasional thunderous rage, she was not the least bit afraid of any of the four of them. Not one had ever made the slightest move to harm her in any way, and she knew now that they never would. They were good men, these d'Arcys, kinder and more moral than any she had ever known. . . .

"Hello, little girl. And what are you doing on my property?"

Caitlyn had been so lost in thought that she hadn't even noticed the man who stood at the edge of the copse, perhaps ten feet away from where she was herself. Knowing that Connor was within easy hailing distance, she felt no fear but looked at him curiously. He cradled a musket in his arms, and from his apparel and the dead

142

grouse that hung from a strap at his waist, she knew he had been shooting. He was perhaps in his mid-forties, thin rather than lean, and tall, with thinning fair hair and light gray eyes. His complexion was pale, nearly as white as her own. His features were regular, and although he was not precisely handsome, he was not unattractive. She smiled at him, and his eyes widened, then narrowed on her face.

"Who are you?" he asked on a different note.

Caitlyn told him her name, then: "Who are you?"

"Sir Edward Dunne. You're on my land." He indicated the ground she was standing on with a sweep of the musket.

"I thought this was d'Arcy land."

He shook his head. "The stream marks the boundary. When you stepped across it, you came onto my land. Do you live at Donoughmore, then?"

Caitlyn nodded. She would have said more, seeing no reason not to, when Connor spoke sharply from behind her.

"Aye, she lives at Donoughmore. In the house, to be precise. She is our young cousin, newly orphaned and come to make her home with us."

Caitlyn digested that, wondering at the purpose of the lie, and tried not to look surprised. She was perfectly willing to go along with whatever tale Connor told, though she was glad he had arrived when he did or she would have said something very different. The truth, in fact.

Sir Edward's eyebrows went up. "You are to be congratulated, d'Arcy, on acquiring such a . . . cousin. She bids fair to be a right little beauty when she is full grown." There was an undertone of animosity to the words that Caitlyn did not understand.

"She has my full protection, Sir Edward." Connor's voice was hard in reply. Caitlyn looked around at him questioningly. Clearly there was bad feeling between these two. Connor was returning Sir Edward's mocking look with a knife-edged one of his own, his jaw very grim.

"And rejoices in it, I am sure." Sir Edward's response was smooth as silk. Caitlyn could not fathom the cause of the undercurrents at play in the conversation, but instinct sent her stepping back across the stream, closer to Connor. He looked down at her, unsmiling, his hands coming up briefly to rest on her shoulders.

"We'll be on our way. Good day, Sir Edward." Connor was abrupt.

"Good day, d'Arcy. It was a pleasure making your acquaintance, my dear Miss O'Malley. Oh, ah . . . by the by, has dear Meredith had the pleasure of meeting your young . . . ah, cousin yet, d'Arcy?"

"Not yet," Connor replied tightly, his hands dropping from Caitlyn's shoulders. One closed over her arm, drawing her back the way they had come.

"I shall take pleasure in informing her of the newest addition to your family," Sir Edward called after them, laughing. Then they were up in the open meadow again, and Sir Edward was separated from them by the trees.

After a sideways look at Connor's grim face, Caitlyn remained silent until he had tossed her up in the saddle and mounted himself, heading back in the direction of Donoughmore. Then she ventured, "Who is he?" She nearly added, "Connor," but bit it back. Although she called Cormac, Rory, and Liam by their first names, as did everyone at the farm, she felt funny being so familiar with Connor. Except by his brothers, he was universally addressed as "your lordship." Only she felt funny saying that too, so usually she called him nothing at all to his face, and Connor in her mind.

"Sir Edward Dunne. He owns Ballymara, the property bordering Donoughmore on the north."

That told her almost nothing, and from the grim set of Connor's mouth there was a great deal more to be told, so she persisted.

"Why did you tell him I was your cousin?"

Those aqua eyes swung around to her. "He's a bad man for a young lass to know, especially a young serving lass. He thinks nothing of taking his pleasure where he can, whether the lass is willing or no. By claiming you as my cousin, I at least made him think twice about taking you out of hand the first time he comes across you unprotected."

His eyes were so filled with turbulence that Caitlyn let the subject drop. But when Connor had returned her to the stable, taking off alone on Fharranain like the devil was on his heels, she wasted not a minute in corralling Cormac, who was halfheartedly forcing a potion down the mouth of a sick sheep in the sheep barn.

"Cormac, what can you tell me about Sir Edward Dunne?" she demanded without preliminaries. Cormac barely glanced up. The sheep he straddled was whipping its head about like a snake as he worked to force the yellowish liquid down its throat. From the wet yellowish splotches that liberally adorned his clothes, it was obvious that he had been trying for some time, without success.

"Sit on the bloody beast's head, would you?" he growled. Then, as the sheep lifted a cloven hoof and caught him squarely in the shin, he winced, cursed, and muttered with pent-up passion, "I hate bloody sheep!"

Caitlyn did as he asked, planting her bottom on the sheep's neck and straddling its head with her knees. In this way Cormac finally managed to pour most of the foul-smelling potion down the animal's gullet, then straightened and wiped his forehead with relief. Caitlyn got to her feet, and Cormac quickly jumped away from the sheep, which had begun to bawl. It scrambled to its feet and scurried to the far side of the stall. Cormac exited the stall, and Caitlyn followed him.

"Cormac, tell me about Sir Edward Dunne!" she insisted as he leaned against the outside of the closed stall door for a moment and gazed malevolently at the baa-ing sheep.

This time she got his attention. "So you ran into Sir Edward, did you? Not on your own, I trust?"

She shook her head. "Connor was with me. They didn't seem to like one another overmuch."

Cormac snorted. "Connor hates Sir Edward, and I don't imagine Sir Edward is any fonder of Connor. Sir Edward thought to acquire Donoughmore, you see, when our father died, as the Penal Laws prohibit Catholics from inheriting land. He even made an offer for the property to the Crown. But what Sir Edward had not counted on was that my father raised Connor a Protestant to prevent just such an eventuality. Connor had merely to prove that he was not a Catholic, and he did so. So Connor was allowed to inherit after all."

"Connor is Protestant?" Caitlyn recalled that Mickeen had told much the same tale when she had first come to Donoughmore, but then she had not been as interested in the part of the saga that affected Connor.

Cormac looked at her briefly. "Aye, though the rest of us are Catholic. My father would have done anything to keep the land in the family, and did. He always feared that it would be taken away from him in his lifetime, though that never happened because of our maternal grandmother's connections at Court. But he knew that after his death there would be no way of saving the land

147

if his heir was of the True Church."

"But that still doesn't explain why Connor hates Sir Edward in particular."

Cormac smiled bitterly. "Ah, but you see, Sir Edward has long coveted Donoughmore. It would near double the size of his holding. And our father died violently, at the time the Castle was burned. It's Connor's belief, and the rest of ours as well, that Sir Edward was behind what happened."

The Fuinneog an Mhurdair?" gasped Caitlyn, who had retained that much Gaelic.

"So you've heard that, have you? Aye. But we've no proof, and Connor will not kill a man on suspicion alone. But you stay away from Sir Edward. He's a bad sort."

"That's what your brother said. He told Sir Edward I was your cousin."

The grim look faded from Cormac's face, to be replaced by a fleeting grin. "Did he, now? I think Conn rather likes having a wee lassie about the place. Livens things up. In fact, in the short time you've been with us, you've made quite a place for yourself, young Caitlyn."

Such talk embarrassed caitlyn, who was not used to receiving affection in any degree. She smiled rather shyly at Cormac, then bethought herself of something. The smile rapidly changed to a scowl.

"There's no need for you to be calling me 'young Caitlyn' in that patronizing tone. You're not that much older than I."

"I'm eighteen," Cormac said with the air of one claiming a great age.

"Well, I'm sixteen." Caitlyn replied, her nose in the air. "I'm no' a child, so you can just stop behaving as if I were."

"You're naught but a baby!"

"I . . . !"

"Are you two squabbling again?" Liam had walked up behind them without their hearing him. He shook his head. "Cormac, did you dose that sheep?"

"Aye."

"Well, there are three more down with it, and Rory's brought two of them into the shed. You can dose them while he drives down the third.' "

Cormac groaned but went to do Liam's bidding. Caitlyn trailed along in response to Cormac's request for her assistance. In other words, he wanted her to sit on the victims' heads. With the two of them working in tandem, it didn't take long to pour the medicine down the sheep. When they were through and walking back toward the barn, Caitlyn ventured another question that had been troubling her.

"Cormac, do you think I'm . . . well . . . pretty?"

He looked down at her in the liveliest surprise. Caitlyn blushed to the roots of her hair.

"You, pretty?" he hooted. "O'Malley the beggar-boy pretty? Good Lord, what maggot's in your brain now?"

His rejection of the idea as totally preposterous

fired Caitlyn's temper.

"Sir Edward said that I would be a right little beauty when I'm grown."

Cormac hooted again. "I've always thought Sir Edward lacked a brain. Now he's proved it."

Furious, Caitlyn doubled up her fist and punched him in the ribs with all the force O'Malley would have used. Then, leaving him gasping and rubbing his side, she marched into the house.

XII

A week later, Caitlyn was down with a bad chill. She'd been confined to the house for two days, sneezing and coughing and in general feeling awful. It had been raining without stop for all of that time, so the younger d'Arcys thought and said that she had taken the illness just to get out of her outdoor work. Caitlyn, miserable at being kept indoors with only Mrs. McFee for company, could have told them that she would have traded places in an instant. But arguing took energy, which she didn't have. So she just sniffled and retired to her room, letting them say what they liked.

When she awoke it was past midnight, she judged, and her bedroom was as black as the inside of a cave. The night was moonless, and the rain made the dark seem twice as impenetrable. The steady pattering on the roof just above her head had seemed companionable when she had gone to sleep earlier. But with the discomforts of her illness, she was not sleeping well, and now she had awakened in the middle of the pitch-black night. Thoughts of banshees and ghosties ran through her mind, along with a vivid memory of the ghostly horsemen who haunted the Castle. Shivering, Caitlyn thought that they were likely to be abroad again on a night such as this. She was glad she was not in the Castle to see them.

Such thoughts made the darkness intolerable. Shivering, she reached for the candle on her bedside. The flint and steel she usually kept there were missing, and of course the fire in the small grate had gone out, probably sizzled to death by raindrops coursing down the chimney, so she could not light it. Remaining alone and awake in the dark was too unpleasant, she decided. She would make her way to the kitchen, where Mrs. McFee kept the fire smoored, or banked, so that it would not be going out overnight. From that she would light her candle and her fire.

Since she slept in her shift, she pulled her quilt over that for protection against the night air. She did not possess such a thing as a wrapper, but the quilt served her well, although modesty was a secondary consideration to warmth at the moment. The d'Arcys all slept like the dead, with Cormac in particular rattling the rooftop with his snores, so she was unlikely to encounter one of them on her journey. But it was too cold in the house to go without some sort of covering, even if she had been alone.

Feeling her way in the pitch-darkness, Caitlyn made it down the stairs to the kitchen, lit her candle, and was on the second-floor landing again when it struck her: she couldn't hear Cormac's snores. She couldn't hear anything at all, besides the rain. A sudden conviction seized her that she was the only living being in the house. The notion was chilling. She would never sleep unless she knew for sure that the d'Arcys were where they were supposed to be.

Carefully cupping her hand around the candle, she moved toward the door to Connor's chamber. They couldn't be outside on such a wild, stormy night. . . . Turning the knob carefully so as not to waken him if he should be sleeping within, she pushed open the door and lifted her candle so that light spilled over the bed. It was empty, had not even been slept in. Feeling equal parts indignant and alarmed, she checked the three other rooms in rapid succession. None of the d'Arcys were in their beds. They were not even in the house. What possible explanation could there be for all four of them being absent at the same time? On such a night?

Caitlyn stood pondering for a moment. A suspicion occurred to her — it was on just such a night that she had seen the ghostly riders at the Castle. But those riders had disappeared before her very eyes. They could not have been flesh-and-blood men. They had been banshees, or figments of her imagination, she had decided long since. On the other hand, Connor and Cormac had come to find her, at the Castle, the very next morning, knowing precisely where to look despite the fact that they had been searching for her for three days previously without success. The more she thought about that, the more damning it was. But how had they disappeared? Only banshees could vanish into the air at will. . . .

Making up her mind suddenly, Caitlyn entered Cormac's room. When she emerged, she was dressed as a lad down to the cloak around her shoulders. She would go to the barn first, to see if any horses were missing. If they were — and she expected that — she would mount Belinda and ride out in search of tracks.

By the time she reached the barn, her head and cloak were thoroughly wet. A wetting on top of the chill was not a good idea, but she was too intent on discovering the d'Arcys' whereabouts to give it much thought.

Luckily she had had the forethought to bring a lantern with her. As soon as she threw open the door of the stable, she was able to determine that Fharannain was missing. Making a quick inventory, she discovered that Thunderer was missing as well, as was Balladeer, Rory's horse, and Kildare, Cormac's horse. Aristedes' stall was empty too and for a moment Caitlyn was puzzled. Sticking her head into the little room at the back of the stable that Mickeen occupied, she had her answer: Mickeen was on Aristedes. But where could they have gone?

Caitlyn remembered that Mickeen had said the devil drove Connor, and she remembered too his tale of the Volunteers that had attacked the Castle and killed the old Earl. Was it possible that Connor and his brothers, and Mickeen as well, had joined a rival gang, the Straw Boys, perhaps, or some such? Obviously whatever they were doing was done in the greatest secrecy. No one was supposed to know, and except for herself she assumed no one did. And she wouldn't have known if she had not awakened in the middle of the night with the miserable chill and then failed to hear Cormac's snores. She could have lived at Donoughmore for years and never guessed.

She was still standing in the little room that was Mickeen's when she heard a great rumbling noise. For a moment she thought it was thunder, but then the stone floor began to shake. Eyes wide, Caitlyn stared at the floor. She had no idea what was happening, but she did know that the stable was no place to be. Running, she stopped short just outside Mickeen's room and gaped. At the opposite end of the stable, where the straw had been swept clean, a large square hole was opening in the floor. Even as Caitlyn blinked at it, disbelieving her own eyes, the rumbling ceased. From somewhere came the presence of mind to blow out the lantern she held in her hand. The stable did not go dark; light was shining from the hole. Seconds later, with a clatter of hooves, five horses burst from the earth with their riders. Connor on Fharannain was in the lead.

XIII

"A grand night's work," Connor said jovially, swinging down.

"Aye," Mickeen replied as the rest dismounted too. A flickering lantern swung from Mickeen's saddle horn. He lifted it down and set it carefully on the swept area of the stone floor. The yawning hole through which they had emerged was now dark; clearly the illumination that had shone from it had come from this lantern, which now cast light in a wavering yellow circle around the men. "Though 'twas rough there for bit. Those outriders were handy with their poppers."

" 'Tis a wonder none of us were hit." Liam was stripping the saddle from Thunderer, a wide grin splitting his usually serious face. A black mask with elongated slits for eyes covered the area above his mouth.

Thankful that the circle of light didn't extend to where she shrank against the stone wall, Caitlyn watched quiet as a mouse so that her presence would pass unnoticed. Looking around the group, Caitlyn saw that the others were all masked and cloaked like Liam. The hooded black cloaks enveloped the men to the knees, so that only black riding boots showed, and covered their heads so that their masked faces were deeply shadowed. If she hadn't known who they were, Caitlyn doubted that she would have recognized any of them. Here, then, without a doubt were her ghost riders from that night at the Castle. The secret of their disappearance was now solved too: clearly there was a tunnel beneath Donough-more, and she was willing to bet it had its origin somewhere at the Castle. But what had they been about so late at night, in such weather? What kind of skulduggery had they been up to that could not bear the light of day?

"A bullet whistled so close past my ear that I swear I could hear it whispering my name." Cormac untied his soaking cloak and dropped it and his mask down the yawning hole. Then he turned back to unsaddle Kildare. Liam and Mickeen disposed of their cloaks and masks down the hole as well, then saw to their horses. Rory was the last to dismount and stood leaning against Bal-ladeer, making no attempt to either unsaddle the horse or remove his disguise. Caitlyn frowned as she looked over at him. Like Cormac, Rory was usually laughing and full of jokes; his behavior now was odd.

Connor had taken off his mask and was walking toward the hole as he untied his cloak when Rory's stillness caught his attention.

"What ails you, Rory?" he asked sharply, changing direction so that he was moving toward his younger brother.

"You know the bullet that Cormac said had his name on it? Well, there was one out there with mine too. But it didn't miss." Rory's voice was weak and faintly apologetic.

"What?"

Connor pulled the hood from Rory's head, untying his cloak with quick hands. Rory continued to lean against Thunderer as if the horse were the only thing holding him upright. He submitted to Connor's ministrations without protest, which, given Rory's independent nature, was frightening. Connor let the cloak drop to the floor, revealing Rory's coat, which was soaked with blood from the left shoulder to the elbow. As he looked down at his own bloodied sleeve, Rory's knees gave way.

"Rory!" The cry was Cormac's. He and Liam surged forward with Mickeen close behind. Connor caught Rory's weight and eased him to the ground. Forgetting that she was supposed to be invisible, Caitlyn moved forward too, not quite joining the rest but hovering on the outskirts of the light as the men bent over Rory.

"Damn! Look at me, swooning like a lass!" Rory was faint but still valiant, trying to laugh at himself despite his obvious pain. Connor ignored him, pulling a knife from his boot and slitting the sleeve from shoulder to wrist with quick efficiency, then stripping it and the shirtsleeve beneath away so that the arm lay bare. A small black hole pierced the swollen, purpled flesh of the upper arm. Blood flowed copiously from the hole down the length of the arm to drip on the floor. Rory took one look and turned his head away.

" 'Tis not so very bad. You'll live," Connor said bracingly, lifting the arm with gentle hands to discover an exit wound, which meant that the bullet had not lodged inside. Rory grunted in pain at the movement. In response to that faint sound, Connor carefully put the arm back down, adding, "Though your arm will be hurting you for a goodly while, I have no doubt."

Rory closed his eyes. Connor looked up. "Mickeen, you and Cormac see to the horses. Liam, I'll need your help."

Caitlyn, remembering where she was, instinctively shrank away toward the shadows as the others started to obey Connor's commands. But Mickeen's sharp eyes picked up her movement.

"Look there!" he hissed, his hand on the pistol he wore thrust in his belt. Caitlyn, afraid she might be shot out of hand, stepped out into the narrow circle of light so that she could be identified.

"I — there was no one in the house," she said lamely as five pairs of eyes fixed her with expressions ranging from astonishment to anger to resignation.

"What the bloody hell is she doing out here? Spying?"

"She'll likely be blabbin' her head off now, just like a damned female!"

"Oh, Jesus!"

"What now, Conn?"

Connor stared steadily at Caitlyn for a moment, his devil's eyes unreadable. Meeting his gaze, Caitlyn experienced a tiny shiver of fear. It was just within the realm of possibility that whatever they were doing was so secret that they would kill her for witnessing it.

" 'Tis something I should have expected. You have a nose for trouble, don't you, lass?" Connor's eyes held hers for a moment longer. "You'll be keeping your mouth shut, I trust."

"Oh, aye," Caitlyn agreed fervently. From the looks on the faces of the others, they were considering very unpleasant fates for her.

"Can we be trustin' her, me lord?" Mickeen's face was hard as he stared at Caitlyn.

"Of course we can trust her. She's practically one of us, now that she knows." That was Cormac. Caitlyn managed an uncertain smile at him.

"She doesn't know," Liam said in a warning undertone. "Not anything that matters."

They all looked at her again, even Rory from his supine position on the stable floor.

"She'll keep her mouth shut. And we can use her help," Connor said, dismissing the argument. Then, turning his attention from Caitlyn to Rory, he directed Liam to take his brother's feet while he took his shoulders.

"I can walk, damn it," Rory protested. Ignoring him, Connor and Liam lifted him and started for the stable door.

"Cormac, you and Mickeen clear away in here. Take care to get any bloodstains, mind. Caitlyn, you can come with us. Hold something over his head to keep out the rain."

Caitlyn slid out of Cormac's cloak and held it over Rory's head as the four of them hurried through the rainswept darkness toward the house. She held the back door for them, then followed them to the stairs. Rory's blood dripped all over the steps and floor, leaving crimson smears. Fortunately, the sight of blood did not make Caitlyn feel sick, though she knew it affected many that way. Connor's face was pale and set as he and Liam carried their brother to his chamber. It was nearly as pale as Rory's, who looked as if he might faint at any minute.

"Caitlyn, you go get hot water and linen strips for bandages. Try to use as little light as possible. We don't want to attract any attention to the house."

Caitlyn hurried to do Connor's bidding. By the time she had returned with the required objects, Rory was stretched out in his bed clad in his nightshirt and the windows were securely shuttered to avoid letting out any chinks of light from the candle at the bedside.

"Liam, you can go and help Cormac and Mickeen now. Connor dismissed his brother. "Clean up the blood on the way and make sure everything's as it should be. Caitlyn will help me."

"Aye, Conn." Liam vanished with a single hard look at Caitlyn. She counted Cormac and Rory as friends, but Liam was harder to win over. He still mistrusted her, she knew. But Connor's championship made it impossible for Liam to be overtly hostile even if he wished to be. He and Mickeen, who was troubled by no such qualms of conscience, were the flies in the ointment of her new life.

"Here, hold the basin." Sitting gingerly on the edge of the bed, Caitlyn took the basin on her lap, watching as Connor thoroughly cleaned the wound and applied pressure with a folded pad of bandages. Still the bleeding continued, staining the pad crimson and seeping finally down the arm again.

"Damned thing's a mess, ain't it?" Rory muttered, wetting his lips as he looked at his arm.

"The bullet must have nicked a vein," Connor grunted in reply. After another try with a fresh pad with the same results; he was frowning heavily and Rory was white to the lips. Caitlyn looked at Connor in alarm. He shook his head at her, telling her without words to say nothing that would alarm Rory, and tossed the blood-soaked pad in the bowl she still held. Then he lifted the bowl away from her and set it on the bedside table. Extracting the knife from his boot again, he held its blade to the candle flame until it glowed red-hot.

"This will hurt," he warned Rory, who nodded and turned his face away. The hand on Rory's uninjured side clenched the bedclothes. Caitlyn covered that clenched fist with her hand, and the fingers curved to grip hers instead.

"If you're squeamish, don't look," Connor advised Caitlyn briefly. But she was unable to tear her eyes away, watching with fascinated horror as he brought the red-hot blade up against the open, oozing wound. Rory made a choked sound as the knife sizzled and the smell of burning flesh rose from the wound, but he didn't scream. Instead, his fingers squeezed Caitlyn's until hers were numb.

"Brave lad," Connor murmured to him as he lifted the knife from the wound and returned it to the candle. Cauterized, the wound remained closed. On one side, at least, the bleeding had stopped.

"Jesus, that hurt more than getting the damned bullet," Rory managed faintly.

"I know."

Caitlyn felt her stomach churn as Connor helped Rory turn over so that he could reach the back of the arm. Then, mouth grim, he held the glowing knife to the exit wound. Rory stiffened, groaning loudly as the cauterizing heat stopped the bleeding. His hand squeezed Caitlyn's until she thought she would scream. Just as she felt she could bear the pain no more, Rory went limp.

"Connor!" Caitlyn gripped Rory's lifeless hand in a panic. Connor took the knife away, cleansing it with the flame before returning it to his boot, while Caitlyn hovered frantically over Rory.

"He's fainted merely," Connor said, deftly winding a bandage around the injured arm. "He's not badly hurt, now that we've got the bleeding stopped." He tied the bandage in place, then pulled the sleeve of the nightshirt over it. "Stay with him till he wakes. I have business to attend to that I can't put off any longer."

Connor got to his feet, looming tall beside the bed as he frowned down at his unconscious brother. Clad only in shirt and breeches, booted feet splattered with mud and rain-wet black hair tied in back in a neat club, he emanated raw masculine power. Caitlyn, standing beside him, felt small and almost fragile. She looked up at him uncertainly. This Connor with the hard-set face and purposeful air was unfamiliar to her. The candlelight gleamed off an intricately wrought silver cross that dangled halfway down his shirtfront from a chain around his neck. That was unfamiliar to her as well; she had never before seen him wear an item of jewelry other than his pocket fob. The aqua eyes glinted as brightly as the silver medallion in the bronze of his face. His mouth was set, with deep lines running from it to his nose that she had never noticed before. It struck her then that Rory's injury hurt Connor too, more than she would have thought.

"What — what were you about, to get Rory shot?" she whispered, unable to resist the question. Connor's eyes were on her then, the restless energy that burned in them frightening. She knew he would tell her nothing.

"You know as much as you need, and more. You should have stayed in the house." His voice was rough-edged, his eyes aflame. "A word of advice, Caitlyn: keep your nose out of that which doesn't concern you."

With that, he turned on his heel and was gone. Caitlyn stared after him for a few moments, listening to the sound of his booted feet on the stairs. Then, as Rory stirred, she settled herself beside the bed. Her mind was awhirl with questions to which she could find no satisfactory answers.

XIV

The work was near done when Connor strode back into the stable. The trapdoor was closed, with straw swept over it so that none would ever guess of its existence. The take had been divided up; Fharannain was still saddled, and Cormac and Liam were tying the filled saddlebags to the horn. His cloak and mask rested across the saddle. Mickeen was scooping what was left into the strongbox that stayed hidden in the barn. That was something else for Connor to take care of, but later.

As he entered, shaking the rain from his hair, Cormac and Liam turned from their task to look at him. Anxiety was plain in both faces. Connor allowed himself a brief moment of self-congratulation. Whatever else he had done, or not done, he had raised his brothers well. They cared for one another truly, as a family should.

"Rory?" Cormac asked quietly as Connor came over to check Fharannain's girth.

"He's well enough. He'll suffer no lasting harm."

Liam looked as relieved as Cormac. Mickeen, having finished what he was doing and now in the act of carrying the strongbox to the place where it was customarily secreted, said over his shoulder, "Aye, and didn't I tell you that only the good die young? Young Rory should have a grand long life."

The three remaining d'Arcys grinned. Mickeen, for all his gruff exterior, was as fond of Rory as they were. The old ostler had been with them from the beginning and would lay down his life without hesitation for any one of them.

"What about Caitlyn? Did you . . . tell her anything?" Cormac asked as Connor donned cloak and mask and swung into the saddle.

"Nothing. And you're not to, either of you. Not that I don't think we can trust her, but the fewer people who know the truth the safer we are." He signaled with his knees to Fharannain to move out, adding over his shoulder, "Go on up to the house now and get some sleep. Your part is done for tonight."

Then he was out in the rainswept darkness, setting Fharannain at a canter over the hills toward Navan. Fortunately, he knew tonight's route as well as he knew the layout of his own house, as did the great black beast beneath him. Fharannain flew effortlessly over fences and streams that both could barely see, leaving Connor's mind free to wander.

Rory had taken a bullet. It was the first time in the years they had been riding with him that one of his brothers had been hurt. Connor felt a deep anxiety as he thought about it. Mayhap he should put a halt to things now, while he could with all of them whole. His brothers were, and always had been, his first concern. His father had given them over to his keeping on the night he died, and Connor had honored his promise to his sire to care for them to the best of his ability ever since.

They had been rough years, those first ones. There was no money, only the land and the few pieces of furnishings and gewgaws that could be salvaged from the charred ruins of the Castle. As a lad of twelve, left with three young brothers ranging in age from four to seven to provide for, to say nothing of the peasants who had traditionally depended upon Donoughmore for support and now were forced to make their own way with much hardship and suffering, Connor had been at his wit's end. At first he had sent Mickeen to Dublin to sell what few possessions they retained that were worth anything, but he had known that when the possessions ran out, the money would too.

In a desperate search for some means of earning a living for his new responsibilities, Connor had gone to Dublin on his own and had quickly discovered that thievery or buggery was the only way for a lad his age to get money. As he was not inclined to permit some fat roué the use of his body, he had turned to thievery. In the intervening two years he had spent at least half the time in Dublin, leaving Mickeen behind at the farm to care for his brothers, picking pockets and thieving from market stalls and stealing whatever he could find that could be converted to cash. With no small degree of success, either. He had kept his brothers alive and the farm going while the injustice of it all burned at him. He, Connor d'Arcy, Earl of Iveagh, should by rights have been master of a handsome estate, with a fortune to command. His brothers would have known a life of ease and plenty. Instead they were poorer than the poorest peasants, often hungry and in rags, with only a lad not much older than they to provide for them. His hatred of the bloody Anglicans who had stolen everything of value from the Irish and killed his father besides became a living thing inside him. One day, he vowed, he would have his revenge. And that day had come, though the vengeance was small compared with the magnitude of the grievance. . . .

Seamus McCool was standing in the mouth of the cave where they always met. Connor reined in Fharannain, untied the saddlebags, and tossed them to the bluff Irishman. Seamus would see to it that the items were sold and the money distributed to those whose need was greatest.

"Lord keep you, sor," he said fervently to Connor, his eyes bright in the darkness as he hefted the bags to test their weight.

"And you, Seamus," Connor replied, wheeling Fharannain about. He rode back into the night, his business concluded. Until the moon waned again.

XV

✼ ✼ ✼ ✼ ✼ ✼ ✼ ✼ ✼ ✼ ✼ ✼ ✼ ✼ ✼

A band of horsemen rode into Donoughmore early the next day. Connor had stayed close to home, ostensibly to supervise the slaughter of sheep. In reality, Caitlyn suspected he wanted to keep an eye on Rory, who was a trifle weak and more than a trifle testy, but surviving. Mrs. McFee had been told merely that Rory had come down with Caitlyn's chill, and she seemed to think no more about his being confined to bed. As for Caitlyn herself, the excitement of the night before had an unexpected benefit: she was completely restored to health by the morning and thus was able to go about her business as usual.

When the half-dozen riders appeared in the lee of the Castle, Cormac's hail brought Connor out of the sheep barn with his shirtsleeves still pushed above his elbows to stand watching their approach. Caitlyn, covertly eyeing the pair of them from the trough where she had been dispatched to scrub the wool pelts, could see the tension in Cormac's face. Connor looked impassive as the riders clattered down into the barnyard. They were disheveled, their horses splattered with mud as though they had ridden long and hard. Caitlyn recognized only one: Sir Edward Dunne.

"What business brings you to Donoughmore,

Sir Edward?" Connor asked brusquely as Sir Edward nudged his horse away from the milling pack and approached him.

"We're tracking some damned highwaymen," Sir Edward said, excitement lending a glitter to his gray eyes and a coarse edge to his patrician accent. "We followed their trail onto your property but lost them on the far side of the Castle. Did you or your people hear anything out of the ordinary last night? Or see anything?"

"I heard nothing at all, nor has anything untoward been reported to me." Connor, barely civil, cocked a head at Cormac, who shook his head. "How come you to be chasing highwaymen, Sir Edward? Has fox hunting begun to pall?"

The sneer was such that Sir Edward could hardly miss it. Apparently he chose to ignore Connor's gibe, because his voice was even enough as he replied: "Lord Alvinley was the victim. As you know, he's my uncle. He came to my house afterward, and we immediately set out in pursuit of the bandits, who made off with considerable booty. My uncle had the rents on him, you see, and his wife's jewel case too, as he was bound for Dublin to join her. His bailiff had just finished collecting from his tenants, so it was a goodly sum. And the jewelry was very fine."

"Obviously someone was well aware of Lord Alvinley's plans. Your uncle would do well to look amongst the people close to him for the rogue."

"My uncle swears the villain was none other than the one the peasants call the Dark Horseman. He said the gang was dressed all in black, and the leader wore the Cross of Ireland on his clothes. I've always thought that the Dark Horseman was nothing more than a tale made up by the peasants to frighten their landlords, but Lord Alvinley is convinced that the man exists and that he was robbed by him. In any case, he had a piece of luck: one of my uncle's outriders winged one of the bandits. There were drops of blood along the trail we followed." There was a brief pause, and then with a barely veiled taunt Sir Edward added, "You might consider joining the search, d'Arcy. There's considerable bounty at stake if our quarry truly turns out to be the Dark Horseman. My uncle has doubled the price on the man's head. And sheep farming cannot provide a very lucrative living."

"Unlike you, I don't care for blood sports. And sheep farming provides sufficient for my needs."

The sudden glint in Connor's eyes would have cowed a braver man than Sir Edward, who backtracked to a safer topic immediately. "Yes, well . . . Are all your tenants sound this morning?"

"All that I've seen. Would you care to search amongst them for the rogue?" This was uttered in such a blighting tone that Sir Edward's hands tightened on his horse's reins, causing the beast to back nervously.

In the moment it took for Sir Edward to quiet his horse, Cormac seemed to hold his breath.

But Sir Edward clearly had decided no good would come of further antagonizing the master of Donoughmore. His tone was conciliatory as he said, "No, that won't be necessary. You will send word if anyone is laid low or is not working as he should?"

"You may be sure of it."

"We'll be off, then. I have this feeling that they are near at hand, perhaps holed up somewhere to care for their wounded. Good day to you, d'Arcy." He nodded at Connor and Cormac, tipped his hat to Caitlyn, who was staring at him, sheep pelts forgotten, then wheeled his horse and headed out of the barnyard toward the road, the others following.

Caitlyn looked after them, eyes wide. Absent-mindedly she brushed stray stands of hair back toward the kerchief covering her head, completely forgetting her wet hands, which dripped water on her face. With a muttered imprecation she dried her hands on her yellow-striped skirt and lifted the hem of it to wipe the droplets from her face. Then she turned to stare at Connor and Cormac, who were moving back toward the barn. They had been out last night, cloaked and masked. Connor had spoken of a good night's work. Rory had been shot. And in Rory's room last night, a silver medallion in the shape of a cross had gleamed around Connor's neck. She had never seen it before or since. Enlightenment dawned in a blinding flash.

Abandoning the skin she had been scrubbing

to float in the muddy water, Caitlyn followed the d'Arcys into the barn. Connor and Cormac stood together just inside the door, watching from the safety of its shadows the riders crest the hill. Two pairs of eyes glanced at her as she entered, then narrowed. Her eyes were enormous, her expression a mixture of astonishment, disbelief, and knowledge.

"What ails you, lass?" Connor asked, his eyes moving over her face with disquieting swiftness.

" 'Tis you, isn't it?" she demanded, speaking scarcely above a whisper as her eyes fixed Connor and Connor alone. "You're the one they call the Dark Horseman!"

Connor returned her look for look, his devil's eyes taking on a warning glint. "You've been out amongst the sheep too long," he said tightly. Then as she continued to stare at him a little muscle beside his mouth jerked and he strode from the barn. Caitlyn watched him walk away, her eyes taking in every bit of him from the curling black hair confined by a black ribbon to the broad shoulders straining against the white linen of his shirt to the lean hips and long, powerful legs in their buff breeches and black riding boots. Connor d'Arcy, Earl of Iveagh, lip-service Protestant to protect his land, expert swordsman, kind paterfamilias, Irishman, gentleman, was the Dark Horseman. She felt she should have known it, should have guessed. He was everything she and Willie and the others had always imagined the Dark Horseman would be.

But she had never dreamed . . .

Her eyes swung to Cormac, who was watching her rather as one would a coiled snake.

"Your brother is the Dark Horseman," she said with certainty. Cormac opened his mouth to reply, then, meeting the conviction in her eyes, closed it again.

"Aye," he said slowly, then with a burst of pride added: "Aye, he is."

XVI

Over the next ten months, Caitlyn fulfilled Sir Edward Dunne's prophecy and grew into a beautiful young woman. With good food and affection, she blossomed, gaining three inches in height so that the d'Arcys no longer towered over her and developing pleasing curves where females were supposed to have them. Despite the soft rounding of her breasts and hips, she still remained slender as a wand, with an impossibly small waist and endless legs. Her hair grew until it reached the middle of her back, thick and smooth and glossy as satin, and black as a raven's wing. She was careless about dressing it, rarely taking the time to do more than tie it back with a ribbon, but its beauty was such that no artifice was required to show it off. Her enormous kerry blue eyes no longer seemed too large for her small-boned face. Framed by thick lashes like lavish black fringes, set off by slanting black brows, they glowed against the camellia whiteness of her skin. Her facial structure was delicate, with the exquisite modeling of the bones readily apparent: high, smooth forehead from which her hair rose in a widow's peak, high cheekbones, rounded jaw and chin. Her nose was small and straight, her mouth soft and perfectly formed, her neck long and slender. At just turned seventeen, she was a woman grown, and O'Malley the thief was nothing more than a dim memory to everyone but Caitlyn herself.

Word of her beauty spread over the countryside, and males for miles around came to see and be dazzled. The former reigning belle of County Meath, Mrs. Congreve, had her nose put decidedly out of joint as most of her admirers deserted her to worship at the shrine of Caitlyn's youthful freshness. Connor was the only eligible male in the vicinity who seemed completely unaffected by Caitlyn's blossoming. He still treated Caitlyn like the young cousin he called her, and continued to visit Mrs. Congreve at her home, his visits increasing in frequency as he oftimes absented himself overnight. His brothers expressed vociferous fears of an imminent wedding. The suggestion made Caitlyn so cross she wanted to spit.

"He would never be so stupid," she informed Cormac, who had expressed just those fears as they rode together along the grassy banks high above the Boyne. Like herself, Cormac had grown up considerably in the past few months. He was no longer the gangly youth she had fought with upon coming to Donoughmore more than a year before, but a well-knit man of nineteen. For the last six months or so, he and Rory had been brangling mostly good-naturedly over the attentions of Lisette Bromleigh, daughter of a baronet in the neighboring county of Cavan. Lately, though, the younger d'Arcys had given signs of becoming aware of the beauty blooming in their midst, and Caitlyn was getting a wee bit tired of the sudden upsurge in chivalrous attentions they were directing her way.

"A beautiful woman has a way of making the most intelligent man stupid," Cormac said gloomily. Then his eyes slid sideways at Caitlyn. "Just look at the way all the men within riding distance make fools of themselves over you. I thought Conn was going to pitch a fit when he came home the other day to find both John Mason and Michael McClendon helping you salt mutton. They were some sight, with Mason dressed to the nines and both of them up to their arses in brine, while you, you little minx, sat on the barn rail and watched them do your work."

"Connor was extremely rude," Caitlyn said with her nose in the air. She sat stiffly upright in the sidesaddle, presenting a rigid spine to Cormac for his criticism. If one disregarded the crumpled state of her blue linen skirt and the stray hairs that had escaped the black velvet ribbon at her nape and were tucked haphazardly behind her small ears, she was the epitome of all that was lovely. "As were you all. I suppose I may have friends, just as you do."

"Friends!" Cormac hooted. " 'Tis not friends they're wishing to be with you, my dear. Though you're too young and innocent to know what I'm talking about, of course."

Caitlyn shot him a glinting look. "Don't you patronize me, Cormac d'Arcy! You're only two years older than I am! Besides, you're as bad as any of them! Don't think I haven't noticed the way you look at me! Aye, and Rory too! And even Liam!"

"That's ridiculous!" Cormac fired back, going red to his ears.

" 'Tis not! I've seen you! Yesterday, for example, when we were having tea."

"Well, anyone would look at you in that dress you wore yesterday. It was cut so low in the bosom that you almost fell out! In front of Mrs. Congreve too! No wonder Conn was mad!"

"Connor has no right to criticize what I wear. Nor do you! Any of you!"

"He bought the dress," Cormac pointed out reasonably. "I guess he can say something if you go taking scissors to the neck of it so that 'tis indecent!"

" 'Twas not!"

" 'Twas!"

Caitlyn glared at him and kicked her mount into a canter. "You can just ride by yourself, Cormac d'Arcy! I can do without your company and your insults!"

"Dash it, Caitlyn . . . !" But he was talking to thin air. Caitlyn was galloping up the hillside in the general direction of the farm. He cursed again and spurred his horse after her. But the gelding Connor had bought her some three months before was fleet of foot and not easy to overtake. He gave it up, cantering just so as to keep her in sight and make sure she came to no harm.

Caitlyn was furious as she leaned over Finnbarr's neck, urging him to greater speed. Men were vile, the lot of them. Here was Cormac making a fool of himself over what was no more than a slight change in her looks, and Rory and Liam were no better. They had practically tripped over each other when she had appeared in her altered dress, which was certainly cut no lower than the one Mrs. Congreve had been wearing as she sat in the parlor flirting with Connor. There had been no need for Connor to poker up like that, or to send her off to her room to change as if she were a naughty child. He had been looking down the front of Mrs. Congreve's dress earlier — she had seen him! He hadn't appeared to think that Mrs. Congreve was indecent. But it was all of a piece. Connor treated her like a bairn! Cormac's and Rory's and Liam's eyes had popped at her cleavage, while Connor had done nothing more than scowl at her as if he were her da! After scolding her like a babe in arms right in front of Mrs. Congreve, the old cat, and sending her up to change, he had driven his lady friend back home himself, leaving the work to the rest of them to do, and stayed away all night! He certainly had no grounds to criticize her behavior! Could she help it if John Mason and Michael McClendon had insisted on doing her work the other day? Could she help it that Tim Regan had brought her a gift of a little heifer calf, completely disregarding the fact that Donoughmore was a sheep farm? Could she help

180

it that the recently widowed Lord Alvinley had brought her a book or that Reverend Lamb, the little parson from the village, had publicly likened her to a pearl among swine, meaning the Catholic (except for Connor) d'Arcys? No, she could not!

The rush of air in her face cooled her temper somewhat as she approached the farm, but the sight of Fharannain's empty stall set it simmering again. Connor was not back yet, and it was well past midday. Making a face as she reined in Finnbarr, Caitlyn mentally replayed Mrs. Congreve's mincing words of yesterday. The lady still feared the Dark Horseman, she had protested coyly as she had begged Connor's escort, which was hugely laughable if Caitlyn had been in the mood to laugh. The Dark Horseman wouldn't hurt a hair on that powdered head!

Of course, it was Connor's perfect right to have a lady friend. Rationally, she knew that at twenty-seven, he was overdue for marriage and children of his own. But Mrs. Congreve . . . ! Caitlyn shared his brothers' dislike of his choice. Or rather, Mrs. Congreve's choice of him. As an impoverished Irish Earl, Connor could not ordinarily look to the ladies of the Ascendancy for a bride. As Cormac had told her, they had originally suspected that Mrs. Congreve would be no more than their brother's mistress for a time, and they had found naught to object to in that. But Mrs. Congreve, whom Caitlyn suspected was not of such high estate herself, had clearly decided to overlook the handicap of Connor's nationality and lack of funds in favor of his virile good looks. In short, the simpering vixen was on the catch for a husband for fun, having already married one for money with great success. Picturing Connor lean and dark in Mrs. Congreve's bed made Caitlyn's stomach churn with displeasure. The mere thought was sickening. There were many other lasses he could have favored, from the village schoolmaster's prim daughter to Sir Edward Dunne's own niece, who was dazzled enough by a handsome face and form to overlook the fact that Connor was native Irish, though it was doubtful her family would let her infatuation come to marriage. But Connor was a handsome man, and a charming one, and it was likely that if he decided to wed Miss Dunne she at least would not object. But picturing Connor with red-haired Sarah Dunne didn't satisfy Caitlyn either. She was not Connor's type any more than was Mrs. Congreve.

At least Connor's absence meant he wouldn't be home to see her returning from her ride unescorted, Caitlyn told herself as she slid from the saddle and turned to take care of Finnbarr. After a pair of "accidental" encounters with Sir Edward Dunne, who was lavish in admiration of her beauty and had taken to riding about the grounds of Donoughmore at just the time when she normally took her daily ride, Connor had decreed that she was not to ride alone. And Connor's temper was short of late. Annoyed as she was at him, she would not care to provoke a confrontation when he was in his present bad humor.

Of course, it was getting near to the waning of the moon. That was when the Dark Horseman rode, and Connor had much on his mind. He had ridden out only four times since Rory had been shot, and she knew that he debated the wisdom of riding at all. For himself, he counted no risk. But for his brothers, she thought he was afraid.

Caitlyn knew that there were many who needed his assistance — poor widows with rent to pay, men who had been injured and could not feed their children, orphanages run by the priests. They all hailed the Dark Horseman as if he were a saint, accepting his largesse with tears in their eyes and blessings on their lips when the distributions came through the mysterious channels that had been set up. Though he was far from being a wealthy man, the farm just making enough to support them all with little left over, Connor kept only what was needed from their hauls and gave away the rest to the poorest of the poor: the oppressed of Ireland. That made him a hero throughout the length and breadth of the land. And it made him a hero to his brothers and Caitlyn, too.

More than anything she wished to ride with them. Connor had strictly forbidden it the one time she had dared to make the suggestion, even dressing down poor Cormac for confirming her suspicions to boot. But Cormac, out of Connor's hearing, thought the idea was a lark. He told her tales of the Dark Horseman's exploits, hinting broadly when they were to ride, so that the last time she had managed to hide herself in the stable and watch them go. The next time they took to the High Toby, she was determined to follow, to see for herself the Sassenach oppressors brought low. Cormac had agreed to tell her when it was to be. Caitlyn guessed it would be soon. Connor was seething with restless energy, the landlords were growing more ruthless with their collection of the rents by the day, and the waning of the moon was at hand. This time, she meant to see the Dark Horseman's noble deeds for herself; the hero worship that Willie had never outgrown (how she wished she could tell him how close at hand his idol was!) now infected her as well.

She had it all planned: she would join the gang. Like the d'Arcys, she would lead a double life. She would be a beautiful, feminine young lady for three hundred and fifty-three days a year. On the other twelve, she would transform herself into a mettlesome lad who rode at the Dark Horseman's side. It was her favorite daydream, and in preparation for the night when it became a reality at last, she had given up her breeches and male ways almost entirely. When the time came for her to be a lad again, none outside the family would have reason to suspect that the Dark Horseman's newest rider was a female.

"Where's Cormac?" Caitlyn had just swung

the saddle off Finnbarr's back when the question made her jump. She had thought for a moment that the question, uttered in a disapproving voice, had come from Connor. Swinging around, she saw Rory and scowled at him. Really, it was disgusting how all the d'Arcys thought they had the right to boss her around!

"I decided to finish my ride without him. He was being most unpleasant," Caitlyn said huffily, walking toward the tack room with the saddle in her arms.

"Here, let me do that! It's too heavy for you." Rory overtook her and removed the saddle from her arms. Caitlyn scowled at his back as he carried the saddle into the tack room and hung it up for her. Turning back to Finnbarr, she was slipping the bridle from his head when Rory's hand closed over hers. "You know what Conn said about you riding alone. Cormac obviously is useless. From now on, I'll go with you."

"I don't want you! Or Cormac either! Or Liam! Or anybody!" She was impatient. Rory looked down at her with a superior frown, moving her hand aside and removing the bridle himself. Finnbarr stamped his foot and snorted when he was left with only his halter. Caitlyn felt a little bit like stamping her foot and snorting herself. This was getting too absurd for words!

"You know you can't ride alone." Rory's tone was stern.

"And just who are you to tell me what to do?"

Caitlyn grabbed Finnbarr's halter and marched him toward his stall. Sure enough, Rory came up and tried to do that, too. She elbowed him in the ribs, hard, and he grunted, rubbing his ribs as he let go.

"Connor said . . ."

"Bother Connor!" She put Finnbarr in his stall and closed the door with a snap, turning back to glare at Rory.

"Caitlyn . . . !" Cormac rode into the barn, eyes narrowed against the sudden darkness. Spotting her as she stood with arms akimbo, glaring at Rory, he sighed with relief. Then he saw Rory standing in front of her, still rubbing his ribs, and his eyes narrowed again.

"I thought you were supposed to be helping Mickeen with the sheep!" Cormac's eyes accused his brother.

"Well, I thought you were supposed to be keeping an eye on Caitlyn!" Rory retorted, returning his brother's look with interest.

"I was!" Cormac slid from Kildare's back and started unsaddling the horse, glaring at his brother all the while.

"Looked like it! She was all alone when she rode in here!"

"I was watching her all the time! She got mad. . . ." Cormac lugged the saddle and bridle to the tack room and then returned to put Kildare into his stall. Rory matched him step for step, hectoring him all the way.

"What did you do to her to make her mad?"

There was a note in Rory's voice that Caitlyn didn't like.

"What did *you* do to her to make her mad? I see you're rubbing your side! She wouldn't hit you for nothing!" Cormac turned from putting Kildare up to scowl at Rory.

"She didn't hit me! She —"

"Stop it, the both of you!" Caitlyn had had enough. "You're both behaving like bairns! I don't need either one of you to look out for me! I can take care of myself!"

The brothers shifted their attention to Caitlyn as she flared at them. Although she didn't know it, she was a magnificent sight with her cheeks flushed pink with anger and a militant glitter in her blue eyes. Her fists rested on her hips, her skirt swayed about her slender body as she berated them, and her black hair tumbled in silken tendrils around her face. Much struck with her beauty, they both stared, their faces wearing identical expressions of bedazzlement.

"Oh, honestly!" At their mooning looks, she turned on her heel and flounced from the barn. Immediately Cormac and Rory came after her.

"Caitlyn!"

"Caitlyn, don't be mad!" Rory caught hold of her sleeve. Caitlyn, whirling on him, jerked it from his hold so violently that it tore. Rory stood looking down in stupefied amazement at the scrap of blue linen he held. Cormac's face flushed with rage.

"Now look what you've done, you looby!"

Caitlyn was inclined to laugh, her anger turned to amusement at the horrified expression on Rory's face.

"Caitlyn, I never meant . . ."

"You tore her dress!" Cormac took a less sanguine view of the situation than did Caitlyn. His fists balled, and a belligerent spark lit his eyes as he glared at his brother.

" 'Twas an accident — and none of your concern!" Rory's initial contrition turned to belligerence as he met Cormac's hostile glare.

"More mine than yours!"

" 'Tis not!"

"Would you stop?" Caitlyn almost shrieked the words, stepping hastily between the two when it appeared they would come to blows. She felt like tearing out her hair with vexation — or tearing out theirs. Glares were exchanged over her head. Cormac tried to step around her, his fists balled and his jaw clenched. Caitlyn performed a little dance step to stay in front of him, her hand resting on his shirt front. Behind her, Rory slipped to one side and shoved his brother's shoulder.

"Think you can take me, do you, little brother?"

That taunting question lit fires in Cormac's eyes. He again tried to get around Caitlyn, who had both hands on his chest now while she angrily told Rory to leave off. Neither seemed inclined to mind her, and she was on the verge of shrugging and permitting the thickheaded numbskulls to kill each other when Connor rode into the stableyard on Fharannain. Cormac, seeing his eldest brother, slowly unclenched his fists while still favoring Rory with a sizzling look. Caitlyn, also seeing Connor — who dismounted, tied Fharannain to a post, and headed in their direction with narrowed eyes — stepped out from between the two of them and tried to look as if nothing at all was amiss. It was left for Rory, who clearly had no notion that Connor was anywhere in the vicinity, to take advantage of his younger brother's disengagement and get off a round-house punch. Fortunately, Cormac ducked and the blow went whistling harmlessly over his head.

"What in the name of Patrick ails you?" A lean, powerful hand fastened inside the neck of Rory's shirt and dragged him back a few paces. Connor, still some two inches taller than Rory, who at twenty-one had attained his full growth, glared down into the face of his younger brother. Rory blinked. Then Connor looked over to where Caitlyn was standing next to Cormac. The expression in those devil's eyes made even Caitlyn, the innocent party in the fracas, feel about two inches tall.

Nobody said anything. Connor's eyes moved over the three of them, their aqua depths measuring. After a moment, he let Rory go.

"Never, for any reason, do I want to see such a thing again. D'Arcys don't lift their hands to one another. Is that clear?"

"Aye."

"Aye."

Both Cormac and Rory looked sullen, but they didn't argue with Connor's pronouncement. It was left to Caitlyn to glare at him, which she did, with real venom. His eyes widened as they met her gaze.

"Now, how have I offended you, my wee lassie?" This was said with such amusement that Caitlyn's annoyance increased. He sounded as though he was humoring a child, which she was not.

"If you had half a brain in your head," she hissed, still glaring at him, "you'd see I'm no wee lassie!"

Then she turned on her heel and stalked off, leaving all three d'Arcys staring after her, their faces reflecting identical expressions of bewilderment.

XVII

Two days later, the time had come. Caitlyn was sure of it as day wore into evening. There was an edginess to Connor and an air of suppressed excitement about the others. Even the horses were stamping in their stalls. After supper, when Mrs. McFee had left, the d'Arcys retired immediately to bed instead of sitting around the parlor swapping tales as was their wont. Then Caitlyn was certain sure. She could barely contain her own excitement as she retired to her room in the attic, ostensibly to sleep but instead to dress herself in the clothes she had purloined a piece at a time from Mrs. McFee's basket of mending: Cormac's old breeches, which she had unhandily taken in so that they more or less fitted, a shirt of Rory's, Liam's jabot with the torn lace frill, and a rough gray frock coat that she suspected had once belonged to Mickeen. She wore her own riding boots, which were much like a man's, and twisted her hair into a loop at her nape so that it might be mistaken for a man's club. The hooded cloak and mask she had had to improvise, clumsily ripping up an outmoded dress of black silk which she had found in the attic along with other woman's things. (She suspected that the trunk had once belonged to the d'Arcys' mother.)

Stitchery was another of the womanly arts at which she did not excel, but she had managed to fashion a serviceable hooded cloak and a mask for herself.

Dressed, she waited for more than an hour while the house grew quiet as a grave. Finally, she could contain herself no longer. Caitlyn bundled the coat and mask under her arm and stole down the stairs. A rolled quilt lay under the covers of her bed just in case one of them should take it into his head to check on her before they left. She could only hope that Cormac would not alert her to their going, as he had done once before. She did not think he would. He had been rather on his dignity with her since that afternoon when he and Rory had quarreled. But leaving the dummy in her bed was a chance she had to take. If she was to have any hope of riding along with the Dark Horseman, she had better be in place when the gang of them set out. Cormac had told her that Connor set the devil's own pace, and she believed it. She had seen him ride.

The night was so black that she could just make out the shape of the stable. If she hadn't known where it was, she might have missed it in the dark. A stiff wind blew from the east. Except for the rustling of the moor grasses and the leaves overhead as the wind passed through them, all was silent. Even the sheep seemed to have sensed something was afoot, for she heard none of their plaintive bleats.

The d'Arcys were still in the house, windows

darkened as though they slept. Caitlyn prayed that they would stay where they were until she was safely out of sight. She thought that they would not leave for an hour or so yet, but she couldn't be sure.

It had occurred to her that it would be impossible for her to follow them through the tunnel without their knowledge; the door to the passage was open only long enough to permit the five of them to pass through. If by chance she should manage to sneak inside the tunnel, she would doubtless be trapped there by the door closing at the other end. So she had decided that her best course would be to take Finnbarr to the Castle and await the emergence of the Dark Horseman from the tunnel there. Then she would follow, keeping behind a goodly way so that she could watch without being seen. They would not be expecting a sixth rider and, with luck, would not become aware of her presence — or if they did, at least not until it was too late to send her back.

Finnbarr nickered once as she quickly saddled him, but she shushed him with an apple she had saved for just that purpose. As he munched contentedly, she got him ready and then led him through the stableyard, her hand on his nose to prevent any other sounds from him. But Finnbarr was as good as could be. When they were well away from the farmhouse and she had climbed on his back, she rewarded him with a pat on the neck. She had grown to love the roan gelding dearly. He was a beautiful animal, sleek and intelligent and fast as the wind. Although Connor would never confirm it, Caitlyn knew that Finnbarr must have cost him a dear price. She was touched to the heart that Connor would bestow so magnificent a gift on her, who, despite the fact that he protected her by claiming her as cousin, was not the slightest degree of kin. Like his brothers, he treated her as family. The grace of God had been with her the day she had tried to pick his pocket. She felt as if her true life had started from that day.

The Castle was as eerie as ever, ghostly and full of whispery sounds on this darkest of nights, but Caitlyn felt no more than a single shiver crawl up her spine as she dismounted and led Finnbarr inside the bawn. Like the living members of the d'Arcy family, she had taken their ghosts as her own. Now when she pictured the Castle haunts, she imagined them as a legion of specters riding at her back instead of threatening her.

She had chosen the stone arches of the covered walkway along the far wall as the best place to wait. The tunnel opening was, she had guessed, in the dungeons that lay beneath the Castle, but the dungeon was one place she preferred not to go, especially alone at night, unless she was forced to. In any event, she had seen her ghost riders disappear through the Castle itself. It was probable that they would emerge the same way.

They did! The muffled thudding of hooves on stone that she had once thought was the beating of a ghostly drum was the only warning she had before the riders burst through the door of the Castle, pounded through the keep, and disappeared over the wall, Fharannain in the lead. Prepared as she was, Caitlyn was so fascinated by what she saw that she almost forgot to go after them. The silent emergence and thunderous swift passing of the black-cloaked figures reminded her of stories she had heard of what had happened once upon the opening of the gates of Hell. . . .

Finnbarr called after his mates, sidestepping nervously. It was enough to bring Caitlyn back to her purpose. Clapping her heels to his side — she rode astride — she sent Finnbarr sailing after the rest, her heart pounding with excitement in rhythm with his hoofbeats as he cleared the tumbledown wall and galloped over the moors in the wake of the will-o'-the-wisps ahead.

She rode at breakneck pace for nearly three-quarters of an hour, careful not to get too close or so far away that she should lose them altogether, relying as much on intuition as on her sense of sight to tell her where to go. The moors were treacherous riding with their hidden bogs and holes, but Finnbarr was sure of foot and did not stumble. The blackness of the windblown night was her protection as they and she forded the Boyne at a low spot where the water, for all its icy swift current, came no higher than Finnbarr's knees. When the riders surged out of the river to disappear into a copse of trees, she was upon the copse before she realized that they had pulled up.

"Stand and deliver!" The hoarse command shouted some little way ahead was followed by the blasting of a thunderbuss. For a dreadful instant Caitlyn thought that they had mistaken her for a stranger and were firing at her. Then she burst through the trees, her head low over Finnbarr's neck as she tried to slow him down. Sensing the nearness of his stablemates, he fought for his head.

"Sweet Mother Mary, what's that?"

Caitlyn managed to pull Finnbarr up just as the little party on the Great Road below became aware of her presence. To a man, the masked faces, and the unmasked ones too, swung in her direction.

"Jesus, don't shoot! It's —" Rory bit off the words before he blurted out her name.

A lantern-lit coach was stopped in the road, its gilt work and the coat of arms on its door bearing testimony to its richness as a prize. Two elaborately gowned ladies clinging nervously to the arm of a single spluttering gentleman stood by the coach's side. Its roof was loaded down with luggage; the group was obviously bound on a journey of some length. Liam, still mounted, kept his pistol trained on them. One of the ladies was weeping; the other looked on the verge of it. The gentleman seemed equally terrified. They would pose no problems. The driver had thrown down his weapon; it lay on the road by the lead horse. The guard had not; he took advantage of the distraction caused by Caitlyn's advent to swing his rifle up . . .

"No!" she screamed. A rifle boomed. For a dreadful instant Caitlyn waited with heart in mouth for one of her family to crumple and fall. Instead, the guard moaned and toppled from his seat to lie facedown in the road. She watched, horrified, as at a gesture from Connor Rory got down to check the condition of the fallen man.

"He's dead," he reported briefly, nudging the corpse with his booted foot.

Caitlyn stared at the sprawled body and felt sick. But there was no time to think. Connor, cloak swirling, face masked so that even she who knew him well identified him primarily by Fharannain, rode up to the side of the coach. The silver Cross of Ireland glinted briefly against the night blackness of his cloak. As he approached, the terrified driver shrank away from him.

"Throw down the bags."

"Aye. Aye, your worship," the driver responded nervously, clearly not eager to share the fate of his fellow. Keeping a wary eye on Connor, he stood up and began pitching the luggage into the road. When they were all down, Mickeen dismounted and began forcing them open, rifling though them. The items he deemed worth keeping were crammed into a quartet of leather bags around his neck. Liam assisted him in his search, filling his own leather bags in short order. When the last piece of baggage had been thoroughly rifled, the leather bags went bulging. Mickeen took Liam's as well as his own and slung them over Aristedes' whithers.

"Please don't hurt us!" The whimper focused Caitlyn's attention on one of the women, who was stripping off her jewelry and holding it out with shaking hands. As he took it from her, Cormac laughed, the sound chilling as it emerged from beneath the black mask. It was as if, with the donning of their disguises, he and the others had taken on different personas. They were highwaymen, dangerous and desperate, certain to pay with their lives if they were caught. Caitlyn realized with a sudden chill that what Connor did as the Dark Horseman was no game.

"Mount and let's away!"

Cormac, the only one still unhorsed, swung back up on Kildare. At a nod from Connor, Mickeen and Liam rode over to the pair of horses that drew the coach and cut their harnesses so that they were freed. The horses were driven off and the coach was left helpless in a matter of moments, with neither the driver nor the passengers daring so much as a word of protest. The fate of the man sprawled in the road was too gruesomely plain.

"You." Connor was suddenly beside her, his whisper grim, his eyes glinting like icy lights through the slits of his mask. "Stay by me!"

The time had come to pay the piper. Caitlyn wet her lips. The last time he had sounded like that was just before he had turned her over his knee all those months ago. Of course, he

198

wouldn't dare to do such a thing to her now that she was grown, but . . .

"Let's go!"

They were off, Liam in the lead as Connor paced Fharannain to stay at her side in the middle of the pack. Nervous as she was of what would come when they were safe at home, Caitlyn was glad to have him there. Angry or not, he was the most important person in her life, and she had seen too little of him of late. Gradually, as Finnbarr raced beside Fharannain over the treacherous moors, she forgot Connor's anger and its probable consequences. Adrenaline began to flow like wine through her veins. Soon she had forgotten everything but the wonder of racing along at Connor's side through the wind-tossed night.

She urged Finnbarr to greater speed, galloping past Liam and Rory and the others. Finnbarr's hooves barely seemed to skim the ground. He took a low wall effortlessly with Fharannain still beside him. Laughing, Caitlyn looked over at Connor to see if he shared her intoxication. His mask obscured most of his face, but there was no mistaking the grim set to his mouth.

"Pull up!"

Even as he was mouthing the words he was leaning over, his hand grasping her reins just behind Finnbarr's tender mouth. Indignant, Caitlyn fought his hold on her mount, but Finnbarr shuddered to a halt, as did Fharannain.

"You little fool, you missed the spot." Connor

was speaking through his teeth as he released her rein to turn Fharannain about. Caitlyn, shivering, looked over her shoulder to find that she and Connor were, as far as she could see, alone on the moor. The others had simply disappeared. Following Connor, she was amazed to see him ride straight at what appeared to be a solid rock cliff. At the last minute she saw the narrow black fissure into which he disappeared. Holding her breath, she followed him into a lantern-lit cave. Mickeen, on the ground just inside, rolled a huge rock into place, blocking the fissure as she passed. The others were already ahead, the sound of hoofbeats and the vague glow of lantern light in the distance telling her that they were riding down into the earth. She followed Connor on Fharannain, the pace in here on slippery wet stone far slower than it had been on the moors. Mickeen, with the last lantern, brought up the rear.

The cave turned into a passageway obviously built by man. Its stone walls ran with water as it twisted ever downward, and a curious rushing noise sounded constantly overhead. Caitlyn realized with a little shiver of fright that they must be passing beneath the Boyne. But it was obvious that Connor and the others felt no anxiety, that they had passed this way many times. She swallowed her fear, keeping her eyes fixed on the broad, blackcloaked back ahead of her for comfort. No real harm could befall her with Connor so near. . . .

Finally the passageway started turning up again, and at last leveled out. They passed through another entryway, which Mickeen closed by the simple expedient of pulling a chain on the wall, though the huge stone slab shrieked in protest as it rumbled into place behind them. Caitlyn realized that they were in the dungeons of the Castle, and the shrieks of the passage opening and closing were the ghostly cries she had heard that night when she had first seen the Dark Horseman ride. Then they were riding through yet another entryway into another tunnel with Mickeen closing yet another protesting door behind them. Moments later, the passage turned steeply up, and they burst through to the lantern-lit stable.

XVIII

❋ ❋ ❋ ❋ ❋ ❋ ❋ ❋ ❋ ❋ ❋ ❋ ❋ ❋ ❋

"Get down!"

Connor reached up and caught her under the armpits, dragging her from Finnbarr's back. He had torn off his mask even before he had dismounted. His face was white with rage, his aqua eyes ablaze. Faced with that sizzling anger, feeling the strength of his grip on her because she did not dismount fast enough to suit him, Caitlyn felt the exhilaration she had experienced on the ride dissipate under a cloud of real fear. Connor looked furious — and Connor in a black temper was formidable indeed.

She was standing in front of him now, her head tilted back as she met that inimical glare. Although she had grown, he was a tall man and she came up only to his chin. His scowl deepened as he glared at her. Then his hand came up to yank her hood down and strip off her mask, which he threw on the ground. Her hair tumbled from its confinement to tangle about her face in a silky black cloud. She brushed it back with an unsteady hand. Caitlyn was slightly unnerved by the suppressed violence of his movements, which told as no words could have done just how extremely enraged he was.

"Connor, I —" She started to explain that she

had just wanted to watch, but the sound of her voice seemed to madden him further. His mouth twisted, his eyes shot fire like twin volcanoes, and he reached out to catch her by her upper arms as if he meant to shake her. He didn't, but his grip hurt.

"I ought to take a whip to you," he growled. "And I may! Have you any notion what a bloody stupid thing you did? You could have been killed! You could have gotten one of us killed! What the bloody hell did you think you were about?"

Then he did shake her, a little hard shake that whipped her head back once. Caitlyn's hands came up involuntarily to grasp his wrists. Her eyes were wide as she met his furious gaze. As she met those flaming devil's eyes, anger and something else took root inside her: a queer kind of tension to which she could not put a name.

"You let her go!" The words were Cormac's and were directed at Connor. Caitlyn had been so focused on Connor that she had forgotten the presence of the other four, who had dismounted and were watching or trying not to watch as their temperaments dictated. Judging by his reaction to Cormac's challenge, Connor had apparently been equally caught up by the rage he meant to vent on her. At the interruption, both principals looked around at the speaker in some surprise. Cormac was standing close to Connor's shoulder, his mouth set grimly and his eyes resolute. Though not as tall or leanly muscled as Connor, he was much stronger than he looked, as Caitlyn knew from watching him work. Like Connor, Cormac still wore his black cloak, although he had discarded his mask. A riding whip was clutched in his right hand.

"What did you say?" Connor barely breathed the words, the flames in his eyes flaring higher as they focused on his youngest brother. His hands still gripped Caitlyn's upper arms hard, the strength of his grasp apparently forgotten in his amazement at this challenge from the youth who had always hero-worshipped him.

"I said, let her go. You're hurting her!"

Connor's hands tightened on her arms, and Caitlyn had to hold back a squeak. She knew he had forgotten that he was holding her, that he was not hurting her deliberately. His attention had shifted from her to Cormac, his expression dangerous.

"This is naught of your affair. Stay out of it," he bit off, then swung his eyes back to Caitlyn again. She moistened her lips, but before she could say anything Cormac jumped back into the fray.

"Let her go, Conn!"

Connor's eyes shifted back to Cormac as if he couldn't believe what he was hearing. Caitlyn could feel anger emanating from him in waves. If nothing else, Cormac had managed to divert some of that rage from her to himself, but Caitlyn was not thankful for the intervention. The relationship between the brothers had always been too close, too special, for her to want to see it damaged. Especially if she was the cause.

"Get on about your work, Cormac. This is between Caitlyn and me." Connor was holding back the imminent explosion with a considerable effort, Caitlyn knew. Those aqua eyes burned as they lifted from his youngest brother to the others, who had frozen in place to watch the unprecedented drama being played out in front of them. "That goes equally for the rest of you. Rory, see to the horses. Liam, you and Mickeen sort through the take and keep what we need. And be quick about it. I've an appointment with Father Patrick at St. Albans, and he's like to worry himself into the grave if I'm a minute late. Which," he said, his eyes shifting grimly back to Caitlyn, "I don't mean to be. As for you, lassie, you can explain yourself at length later. I've no time to listen now. But I want one thing clearly understood before I go. You are never, under any circumstances, to try such a trick again. I want your promise."

His eyes bore into hers. She wet her lips again, half inclined to say what he wished her to and get the whole anger-charged episode behind her. But she had no intention of remaining tamely in the house while they rode the High Toby without her. And her respect for Connor was too great to allow her to give him her word if she had no intention of keeping it.

"I'll have your promise!" His hands were tightening on her arms again. Caitlyn met that devil's gaze with apprehension, but she was no less determined for all that. Despite his temper and his strength, which was obviously many times hers, she did not physically fear Connor. He would not hurt her, she knew. The only consequence of her defiance would be a furious blaze of temper — and that she could deal with. She hoped.

"That I cannot give." Her voice was low, but there was no doubt that everyone present heard her words. An appalled silence filled the air. Every eye was trained on her. Her own eyes never left the man before her.

At her reply, Connor practically gnashed his teeth. Staring up into that dark, lean face, feeling the sheer force of the body bending over hers, she knew a moment's craven wish to take back her rash words. But she reminded herself again that this was Connor. Despite his vibrating rage, she was in no danger of bodily harm.

"Your promise!"

"Don't you hurt her, Conn!"

"You stay out of this, young idiot!" Connor hissed at Cormac, who had stepped forward as he bent threateningly over Caitlyn. But even as he was rebuking Cormac, Connor's eyes never left Caitlyn, who was practically hanging from his hands as he lifted her onto her toes by the strength of his grip on her. "Your promise!"

"I cannot give you a promise I don't mean to keep." The words were breathless but valiant. Caitlyn sensed the collective indrawn breaths of her audience. Connor stared down at her for a moment, mouth tight, eyes smoldering. She went on desperately: "I want to ride with you. All of you. You're my family now. I can help. . . ."

"I'll hear no more bloody talk of helping!" Connor roared, the sound so loud that it almost deafened Caitlyn for an instant. The lid was off his temper now, and no mistake. "You'll damned well do as you're told, and I'm telling you that if you ever, ever, pull such a stunt as tonight's again I'll whip the skin from your bloody bones! You'll stay safe in bed, and there's an end to it!"

"I won't!" Caitlyn's temper was beginning to heat in its turn. She glared up into the aqua eyes that flamed so close to hers. "Why can't I ride with you? I can ride as well as Liam and a sight better than Mickeen. I can learn to shoot —"

"No!" Connor was nearly beside himself.

"Conn, she really is a good rider." Cormac had been in favor of having her come with them ever since she had discovered their identity. "I'll watch out for her. It'll be a lark, having her along."

Connor released Caitlyn abruptly and turned on his brother. His jaw was clenched with the force of his anger. "Aye, and will it be a lark watching her get shot or hanged? She's a bloody lass, and she'll stay in the house where she belongs! And that's my last word on the subject!"

"I'll not stay in the house! I'll not! I don't care what you say, I'll do as I please." Caitlyn moved forward, hands balled on her hips, spitting her defiance at the back of that black head.

Connor whirled on her so fast that she had no

chance to jump out of the way. The back of his hand caught her face with numbing force. She cried out as the blow sent her tumbling backward into the straw, her hand raised to cradle her injured cheek. She barely had time to register Connor's stunned expression before Cormac leaped forward with an inarticulate cry of rage and brought his whip whistling around toward his brother's head. Connor fended off the whip with an upraised arm, then responded with a lightning jab to the stomach that sent Cormac flying to the straw alongside Caitlyn. He lay holding his stomach and groaning. Caitlyn sat up, glaring at Connor, her eyes blazing as vividly as the scarlet patch that marred her right cheek. Though she was quite sure that the blow to her had been an accident, knowing that did nothing to calm her temper. But she did not quite dare give voice to the many unflattering epithets for him that crowded her tongue. Fists still clenched and jaw hard, Connor looked ripe for murder.

"I'll have no more bloody sass from any of the lot of ye!" Connor spoke through his teeth as he glared at the two he had put on the ground. "You'll do as I say, or you'll get the hell out. All of you."

He swept Mickeen, Rory, and Liam with his eyes, stalked over to Fharannain, and with a single fluid motion leaped into the saddle. Mickeen hastily finished tying on the last of the saddlebags and stood back. With a last blistering glare at the insubordinate pair in the straw, Connor set his heels to Fharannain's sides and rode out into he night.

His leaving seemed to break the spell that held them all in place. Rory came over to give Caitlyn a hand up, and Liam bent over Cormac. Only Mickeen went on with the business of caring for the horses and cleaning up after the raid.

"Connor's in the right of it, you know," Liam said seriously to Cormac. "Caitlyn has no business riding with us."

"Jesus, what bloody maggot got into your brain to make you go for Conn with that whip, little brother? You know he didn't mean to knock Caitlyn down. Conn would never hit a female. He's never even hit you before, and you've deserved it more times than I can count." Rory spoke to Cormac even as he pulled Caitlyn to her feet.

"I knew the bloody lad would be nothing but trouble the first time I clapped eyes on him," Mickeen put in sourly from where he was sweeping straw over the closed door to the tunnel. "If I'd known he was a bloody lass, I'd have left him by the road afore ever we came within ten miles of Donoughmore. Lassies are worse than poison to young lads."

"Even if he didn't mean to hit her, Conn had no business shaking Caitlyn like he did. She's a female, for Christ's sake! And if he wants me to leave his bloody precious Donoughmore, I will." Cormac was still angry as he got to his feet.

"Connor's in the right of it," Liam repeated

stubbornly. "Though that was temper talking at the end. Still, he deserves better than for you to attack him, Cormac. After all he's done for you — indeed, for all of us! — I'd think shame on myself if I were you!"

Cormac glared at Liam for a moment. Then some of the temper faded from his eyes. "I don't know how I came to do such a thing," he admitted. "I never meant to. It was just . . . seeing him hit Caitlyn. I think I went a wee bit crazy."

"It's all the fault of yon toothsome lassie," Mickeen said, eyeing Caitlyn with severe disapproval. "Many's the brothers who've been parted by such. Deadly as poison, they are."

"I'll beg Conn's pardon tomorrow." Cormac sounded genuinely contrite. Then he added with a final touch of truculence, "If he first begs pardon of Caitlyn."

"I've no need of your championship, Cormac." Caitlyn brushed the straw off her breeches and moved to take charge of Finnbarr, who had still not been put in his stall. Her cheek tingled faintly, and she did not doubt that Connor's hand had left a mark on it. Still, it was nothing to the mark the altercation had left on her soul. The sudden fierce flaring of violence between the brothers had shaken her to the core. And making it worse was her secret concurrence with Mickeen's assessment: what had happened was all her fault. "You make your peace with Connor, and I'll make mine. In my own time, and in my own way."

Mickeen looked at her sharply. Out of the corner of her eye Caitlyn could see him shaking his head.

"Nothing but trouble," she thought she heard him mutter. And then he was turning his attention to his task and leaving her to hers.

XIX

❊ ❊ ❊ ❊ ❊ ❊ ❊ ❊ ❊ ❊ ❊ ❊ ❊ ❊ ❊

Tensions still ran high at Donoughmore the next day. For the first time since she had known him, Connor stayed in bed until nearly midday. Since he had not returned to the house until after dawn — Caitlyn knew, because she had been unable to sleep for listening for him — that in itself was not remarkable. But when he did arise, he was blood-shot of eye and short of temper. Even Cormac's apology was received with not much more than a grunt, although Connor did not appear to harbor a grudge against his brother. His ire seemed to focus entirely on Caitlyn. He spoke not so much as a word to her all day. And she, for her part, spoke not a word to him. If there was any apologizing to be done, she told Rory with a sniff when Rory urged her to it, it was for Connor to do, not her.

Connor's ill-temper affected everyone. From Mrs. McFee in the house to Mickeen in the stable to the peasants in the field to the younger d'Arcy brothers, all walked carefully under the dark cloud of the Earl's displeasure. Mickeen blatantly regarded the whole fiasco as being Caitlyn's fault. His muttered asides on her character, antecedents, and sex made her long to take a stout stick to his head.

Fharannain had evidently picked up a stone in his hoof during the last part of Connor's solitary ride the night before; this was added to the list of grievances for which Caitlyn felt she was being blamed. Angry at the world, she left her chores half done midway through the afternoon and struck out across the meadow. The cure for her megrims — besides clouting Connor, and to a lesser extent Mickeen — lay in fresh air, and lots of it, she decided. What she needed was a long, solitary walk.

She was gone about two hours, and when she returned she did feel better. The stable was deserted of human habitation, as was the sheep barn, she discovered upon checking. The d'Arcys and Mickeen were nowhere to be found. Willie had long since taken up with the O'Learys, the peasant family with whom he slept and ate, and was doubtless with their menfolk cutting peat. These days she saw him very little; their relationship, slowly but inexorably as O'Malley the thief was all but forgotten, had greatly changed. Mrs. McFee was in the house, and since Caitlyn was in the mood for neither her conversation nor her chores, she was left with no one but herself for company. So she climbed into the stable's loft and lay in the soft straw, staring out the open door at the near cloudless blue sky. Wisps of white fleece floated into her line of vision, then disappeared. She amused herself by making pictures in them. And thus she fell asleep.

"She's here!"

The words penetrated her sleep, which was deep because of all the hours she had missed the night before while listening for Connor. Swimming up through the mists that held her, she opened her eyes to find Cormac standing over her, a frown on his face. Caitlyn smiled up at him, a slow, sweet sleepy smile because he did so resemble Connor and for a moment she was imagining they were friends again. The frown faded from Cormac's face.

"She's been here sleeping all the time," Cormac said over his shoulder in an excusing tone. Caitlyn was still only half awake, but she became aware that her legs were sprawled immodestly, with a considerable amount of calf showing beneath her skirt. Sitting up, she rearranged her skirt, her movements lethargic with the aftereffects of sleep. Cormac smiled indulgently at her and reached down with both hands to help her to her feet. Caitlyn took his hands and let him draw her up, then smiled her thanks at him as she blinked to get her bearings. He didn't release her immediately but stood holding her hands and staring at her sleep-flushed face with a besotted smile on his face.

Not having the energy yet to engage in the tug-of-war it would take to free her hands, she let them remain in his as she struggled to banish the remnants of sleep. A sound that was somewhere between a grunt and a growl caused her to look beyond Cormac toward the tall shadow to which he seemed to have been talking earlier.

The shadow stepped forward and resolved itself into Connor. He seemed to be in a temper again, his arms crossed over his chest and his aqua eyes glinting unpleasantly as they rested on Cormac's hands holding hers. Registering the thunderous expression on his face, Caitlyn felt the peace her solitary afternoon had given her recede, to be replaced by an anger of her own.

"So, you've been sulking in here, have you? We've spent most of the past two hours searching for you!" There was a furious note to his voice, more furious than the situation justified. Caitlyn wondered if he were still nursing a grievance from the night before, and ruefully supposed that he was. Then he lifted his gaze from her hands, still linked with Cormac's, to her face, and she was taken aback as pure rage flared at her for a moment from those devil's eyes. Caitlyn blinked at him in surprise. His lids dropped, and when they lifted again the emotion was carefully banked. An idea hit Caitlyn with the force of a brick. As she considered it, her heart began to pound. Meeting Connor's smoldering eyes with a limpid look of her own, Caitlyn switched her attention to Cormac, smiling warmly at him. She meant to test this new notion of hers without delay.

"Have you been searching for me?" she asked sweetly, beaming her nicest smile on Cormac. Never before had she had occasion to use her female attractions, but she found that the knack came to her instinctively, without her even trying for it. " 'Tis sorry I am if I worried you." She

215

squeezed his hands slightly. Cormac looked dazzled.

"I — I — it was Conn," he blurted.

"Oh, Connor," Caitlyn said in a dismissive
tone, as if Connor didn't matter in the least.
Flicking a sideways glance at the object of her
experiment, she was pleased to see that Connor
looked increasingly grim. It was all she could do
to contain a triumphant smile. She was nearly
certain now that her intuition was right on target:
what had exacerbated Connor's temper past the
point of control the night before and made him
so angry now was Cormac's attention to her.
Connor didn't like it. Why, she hadn't quite
decided, but it was an extremely pleasant notion
and she meant to take full advantage of it.

"The next time you decide to take a nap in
the straw, you might have the kindness to tell
someone first. We've lost half a day's work looking for you." Connor growled the rebuke. Glancing over at him, Caitlyn saw that his hands were
balled into fists and jammed into the pockets of
his breeches. A little flicker of excitement flamed
to life inside her. This new game of baiting Connor could prove extremely interesting.

"Why did you bother? You must have known
that I was somewhere about."

"I thought you might have taken it into your
head to run away again." The admission was
gruff. A patch of shadow had shifted so that
Connor once again stood in darkness, making it
difficult to tell too much about his expression in

the brief look she allowed herself. Cormac was still holding her hands; Caitlyn's fingers were going numb from the pressure of his grip. She tried to disengage without being too obvious, but in the end she had to tug her hands from Cormac's hold. Cormac let her go with obvious reluctance.

"Now, why would I do a thing like that?" Caitlyn smiled at Cormac, looked fleetingly at Connor again, and started for the ladder. The skirt of her yellow-striped dress swished against the straw covering the boards of the loft as she moved.

"Why indeed?" Connor's voice was ironic as he watched Cormac follow Caitlyn, giving every indication that he wished to tenderly assist her down the ladder. She managed to get down without his help, though she purposely gave him a sweet smile for offering it. Cormac climbed down behind her, with Connor swinging down last.

Outside it was just dusk, though the inside of the stable was full dark. Caitlyn did not need Cormac's guiding hand on her elbow as they made their way out into the open air. She would have told him so too, in no uncertain terms, if it had not been for the game she was playing with Connor. As he was walking on her other side, she wasn't even sure that he knew of Cormac's tender grip on her elbow. But then, knowing Connor, she rather thought he did.

As the three of them walked toward the house,

no one spoke. When they reached the stoop and Cormac finally let go of her elbow so that she could climb the stairs, Connor said abruptly, "I'd like to see you in my office after supper, Caitlyn, if you please."

She deliberately climbed the stairs to the stoop before she turned back to face him. Cormac was ascending behind her, and she stood aside for him to pass. He stopped right behind her, waiting, listening. Caitlyn paid him no heed. Her attention was all on Connor, who still stood on the ground looking up at her. With three steps between them, she was the taller by a head. Looking down into those narrowed aqua eyes, she allowed herself the smallest of pensive smiles.

"If you're meaning to apologize for your behavior last night, there's really no need," she said with sweet provocation. "I've already forgiven you."

Then with that masterly shot she turned on her heel and went into the kitchen for supper.

Connor did not speak to her again during the meal, so she occupied her time by flirting impartially with Rory and Cormac. Liam was rather harder to flirt with — he had a disconcerting habit of looking at her suspiciously when she smiled at him — but still she tried her best. It was amazing how easily flirting with males came to her, she thought, considering that she had been the next thing to one herself less than a year and a half before. But there was nothing complicated about it: a smile and a sideways glance, a touch of her fingers on a hand or a shoulder, and Rory and Cormac at least seemed enslaved. Mickeen watched this byplay with sour disapproval, while Mrs. McFee expressed her opinion with a series of loud sniffs. Connor, if he noticed it, seemed not to. Caitlyn vowed to redouble her efforts, and succeeded in bedazzling Cormac into pouring gravy all over the table instead of on his plate as he stared at one particularly blinding smile.

When supper was over and the d'Arcys and Mickeen stood up to leave the table — much as Caitlyn hated it, it was part of her duties to help Mrs. McFee clean up — Connor glanced over at her.

"In my office, Caitlyn," he said softly. Caitlyn returned his look for look. It entered her mind to refuse, just to see what his reaction would be, but she rather wanted to hear what he had to say, and besides, she hated kitchen duty. So she meekly followed him up the stairs, conscious of the younger d'Arcys' eyes on her until she was out of sight.

Connor opened the door to the office and stood back for her to precede him. Unused to chivalrous gestures from him — Connor was far more likely to treat her like another of his young brothers than like a lass — Caitlyn still managed to walk past him with aplomb. He closed the door behind her, his movements deliberate. She watched with growing uneasiness as he lit the lamp on the scarred desk with the taper he was carrying, then blew the candle out and set it aside. She was not quite at ease with Connor all of a sudden. He seemed almost a stranger to her, a tall, handsome, masculine stranger. Watching the play of candlelight on the lean planes of his face, she was struck by how grim he looked. Grimmer than she would have expected him to be if all he meant to do was dress her down for her role in the fiasco of the night before. Perhaps she had carried her flirting with his brothers just a little too far. . . .

"Sit, please." His tone told her nothing as he indicated the worn leather chair in front of the desk.

Again, by not sitting down until she was seated, he was treating her as he would a full-grown lady. She had seen him perform such courtesies for Mrs. Congreve and had secretly sneered. But she found that it was very pleasant being on the receiving end of his good manners and essayed a tentative smile at him as she sat down.

Connor did not return her smile as he took his own seat in the matching leather armchair behind the desk. If anything, he looked bleaker than ever. Propping his elbows on the desk, he clasped his hands together and rested his chin on his hands. For a long moment he considered her without speaking. Caitlyn finally squirmed under his unrelenting gaze. As if that were the signal he had been waiting for, he leaned back, pushing the chair a little away from the desk so that he could stretch out his long legs comfortably in front of him. The chair gave a creak of protest at his posture. His fingers drummed on the wooden arms. His eyes met hers again, distant under frowning brows.

"Caitlyn." He finally broke the silence with her name, then said nothing else. His eyes never left her face as he seemed to mull something over in his mind.

" 'Tis my name." His uncharacteristic hesitancy was making her nervous. To conceal her apprehension from him, her response was flippant. She met his eyes, questions and defiance mixed in her expression.

Finally he spoke, the words careful, measured. "First I must admit: you were in the right of it. I owe you an apology. I regret having struck you, though 'twas an accident, as I'm sure you know. Even so, had I kept a tighter rein on my temper it would not have happened. I beg your pardon."

The very formality of his apology disturbed Caitlyn. She eyed him uncertainly.

"You were provoked." She had thought that an apology would give her the upper hand. Now she found that the game was all his, as it had ever been. In the face of Connor's baffling behavior, she was fast being reduced to a nervous child. He smiled a little at her unthinking admission, but still his eyes were bleak. He did not seem like himself at all, and the fact had her increasingly frightened.

"Aye, I was provoked. You seem to have a knack for doing that."

She thought she detected a note of humor in his voice and tried a faint smile while she searched his eyes in vain. He did not smile back at her, and if there had been humor in his face it was gone now. He looked completely serious, even a little melancholy.

"Caitlyn." The very way he said her name worried her. It was as if he had bad news to impart and was concerned how she would take it. Her eyes, suddenly huge, searched his. The black ring around his irises seemed to enlarge, making his eyes appear almost dark.

"We have a problem, lass," he continued after a brief hesitation. "It seems I should have foreseen this difficulty earlier, but surprisingly enough, I did not."

"What difficulty?" Apprehension was making it difficult for her to talk. From the regretful way he was looking at her, she could almost suppose herself dead and in her coffin.

"Raising a lassie in a male household. Lassies are different from lads by their very nature, and lads are different when lassies are around. 'Tis natural for you to want to test your femaleness, and 'tis natural for them to respond to you. I want you to understand that no blame attaches to you for this. You've done nothing wrong."

"What are you saying?" A terrible weight seemed to have settled in her chest.

"For your own well-being I must send you away, lass." It was said with awful gentleness. Caitlyn stared at him, kerry blue eyes huge in the whiteness of her face, her hands clenching in her lap until the nails dug into the soft flesh of her palms. Her agitation was such that she didn't even feel the pain.

"What?" The statement was so unexpected that it temporarily bewildered her.

He went on quickly, ignoring her interruption and the distress in her face. " 'Tis no great tragedy, Caitlyn. I've no intention of turning you back into the world on your own. The good Sisters at St. Mary's in County Longford have a school for lassies. They'll take you in; I've a friend who said he'd see to the necessary arrangements. They'll teach you things: how to run a household, manners, how to go on. There are many things females need to know that we males have no notion of, it seems."

"No!"

" 'Tis all arranged, and 'tis for the best, lass. Believe me. I'd not do it otherwise."

"No!"

He went on swiftly, as if to head off her protests with reasoned words. "No good can come of you staying here with us. A lassie's place is amongst other females, not randy young bucks. You'll have tomorrow to gather your things and say your good-byes. We leave for St. Mary's early the next day."

Caitlyn felt as if a giant hand were squeezing her heart. Connor's eyes were on her face; they were dark with compassion. Compassion, when he was hurting her so badly that all she wanted to do was scream!

"You can't — you can't do this. If 'tis because of — of what happened the other night, it'll never happen again, I promise. I'll stay safe in the house when you ride out, and I'll never even look at Cormac, or Rory, or Liam, or anyone else you don't want me to, and I'll —"

He stopped her increasingly frantic babble with an upraised hand. " 'Tis not because you rode after us the other night, or what happened after. 'Tis not because of anything you've done. 'Tis because of what you are. You've grown up into a beautiful lass, Caitlyn, and we're all men here. Men, even the best of them, which I hold my brothers to be though I can't always claim the distinction for myself, can lose their heads easily around a beautiful lassie. There's trouble now, but it can be nipped in the bud. Think of the havoc you'd wreak if you stayed."

"I wouldn't . . ."

"You couldn't help it." The pronouncement was heavy. "Besides, think of yourself. The day will come soon when you'll want to marry and have bairns of your own. What decent man will take you when it's known you've been living here with us alone? They'll think you've little virtue, and if one does take you, he'll likely value you less because of it. With the holy Sisters, your good name will be safe. And we won't be totally abandoning you, lass. We'll visit and bring you presents, and when the time comes for you to wed, I'll even provide you with a bit of a dowry. How's that?"

"No!"

"I'm sorry, lassie. 'Tis the way it has to be."

Caitlyn's lips trembled as she searched his face and found not the faintest hint of relenting. He meant to do this. He would really send her away. . . . The sting of tears burned her eyelids, but she blinked them back. She would not cry. She would not!

"I thought you . . . cared for me." The words were heartbreaking. Connor's mouth tightened and he reached out a hand toward her, only to pull it back. He looked very stern, his thick black brows drawn together until they almost met over his nose, his strange light eyes dark with regret as they fixed on her face. Looking in agony at that lean, handsome face that had become familiar to her as her own and dearer than she had dreamed, Caitlyn sobbed once, pitiably. A muscle beside Connor's mouth twitched as he watched her force the tears valiantly back.

"We all love you like a wee sister, child. Never doubt it."

"Then why —"

"The fact is that you're not our sister. You're no blood kin at all. You're a beautiful, nubile young woman, and we're four healthy men. 'Tis a recipe for disaster, Caitlyn. Thank the good Lord I'm old enough to see it before it hits."

She took a deep, shaking breath. "Do the others know?" She had a faint hope that his brothers would champion her cause. Which they probably

225

would, but in the end there was little they could do to alter Connor's decision. Connor was the master of Donoughmore, the Earl, the head of the family. Like it or not, in the final reckoning what he decreed was the way it would be.

"Nay. I thought to tell you first."

There seemed little doubt that he would do as he said he would. Hopeless, Caitlyn stared at him, making a mute plea for a stay of sentence. A single tear spilled from each eye. He got up and went over to her. A muscle twitched beside his mouth again as he lifted a hand to brush away the moisture that streaked the cheek he had bruised the night before. He caught the tear on the tip of one finger. Caitlyn felt the brush of his hand against her cheek and looked up at him with silent pleading. He was not looking at her. For an instant only he stared down at the tear he had caught; then with a sudden, involuntary grimace his hand clenched into a fist as if to make the visible sign of the pain he inflicted go away.

"I have no more to say. You're free to go."

Caitlyn got to her feet, moving stiffly like a very old lady. With an almost unendurable sense of loss she realized how very much she had come to consider Donoughmore her home. She loved every blade of grass, every bleating sheep, every hillock and tree and stream. She loved the d'Arcys, one and all. Even this harsh stranger who was sending her away. This was her home, and they were her family. Her heart throbbed in her chest as though it swelled with pain.

"Please don't do this, Connor," she begged brokenly, her eyes meeting his in one last attempt to sway him.

" 'Tis done already. And for the best," he answered through stiff lips. Then, as if he could no longer bear the sight of her, he walked out of the room, leaving Caitlyn to sink back down into the worn leather chair and sob as though her heart would break.

XX

❋ ❋ ❋ ❋ ❋ ❋ ❋ ❋ ❋ ❋ ❋ ❋ ❋ ❋ ❋ ❋

It was near dawn. Connor had tossed and turned in his bed all night, so far without getting a wink of sleep. Every time he closed his eyes he could see Caitlyn's stricken face. He had wounded her to the heart, he knew. But it had been necessary for the future well-being of them all.

As he had told her, her continued presence at Donoughmore was nothing more than a recipe for disaster. Already she had succeeded in making them turn on one another. The previous night's debacle between Cormac and himself was but the final straw. Cormac and Rory were lately at each other's throats constantly as they vied for her favor, and even staid Liam had been seen to give her more than one long look. As for himself, he was too old at twenty-seven to be led around by the nose by tricks from a new-hatched chick. But he would be less than honest if he refused to admit to being swayed by the extraordinary beauty that had grown so unexpectedly in their midst. After all, he was not a saint, not a priest, not a eunuch. He had all the normal male instincts. Fortunately for her, he also had a conscience, and was old enough and experienced enough to follow it. His brothers were younger; in her presence they reminded him of young stags jousting with their antlers. Even among the four of them, close as they were, there was real potential for violence. And when the other males who flocked around Donoughmore now that word of Caitlyn's loveliness had spread were counted into the equation, it was more than a recipe for disaster. It was a prescription for bloodshed. The worst thing about it was that it was no one's fault, yet Caitlyn was going to bear the brunt of the punishment. But he'd been unable to come up with a more palatable course of action than to send her away.

Family had to come first. His family. No matter how winsome or lovely, an outsider could not be allowed to drive a wedge between brothers. Since his father's death, they'd been the world to one another. He had used every last ounce of his strength and ingenuity and passion to keep them all together. There'd been some who had thought to put them on the parish after their father's death, thinking that the young lads would certainly starve on their own. He, Connor, had in his darkest hours thought the same. But he had nevertheless managed to keep them all together, body and soul. A family.

It had been a rough haul. But the worst was behind them. Now he had to concentrate on getting his brothers creditably settled and restoring Donoughmore to what it had been. And there was also the matter of avenging the murder of his father. That he meant to see to once the others were done. Caitlyn had no place in any of these plans. Her presence served merely to confuse the issues. Again he thought that he should have foreseen the complications as soon as he discovered her true sex. But he hadn't. And now the time had come to rectify that mistake. Mickeen was in the right of it, he knew; at Donoughmore, Caitlyn was nothing but trouble.

The holy Sisters would be good to her, teaching her feminine ways and things she should know. Despite her fetching looks and recent foray into flirting, she was still near as much lad as lass, and the fault was to some degree his. He simply didn't know anything about raising a lassie. He'd treated her as one of the lads as long as he could, and when that had become impossible he'd floundered for a bit. The whole situation had somehow gotten beyond him in a matter of a few weeks.

Then, as he'd ridden over the moors the night before, making the expected delivery to Father Patrick, he had had a sudden vision of the way Caitlyn looked defying him in the stable. He had pictured her in his mind's eye as clearly as if she stood before him, pictured the heart-shaped face framed by disheveled masses of raven hair, the flashing sapphire blue of her eyes, the whiteness of her skin, the softness of her pink mouth. He'd pictured the shape of her, clearly apparent in the boy's garb that did as much to reveal as to hide: the long, slender legs that looked all the more shapely and feminine when outlined by the worn material of Cormac's oldest breeches; the slim hips and tiny waist, cinched by a rope of all things; the roundness of her small bottom; the thrust of young tender breasts against the thin linen shirt. And, picturing that, he had felt a fierce stab of lust. God forgive him.

There was the crux of his dilemma: the age-old desire of a male for a lovely young female. Though he had managed to successfully banish that shameful pang of lust — largely by dwelling on his fury at the headstrong lass who provoked it — he had not banished the uneasy feeling that it had caused. His brothers must be experiencing much the same thing, but they were younger, less disciplined. It was entirely within the realm of possibility that they would find such strong urges uncontrollable. And the consequences of that he shuddered to contemplate. He was left with a firm conviction: the situation as it existed was impossible.

Father Patrick was an old friend of the family, one of the handful in the Dark Horseman's far-flung distribution network who knew the high-wayman's real identity. As the old Earl's confessor, Father Patrick had known Connor and his brothers from birth and did not hold his expedient Protestant upbringing against him, re-alizing that in Connor's heart and soul he was a son of the True Church. While sitting in the vast dark kitchen of the monastery orphanage that the good Father ran, enjoying a wee dram before setting off for Donoughmore again, Connor had found himself unburdening his dilemma, sinful thoughts and all. It was Father Patrick who had suggested the Sisters at St. Mary's, and it was Father Patrick who had volunteered to make the arrangements. Connor, well into his dozenth wee dram by that time, had been pleased to agree. Caitlyn was a problem that had to be dealt with. She was disrupting his life, his brother's lives. Her good name was in grave danger of being sullied, to say nothing of her virtue. The Father's suggestion was a good one; if Connor wished now that he had searched for some alternative solution before agreeing, well, that was because he was allowing his heart to rule his head, which was always a mistake.

But her crying had smote him hard.

Connor turned over in bed, trying in vain to find a spot that would induce sleep. The faintest suggestion of silvery moonlight spilled through the shuttered windows. The moon was waxing full again. . . .

He rolled onto his back, kicking at the covers that confined him. As he did so, he saw something move at the foot of his bed. He froze, barely daring to breathe. Someone was in his room, standing at the foot of his bed, watching him. Stealthily, hoping that the person's eyesight was no better than his in the darkness, he slipped his hand beneath his pillow where he kept his loaded pistol. Not for the first time would the habit stand him in good stead.

"Connor."

He would know that voice in the darkest pit in Hell. His fingers abandoned their quest for the pistol to grab the bedclothes. Sitting up abruptly, yanking the covers securely over his lap, for he slept naked, he glared through the darkness at the source of his sleeplessness.

"What the devil are you doing in my bedchamber at this hour?" The question was a surly hiss. On top of his recent shameful thoughts, her presence was as welcome as potato rot to a farmer.

"I want to make a bargain with you." Her voice was determined, but her form was shrouded in darkness. Connor gave vent to a long-suffering sigh and reached for the tender he kept on the bedside table. In moments the candle was lit. The flickering light cast strange shadows in the corners of the room. He looked down the length of the bed at Caitlyn and felt another twinge in the region of his heart. Her nose was as red as the worst tippler's, her eyes were swollen and damp, and her black hair straggled about her colorless face like the hair on one of the witches of All Saints. Clad in a long-sleeved, high-necked white nightdress, she looked the veriest child. The fatal beauty that had so alarmed him was superseded by innocent pathos. But as he looked closer, he saw that there was an air of triumph about her that belied the evidence of recent copious tears.

"A bargain?" He was wary. With her, he had learned to be.

"Aye, a bargain. You don't send me away —

233

and I won't tell anyone that you're the Dark Horseman."

Connor was struck speechless for a moment. He leaned back against the intricately carved rosewood headboard and stared at the hard-hearted little minx who was very calmly threatening his life and the lives of all those he held dear. He had never envisioned this possibility, and it flummoxed him. Slowly, carefully, he worked it through. It all boiled down to one inescapable conclusion: she had him. Even as he recognized the fact, a spurt of relief mixed with his anger that it should be so.

" 'Tis bloody ungrateful you are, isn't it?" he demanded, nettled.

She lifted her chin at him. Connor could not help but notice the thrust of her breasts against her nightdress. To his angry embarrassment, his body responded as nature had intended that it should. Damn, there would be hell to pay if she stayed. And he was thrice a fool for allowing himself to get caught in this predicament, though he still did not see quite what he could have done to prevent it coming about. He gave up on that for the moment and focused his attention on keeping his eyes on her face. If she was to remain with them, then all of them — himself included — would have to keep a tight rein on their baser instincts.

"I don't want to be sent away." It was an explanation. Connor tucked the covers more se-curely about his waist, crossed his arms over his bare chest, and eyed her.

"I've a notion you're bluffing."

"Try me." Her eyes met his with a cool look that reminded him of men he'd faced on the dueling field at dawn.

"You'd really see me hang? And Cormac? And Rory? And Liam? To say nothing of poor Mickeen?"

She moistened her lips. Connor watched the movement of that small pink tongue with interest, which was quickly followed by lively dismay. Looking only at her face wasn't a solution, it seemed. He tried to narrow his focus to nose and eyes.

"I wouldn't like to. But I don't want to leave here either. Donoughmore is my home now."

Disgruntled, he stared at her, hoping to shame her for what was blackmail pure and simple. She stared right back at him, not giving an inch. Connor had the disquieting notion that in this impertinent slip of a lass his vaunted iron will had met its match.

Keeping his eyes from slipping downward was something of a strain, and he was glad when she crossed her arms over her chest, from either nervousness or cold, he couldn't be sure which. Despite his best intentions, it had been impossible for him to miss the faint movements of her breasts inside the loose gown.

The only possible solution that didn't involve either her winning or putting his brothers in danger occurred to him. He dismissed it out of hand, but she couldn't know that.

He smiled at her with slow relish. "I could kill you, you know. To keep you silent." That should put a scare into the little viper, he thought with satisfaction.

She smiled faintly in turn and shook her head. "You wouldn't." The statement was positive. Her eyes met his fearlessly.

Annoyed, Connor pursed his lips. "Well, now, we're at a stalemate, it seems. For I don't think you'd turn in the Dark Horseman either."

That rattled her a little, he could see. Her eyes widened, and she moistened her lips again. Then she frowned, so that her lovely silky black eyebrows met in a line over her small nose, and looked at him levelly.

"But then you could never be sure, could you?"

She was calling his bluff, just as he had called hers. And for all that he was fairly certain that a bluff was all it was, he was going to permit her to get away with it. If "permit" was the right word.

"So you'd make me a bargain: your silence if I allow you to stay."

"Aye."

His mouth twisted with derision that was largely self-directed as he glared at her in not-quite-unwilling surrender. " 'Tis a spawn of the devil you are, Caitlyn O'Malley. Very well, you've got your bargain. I wish you the joy of the consequences."

She sagged with relief. A tentative smile teased

the corners of her mouth. Watching her, Connor felt a renewed twinge of foreboding. Every grain of sense he possessed screamed that he was looking at a gargantuan catastrophe in the making.

"Are you angry with me, Connor?" She was peeping at him through the incredible fringe of her lashes, her head slightly atilt. It was an enchanting trick, one that she employed frequently of late and, he thought, unconsciously. He shook his head at himself, remembering the cocky, ragamuffin lad he'd thought he'd brought home with him from Dublin. How could he have ever imagined that those eyes belonged to anything but a lass?

"Furious."

She eyed him. Then the tentative smile turned into a real one. Before he realized what she was about, she ran around the side of the bed, leaned over him, put her hands on his bare shoulders, and planted a soft kiss on his unshaven cheek. He almost reeled at the sudden assault on his senses. The very unexpectedness of it saved him. Before he had time to respond in any fashion, she straightened. If there was anything untoward in his expression — and if his body was any indication, there must have been — she didn't seem to notice.

"You're not." She was turning to leave. Silent, he watched her cross the room, infuriated, amused, alarmed — and faintly bedazzled by the swing of her small backside beneath that loose gown. At the door, she turned back to look at him, one arm lifted to rest against the jamb. Masses of black hair hung in a silken tangle down her back. Her deep blue eyes slanted sideways at him. He was again conscious of a twinge of premonition. She was too lovely by half, without trying in the least. For him, for his brothers, for Donoughmore itself, this lass spelled trouble. Yet he was letting her stay.

"Thank you, Connor," she whispered. And then she disappeared into the darkness of the hall.

XXI

❀ ❀ ❀ ❀ ❀ ❀ ❀ ❀ ❀ ❀ ❀ ❀ ❀ ❀

The next few weeks passed in relative peace and tranquility. No more was said about Caitlyn's leaving, and it was as if the suggestion, with its resulting answer and all that had gone before it, had never been made. It was autumn now, time to cull the flock before winter, and all the d'Arcys were busy in the fields. Connor had set Caitlyn to helping Mrs. McFee make soap and candles out of mutton fat, so she passed her hours by alternately stirring a large kettle suspended over a fire in the yard and dipping wicks into hot liquid tallow over and over again. The work made her hot, sweaty, and irritable. She had a suspicion that Connor had set her to it just to keep her out of the way. But for the moment she was wary of antagonizing him. They had achieved a kind of truce, and she did not want to be the one to break it.

To tell the truth, she was shy of him now. Shy, and something else. Just thinking about him made her heartbeat quicken; the sight of him was enough to bring a blush to her cheeks. What ailed her exactly she didn't know, but it was uncomfortable and she wished it would go away. More than anything in her life, she wanted to be Connor's friend. But he seemed to go out of his way to avoid her, and of course she knew the reason why: he hadn't taken kindly to her blackmail. She was a little ashamed of it herself, but it had been the only way she could think of to stay on at Donoughmore.

The younger d'Arcy brothers were keeping their distance too, and Caitlyn wondered if Connor had had a talk with them. Or maybe it was only that all of them were so busy with the slaughtering. Whatever, she was missing them all, and Mrs. McFee's grumpy companionship was no substitution.

"I've more fat for you, Caitlyn."

Caitlyn straightened away from the huge iron kettle she was stirring with a stick, a hand rubbing the aching small of her back as she digested that unwelcome information. More fat! That meant more soap and more candles. More work. More aching back.

"Aren't sheep made of anything but fat?" she groaned, looking around at the bearer of the glad tidings, who happened to be Willie. He grinned at her sympathetically, proffering the huge basin he carried in both hands at her. Caitlyn stared at it and groaned again.

"Just set it on the ground," she said without enthusiasm. "I've no doubt that Mrs. McFee will have a hundred uses for it. But at the moment, I don't."

"Think you've got it bad, do you? I'm helping his lordship skin the bloody beasts. 'Tis hard work, it is."

Caitlyn leaned on her stick as it rested in the middle of the pot and looked at Willie, the germ of an idea forming in her mind. She was dying to get away from the heat and smell of the soap-making, and she was not loath to have a chance to talk with Connor either. A small, coaxing smile curved her lips.

"Willie," she began, "you're dead tired of skinning, and I'm dead tired of making soap. I propose we consider a trade."

"I don't know . . ." Willie frowned at her uncertainly. He and she were still approximately on eye level, she noticed, which meant that he had grown approximately the same amount as she. But at seventeen she was full grown, while at fourteen he had a way yet to go. Willie might become a good-sized man one day. If only his brain had not kept up with his height.

"What's to know? We'll just trade jobs. Nothing could be simpler."

"His lordship might not like it."

"His lordship won't care a button. Now, all you have to do is stir this — this mess with this stick so it doesn't burn or overflow. Here, like this."

Willie had always been overwhelmed by the sheer force of her personality, and this was no exception. He took the stick, looking unhappy, but obediently began to stir. Caitlyn beamed at him encouragingly.

"His lordship is in the sheep barn?"

"Nay. We finished the skinning. He's out behind it scraping the hides."

The wool and bits of debris that remained after skinning had to be scraped from the hides before they could be made into leather. Caitlyn had never participated in the scraping, but she had watched and knew it for hard work. Still, a change was as good as a rest, and at least she would be near Connor. She had something she wanted to say to him.

"Thanks, Willie." With a nod she left the red-headed lad halfheartedly stirring the thick mixture in the kettle and walked toward the sheep barn. Her step was brisk, for she expected to hear Mrs. McFee's indignant voice calling after her at any minute. But she made it around the barn and out of sight without mishap, then slowed her steps as she drew near the back of the barn. A few yards away she could see Connor, down on one knee as he scraped briskly at a hide stretched over a stone. Despite the mildness of the day, he was stripped to the waist. A fine sheen of perspiration gleamed on the skin of his bare back.

Caitlyn stopped at the corner of the barn and leaned against it, watching. She had seen Connor without a shirt on before — indeed, the night in his bedroom when she had played her trump card rose immediately in her mind — but always before her thoughts had been on other things. Now it struck her suddenly that there was nothing she would rather do than stay in the shadows and watch Connor at work, and that was just what she did.

He was facing away from her, clad only in dusty black breeches and dustier boots, a sharpened scraping tool in his right hand. His black hair formed deep waves about his head, its natural curl increased by his exertions. Confined by a narrow black ribbon, it curled into a tail at the nape of his neck. The broad, powerful shoulders and lean back rippled and flexed as he worked. Her eyes followed the ridge of his spine as it disappeared into his breeches.

He moved, shifting sideways a little so that she could see his face and chest. The skin of his face was darker than that of his chest and back, which rarely saw exposure to the sun. His lashes made stubby dark crescents against his cheeks as he looked down at the hide he was cleaning. Seen at a three-quarter angle, his features were lean and hard, almost austere. The faintest shadow of a blue-black beard darkened his jaw.

Caitlyn's eyes fell from his face to his chest. From that night in his bedroom, she had retained an impression of hard muscles and fine black hair. Now she saw that a wedge of hair curled in a V across his chest to narrow over his muscle-ridged abdomen into a trail that disappeared beneath his breeches. She caught her breath, admiring the sheer masculine beauty of him. Just looking at him without his shirt on made her heartbeat quicken. She was conscious of a sudden urge to walk over to him and place her hand on his bare chest. Would the hairs there be soft or wiry . . . ? Then she must have made some sort of movement, because he looked up to meet her eyes. Caught, she could only stare back helplessly, her cheeks aflame at the guilty tenor of her thoughts. He stared at her for a long moment, eyes narrowed. Then he got slowly to his feet.

"That's the last of them, Conn." Rory walked out of the barn, wiping his hands down the backs of his breeches. Connor's eyes shifted to him, breaking the invisible thread of tension that had bound him to Caitlyn. Caitlyn swallowed, both glad and sorry for the interruption. There had been something disquieting in Connor's eyes. . . .

"Aye, and I'm for a swim. Rory stinks like a dead sheep, and I've a notion I do too. Care to join us, big brother?"

"I've still some things to do. You go ahead." Connor's voice as he answered Cormac was completely normal. Caitlyn wondered if she had imagined the way he had just looked at her. The idea that he might have guessed her thoughts was mortifying. She found that she no longer wanted to talk to him after all.

Melting away from the barn while he was still talking with his brothers, she headed down toward the line of trees that marked the stream. The spring house was there, a small stone building erected over the place where icy water bubbled up from the ground. Butter and milk and cheese were kept inside. Caitlyn felt a sudden urge for a cold drink. Her cheeks were flushed and she felt as warm as if she had walked for miles instead of yards. Of course, she had been working hard all afternoon. Her sleeveless blue dress was splotched and wrinkled and the once-spotless shift she wore underneath felt damp against her skin. The exposed sleeves of the shift were pushed up over her elbows, but still she felt miserably hot. As she entered the spring house she reached up to pull the blue kerchief from her head. Shaking out her hair so that it spilled unconfined down her back, she felt a trifle cooler as air reached her scalp.

The interior of the spring house was dark and cool. Leaving the door open behind her, she walked down the half-dozen steps to the spring. A long-handled tin cup hung from a nail driven into the stone wall just above her head. Standing on the stone platform, she reached up for the cup and then knelt to dip it into the spring. Still on her knees, she lifted the icy water to her lips and drank deeply. It felt wonderful as it flowed down her parched throat.

"I'll just be a minute, so keep your breeches on." The voice was Cormac's, and it came from outside the spring house. A moment later he was inside, coming down the stairs. Caitlyn got to her feet, smiling at him. She hadn't seen Cormac to speak to since she had made her devil's bargain with Connor.

"Caitlyn!" He checked a minute, hazel eyes alight as he took her in. He looked delighted to see her, and Caitlyn's smile widened. Despite his occasional peskiness, she had grown genuinely fond of Cormac. Her feelings toward him were sisterly, pure and simple, untroubled by the dark overtones that sometimes colored her feelings toward Connor. "Where've you been hiding, eh?"

"I've been hard at work. Making soap," Caitlyn answered with a comical grimace. He reached the platform and she stood back to make room for him. He grinned.

"Conn's demanding, ain't he? He's had Rory and me working so hard that we scarce make it to our beds at night before we're asleep. If he doesn't let up, we'll be sleeping in the barn soon, which he'd probably like. No more time wasted shuttling between house and barn."

Caitlyn laughed and held the cup out to him. He shook his head, his hazel eyes twinkling roguishly at her.

"I've something a bit more to my liking in here," he said confidentially. She lifted an eyebrow at him. "A jug of good home-brewed ale," he responded to her unspoken question. "I put it in the spring this morning. It should be just right by now. Rory'll think he's died and gone to heaven."

He knelt to fish in the spring as he spoke. Finding what he was after, he straightened, waving the dripping wet jug triumphantly as he got to his feet. His upraised arm caught Caitlyn's shoulder, making her stagger. With horror, she realized that she was tottering over the spring. . . .

"Oh, no!" Her arms windmilled wildly. Cormac dropped the jug with a crash and a curse and grabbed for her. He caught her just as she was about to go in the drink.

"Christ, I'm sorry!" Her heart was still pounding with fright as he pulled her close against his chest, wrapping his arms around her and hugging her to him. She rested her head against him for a minute, closing her eyes. Although the shelf closest to the platform was shallow, the larger pool beyond was deep. And she had never learned to swim.

"Oh, your ale!" she said after an instant as a pungent smell assailed her nose, and she opened her eyes to discover its source. The jug that he had recovered with such triumph only minutes before lay shattered on the stone, while the frothy yellow of its contents rolled toward the spring.

" 'Tis nothing." Cormac's voice was husky. His arms around her were hard. Alarmed, Caitlyn leaned back against them, pushing firmly against his chest. He did not let her go.

"Caitlyn . . ." he began. He was breathing rapidly, and his hazel eyes were dazed as he looked down at her. Her initial instinctive alarm was rapidly being replaced with annoyance. This was Cormac, after all.

"Let me go, Cormac," she ordered firmly. He shook his head, and his arms tightened the tiniest bit.

"You're so beautiful," he said, his eyes moving with feverish intensity over her face. "I could hold you like this forever. Do you feel that way about me too, Caitlyn?"

"No, Cormac, I do not. Now stop being so silly and let me go. I mean it."

"I will," he promised, tightening his arms and moving his head down toward hers. "If you'll first let me kiss you."

"No!" Caitlyn shoved harder against his chest, turning her head away from his proposed assault. " 'Tis a bloody nuisance you're making of yourself, Cormac, and no mistake! I don't want to kiss you!"

"You will," he promised and, maneuvering adroitly, managed to place a sloppy kiss against the side of her averted mouth.

"You dirty rotten son of the devil!" The sound of another human voice was one of the most welcome things Caitlyn had heard for a long time. That is, until she figured out that the voice belonged to Rory and he was charging down the spring-house stairs two at a time. "You low-life snake! Take your hands off her, you dog!"

Cormac did take his hands off her just in time to meet his brother's rush with a roar. Caitlyn jumped back against the wall, for a second time barely avoiding being knocked into the pool. The two brothers clenched with violent snarls, trading punches furiously. Caitlyn watched with a combination of disgust and aggravation. She hoped they beat each other black-and-blue. The pair of them were getting to be nothing more or less than confounded pests.

She became aware of Connor coming down

the stairs just as Rory got off a roundhouse punch that sent Cormac sailing into the pool. Rory barely got a glimpse of his older brother's furious face before he found himself lifted by the collar of his shirt and the seat of his pants and tossed into the pool after Cormac. Caitlyn, watching wide-eyed, was the recipient of a single blistering look from Connor before he turned his attention to his brothers, who had just surfaced, spluttering.

"Jesus, Conn, 'twas Cormac! He was kissing Caitlyn, for pity's sake!"

"I . . ." Cormac started to defend himself. Both brothers glared at each other as they treaded water in the middle of the pool.

"I've had more than enough of your foolishness," Connor bit off, with the air of a man goaded to the limits of endurance. "You're naught but moonlings, the pair of you. But I'm telling you now that I'll not be having any more of it." He reached out and caught Caitlyn by the arm, dragging her over to stand beside him. She stumbled but managed to right herself. His hand hard on her arm, Connor pushed her forward as if she were a prize exhibit. Nervously she looked down at Cormac and Rory in the water. They looked just as nervously back at her. Connor continued. "From this moment on, the lass belongs to me. If I catch any of you mooning about her, I'll break both your arms and your legs, and maybe your neck. Do I make myself clear?"

This last was said in a muted roar that caused

his brothers' eyes to widen. Caitlyn felt as though her eyes must be the size of saucers themselves. Had Connor really meant to claim her for his own? Her heart began a slow hammering.

"You don't mean it, Conn. Do you?" Astonishment, confusion, and resentment mixed in Cormac's face as he gaped at his oldest brother. Soaked to the skin, treading water, his hair slicked back around his face and dripping water, he looked very young all of a sudden.

"As God is my witness, I do." Connor sounded grim. His grip on her arm tightened enough to hurt. She could not forbear a wince, which he must have seen because his hand immediately loosened, though he did not seem to be looking at her. His scowling attention was focused on his brothers in the water.

"She's not a bloody chattel," Rory objected reasonably. "You can't just claim her, Conn. We've a right to have a chance at her too."

"Rory's right, Conn. She should be allowed to make up her own mind, in her own time. You're not some feudal lord, you know, even if you are an earl."

"I — I have made up my mind." Caitlyn was astonished that her voice didn't shake. All three brothers looked at her rather as if a mounted moose's head had spoken, but she went on doggedly. "I choose Connor. And 'tis my hope that the rest of you will honor that choice."

There was a thick silence as Rory and Cormac stared at her. Caitlyn did not dare look over her shoulder at Connor, who stood silently behind her, his hand heavy on her arm.

"As you wish, of course," Rory said stiffly after a moment, and swam the two strokes needed to bring him to the side of the pool. Cormac was right behind him. They hauled themselves dripping from the pool. Without another word, trailing water as they went, they climbed up the stairs and walked out of the spring house. Caitlyn was left with Connor. The moment they were alone his hand fell from her arm. Caitlyn was half frightened to do it, but she did it anyway: she turned to face him.

He was frowning at her, not scowling but frowning. He had shrugged into his shirt after she left the barn, but it was unbuttoned and hung free of his breeches. His chest was bare, and as Caitlyn looked at the sweat-filmed muscles roughened with dark hair she felt her heartbeat quicken.

"So you were kissing Cormac, were you?" he asked, his eyes narrowing at her.

"I . . ." Caitlyn began, meaning to defend herself. Then inspiration took her. "I just wondered how it would feel," she finished with demure provocation.

His frown deepened. That tiny muscle began to twitch again beside his mouth. Looking at him, Caitlyn felt her own mouth go dry. She swayed toward him, the movement almost involuntary. He reached out and caught her upper arms, pulling her closer but still holding her away from him.

"So you just wanted to know how it would feel," he repeated with soft bite. Then his eyes narrowed further and focused with sudden blazing intensity on her mouth. "Caitlyn, lassie, if 'tis kissing you want to try, then come kiss me."

XXII

❀ ❀ ❀ ❀ ❀ ❀ ❀ ❀ ❀ ❀ ❀ ❀ ❀ ❀ ❀

He pulled her slowly closer until her breasts just brushed the mat of hairs on his bare chest. His eyes never left her face, and her eyes drowned in his. Her heart was pounding so hard that she could scarcely hear anything over it. When his hands released her arms to slide around her small waist, she wet her lips. He took a quick, deep breath.

"Put your arms around my neck." His voice was faintly hoarse. Tiny flames lit the backs of his eyes. Caitlyn felt her knees go weak as she obediently lifted her arms. At the first tentative touch of her hands on his neck he stiffened. Caitlyn felt the warm dampness of his skin under her fingertips and trembled. Her arms slid slowly around his neck, her fingers touching the curly tail of hair at his nape. He bent his head. She closed her eyes.

The first touch of his mouth on hers made her dizzy. His lips pressed against hers gently, warm and dry, nuzzling her mouth. She felt a quickening deep inside her, a longing so intense that she thought she might faint with it. Her chest heaved as she drew a long shuddering breath, and then his tongue was inside her mouth.

She moaned. Never in all her life had she

imagined that kissing a man would be like this. She felt lightheaded, intoxicated, enthralled as his tongue softly, gently, explored her mouth. When he removed it and lifted his head, she dug her nails into the back of his neck in protest even as she opened her eyes.

"Gently, lass." He was breathing unevenly too, she saw. Her arms were still around his neck, and his arms enwrapped her waist. If it hadn't been for this support, she didn't think she would have been able to stand. Her knees had melted to butter, and her insides were all aquiver. The look in her eyes was both languorous and urgent as she lifted them to his.

" 'Twas marvelous. Do it again." It was a soft murmur.

"Sweet Jesus." His eyes blazed down at her for an instant before he bent his head to hers and took her mouth with a ferocity that lit brushfires of need inside her. He pulled her up on tiptoe, bending her backward so that her head was pillowed on his shoulder as his tongue plundered her mouth. Caitlyn locked her arms around his neck and kissed him back, relying on blind instinct to teach her all she needed to know. Boldly her tongue stroked his, slid inside his mouth. A fine tremor shook the arms that strained her to him. His hands slid down to cup her bottom through the layers of skirt and petticoat and shift, pulling her up against him as he pressed boldly into her. She felt the rock hardness of him grinding against her belly, felt the kneading of his fingers on her bottom as they drew her closer yet, and moaned his name into his mouth. He groaned in answer and shifted his hold on her, so that she thought he would lower her to the stone floor beneath. Then he muttered a vile word into her mouth, pulled her upright again, and tore his mouth from hers, still holding her close while his heart pounded against her breasts and his face rested against the top of her head.

"Connor!" This time his name was a soft protest. She felt him draw a deep breath. Then his arms slid from around her waist and he took a step back from her, his hands closing over her forearms where they were linked behind his neck.

"You are a menace," he said through his teeth, spacing the words out. When she still swayed toward him with invitation, he pulled her arms from around his neck and held her away from him by his grip on them. "Stop it! Do you want to end up as my mistress, taken right here on the bloody floor?"

Caitlyn smiled at him. Her insides were aclamor, her head awhirl. There was only room for one thing in her thoughts: Connor himself. He looked so incredibly handsome as he stood there scowling at her, his eyes narrowed beneath frowning brows and his mouth, his marvelous mouth that could do the most incredible things to her, fierce. His black hair was escaping untidily from its ribbon, and she supposed that she had caused that when she had stroked its silken waves. His broad shoulders were set rigidly as though to hold her off, but his chest heaved beneath his open shirt as if he were having trouble drawing breath. Caitlyn stared at that hard-muscled, sweat-filmed chest for a long moment before she lifted her eyes to his again.

"If you like," she said simply and lowered her eyes to his chest once more. That broad, hair-roughened expanse fascinated her. Of its own volition her hand came up to rest gently over his heart, and she had the answer to the question that had troubled her: the mat of fine hair was as soft as a kitten's fur.

"Holy Mother of God!" Connor yelped, jumping back as if stung by her gentle touch. Then, before Caitlyn knew what was happening, he was tottering on the edge of the pool. Instinctively she reached out a hand to him, but it was too late; he fell in.

She was staring wide-eyed at the spreading ripples on the dark water when he surfaced what seemed like eons later. Treading water, he scowled up at her, brushing the strands of sopping-wet black hair from his eyes. Then the sheer ridiculousness of it coaxed a reluctant grin from him.

"I should have listened to Mickeen from the beginning," he told her, swimming for the edge of the pool and hoisting himself up. "You've been nothing but trouble to me from start to finish, young Caitlyn, and it seems the more I try to get out the deeper I get into the coil. And you are no help at all."

"What are you talking about?" She stared at him, bewildered, as he stood up and looked ruefully down at himself. He was soaked to the skin, his boots doubtless ruined, the ribbon securing his queue left behind to float on the surface of the spring. Water poured off him like rain. He looked up at her, his expression wry.

"I never meant to lay a finger on you, lass, and 'tis ashamed of myself I am for doing so. With a little cooperation from you, I'll undertake to make certain that it does not happen again."

"But — but —" Caitlyn sputtered at him, unable to believe her ears. "You said — you told Cormac and Rory that you — that I was your property. I thought — I thought . . ." What she had thought trailed off into nothingness as she found herself unable to put it into words. Connor looked at her steadily.

"What I said was merely my own clumsy way of trying to keep my brothers from killing each other over you. I never meant to claim you truly. Only to keep you safe."

"Oh!" Her cheeks burned with mortification. Her hands flew to them and she stared at him in dawning horror. Remembering every little thing she had said and done, she wanted to die. And with shame came flaring, healing anger.

"Caitlyn . . ." He said her name in a gentle tone, reaching for her. She glared at him, her hands dropping away from her cheeks to clench at her sides.

"You are a vile beast, Connor d'Arcy!" she

hissed, and as he took a step toward her she shoved him so hard that he tumbled backward into the spring. Even as the water from his fall splashed over her, she was turning away with a swirl of skirts and rushing up the stairs. If she was lucky, she thought, fuming, maybe he'd drown in the bloody pool!

XXIII

By the following morning, having spent the night giving considerable uncomfortable thought to the previous day's happenings, Caitlyn had decided that neither suicide nor murder was the answer to her problem. Vile beast though Connor certainly was, she did not really want to see him dead and doubted her ability to bring such a thing about in any case. And she certainly had no intention of killing herself and thus ridding him of his problem. She had also reached a conclusion. No matter how much he tried to convince her and himself otherwise, Connor found her desirable. There had been no pretense in that soul-shattering kiss.

At that moment she would have let him do anything he wanted to her and reveled in the doing. That was mortifying to admit, but true. She had been butter in his hands, and she suspected that if the situation were repeated again, even with the humiliating knowledge of his motives that she now possessed, she would respond in exactly the same way.

Without knowing it, she had longed for his kiss for weeks. The reality, when it came, had been more dazzling than any daydream. And the simple truth of the matter was, she wanted him to do it again.

She wanted Connor d'Arcy. The knowledge came to her with the blinding light of truth. She wanted him to be hers, her man. For months feelings of possessiveness toward him had been growing inside her undetected. Now they sprang forth in full bloom. He was hers, like it or not. He just had not yet acknowledged his downfall. The problem was, how was she to go about making him do so?

Still pondering the matter, she went downstairs to breakfast only to discover that Connor had gone with Mickeen to Dublin. He did not return for three full days.

During that time, Caitlyn kept her distance from the younger d'Arcys. Cormac and Rory appeared to have taken Connor's threat to heart, for they barely spoke to her. Liam was caught up in doing the farm's books. She was not sure he was even aware of the prohibition, but he was so abstracted most of the time that she doubted that he saw her or anyone else.

She did her chores and rode Finnbarr, and if she was unhappy none knew it.

On the afternoon of the third day, Caitlyn saddled Finnbarr and went for a ride. Since the younger d'Arcys were still sulking and Mickeen had gone with Connor, there was no one to tell her not to ride alone. In fact, she had been doing so every day and almost enjoyed the freedom. Although if she were to be honest, she missed the free and easy exchanges with Cormac and

Rory, and even Liam's wry wit. And she missed Connor, though she was growing angrier at him by the day.

She took her familiar route down toward the Boyne. The day was brisk, and Finnbarr was frisky. Pulling the kerchief from her head, she let her hair fly free behind her and gave Finnbarr his head. He soared over the turf toward the misty hills that rose to the north.

After a while she pulled him in and turned him toward home. The ride had been exhilarating, but she did not want to tire Finnbarr and held him to a walk. When they came to a stream, she stopped.

He drank thirstily. Caitlyn patted him and settled herself comfortably in the saddle, whiling away the minutes with a daydream: Connor down on his knees to her, slathering kisses over her lily-white hands . . .

"Well met, Miss O'Malley!" The hail almost made her tumble off Finnbarr's back. Startled, she straightened and turned her head to find Sir Edward Dunne riding toward her on a big roan.

"Good day, Sir Edward." Caitlyn was polite even as she groped for Finnbarr's reins. Of course they had somehow managed to unwrap themselves from the pommel and slide down the animal's neck. She leaned forward as far as she could, but she couldn't quite reach them.

"Allow me." Seeing her predicament, Sir Edward dismounted and trudged through the shallow stream, leaving his horse behind with its reins trailing, to retrieve her reins for her. Caitlyn watched his approach a trifle uneasily. After all that Connor and the others had told her about this man, she did not like being alone with him so far from home. But then, the main road was nearby, and in any case surely he was not as black as the d'Arcys had painted him. And even if he was, the mantle of Connor's protection should be an adequate safeguard from any unwelcome advances.

"If you'll permit me to say so, you're growing lovelier by the day." Sir Edward made no move to hand her reins up to her immediately. Instead he stood slapping them idly against his palm as he gazed at her, seemingly heedless of his booted feet in the stream.

"Th-thank you." She was becoming increasingly nervous and held out her hand for her reins. He shook his head and kept them out of reach, smiling teasingly up at her.

"Surely you can stay and chat a while? It is rare that I see you without one of your — ah — cousins in tow."

"I really have to get back. Conn — Connor will be looking for me." Again she reached for her reins. She did not like the look in Sir Edward's eyes, or the too-familiar tone of his voice. She hoped to instill in him the worry that Connor might appear in search of her at any moment.

"Really?" Sir Edward affected surprise. His smile widened. "Strange, I just returned from Dublin this morning, where I had the privilege of attending a ball at Dublin Castle. While I was there I encountered d'Arcy, who had just concluded a waltz with Meredith Congreve. He informed me that he meant to spend the rest of the week in town, and from the way the divine Meredith was clinging to him, I have little doubt that he meant it."

"I meant Cormac, of course." As unsettling as the information he had just given her was, she had no time to do more than register it with an unpleasant jolt and file it away for future reference. All her attention had to focus for the present on getting away from Sir Edward. She was growing more frightened of him by the moment.

"Ah, but young Cormac is a very different kettle of fish. If d'Arcy has passed you on to his baby brother already, then I see I need have no more scruples. I'd like to make you an offer, my dear."

"An offer?" Caitlyn looked down at him rather wildly. Short of jumping from Finnbarr's back and running for it, she could conceive of no means of escape. And to put herself within Sir Edward's easy reach would be foolhardy.

"I'm a far richer man than Connor d'Arcy, my dear, to say nothing of the rest of the pack. And you'll find that I'm extremely generous when I'm pleased. A young lady such as yourself should have the finest clothes, jewelry, a chance to shine in Society. I could give you all that, and more."

"I haven't the faintest notion what you're talking about," Caitlyn said, genuinely bewildered.

Sir Edward's mouth tightened impatiently, and he shaded his eyes with his free hand as he looked up at her. Caitlyn noticed that the features she had thought not unattractive before now looked pinched and cruel.

"Come, come, Caitlyn. I may call you Caitlyn, may I not? Surely you did not think that I or anyone else would swallow that nonsense about your being the d'Arcys' cousin! It's patently obvious that you were mistress to Connor at least, and probably passed down the line. I can certainly offer you better than that. Your own house in Dublin, if you wish."

"You are mistaken, sir," Caitlyn said in a suffocated voice, holding out her hand imperiously. "Now if you will please hand me my reins . . ."

"Oh, ho, holding out for more, are you? Well, let's see how you price yourself when the deed's done, my girl!" With that he reached up to catch her around the waist, pulling her off Finnbarr's back with a jerk. Caitlyn screamed once, shrill as a whistle in case anyone should be nearby to hear. Then, as Sir Edward twisted her into the circle of his arms and bent his head toward her, she kicked him as hard as she could in the shin.

"Oww! A little she-devil, are you? No wonder d'Arcy's kept you around so long." Although his grip had slackened from her kick, he was pulling her close again. Caitlyn had just enough time to wrest her arm out from between them. As he bent his head toward her she drew back her fist and punched him in the face. Her fist made jarring contact with his left eye. He howled, staggering back without releasing his grip on her. Caitlyn tried to punch him again, but he warded off her blows.

"I'll teach you to fight me," he growled with relish. Then he slapped her as hard as he could across the face. Caitlyn reeled back, feeling her lip split. Catching both her arms, he dragged her into his embrace and ground his mouth against hers with no regard for the lip he had injured.

A pistol went off near at hand. Sir Edward jerked upright at the sudden explosion of sound. Caitlyn, no longer subject to his assaultive kiss, looked frantically around. To her immense relief, she saw Connor sitting astride Fharannain not ten feet away. The look on his face was menacing as he lowered a smoking pistol. Drawing its mate from his belt, he leaned over the horn of Fharannain's saddle and pointed it squarely at Sir Edward.

"Let her go or die," he said, and Caitlyn at least had no doubt that he meant it.

Sir Edward let go. Caitlyn stumbled away from him toward Connor.

"I was merely offering to take her off your hands, d'Arcy. You must have tired of her by now, and I'm prepared to make a generous settlement on you as well as on her if she comes to me." Sir Edward's voice was nervously placating. Connor ignored him, dismounting and putting a hand beneath Caitlyn's chin as she came up to him. Even as he lifted her face for his inspection he kept the gun trained on Sir Edward.

"He hit you." It wasn't a question. Caitlyn was frightened by the ominous sound of those three words. Connor was so angry he was icy with it. Knowing the white heat of his usual explosions, she realized that this was different, and far more dangerous.

"It doesn't hurt. Not really." She might as well have been speaking to Fharannain for all the notice he took. Those devil's eyes fixed on Sir Edward.

"You've made a serious miscalculation," he said, and smiled. That smile was enough to chill Caitlyn's blood, and it must have had a similar effect on Sir Edward.

"If you kill me you'll hang for it, d'Arcy."

Connor looked down at Caitlyn fleetingly. "Get back on Finnbarr and go home."

"You'd better stop him, Miss O'Malley. Unless you want to see him hang!" Sir Edward sounded close to hysteria, and looking at Connor, Caitlyn didn't blame him. Connor looked ripe for murder.

"Please don't kill him, Connor," she pleaded in an undertone, her hand resting against his upper arm. The brown riding coat he wore was smartly cut but dusty, its texture rough beneath her hand. " 'Twas a kiss, nothing more. A kiss isn't a killing matter."

Connor's eyes slanted down to meet hers briefly before returning to Sir Edward.

"You see, d'Arcy? Just a kiss. If I — I got a little rough, I apologize to the young lady. See? That's all there is to it!"

"Get on Finnbarr and go home," Connor repeated. The deadly gleam in his eyes had not lessened.

"Connor!"

"I won't kill him," he promised. Then he gave her a little shove. "Now go!"

Despite Sir Edward's frantic protests, Caitlyn obediently walked back to Finnbarr and mounted. At a gesture from Connor, she turned the horse and rode away. But only as far as a copse of pines halfway up the hill, where she turned Finnbarr and sat watching, hidden by the screen of fragrant branches.

Connor kept his pistol trained on Sir Edward as he approached him. Caitlyn was too far away to hear what he said, but whatever it was made Sir Edward go white to the lips. Then Connor was within arm's length of him. Thrusting the pistol into his belt, he reached out and grabbed the Englishman by the coat. The bloody pommeling that followed could not really be termed a fight. Sir Edward got off a few feeble punches, but Connor beat him to his knees with a series of savage blows that made Caitlyn, watching, feel queasy. Sir Edward swayed as he knelt, saying something to Connor which Caitlyn guessed was a plea to stop. Connor responded by twisting his hand in the man's coat front and lifting him halfway to his feet. Then he punched Sir Edward viciously in the head, letting go of his coat at the same time. Sir Edward fell sideways as if he had been poleaxed and lay unmoving in the grass. Connor stood over him for a minute, breathing heavily. Then he drew back his booted foot and kicked Sir Edward brutally in the ribs. Watching, Caitlyn winced. As Sir Edward still lay unmoving, Connor spat on him, then walked back to remount Fharannain. And he rode away, leaving Sir Edward lying bloody and unmoving in the field.

Caitlyn was so unnerved by what she had witnessed that she forgot that Connor had told her to go home. When he rode into the copse and saw her, she could only stare at him wide-eyed. A gash had been opened in his cheek and blood dripped down his face. Besides that, she could see no other mark on him.

"Your face . . ." she said, riding to meet him.

"He caught me with his damned ring," Connor growled, his eyes glinting as they rested on her swollen lip. " 'Tis nothing. I thought I told you to go home."

"I was afraid he might hurt you."

Connor snorted. Caitlyn turned Finnbarr to keep pace with Fharannain as they rode out of the trees and across the hill toward the farm.

"Should we just . . . leave him there?" She looked back over her shoulder toward where they had left Sir Edward.

"I'll send word to his people to come and get him. He won't bleed to death before then." Connor shrugged indifferently.

"But . . ."

"But nothing. 'Tis lucky he is that I didn't kill him outright. He deserved it."

"It was only a kiss. And a blow. I've suffered worse."

Connor glanced over at her, his eyes glinting. "The man's the worst kind of bastard; your lip's as fat as a sausage. And 'twas only a kiss because I came when I did. Had I not, he'd have raped you. Don't tell me that wasn't his intention."

Caitlyn knew that was true, but she refrained from agreeing for fear of inciting Connor's rage again. It wouldn't take much for him to go back and finish what he had started, she feared. Not that she would bemoan Sir Edward's demise, but as the Englishman himself had pointed out, Connor could well hang for it.

"How did you come to be around to rescue me, by the by? I thought you were in Dublin — dancing with Mrs. Congreve." The last words, dripping sarcasm, forced their way out of their own volition. Caitlyn could have bitten her tongue through. She sounded for all the world like a jealous female — which, of course, she was.

The faintest hint of amusement showed for an instant in Connor's eyes as he slanted a sideways look at her. "I danced with many ladies, Mrs. Congreve among them," he said sedately. Then he added: "Fortunately for you, this morning I decided that I'd been away from Donoughmore long enough. I left Mickeen to get the rest of the supplies and set out. I was on the road when I heard a woman scream. Ever the chivalrous gentleman, I investigated and found — you."

He looked furious all over again. Caitlyn started to say something, but he turned such a blistering gaze on her that she was silenced.

"If you ever, ever ride out alone again, I'll sell the damned horse and send you to the nuns, blackmail or no," he told her fiercely, then set his heels to Fharannain and galloped for home.

XXIV

Two days later, Connor's gash had healed to a raw scar across his cheekbone, and Caitlyn's lip was back to its normal size. There had been no word from Ballymara, though, true to his promise, Connor had sent a message to Sir Edward's home advising that Sir Edward had suffered an "accident" and where he could be found. Caitlyn had been afraid that Sir Edward would not allow the matter to rest there. But nothing untoward happened and she tried to put the incident from her mind.

Connor's temper had not improved with the passage of time. When his brothers exclaimed over the state of his cheek and Caitlyn's lip, Connor had seized the opportunity to upbraid them for not keeping a closer watch on Caitlyn. When Caitlyn had rather miserably tried to smooth things over, Connor had snapped her head off, and the younger d'Arcys had not appeared particularly appreciative of her efforts. After that, Connor was busy. No matter when or how she tried to approach him, he brusquely cut her short. She found it hard to believe that he was so angry at her merely because she had ridden out alone and had gotten into trouble, but if the cause was other than that, she didn't know, because Connor wouldn't tell her. The effect of his silent anger was to make her miserable, and everyone else wary.

"For the Lord's sake, what've you done to the man?" Rory demanded of her after Connor had bitten everyone's head off during the midday meal before stomping off to harass the peasants in the fields. " 'Tis like living with a wolf with a sore paw!"

They were getting up from the table. Caitlyn had elected to muck out stalls rather than help with the clearing up, so she was leaving the house with the men. Mrs. McFee paused in the act of removing the plates to look sharply at Caitlyn as if listening for evidence that the evil she had always predicted was occurring under Donough-more's roof.

"Hush," Caitlyn muttered to Rory, who was obediently silent until they were safely on the stoop. Then he looked at her, eyebrows raised while he waited for an answer.

"I haven't done anything to him," she said defensively, lifting her skirts clear of her feet as she stepped to the ground.

Behind her, Cormac snorted. "Like as not, that's the problem."

Caitlyn, not understanding, stared at him as he fell into step beside her. Liam, trailing behind, went red to his ears. Rory, on Caitlyn's other side, looked at Cormac reproachfully.

"You shouldn't say things like that in front of Caitlyn. 'Tis not proper," he rebuked his brother.

Cormac shrugged. "Why not? If she's sleeping with him, then she's no innocent to have her ears sullied. And if she's not, why then, I'd say that's the problem."

There was a bitter note in his voice that told Caitlyn that he still resented Connor's edict. Impulsively, she put a hand on his forearm, bare where he had rolled the sleeves of his shirt past his elbows, stopping him. The others stopped too, watching as Caitlyn gazed earnestly up at Cormac.

"Can't we please be friends, Cormac?" she asked softly. "Just because I — I feel a certain way about Connor doesn't mean that I don't care for you too. And Rory. And even stodgy Liam." She favored Liam with a fleeting smile. "As brothers. We've been friends — good friends — for more than a year. Just because we're all growing up is no reason that has to change, is it?"

Cormac looked at her for a moment, the beginnings of a sulky frown on his face. Then he grinned reluctantly.

"Oh, I suppose not," he said. "Though you are certainly more interesting as Caitlyn the beauty than O'Malley the beggar-boy."

Rory and Liam laughed, and Caitlyn did too. A tiny corner of her heart healed to know that she was on good terms with the younger d'Arcys again. If only repairing her relationship with Connor were this easy. . . .

"Thank you, Cormac," she said softly, planting a quick, sisterly kiss on his cheek. Then she did the same to Rory and Liam.

"Mighty free with your kisses, aren't you?" an all-too-familiar voice snarled behind her. Caitlyn and the three d'Arcys all whirled guiltily to find Connor standing a few paces away, a pitchfork in his hand and an ugly scowl marring his face. Like Cormac, he was in shirtsleeves, which he had rolled up past his elbows and left unfastened at the throat so that a wedge of hair-roughened bronzed skin showed there. He was wearing his oldest breeches and a pair of scuffed boots, and from the perspiration beading his brow and dampening his shirt, it was obvious to Caitlyn that he had beaten her to the task of mucking out the stalls. She felt herself flush with chagrin as she lifted her eyes to his face; the unspoken implication was that she should have done the work sooner.

"But, Conn . . ." Liam said plaintively. Connor glowered even at this brother who rarely provoked his ire.

Before more could be said, they were interrupted by the sound of a carriage approaching. Mrs. Congreve's gig rolled into the stableyard with the lady herself at the reins. Unable to stop herself, Caitlyn glared at the intruder and was pleased to note that the younger d'Arcys did the same. Connor's eyes narrowed on the newcomer, but it was impossible to tell if he was pleased at her arrival. In any case, Mrs. Congreve appeared to notice no lack in the greeting afforded her, because she waved cheerily. Changing the direction of her horses, she drove over to where the five of them waited, drawing rein smartly when she was just a few feet away.

"Mucking out the stables, darling?" she called gaily to Connor, whose scowl had faded with her approach. He actually smiled as he crossed to her, pitchfork in hand. Caitlyn's glare deepened as she took in the lady's pristine beauty. Even on this hot summer day, not a hair was out of place on that powdered head. Mrs. Congreve was dressed in pink silk today, with flounces of silver lace and a pink feather drooping saucily from the side of her enormous hat. Looking self-consciously down at her own much-mended dress, Caitlyn felt her ire rise in direct proportion to her dowdiness.

"I'm a working farmer, you know, Meredith," Connor replied. He sounded jovial, which he hadn't been to any of them in days. Mrs. Congreve simpered at him, and Caitlyn felt her temper rise some more.

"I hope I haven't called at an inconvenient time," the woman went on, extending her hand to Connor. "But I heard from Sarah Dunne that you and Sir Edward had some sort of — er — contretemps, which left Sir Edward quite badly hurt. I had to see for myself that you weren't in like case, though I should have known there was no chance of that. Darling, I do hope I wasn't the cause of your disagreement?" She ended it as a delicate question, her expression telling Caitlyn that, contrary to her claim, she very much hoped she had been.

"Ah, that would be telling." Connor smiled charmingly as he took her hand and lifted it to his lips. His eyes met Caitlyn's over the lady's white hand. She glared at him as he pressed his lips against the whiteness, and his eyes went hard in return. Then, still holding the lady's hand, he deliberately leaned over the edge of the gig and kissed Mrs. Congreve's soft cheek.

There was a collective indrawing of breath among the younger d'Arcys, and three pairs of eyes turned to Caitlyn to see how she would react to that. Caitlyn stiffened, her eyes fastened on the twosome by the gig. Pure animal rage flooded her veins; she clenched her fists as bright flags of color flew to her cheeks. Her eyes blazed dangerously. Deftly sidestepping Liam's hand lifted to stop her, she marched herself over to the gig, stopping when she was no more than a foot away from Connor's side.

"Oh, Connor, darling," she drawled in broad parody of Mrs. Congreve's mincing tones. When Connor turned to look at her, brows lifted, she drew back her hand and slapped him very deliberately across the face.

There was a moment's awful silence, broken only by the ringing sound of the slap. Then Mrs. Congreve gasped, Connor's hand went to his abused cheek as he stared furiously at Caitlyn, and the younger d'Arcys, moving almost as one, took a single protective step forward. But before Connor could respond with more than a look,

276

Caitlyn turned on her heel and stalked into the stable, climbed into the loft and threw herself down on her stomach in the straw. And with a mixed sense of doom and satisfaction, she waited.

She had not long to wait. She sensed his presence even before he stepped off the ladder, even before she heard his booted feet on the floor of the loft. Still she continued to stare out the window, refusing to look at him even when he stood directly beside her.

"I hope you're bloody pleased with yourself," he began furiously.

"Shouldn't you be with your lady friend?" she said, putting sarcastic emphasis on the last two words as she rolled to one side and sat up, crossing her legs beneath her. Her reddened handprint was still plainly visible on the same cheek that had been cut by Sir Edward's ring. Above it, those aqua eyes gleamed at her with devilish anger.

"Aye, I should be!" He bit the words off, then made a palpable attempt to control his temper. When he spoke again, the anger was less apparent. "What maggot entered your brain to cause you to slap me? You've convinced Meredith that you're my mistress, and what Meredith knows the whole countryside knows soon afterward!"

"I don't care." She folded her arms over her breasts and looked stubbornly out the window.

"Well, I do!"

"Oh, is she angry at you?" Caitlyn asked venomously. "Good!"

There was a moment of charged silence.

Caitlyn could feel the heat of Connor's eyes boring into her averted face. His next words held an aura of carefully invoked patience.

"Caitlyn, you've no business to be jealous of Meredith. What is between her and me is no concern of yours. We are both adults, and you are naught but a child."

She looked at him then, her eyes blazing. "Oh, really? Doubtless 'tis merely my imagination, but I seem to recall that you thought I was an adult not so many days ago. Or do you always go around kissing children like that?"

His eyes narrowed, and his arms crossed over his chest as he met her furious stare. For a long moment he only looked at her, and the final traces of fury faded from his face. When he spoke, his voice was gruff. " 'Twas a mistake and nothing more."

"A mistake! A mistake!" As his anger faded, hers was reborn. Caitlyn surged to her feet, her hand swinging in a wild arc toward his face again. Connor, ever fast on his feet, caught her hand before it could make contact with the self-same cheek it had smacked before and held it tightly.

"Caitlyn!" There was taut warning in his tone.

She ignored him, raging. "Why don't you admit it, Connor d'Arcy? You liked kissing me! I could tell you did! And if I'm jealous, you are too! 'Tis so jealous you are of your own brothers that you're practically green with it! Don't tell me that you didn't kiss that — that — Mrs. Congreve because you saw me kissing Cormac and Rory and Liam. And perfectly innocently too, which is more than you can lay claim to!"

"Caitlyn!"

"Don't you Caitlyn me!" She swung on him with her other hand, but he caught that one too.

"Damn it, Caitlyn, if you hit me again I'm likely to turn you over my knee and tan your backside for you!" He was glaring at her even as he held her captured hands prisoner.

"When will you get it through your head that I'm too old for you to spank?" she hissed at him. "I'm a woman grown, Connor d'Arcy, and you know it! You're just afraid to admit it!"

He stared at her for a moment, his mouth tight. Those light eyes flickered with anger and something else as they moved over her flushed face. Then his eyes moved down her body in its well-patched green dress, resting for a moment on heaving breasts and tiny waist before coming back up to the faded green kerchief that drew her raven hair back from her widow's peak. At last he met her eyes.

"Be glad that I am," he said quietly. "If I were to treat you as a woman grown, there'd be hell to pay!"

She looked up at him, arrested. There was an underlying edge to his voice that gave her renewed hope. Her anger faded, and she stopped tugging at her hands in his.

"I want you to treat me as a woman grown," she almost wailed, her eyes wide.

"You're too young to know what you want."

His eyes narrowed on her face. There was a restless glint in them. She fastened on that and tried not to hear the grim note in his voice. " 'Tis thankful you should be that I have more sense than you."

Clearly he was determined to keep her at arm's length. Scowling, Caitlyn studied that lean, handsome face that frowned so sternly back at her. His hold on her hands had slackened now that she no longer seemed hell-bent on hitting him. Their fingers had intertwined apparently of their own volition, completely oblivious to the angry words that were being exchanged.

"I hate you," she said petulantly, tugging at her hands again.

"Good." His reply was heartless. But he did not release her hands.

"Let me go! Beast!" She pulled at her hands to emphasize her words.

He sighed, the anger gone from him now. "Caitlyn, you're a beautiful lass, and I'm a normal man. 'Tis you I'm trying to protect."

She stopped tugging on her hands and studied him. "I don't want to be protected. Not from you. And I don't hate you. I — I love you, Connor."

She made the admission shamelessly. His eyes widened, then narrowed again. His voice was harsh.

"You're naught but a child. You don't know what you're saying."

"I do! I do!"

280

He said nothing, just looked at her for a long moment while tiny flames flickered in the backs of his eyes. His fingers tightened around hers almost painfully. Caitlyn gladly tolerated the small hurt.

" 'Twould be very wrong of me to take advantage of the way you think you feel. You —"

"I'm not a child, Connor!" she snapped, exasperated. Then she walked right up to him with their fingers still entwined. "I want you to kiss me. Now. Please."

"Caitlyn . . ."

Despite the restless flaming of his eyes, he was still reluctant. So Caitlyn boldly rose up on her tiptoes and pressed her lips to that hard mouth.

"Caitlyn . . ." Belying the attempt at protest that was her name, he was not putting her away from him. Encouraged, Caitlyn tilted her head sideways, closed her eyes, and pressed her mouth more firmly to his. Her heart began to pound; her breathing quickened. His lips felt firm and warm beneath hers. Greatly daring, she stroked the line where they met with the tip of her tongue.

For a moment longer he resisted her gentle assault. Then his breath drew in in a long, shuddering sigh, and his hands freed themselves from hers to slide around her waist.

"On your own head be it, then," he muttered against her mouth. And then it was he who was kissing her.

He kissed her fiercely, as if he were starving for the taste of her mouth. Wrapping her arms around his neck, Caitlyn kissed him back. Her heart was pounding so loud that she could barely hear his harsh breathing. A quickening started in the pit of her stomach. Her knees grew weak. She clung to him as the only solid thing in a whirling universe.

"Ahh, Caitlyn." He lifted his mouth from hers to trail kisses across her cheek to her ear. Caitlyn took a deep, shuddering breath, burying her face in his neck. The warmth and male smell of him enticed her. Parting her lips, she touched her tongue to his throat.

His arms tightened around her and he pulled her up on her toes as his mouth traced a blazing path down the side of her neck. When he reached the place where her neck and shoulder joined, he paused for a long moment while his mouth seemed to burn through her skin. Her nails dug into his shoulders, her mouth opening against the side of his throat. Then he lifted her off her feet and laid her down in the straw.

She raised her arms to him, her eyes drugged with longing, but there was no need. He was already coming down in the straw beside her, his hard body close against hers as he bent over and took her mouth again.

Enthralled, she stroked his shoulders through the thin linen of his shirt, traced the line of his spine, burrowed beneath his collar to touch the bare skin of his nape. When his hand slid from her waist to close over her breast, she gasped and trembled at the wonder of it.

"I love you, Connor," she breathed in his ear and felt the hand on her breast clench for the merest instant. Then his hold loosened again and his mouth lifted from hers.

"My lovely Caitlyn," he said unsteadily, raising himself a little bit above her and looking down into her face.

"Don't stop," she whispered, sliding her hand from his shoulder to rest over his hand where it lay on her breast. She pressed his fingers harder into her softness. His lips parted slightly and his eyes blazed anew.

"Even if I wanted to, I could not," he confessed with the barest glimmer of a smile. And then he was kissing her again with increasing hunger as his arms slid around her and he fumbled for the buttons at the back of her dress.

Caitlyn could scarcely breathe as he slipped the dress and then the shift down her shoulders. Watching him, she saw his eyes flame as he slowly, tenderly, bared her breasts. Then he touched her, stroking the hardness of a small strawberry-pink nipple with reverent fingers. The ensuing jolt of feeling made Caitlyn moan and arch her back.

"Easy, my own." He murmured the words to her, his eyes on her face now, watching the passion shine from her. Her head rested back on his forearm as he leaned over her, tracing a line from one taut nipple to the other. She thought she would die from the sheer wonder of it.

Then he lowered his head.

Caitlyn watched, eyes glazed with need, as he touched her nipple with his tongue. He repeated the butterfly caress on her other nipple, and she cried out his name.

At her cry, she felt the muscles of his shoulders clench beneath her hands. Then his mouth was on hers again, hard and hot and demanding, and he was crushing her back into the straw. His hands slid down the length of her body to tug at her tangled skirts.

XXV

"Conn!"

The voice belonged to Liam. Connor's hand, in the act of sliding up Caitlyn's bare thigh, tightened and stilled. Her whole body stiffened as she tried to shut out the intruding sound. She whimpered, wordlessly begging him not to stop. Connor's broad shoulders blocked the rest of the loft from her view as he looked toward where the ladder ascended into the loft. Liam's voice had come from the foot of it. Willing him to ignore the intrusion, she twined her arms tighter around his neck. He spared her a flickering glance, his eyes moving from the soft whiteness of her thighs, bared by the skirt he had pushed out of his way, to the pink-tipped, quivering breasts above the lowered bodice. She was nearly naked beneath him. The knowledge melted something deep inside her. She quivered, and Connor's eyes, as hot as the midday sun, lifted to meet hers.

"Connor!" Liam called, insistent. Connor tore his eyes away from her to look toward the source of the sound again.

"Aye, what is it?" he answered, his voice not quite steady. Then, as if he couldn't help himself, his eyes returned to her. They moved over her once more, fixing finally on the thigh where his hand rested in dark contrast to her ivory skin. Those aqua eyes darkened. An instant later his mouth twisted violently. Despite Caitlyn's mewling protest, he removed his hand. With methodical precision he pulled her skirt down, smoothing it over her legs. His face was a study in passion, regret, and something else that Caitlyn finally recognized as resolve.

"Fools and children," he muttered under his breath. Caitlyn remembered him saying something similar once before. Before she could quite recall the context, Liam's voice interrupted her chain of thought.

"Ah — your visitor is taking tea in the parlor. She's wondering where you've got to." He was still speaking from the foot of the ladder.

"Damn, I forgot all about her!" Connor followed this appalled statement with a string of muttered curses. Then he disengaged Caitlyn's arms from around his neck and sat up, running unsteady fingers through his hair. At the reminder of Mrs. Congreve, Caitlyn scowled. The passion that burned in her eyes was joined by smoldering anger.

"Keep her occupied, will you? I'll be right there," Connor called down to Liam.

"Aye." There was the sound of muffled footsteps, and Liam was gone. Caitlyn sat up, pulling her bodice up with angry jerks, glaring at Connor all the while. The flush that passion had brought to his cheekbones faded as he quickly retied the ribbon that held his hair. That he could go from her to that — that *woman* made Caitlyn want to bash him over the head with the nearest deadly object. Fortunately — or unfortunately, depending on one's point of view — there was no deadly object within reach. Lip curling into a sneer, Caitlyn reached out and plucked an errant straw from those black waves. Connor looked at her, his brows lifting.

"We wouldn't want your lady friend to think you've been doing something you shouldn't, would we?" she asked with bite, holding the straw aloft before dropping it disdainfully to the floor. Connor's eyes hardened as he took in her anger.

" 'Tis you I'm thinking of," he said grimly. "Do you want it all over the county that I've been making love to you in the hayloft in the middle of the afternoon? 'Tis your name that will suffer, not mine."

"Do you think I care?" Her voice was fierce. Connor glared at her, his temper ignited by hers.

"You're a fool, Caitlyn O'Malley, and I'm a bigger one. But I've no time to discuss it now." With that he surged to his feet. For a moment he stood, hands balled on hips, glaring down at her as she sat at his feet. He looked very formidable as he towered over her, every inch the virile male from the still-rumpled waves of his black hair to the toes of his scuffed boots. Beneath scowling black brows, those aqua eyes impaled her. Even the set of his chin spelled trouble. But Caitlyn was not intimidated. She scowled back at him mutinously, her arms crossed over her breasts. What had been wonderful only moments before was soured now by anger.

"What are you standing around for? Go on! Meredith is waiting for you." Venom dripped from every word. Connor's eyes glinted dangerously at her for a moment. Then he took a deep breath. Reaching down, he caught her arms and hauled her unceremoniously to her feet. Without the protection of her hands holding it in place, her bodice gaped indecently away from her chest.

"Let go of me! What do you think you're doing?" She tried to catch the falling bodice and at the same time shake free of him as he whipped her around. The neckline slipped off her shoulders and drooped dangerously near her waist. Only her thin shift saved her from utter indecency. Furious, mortified, Caitlyn yanked the bodice of her dress back into place and held it there with both hands.

"Buttoning your dress," he said through his teeth. He steadied her in front of him, her back to him. His hands on her shoulders gave her a hard warning squeeze before he let go and started to do up the back of her dress.

"Had lots of practice acting as lady's maid, have you?" she asked nastily as he completed the job in record time. As soon as his fingers had secured the last button, she jerked away and turned to glare at him. He crossed his arms over his chest and gave her scowl for scowl. Then something in her expression caused his anger to fade.

"I told you, you've no reason to be jealous of Meredith. What is — or is not — between her and me has nothing to do with you. Nothing at all."

"I'll not share, Connor. I warn you." He looked at her silently for a moment, his eyes narrowing, his lips compressed.

"You're taking entirely too much for granted, Caitlyn O'Malley. If you're bound and determined to be my mistress, you should know that a mistress has no rights over a man at all. Only a wife has that."

"Then I'll be your wife." As soon as she spat the words at him, Caitlyn knew that it was exactly what she wanted: to be his wife.

" 'Tis considered proper to wait till you're asked." Connor's voice was dry.

"Then I'm not proper!"

"Amen to that!"

They glared at each other, neither giving an inch. Then Connor shook his head impatiently. "I've no more time to bandy words with you now," he said, turning away.

"Mustn't keep dear Meredith waiting, must we?" she shot after him as he headed toward the ladder.

He swung back to look at her. "Damn it, Caitlyn . . ." he began furiously. Then, with a muttered curse, he stepped onto the ladder and disappeared from sight. Caitlyn stamped her foot. If there had been anything close at hand to throw, it would have gone sailing through the air. But straw made a poor projectile. Impotently she stamped her foot again, mentally castigating Connor d'Arcy as three kinds of sons of the devil.

XXVI

She saw Connor again at dinner. Though she stuck her nose in the air and studiously ignored him, she was secretly relieved to see him there. She had been more than half afraid that he had escorted Mrs. Congreve home, or perhaps disappeared to Dublin again, as he had done after their last aborted lovemaking session. But there he sat, at the head of the table as always, scowling and silent to be sure, but present. Caitlyn felt a great surge of relief.

It was hard to ignore a man when one was serving his dinner. Banned from helping with the cooking by popular request (by all four d'Arcys, who had been unanimously appalled at the various lumps and foreign objects which her unskilled hand had caused to appear in their food when Mrs. McFee had undertaken to teach her the rudiments of cookery), Caitlyn had been drafted into helping dish up the food. Now she made her way around the table, dropping big ladles full of boiled potatoes onto china plates. A scowl was fixed on her face, and the potatoes landed with an audible plop and considerable splattering.

Although Connor, as the head of the household, was usually served first, she had deliberately left him for last as a small measure of revenge. Her lip curled with satisfaction when she discovered that, by the time she held the ladle poised over his plate, there were only three smallish potatoes left.

"Here, now, watch what you're about!" Mrs. McFee scolded sharply as the meager helping nearly missed Connor's plate altogether. Connor sent Caitlyn a sharp look, his expression as ill-tempered as her own, but said naught. The misshapen potatoes landed scant millimeters from the edge of his plate, where they teetered precariously for a moment before skittering toward the slices of mutton at the center.

"Caitlyn's out of temper," Cormac observed teasingly, his hazel eyes glinting at her as she set the empty bowl on the sideboard with a clatter before taking her seat.

She scowled at him across the table by way of a reply. He grinned and opened his mouth to say something further. A surprised look came over his face.

"Here, what are you kicking me for?" he demanded, sounding amazed as he looked over at Liam.

"Just shut up, idiot," Liam advised him in an undertone. Connor's attention was directed momentarily at Rory, who was asking him something about the sheep and earning for his pains a growled reply. Liam seized the chance afforded by his older brother's averted eyes to cast a significant look at Connor, then at Caitlyn. Caitlyn, who didn't miss the telling look or its import, flushed. Cormac's eyes widened as he looked from Connor's tight expression to Caitlyn's nearly identical one.

"What are you two whispering about?" Connor's question had an edge to it. Pinned by his oldest brother's inimical stare, Cormac hesitated, then shrugged and returned his attention to his plate. Liam too was silent. Connor looked at the two for a moment, then focused on his own food. No one spoke except to say things like "Please pass the bread" for the rest of the meal.

They were just getting up from the table when Mrs. McFee appeared, a pair of soft kid driving gloves in her hand.

"I found these in the parlor, yer lordship. The lidy left them." She directed a triumphant look at Caitlyn as she spoke. Caitlyn's eyes narrowed, and she stiffened. Because she was in the act of rising, this caused her chair to slide back with a clatter and nearly overturn. Liam caught it in the nick of time, returning it to an upright position. Caitlyn scarcely noticed. Her eyes, burning with outrage, were fixed on Connor. He was looking at Mrs. McFee and holding out his hand for the gloves.

"Thank you." He accepted them with no perceptible change of expression and carried them with him as he left the room.

Caitlyn's face grew fiercer by degrees as she helped Mrs. McFee clear the table and wash the dishes. Of course Connor would return the hussy's gloves to her, and nothing loath either! He might even do it that very evening — and spend the night in the simpering tart's bed while he was about it! That was certainly what she had been angling for when she had left her gloves in the parlor. Not for a moment did Caitlyn believe that the gloves had been left accidentally. It was a deliberate ploy, and Connor was going to fall for it! Not that "fall for it" was the right expression. Connor was a grown man, and no fool, and would know full well what Mrs. Congreve was about. He would not be tricked into doing anything he did not wish to do. Which left Caitlyn with the uncomfortable conclusion that if he ended up in Mrs. Congreve's bed, then it was precisely where he wished to be. And she very much feared he did wish it!

Mrs. McFee's silent gloating did nothing to improve Caitlyn's temper. Although the woman had no idea of the extent of the relationship between Caitlyn and her employer, she would have had to be deaf, dumb, and blind to have remained unaware of the tension that had sizzled lately whenever the two had occupied the same room. Mrs. McFee had been convinced from the beginning of Caitlyn's designs on Connor. Now that it seem her worst predictions might be coming true, she was doing everything she could to spite what she perceived as Caitlyn's evil plans. Which was why, on this particular night, the washing up took fully twice as long as it ordinarily did. Mrs. McFee meant to hold Caitlyn in the kitchen just as long as she possibly could.

Finally Caitlyn had had enough of the sly looks and turtle-paced work. She slammed down the plate she was drying with a clatter. "If you want to go ahead home, I'll finish this myself," she said with tart meaning.

"Eh, it's not for you to tell me when to go home. I work for the family, I do, and his lordship in particular. Not some little upstart twit who's no better than she should be."

Caitlyn stared at Mrs. McFee for a long moment, mentally struggling to control the urge to hurl the plate she had just finished drying straight at that dour face. Mrs. McFee's insults and dire predictions of the evils her presence would bring down upon all those at Donoughmore were more or less constant, and Caitlyn was in large measure used to them. The woman had never liked her. Her quarrel this night was with Connor, not with Mrs. McFee. The plate that she itched to throw should rightly be hurled at Connor's head, not at the serving woman's.

"You can finish up yourself, then. I've more important matters to see to."

"Hummph! 'Tis precious little help you are, any road," Mrs. McFee said to Caitlyn's departing back. Caitlyn gritted her teeth and willed herself to ignore the woman. In a few moments Mrs. McFee would wind her scarf around her head and set off for her home in the village, not to return until morning. In the meantime, Caitlyn would vent her anger on its proper recipient. The very idea of Connor exchanging with Mrs. Congreve the kind of intimacies she had shared with him in the loft made her burn with fury. He was a pig, and she meant to tell him so!

The d'Arcys generally congregated in the parlor after supper. Rory and Cormac were there, seated in faded gold brocade armchairs that ordinarily graced either side of the huge fireplace. At the moment, the chairs had been dragged forward so that they faced each other in front of the fire with a table between them. A chessboard had been set up on the table, and Cormac and Rory were arguing in spirited but subdued voices over the game they were engaged in. Connor was missing, as was Liam.

"Where's Connor?" Caitlyn demanded, belligerence rising as she considered the possibility that he might have already left to return Mrs. Congreve's gloves.

"Believe me, you're not wanting to see Connor just now," Rory said positively, looking around. "Just since dinner, he's quarreled with both Cormac and me, and right now he's upstairs tearing a strip off Liam for some error he made in the books."

"Oh, he is, is he?" Caitlyn turned on her heel, meaning to march straight up the stairs to confront Connor in the office. If he was spoiling for a fight, why, he'd get one!

"He's in a foul temper. I'd leave him be if I were you," Rory called after her.

"Being that she's the cause of it, I'd say she

deserves it if he lets fly at her," she heard Cormac say to Rory.

The door to the office was slightly ajar. Without even the courtesy of knocking, Caitlyn thrust it open to find Liam seated behind the desk and Connor leaning over him, pointing something out in the ledger opened on the desk before them. Both of them looked up at her unceremonious entrance. Liam's inquiring expression quickly changed to one of trepidation, while Connor's frown deepened into blackest foreboding.

"I want to talk to you," she said to Connor, completely ignoring Liam.

"I've no time for children's tantrums now. As you can see, I'm busy." Connor's tone was as harsh as his words.

Children's tantrums, eh? How dared he! "So I'm back to being a child, am I? You're naught but a hypocrite, Connor d'Arcy, and that's the truth of it!"

"And you're the most persistent little wench it has ever been my misfortune to run across!" Connor roared. He straightened and took a single hasty step out from behind the chair before stopping with a visible effort, his hands clenching at his sides.

"Coward!" She faced him with fists on hips and eyes flashing. At her insult his eyes flamed at her.

"Jezebel!"

"Jezebel?" Outraged, Caitlyn could barely get the echo out. "Jezebel!"

"Aye, Jezebel! Only a Jezebel would go on tormenting a man who clearly wants no part of her!"

"Conn — !" Alarmed, Liam tried to intervene, an appalled expression on his face.

"So you want no part of me, do you? That's a lie, and you know it, Connor d'Arcy! You do want me, you do! You're just too much of a coward to take what you want!"

"If you will continually throw yourself at my head —"

"Throw myself at your head?"

"Conn!" Liam was sounding increasingly outraged. He looked rather desperately from his brother to Caitlyn and back again, only to be ignored.

"What would you call it? 'I love you, Connor; I want you to kiss me, Connor,' " he mimicked cruelly, his eyes blazing into hers. "If you heard another female say that to a man, wouldn't you consider that she was throwing herself at his head?"

At this low blow, uttered in front of Liam, whose reddening ears bespoke his discomfort, Caitlyn was so furious she could not speak for a full minute. If during that time her anger was joined by an aching hurt that grew more painful with every passing heartbeat, she refused to let anyone see it, or to acknowledge it to herself.

"You bastard!" When she could talk again, she threw the words at him like stones. His eyes flared back at her.

"You go too far, Connor!" Liam said urgently, jumping to his feet and laying a hand on his brother's arm.

"The hell I do!" Connor's voice was savage; his eyes never left Caitlyn's whitening face. Then something about her expression made his mouth tighten, and he looked down at his brother's restraining hand with violence in his eyes.

"Get out of my way," he said through his teeth. When Liam made no move to do so, Connor shook him off and strode past him and Caitlyn and out the door. Caitlyn and Liam stared at each other as the sound of Connor's boots on the stairs echoed about their heads.

"He didn't mean it, you know," Liam said uncomfortably after a moment's charged silence.

"Did he not?" Caitlyn's voice was hard.

"You know he didn't. You know Conn." Liam shook his head and walked toward her to pat her shoulder in clumsy consolation. "He flares up, says things he doesn't mean, and then 'tis all forgotten."

"Not by me," Caitlyn said with icy conviction. "Not this time. Your precious brother can go to the devil for all I care!"

XXVII

It was sometime after midnight. Caitlyn could not sleep, though the rest of the household was long abed. Connor had ridden off on Fharannain after stomping out of the office and had not yet returned. She was becoming more and more convinced that he would not return that night. Visions of him in Meredith Congreve's bed made her grit her teeth. Huddled in a quilt before the banked fire in the kitchen, she waited, her expression increasingly grim. But it was beginning to look as though his comeuppance would have to wait for another day. At the thought, she wanted to gnash her teeth.

For hours the scene in the study had replayed itself in her mind. How dared he say such things to her, and before Liam too! Besides being a coward and a hypocrite, he was a cad! And she meant to tell him so before he was very much older! And if it turned out that he had spent the night making love to Meredith Congreve, she might well split his skull for him and be done with conversation altogether!

Honesty forced her to admit that there was a small grain of truth to his accusation. Some people might just possibly construe her actions as those of a woman throwing herself at his head.

She had done most of the running, and she had asked him to kiss her (though not the first time!) and told him she loved him — but what else could one do with a man like Connor, who through some misguided sense of honor refused to follow his — and her — natural inclinations? She was an innocent, but she knew enough to know that the fire that blazed between them when they touched was no ordinary thing. Even when they were merely within sight of each other, the tension that vibrated between them was a tangible entity. But of course, contrary and pigheaded as always, Connor had to take it into his head that something so elemental and strong was also sinful. She had no such reservations. Despite his faults, which were many and varied and which she could spend the better part of the night enumerating, she loved him. She meant to have him — if she didn't murder him first! Jezebel, indeed!

She was in the middle of a great yawn when she heard a footstep on the stoop. Swallowing the yawn, she stood up, hugging the quilt around herself and looking expectantly at the door. From the parlor, the clock struck two. A fine time to be getting home, to be sure!

Clearly he was trying to be quiet as he stepped into the kitchen, closing the door behind him. Just as clearly he did not at first see her in the shadows beside the fire. Droplets of water shone on the blue-black waves of his hair and clung to his buff superfine coat. It must have started to rain only in the past few minutes, because he was not wet through, merely sprinkled with rain-drops. The banked orange glow of the fire illuminated him faintly, casting a huge black shadow over the wall behind him. Broad-shouldered and tall, his hard-muscled legs clad in close-fitting black breeches and riding boots, he was formidable-looking enough without the added specter of the huge black shadow at his back. But as he came into the room, stepping softly with the object she guessed of not rousing the house, there was something furtive, almost guilty about his movements. Obviously, wherever he had been, he was wishful of no witnesses to his return home. At the realization, Caitlyn's chilled-over temper began to heat anew. For where else could he have been, acting so ashamed, but with his mistress?

" 'Tis a fine time for you to be coming in!" she said shrilly, taking a step forward and fixing him with blazing eyes.

In the act of walking toward the fire to warm himself, Connor started and stopped dead, head swiveling around as his eyes found her. A chagrined look descended briefly over his face before he tried to cover it up with anger.

"What the devil are you doing up?" he growled. His brows came together in a devilish scowl, and his eyes narrowed as they met her accusing gaze. " 'Tis gone two in the morning."

"I'm well aware of the time, thank you. Where have you been?"

He resumed his walk toward the fire. Holding out his hands to the glowing peat, he said over his shoulder, " 'Tis none of your business, miss."

"Is it not?" Incensed, she took a couple of steps toward him, until less than two feet separated them. The accusation emerged of its own volition: "Have you been with that woman?"

He took a long look at her, standing there wrapped ridiculously in a faded blue quilt with just the ruffled neck and hem of her plain white nightgown showing above and below it, bare of foot, her long hair streaming unconfined down her back, her blue eyes blazing at him while she quivered with temper. He sighed. "Stop bedeviling me, lass, and take yourself off to bed. I'm in no kind of mood for your tantrums."

"Tantrums! And I suppose your displays of temper are righteous anger?"

He sighed again as if mightily ill-used and turned away from the fire. "If you won't go to bed, I will. Good night."

"Come back here! I've a great many things to say to you!"

"No doubt you have, but I'm not inclined to listen. You'll have to hold your spleen till morning."

"I . . ." Their conversation was conducted in hissed whispers as she followed him down the hall to the stairs. She broke off abruptly as she watched him lift a foot to the bottom stair, miss his mark, and stagger sideways until his shoulder made contact with the wall and he was able to right himself.

"Connor . . ." she began, frowning. He was

never clumsy. But before she could finish speaking he had found his balance and was climbing the stairs, his movements a trifle slow and deliberate, but adequate. She followed him almost to the door of his room, watching his every move. Was it possible that he was injured, or ill? There was that in his movements that spoke of a carefully orchestrated striving for normalcy. And now that she thought of it, his speech had been somewhat forced too, though nothing that she would have picked up on, had she not been witness to that uncharacteristic stagger.

"Connor, wait!" she said urgently as he entered his chamber without a backward look. When it seemed he would shut the door in her face, she shoved against it. To her surprise it flew open to bang against the wall as he went staggering back.

"Shhh!" he said, leaning against the wall. She could just see the bright gleam of his eyes through the darkness. From his chamber on the other side of the hall, Cormac's resounding snores continued undisturbed, and Caitlyn was sufficiently acquainted with the sleep habits of the rest of the d'Arcys not to fear waking them with anything less than a bloodcurdling scream. Still, just to make sure, she gently closed the door, then turned to lean against it for a moment, looking at Connor consideringly. He didn't move.

"What is wrong with you?" she demanded, stalking toward him.

"Sweet Jesus, how you plague a man! Will you let me be?" But he didn't move away from the wall, and Caitlyn's alarm grew.

"Are you hurt? Are you ill?" She reached up to lay a hand against his cheek to test for fever, her eyes running worriedly over his tall frame, only to have him catch her wrist and pull her soft palm away from his face.

"I'm neither hurt nor ill, and I want to go to bed. Now will you please go away?" Still holding her wrist, he bent his head toward her menacingly as he spoke. For the first time Caitlyn got a whiff of his breath. Whiskey! Standing stock-still, she stared up at him through the darkness. She was close enough so that her quilt brushed his legs. At the expression on her face, he looked suddenly conscious, and lifted his head a little.

"Connor d'Arcy, have you been drinking?"

His eyes shifted. "A wee dram or two with Father Patrick . . ."

"You have been!"

". . . does not constitute drinking, precisely, to my mind."

"You're drunk!"

"I am not drunk. Merely tired. And if you will excuse me, I would like to go to bed. Alone, if you please."

At this barb Caitlyn's anger, forgotten in the face of her worry, flared up again. She pulled her wrist from his hold and stood glaring at him.

"You're a swine!"

"So you've said before. But at least I'm not enough of a swine to dishonor a young girl living under my roof under my protection. Not yet,

305

anyway." This last, muttered under his breath, was obviously not meant for her ears.

"Connor . . ." He was still leaning against the wall. As she spoke he straightened up to stand away from it, not quite steadily on the balls of his feet. His hands were on his neckcloth, untying it and pulling it away from his neck.

"Go to bed, Caitlyn. Please." He dropped the neckcloth on the floor and leaned against the wall again. He seemed so exhausted, or so much the worse for drink, that despite her anger she felt another twinge of worry for him.

"Do you need help getting undressed?" This was asked with all the exasperated concern of a mother for an erring but beloved child.

He laughed, the sound tinged with irony. "Help getting undressed is just what I don't need. Go to bed."

"But —"

"I called you a Jezebel, remember? You should be furious at me, not asking if I need help."

"I was furious." Remembering her grievance, Caitlyn scowled at him. "I am furious. Besides being a swine and three kinds of sons of a dog, you are a loathsome, no-good, dirty spawn of the devil! You —"

"I didn't mean it," he said, stopping her in mid-tirade. Something in the look in those aqua eyes made her heart speed up.

"Connor . . ."

"Go to bed."

"If you think to get away with that meager

excuse for an apology . . . !"

"I'll do better in the morning. Go to bed."

"I don't want to go to bed." The soft protest narrowed his eyes. He straightened up from the wall again, put his hands on her shoulders, and tried to turn her about. She resisted, reaching up to close her fingers around his wrists. With neither of her hands to hold it in place, the quilt slid to the floor, leaving her clad only in her thin nightgown. His eyes slid down her body, seemingly drawn like a magnet despite every effort of will, before returning to her face.

"Caitlyn, for God's sake. . . ." There was an almost desperate look in his eyes as she moved her fingertips lightly against the bronzed skin of his wrists.

"I want my apology now." Her voice was husky.

"I apologize. There, are you satisfied? Now go to bed."

Caitlyn sniffed. "Do you think that little bit will make up for the dreadful things you said to me?"

"I've forgotten what I did say. I was rather angry at the time. Tomorrow I promise you a handsome apology, but —"

"I remember," she said, interrupting him ruthlessly. Her fingers continued to move over the hard bones of his wrists, and her eyes lifted to his. He was frowning down at her, his brows a forbidding V. But there was a restless glitter in his eyes, and he made no further move to turn her out of the room.

"Besides calling me a Jezebel, you accused me of throwing myself at your head."

"Don't you?" The dry murmur was robbed of its sting by the way his eyes watched the movement of her lips, as if mesmerized.

She shook her head. His eyes rose to meet hers, and she felt as if she would be trapped forever in those aqua depths.

"Just because I said, 'I love you, Connor . . .' " Her voice was a soft caress; her eyes never left his. At her words, tiny embers at the backs of his eyes began to blaze. Her hands left his wrists to slide up his arms, her fingers moving lightly over the still-damp cloth of his coat until they touched his shoulders. Then, slowly, her eyes still locked with his, her hands slid behind his neck.

". . . and 'I want you to kiss me, Connor' " — she tilted her face toward his while his hands automatically came to rest on her waist — ". . . that doesn't constitute throwing myself at your head. Precisely."

"Not precisely." His voice was unsteady. Beneath her fingers, the skin of his neck felt as if it would burst into flames at any instant.

"If I really wanted to throw myself at your head," she continued, her words scarcely above a whisper, "I would . . ." She hesitated, her tongue coming out to moisten her lower lip. The blaze in his eyes exploded into a full-fledged conflagration.

"What?" The single word was hoarse.

She smiled at him, tremulously, going up on tiptoe to touch her lips to his.

"Do this," she said against his mouth. And kissed him.

XXVIII

For a moment only he accepted her caress without moving. Then he made a sound like a gasp, as though he were dying, his arms slid around her waist to clamp her to him, and he was bending her back over his arm, kissing her as if he were starving for the taste of her mouth. Dizzy, Caitlyn clung to him, opening her mouth to his endlessly, reveling even in the sharp taste of whiskey which previously she had despised, returning his kiss with a fiery need of her own. Her arms wrapped around his neck as if she would never let him go; her tongue touched his, stroked it, and he shuddered. Then he scooped her up in his arms and took two rather unsteady strides toward the bed. Whether or not he meant to deposit her romantically thereupon, Caitlyn never discovered. What actually happened was that the tipsy creature tripped over his own feet and sent them both sprawling across the feather mattress. The ropes supporting it creaked loudly in protest against such unexpected violence.

Caitlyn lay on her back where she had fallen, staring up at the shadowed ceiling, shocked at the abrupt change in the course of events. After a moment she turned her head, to find Connor lying on his side beside her, one arm pillowing his head as he rested with what appeared to be utter contentment amidst the quilts their fall had disordered. His eyes glinted at her; his mouth curled in the merest hint of a smile.

"Fools and children," he muttered obscurely and flopped onto his back, smiling with rueful charm up at the ceiling.

"Fools and children indeed," she said, sitting up and glaring down at him. "If by that you mean that the good Lord in His wisdom is protecting me from you, then I would say that He uses some peculiar methods. First that shameless hussy, and now what I would guess is a good bit more than 'a wee dram or two' of whiskey! You're drunk as a lord, Connor d'Arcy, and 'tis certainly not the work of the angels! More likely an agent of the devil!"

"Now there you're out. Unless the devil's agent has disguised himself as Father Patrick, who tips a mean decanter. Father Patrick is surely one of the Lord's angels. He says you're a fleshly temptation I must overcome for the good of my immortal soul." Connor's eyes shifted from the ceiling to focus on her face. "Get thee behind me, Satan," he said to her and chuckled.

"There's no getting any sense out of you tonight, I can see." Caitlyn said with disgust, getting off the bed and eyeing him with disfavor. His long legs were sprawled out in front of him, the heels of his boots touching the floor, his torso to the thighs supported by the bed. His arms were flung up over his head, and the remains of a whimsical smile curved his mouth. She had seen Connor in many moods, but never drunk, and despite her annoyance she had to smile at him. With his black hair escaping from its ribbon to curl around his head, his eyes twinkling, and that crooked smile lending a boyish charm to his lean, dark face, he looked so handsome that he took her breath away. He also looked very young suddenly, younger even than she. All this time he had looked after her. For once it was he who needed looking after.

"What are you doing?" He lifted his head from the mattress as she straddled one booted foot, her back to him. The effort was apparently too much for him, because his head fell back almost immediately.

"Taking off your boots. You don't want to sleep in them, do you?"

"I have before. 'Tisn't fatal."

"Well, you won't tonight. I don't think." This last was muttered under her breath as the boot in question resisted considerable tugging. At last she managed to wrest it off, freeing the foot and calf from the long slide of scuffed leather. While that foot flexed its toes, still in the confines of a white stocking, she went to work on the other. By the time she had managed to liberate the second foot, she was panting. Picking up the boots and setting them neatly side by side next to the bed, she turned back to look at him. He was watching her, but with the room cloaked in shadowy darkness relieved only slightly by the

rays from the sickly moon that floated just outside the window, it was impossible for her to read
his expression. She had the impression that he
was making a concerted effort to regain control
of his whiskey-befuddled senses.

"Can you sit up?"

His eyes shifted from their contemplation of
her person to the ceiling. "Now why would I
want to do a fool thing like that?"

"Because you're still wearing your coat, and
'tis damp. If you can sit up, it'll make getting it
off you that much easier."

"And if I cannot?"

"Then I'll cut it off you. There are scissors in
the office."

"That you won't!" He had a partiality for the
coat, she knew.

"Then sit up. Here, take my hands." She
reached out to him. After a moment's hesitation
he grasped her hands. Tugging with all her
might, and with considerable groaning from him,
she just managed to pull him into an upright
position on the edge of the bed. He groaned
again, slumping forward, elbows on knees, his
head immediately sinking into the cradle of his
hands.

"My skull feels as if there's a legion of little
people inside, all going at it with hammers."

"Serves you right," she said without sympathy,
easing the coat from his shoulders. "Strong drink
is its own punishment."

He grunted, lifting his head from his hands so

that he could look at her. "You're no comfort at all."

"Here, raise your arm. It seems you've had comfort enough tonight already. Is that not why men drink?"

Obediently lifting his arms while she stripped the coat from him, he favored her with a wry glance. "I know not why other men drink. I only know what prompts me to it."

"And what is that?" Keeping a steadying hand on his shoulder, she dropped the damp coat on the floor. His shirt felt damp, too, beneath her hand. As automatically as a mother would do for a child, she fell to undoing the buttons.

A crooked smile twisted his mouth. "You, my beauteous Caitlyn. Naught but you."

Her hands stilled and she stared down at him. "I see no reason why I should be held responsible for your foolishness."

"Do you not?" His hands lifted to catch hers where they had stilled on his shirtfront. As his hands closed over hers, pressing them closer to his body, she became aware for the first time of her knuckles brushing the hair-roughened bare chest beneath the shirt. Her breath caught.

"You are a constant temptation and torment to me, my lass, and I wrestle the devil for the salvation of my soul whenever you are within my view. Looking at you, with your soft white skin and rosy mouth, with your slanted eyes and tangles of silky hair black as the darkest midnight, to say nothing of curves that would tempt a saint,

I am almost persuaded to agree with Father Patrick that you are devil-sent. Except that I know something of you that Father Patrick does not: I know your soul, and it is purely angel."

Connor was not a man given to flowery speeches, and yet those were the most beautiful, eloquently spoken words she had ever heard. They touched her heart, moved her to tears.

"Oh, Connor, I do love you so," she whispered, barely managing to get the words out past the constriction in her throat. For a long moment they stared at each other, he seated on the edge of the bed, clad in half-fastened shirt, snug black breeches, and stockinged feet, she standing over him, her hands clenched beneath his and pressed to his heart.

"Ah, well, they do say the road to hell is paved with good intentions," he muttered and pulled her down into his arms.

Caitlyn went with a little mewling sound, curling up on his lap and wrapping her arms around his neck, lifting her face to his even as his mouth lowered to hers. This time he initiated the kiss, his mouth soft and gentle at first and then hardening into fierce passion as she opened her lips to him, giving herself without reserve. She kissed him with all the love that she had bottled inside her for all those affectionless years, and with a woman's passion too; kissed him until she forgot where she was, forgot everything but him and her need of him, her love for him. When his hand found her breast, closed gently over it with only the thin cloth of the loose nightgown between his flesh and hers, she clung to him more tightly, trembling, while his hand fondled her, seeking out and stroking the quivering nipples until they thrust urgently against the confining gown, aching to be free.

"Caitlyn. . . ." He lifted his hand from her breasts. Her eyes opened to meet his, and she could see the battle that raged inside him. Her misguided warrior still sought to fight the urges of his own body and soul. . . .

"I love you," she whispered. His eyes clouded, and his mouth descended on hers again, hungry and yearning. His hand found the buttons at the neck of her nightgown, undid them with unsteady fingers, and slid inside. Caitlyn's heart speeded up until she thought the pounding of it would beat her to death from within. His fingers slid down over her collarbone, over the first swelling curves of her breast to close over the whole, cupping and squeezing and fondling until she was squirming on his lap, delirious with need, on fire for more and still not knowing exactly what more was.

"Let's have this off you, then." He was standing up with her, putting her down so that her bare feet touched the cold planks of the floor. For an instant he steadied her against him while her swimming senses sought to orient themselves. Vaguely she was aware of him bending to catch the edge of her gown. Then he was lifting it, pulling it over her head and throwing it aside to land in a crumpled white heap scarcely visible amidst the shadows that shifted along the floor. She was left to stand revealed before him, gloriously naked and trembling, while his eyes moved over her, an expression in their strange light depths that weakened her knees and shook her heart.

Her hair fell over her shoulder to tumble below her waist, partially veiling her from him. He lifted an unsteady hand to tuck the errant strands behind her ears, smoothing the silken tresses so that they flowed down her back. Still he stared, transfixed by the sight of her, long-limbed and slender, pale as the moonbeams that probed the ceiling, as elusively lovely as the night itself. Her masses of raven hair exactly matched the silky triangle between her thighs. Her high, firm breasts with their pink puckered nipples gleamed in the darkness. Her eyes gleamed too, soft and mysterious and liquid with love as they searched his face. He stared at her, and she turned her head, pressing her lips to his hand where it rested against her ear. He trembled, reaching for her, pulling her close. Her eyes fluttered shut and she wrapped her arms around his neck.

His breathing was fast and shallow as he lowered her to the bed, coming down hard on top of her, their feet still touching the floor. His much greater weight sank her deep into the mattress, her thighs parting of their own accord as the cradle of his hips wedged between them, the wool of his breeches abrasive against her softness as

317

he pressed himself to her. The sensation made her head spin. She caught her breath in a little gasp, and he pressed himself against her again. She could feel the heat and hardness of him, swollen taut and straining against his breeches, rubbing against that part of her that was open and vulnerable and aching for him. She cried out, moving wildly beneath him, her breasts lifting to thrust mindlessly against his linen-covered chest. He was still fully dressed, and it drove her wild. She wanted him naked, as naked as she. Her hands tangled in his shirt front, yanked. The shirt popped open with the sound of flying buttons. She stroked his chest, ran her fingers over the muscles, touched the flat nipples.

"Oh, Jesus, this goes too fast." His mutter was thick and tormented as he bent his head to her sobbing mouth, kissing her with a wild, shaking passion while his hand slid between their bodies to fumble with the buttons on his breeches. At last he was free, pressing hotly against her. Caitlyn cried out, the sound muffled by his mouth, her back arching and her nails clawing at his chest as he probed at her softness, found the hot liquid center of her that throbbed and burned and ached for his possession. With a sudden, uncontrolled thrust he breached the opening, entering a scant inch or so before catching himself and holding back. She could feel the trembling in his arms as he fought to exert control.

"Connor. . . ." His name was not more than

a breath whispered into his mouth. Her hands clenched on his shoulders; her body moved urgently beneath his.

"I don't — I don't want to hurt you." The words were so hoarse they were scarcely intelligible. Then, as if the thought were father to the deed, he groaned and thrust, hitting her maidenhead and thrusting again, convulsively.

She cried out, eyes flying open, caught by surprise by the pain she had not expected as he broke through the barrier to embed himself deep inside her. Sweat beaded his brow, dripped from his jaw. His eyes when he opened them at her cry were hot and glazed. He saw her pain, saw her teeth sink deep into her lower lip, and shuddered before he clutched her close again, his eyes closing as he arched over her.

"I'm sorry. Sorry," he whispered against her neck. But he did not stop, could not stop, thrusting into her again and again with a hungry violence that was everything she had ever suspected the darker side of a man's passion might be. With any other man, she would have been terrified, horrified, repulsed, and disgusted. She would have fought, screaming and clawing, to be free of this pain that threatened to rend her in two. But this was Connor, her love. He would never harm her willingly. This savage act was what men did to women all over the world, from the beginning of time. He had warned her against it, tried to protect her from it. It was the price she had to pay for belonging to him, and she was willing to pay that price. For his pleasure, she would endure pain. Twining her arms around his neck, she shut her eyes, gritted her teeth, and held him while he sweated and pumped and groaned. By the time he was through, spending himself with a wild cry before collapsing, panting, on top of her, the pain had subsided to a dull ache, and she was able to perceive that she would be able to endure this man-woman thing again. For Connor.

Only for Connor.

XXIX

He lay atop her for long moments afterward while she stroked the sweat-damp back of his neck beneath his hair. Finally he lifted his head to look at her. She met that look and smiled at him rather tremulously. He groaned again, shutting his eyes as if the sight of her pained him. Then he withdrew and rolled off her, taking her with him so that she was cuddled against his side, her head on his shoulder, her arm resting on his hard waist just above the opened breeches.

"I should be shot," he said through his teeth, his eyes still shut. His arm tightened around her. Looking up at that lean, dark face, Caitlyn saw his eyes open to slant a look down at her. "I'm sorry, so damned sorry. I just couldn't stop, or exert any control at all. I never meant to hurt you."

"It . . . it wasn't that bad. Really." He looked so angry that she had to reassure him. Timidly she stroked his chest. The hairs felt rough beneath her fingertips, the skin itself warm and moist. His jaw clenched.

"It wasn't that bad," he echoed with a grim laugh. Sitting up, he leaned over her, shirt gaping open, to drop a kiss on her mouth. "My own, I have bedded dozens, no, scores of women in my

321

life. And not one of them has ever said to me afterward, 'It wasn't that bad.' "

"Well, you see, I love you, so that likely makes a difference." She said this so seriously that he could only stare down at her for a dumbfounded moment. Then he laughed again, the sound as grim as before.

"What will it take to make you believe that making love is usually very pleasurable, I wonder? For the woman as well as the man. God forgive me, I should never have taken you at all, but since I did I should have used more care. I've been wanting you so much, for so long. . . . I forgot you're scarcely more than a child. I can only blame the whiskey — and you. You went to my head as much as the spirits did. But I should have gone slow, should have prepared you. The next time, I promise you, it won't hurt. You'll like it. 'Twill get better and better, until you're begging me to make love to you at every opportunity and I'm fighting you off night and day till I'm worn to a bone."

She looked up at him with doubt plain in her eyes, clearly unconvinced.

"I promise," he said. She eyed him. He studied her for a moment, then got to his feet.

"What are you doing?"

"Getting undressed."

"Oh." She sounded as uneasy as she felt.

He suited the action to the words, shrugging out of the shirt she had all but destroyed and sliding out of his breeches. Sitting up and wrap-

322

ping the uppermost quilt around herself, Caitlyn watched with some trepidation and more interest as he sat down on the chair in the corner of the room to roll off his stockings. Though the shifting darkness obscured much detail, she could see that he was magnificently made. Broad shoulders and muscular arms tapered down into a wide chest roughened by a V of dark, curling hair before tapering still more into narrow hips and a muscle-ridged abdomen. Her eyes skimmed over the next part of him, the man part, to move down the long, powerful legs. She was not yet ready to fully see what had caused her pain. He was standing again, naked now, moving toward her. A stray moonbeam glinted off his eyes. He was watching her watch him, and the knowledge made her blush.

"Up with you."

She looked up at him wide-eyed as he held out a hand to her, clearly meaning her to get off the bed. Seeing that he was waiting patiently for her to comply, she scrambled to her feet, still clutching the quilt. Suddenly, inexplicably, she felt horribly shy. But he didn't look at her, busying himself with smoothing the bed and turning down the covers with easy efficiency. Outside, the rain had begun to come down in earnest, the droplets making a rhythmic patter against the roof. The fire in his room had gone out hours before, and it was cold as well as dark. Caitlyn curled her bare toes against the chill of the floor, wondering uneasily if his actions were her cue to take herself back to her own room. Never having been with a man before, she was not exactly certain what one did afterward.

"Climb in." Plumping the last pillow, he turned to her, his eyes sharp as they moved over her face. Caitlyn looked from him to the cozily turned-down bed uncertainly.

"Do we . . . go to sleep together now?"

He actually smiled.

"I thought we'd talk a bit first, if you have no objections."

"N-no." She still sounded doubtful, but he was naked and had to be freezing, and after all, as he himself had said, he'd done this many times before and had to know all the ins and outs by now. But he didn't look the least bit sleepy, he actually looked far more alert than he had when he'd first come home, and as for her, well, she didn't think she'd sleep at all this night. There was too much to think about, too much to weigh and consider. Still, he was waiting patiently for her to do as he'd asked, so she did. When she was settled on her back, lying rather stiffly with her head on the pillow, he reached down to tug gently at the quilt in which she was still wrapped.

"I don't think you'll need this."

For a moment Caitlyn instinctively clutched the quilt close, looking up at him with the tiniest trace of wariness in her eyes, but the slight smile on that handsome, beloved face soothed her fear. After all, he was naked too, and this was Connor, whom she would trust with her life, or her body.

Besides, they had finished the man-woman thing for the night, and she knew that never in any other way would he cause her hurt. So she allowed him to pull the quilt from her without protest. The instant it left her, however, she was tucking her feet down under the bed covers and pulling them over herself, not quite ready to lie naked under his inspection. Then he was climbing into bed beside her, his long, hard length sliding down next to her nakedness. His weight made a hollow in the center of the bed, toward which she inexorably rolled. Before they were settled comfortably, her head was on his shoulder and his arm was wrapped around her. His fingers toyed with her hair, stroking and smoothing it over her bare shoulders, which were just visible above the piled bed covers.

"Are you warm and comfortable now?" He had turned his head so that he could look at her. She nodded. If truth were told, she was so cozy and comfortable cuddled next to his warm bare skin that she could have stayed as she was forever. She found she quite liked this part of the man-woman thing, and thought it would be much easier to endure the next time since she knew this period of wonderful closeness would follow.

"Do you hurt anywhere?"

Caitlyn thought about that. The place between her legs was a bit sore, but she did not really hurt. She shook her head.

"You're not frightened of me?"

As that question penetrated, she came up on

an elbow to look at him in surprise.

"Of course not."

"I just wondered."

"Well, I'm not. I know you would never hurt me deliberately, so you can just quit feeling so guilty. Believe me, I quite understand about the man-woman thing. I know that men get an inordinate amount of enjoyment out of it, and I'm quite prepared to put up with it to please you."

"Thank you," he said gravely, then made a sound as if he were choking. Frowning down at him, Caitlyn saw that he was struggling not to laugh.

"And just what's so funny?" she demanded, indignant. He grinned then, broadly, and tweaked her nose while she drew back with a frown.

"Nothing at all, my own. You are so sweet and so absurd you make me feel like the biggest rogue unhung. If anyone else had done what I just did to you, I'd be putting a bullet in his brain about now. Since I'd really prefer not to do away with myself, I'll do the next best thing: I'll make an honest woman of you."

"What?" Caitlyn blinked at him, not quite certain she'd heard him correctly. She sat up suddenly, clutching the quilts to her so that she was covered to the armpits and he was bared to the hips.

"How do you feel about being a Countess?" His smile was crooked and charming as he folded his hands to rest them behind his head. She had a vague impression of flexing male muscles and dark body hair, but she was far more interested in his words than his appearance at the moment. He grinned up at her, his eyes gleaming as they moved over her face. He seemed very carefree suddenly, and happy, as if a burden he'd carried for a long time had been lifted from his shoulders.

"Are you asking me to marry you?" Excitement shot through her, sparkled in her eyes, colored her voice. His grin broadened.

"I must be. What do you say?"

"Oh, Connor!" She threw herself on top of him, hugging him with such force that he all but choked. But he hugged her back, kissing the side of her neck, before rolling with her so that her back was on the bed and he was looming over her. The coverlets were a wild tangle between and around them.

"I take it that means yes."

"Yes!"

"Then since we are affianced, I need have no more scruples and can properly teach you all you need to know about lovemaking." The suggestion of a teasing smile curled the corners of his mouth.

"Oh, yes. . . . You mean there's more?" Her response shifted from joyous excitement to dismay as the import of his words sank in. She regarded him with a slight frown of consternation. He grinned.

"You are a constant source of delight to me, my own. Yes, there's more. You've hardly got started."

"Oh."

His grin widened until he was actually laughing. "Don't sound so worried. Lovemaking's fun. You'll like it, once you get used to it. You have my word on it."

His laughter ignited sparks of suspicion in her. "Connor d'Arcy, are you making sport of me?"

"Now what makes you think that?"

"A man can't — you can't — we already m-made love for tonight."

"Very true." His tone was solemn, but something about his eyes made her suspect that he was still laughing at her. "That being the case, you've nothing to worry about, have you? Instead, you might want to think about giving me a kiss to seal our betrothal. Kissing is nothing to be frightened of, is it? You've always seemed particularly partial to it."

Caitlyn looked at the handsome face with its aquiline nose and strong jaw, at the hard mouth that was quirked just now with humor and something that looked very much like tenderness, at the aqua eyes that were so strangely light against his dark skin, and felt a rush of love so strong that it shook her. He was hers, now and forever. She would be his wife. Connor's wife. It was her dream, and it was coming true. She lifted a hand to stroke his bristly jaw.

"I'll be a good wife to you," she said, as if she were making a vow. The laughter in his eyes died and he looked down at her intently. Then, without waiting for her to kiss him, he was lowering his head and taking her mouth, kissing her hard and fiercely as if to seal his possession of her, and her arms were going around his neck and she was kissing him back. With an inarticulate murmur of impatience at the quilts that bound them both, he freed her from them with scarcely a pause in the intense possession of her mouth. Then he gathered her to him, skin to skin under the sheltering warmth of the covers.

He held her close, pressing soft little kisses from one corner of her lips to the other, nibbling at her lips, tantalizing her with quick forays of his tongue against her teeth until she was clutching his hair and holding his head still so that she could kiss him properly, as he had taught her. Then he kissed her deep and long until her head was spinning and that now-familiar tightening was coiling deep in her belly and her breasts were swelling and aching against his chest despite what she now knew the ending to this feeling would be. But for the rest of the night she was safe, safe to indulge these wonderful sensations without fear of the ultimate man-woman thing, safe to revel in possessing Connor and having him possess her.

When his mouth left hers to trail kisses across her cheek to her ear, which he nuzzled and tickled with his tongue, she smiled and squirmed and returned the compliment with his ear until he was shaking his head to free it from her encroaching tongue and then moving his head lower, out of her reach. With infinite delicacy he traced a path across her throat, all the while holding her close against his body so that the heat and size and strength of him intoxicated her every cell. She clung closer as he ran his tongue around the hollow of her throat, pressing his mouth to the fast-beating pulse and resting there for a moment while his hands stroked down her spine to her buttocks and then stroked them too, with silky soft caresses over the rounded flesh. The quickening inside her speeded up, and Caitlyn remembered how wonderful it had been, how magical were the feelings Connor had aroused in her body before he had hurt her so unexpectedly in the end. But since she no longer had to fear that, not tonight, she could relax and enjoy the caresses, enjoy the feelings that he was stirring in her, enjoy him. For months now she had longed to have him kiss her, longed to have him make her his, longed to kiss him and make him hers. Now, tonight, with the worst behind her, was her chance to do what she wanted.

Her hands began to explore him, timidly at first and then with increasing boldness, stroking over his chest, discovering the crisp silky mat of hairs over steely muscles for herself, rubbing his nipples until she found to her surprise that they came erect just like her own, trailing her fingers down over his taut belly to find his belly button and meander inside. He permitted her exploration to this point, busying himself with watching her face while she familiarized herself with his body. But then, when she dared a glance down at the man part of him that seemed suddenly much larger and more menacing than it had when she had started, he flipped her onto her back with a shake of his head.

"Turnabout's fair play, you know," he said in a voice that might almost have been teasing except for the husky note that lay under the words. Caitlyn looked up at him wide-eyed, watching as he bent to kiss her, but when his mouth was on hers, her head started to swim and all rational thought fled beneath the intoxicating onslaught of his mouth. His hands slid from behind her to cup her breasts, caress them, hold them captive for his mouth. Her eyes fluttered shut as he slid his lips over the swelling globes, kissing them so thoroughly that by the time he had taken the first nipple in his mouth, she was gasping at the wonder of it. With the part of her mind that was still capable of coherent thought, she wondered how these preliminaries could give her body such pleasure when the ultimate man-woman thing caused pain, but then his hand slid down between her thighs and she ceased thinking at all.

"Part your legs for me, cuilin," he whispered in her ear when she, partly out of instinct and partly out of fear, kept her legs resolutely clamped together in the teeth of that seeking hand. His fingers moved persuasively in the silken nest at the apex of her thighs as he spoke, insinuating themselves deeper, touching and stroking until with a gasp and a sigh she obeyed him, spreading her legs convulsively until he had full access to the deepest secrets of her body. Her eyes were closed tight, her body and legs stiff, her nails digging deep into his shoulders as his fingers searched, explored, and at last found her. They slid inside that place where he had hurt her so short a time before, and she gasped. But not with pain. There was no pain, just a glorious aching that cried out for relief.

She was on the verge of something momentous when he withdrew his hand.

"Gently now," he soothed her as she protested with a wild little whimper. And then, while her senses were disordered with longing and her defenses were breached, he quickly positioned himself over her and slid that man part of him inside her. A single thrust and he was buried deep, stretching her to the ultimate, impaling her. Shocked at the suddenness of it, the unexpectedness of it, she cried out, stiffening with remembered pain. Her eyes flew open. He was enormous again, hot and throbbing, and it wasn't possible, he could not . . .

"Connor!" His name was both protest and plea. Her eyes were huge kerry blue pools as they met his. He was holding himself above her, his weight braced on his elbows, their flesh joined as before. But this time there was a keen awareness of her in his eyes. The corners of his mouth curved tenderly as he looked down at her, slender and naked beneath him, her mouth swollen with his kisses, her midnight hair flowing in silken tangles across the white pillow.

"I thought you loved me." His voice had grown

noticeably huskier.

"I d-do, you know I do, but . . ."

"Then won't you trust me, cuilin?"

Caitlyn stared up at him, near despairing. She did trust him, she did; he wouldn't lie to her deliberately, but perhaps he didn't know how it was for a woman. Or maybe she wasn't like most women. Maybe she was too small to accommodate him; maybe — maybe she was deformed. She didn't know; all she was sure of was that it had hurt before and she feared the pain again. But he was already inside her without causing her pain, and perhaps, just perhaps, this time it wouldn't hurt quite so much. Besides, this was the price she had to pay for belonging to Connor. If she had to endure this five times a night for the rest of her life, she would.

"All right." She closed her eyes tightly, her teeth sinking into her lower lip in unconscious preparation for the onslaught she feared. Her body went rigid. Her hands slid down from his shoulders to close over the hard muscles of his upper arms, her nails digging in. He looked down at her for just a moment, his eyes both rueful and tender. Then, without moving the lower part of his body more than he had to, he bent his head to press a trio of tiny sweet kisses on her mouth.

Her eyes fluttered open, and she looked up at him in some trepidation.

"I'm ready. Go a-ahead," she said bravely. His lips curved up in that tender almost-smile again, and again he bent to kiss her. That part of him that was joined to her burned and throbbed and seemed to swell deep inside her, but he was not moving and there was no pain.

"Don't look so terrified, my own. I'll do no more than this, I swear. Unless and until you want me to. So you can feel quite safe. This isn't hurting, is it?"

"N-no."

"Well, then. Just relax."

Beneath her clutching hands she could feel the tremors that coursed through the arms that held his weight from her, while in his eyes she could see the effort that restraint was costing him. Her heart swelled with love for him. She told him so, and in response he grimaced and sweat popped out on his brow. Still he didn't move his lower body, just kept himself deep inside her, letting her get used to the feel of him. That part of him that so thoroughly possessed her might swell and burn of its own volition, but he was not using it against her, and she realized that he would not. Gradually her body relaxed.

This motionless possession was not really unpleasant, she discovered now that her fear of imminent pain was in abeyance. His hips, cradled between her legs, pressed tightly against her. Heat and friction combined to create a tension within her that wound gradually tighter, sending tiny quivers of awareness along her nerve endings. The tips of her breasts just brushed the soft mat of hair on his chest. Her nipples hardened, puckered, ached. Against her belly she could feel the warmth of his flat abdomen. The soft insides of her legs were abraded by his rock-hard thighs. Beneath her hands the muscles of his arms were like iron. Almost unconsciously, Caitlyn's fingers flexed, began stroking the corded sinews.

He moved then, just a little, and a shaft of pure heat shot through her. She caught her breath, feeling her muscles clench around him. Her heartbeat quickened. Something of what she was feeling must have shown in her eyes, because he gritted his teeth. Caitlyn tensed. Still he made no move to find his own pleasure.

This time, he would do nothing to hurt her. He had given her his word, and Connor was ever a man of honor. Caitlyn's fear disappeared, and in its wake a myriad of sensations began to riot through her body. She drew in a soft breath, shifting her legs. The resulting stab of pleasure caught her by surprise. Her eyes widened, and she moved again, experimentally. His eyes were almost shut now, his breathing harsh. Sweat trickled from his forehead to slide down over his jaw. Still he held himself rigidly still, and Caitlyn knew that he was leaving it up to her to learn about lovemaking as she would. Reassured, she tilted her hips so that they pressed closer against him, then pulled them back again. Her eyes fluttered down, opened again to find that Connor's face was reddening. Tremors racked his arms, coursed through his legs. The knowledge that she could affect him so profoundly was intoxicating. She moved again, with more confidence this time, lifting her hips off the mattress to press boldly into him before allowing them to fall back. At the exquisite friction, she caught her breath.

"Sweet Jesus." He groaned the words under his breath. Caitlyn saw his eyes were closed and his lips grimly compressed. He looked as if he were in physical pain, and she knew a momentary flicker of concern. Then she realized that she was the cause of his discomfort, that he wanted her so badly that he was hurting with the effort of holding back, and a warm glow began to build inside her. Growing ever bolder, she moved her hips again, undulating back and forth, sliding up and down on him while her hands traced a slow path up his arms to lock around his neck.

"Oh, my God." Abruptly his face clenched and he started to withdraw. Caitlyn clutched his neck, her legs instinctively wrapping around his back to hold him in place.

"Caitlyn, let go. Let go, or I won't be responsible. . . ." He was sweating so profusely now that his back was slippery with it. He sounded desperate; his eyes as they opened to meet hers looked glazed. At this visible evidence of the strength of his passion she felt a tremor start deep within her loins. It spiraled outward, infusing her skin with heat.

"I'm not afraid any more. Teach me the rest." The words, barely whispered, had a galvanizing effect on him. He stiffened, shivered, then collapsed on top of her, his arms going around her, straining her to him so tightly that she could scarcely breathe. He buried his face in the hollow between her shoulder and neck, muttering endearments that she couldn't decipher against her skin. His hips ground into her violently, pumping in and out with a driving intensity that caught her up and sent her whirling away with it. She clung to him, back arching, face pressed to his shoulder while pinwheels of wildfire exploded through her veins. It lasted just a few minutes, but when it was over her whole world had changed.

"Oh, my." Those were the first words that she said when she came back to earth. They were breathed close to his ear and surprised a laugh out of him. He still lay atop her, gasping for air as was she, but this made him raise his head and look at her.

"Oh, my?" he echoed, lifting his brows quizzically.

She smiled and said nothing more.

"Well, at least that beats 'It wasn't so bad.' I think."

She smiled again, demurely, and lowered her eyes.

"Caitlyn . . ."

She flicked a look up at him.

"If you don't expand on that fascinating statement, I'm likely to wrap my hands around your lovely neck."

She grinned then, hugely, like a cat who has

just enjoyed a large saucer of cream.

"I think I'm going to quite like being your mistress. I knew I would."

He frowned. "You're not my mistress. You're my affianced wife, which is a very different thing. We're to be wed. There's no shame attached to you for what we did."

Caitlyn studied him. To be his wife was her every dream come true, and yet she found she could not trap him into matrimony. She loved him too much. "You don't have to wed me, you know, Connor. Not because of this."

"What, and would you have me endanger my immortal soul?" He grinned suddenly, lightheartedly. "I'll not spend eternity roasting in Hellfire over the likes of you, you devil's imp. I'd much rather spend eternity making love to my lawful wife, and not a whiff of sin about it. So will you or nill you, we'll be wed as soon as I can arrange it. And I don't want to hear further argument on the subject."

He was more than half teasing, but Caitlyn detected a note of seriousness beneath the banter. He had not said he loved her, yet Caitlyn was content. If he did not love her as she loved him, why, he would. She would see to that. As she had told him earlier, she meant to be a very good wife. Then she bethought herself of something.

"I'll have no more of your visits to Meredith Congreve," she told him, scowling.

He looked down at her for a moment, then

grinned, all traces of seriousness vanishing. "But, Caitlyn, I thought you knew: all married men keep a mistress on the side. 'Tis quite the thing. And after all, 'tis you who'll be my wife."

She doubled up her fist and hit him squarely in the shoulder, though she knew he was but teasing her.

"I'll not share, Connor," she told him with mock fierceness. He bent his head to kiss her.

"Nor will I, my own, so I'll be warned if you will. When we wed, we cleave to one another, for life."

"I'd never play you false, Connor."

"Aye, I know it. You haven't a false bone in your luscious little body." He rolled off her and got to his feet in a single lithe movement, moving purposefully away in the darkness. She rose on an elbow to watch him.

"What are you doing?" she asked, mystified, when he came back with a towel.

"I'm going to give you a bed bath, button you into your nightgown, and carry you back to your own bed. Until we're wed, you'll sleep alone. I'll have no scandal about this marriage."

"Marriage," she said dreamily, hitching herself up so that her back rested against the headboard, oblivious of her nakedness. He came around the bed and bent over her, wiping her face with the towel, which he had wetted at the washstand in the corner. She spluttered, and when he would have proceeded with the impromptu bath, she snatched the towel from his hands.

"I can bathe myself, thank you. If you'll turn your back."

"Still shy, after all we've shared? I'll have you cured of that before the ink's dry on the marriage register."

"We're not wed yet," she said positively. "And some things require privacy. Now turn your back."

He met her adamant look for a moment, grinned suddenly, and capitulated, handing over the towel and turning his back.

"You'll lead me quite a dance, won't you? But be warned: I mean to be master in my own house."

"And I mean to be mistress in mine." Caitlyn spent just an instant admiring his powerful back and taut round buttocks, then turned her attention to her impromptu bath. She washed her body quickly but thoroughly, getting out of bed to wet the towel again after a peremptory order to Connor not to turn around. When at last he did, with her permission, she was clad in her nightgown, demurely doing up the buttons. His eyes moved over her, and he grinned.

"That is the most seductive garment I've ever seen in my life. The last time you wore it in here 'twas all I could do to keep from tearing it from your body."

"I fear you're easily seduced."

He chuckled. "Not easily. Just seduced. And very thoroughly, too."

He was still naked, unashamedly so, and her

eyes feasted on that tall, powerful body. The darkness of the room still veiled most details, which she regretted. Now that she no longer feared it, she was quite eager to see the man-thing. He reached for his breeches, stepped into them.

"Why are you getting dressed?"

"I told you I meant to carry you up to bed. I do."

"Don't be daft. There's no need. I can walk perfectly well."

He finished fastening the breeches, then scooped her up in his arms despite her protests. "You'll have to learn that I mean to be obeyed. I'll not have a headstrong wife who's forever arguing with me."

"And I'll not have a domineering bully for a husband. Connor, put me down. Do you hear?"

"I hear, my own. What a bossy little wench you are! Take care that I don't take a stick to your hide once we're wed."

"You can try. Though you may end up going to your heavenly reward rather sooner that you expected."

He chuckled at that and bent his head to kiss her, right there in the hall. Caitlyn wound her arms around his neck and kissed him back with abandon. So involved was she that she never heard the door open at the end of the hall. The first she knew of Cormac's presence was when she looked up and saw him. He was standing in the doorway of his room, leaning against the jamb, a quilt hitched around his waist and a dumbfounded expression on his face. Realizing how they must look, with her in her nightgown caught high in Connor's arms, cradled against his bare chest while he kissed the life out of her, Caitlyn blushed. Connor, who had become aware of Cormac's presence a scant moment before she had, scowled at his brother over the top of Caitlyn's head as Cormac's brows lifted in an uncanny replica of the quizzical expression Connor wore at times.

"We're to be wed," Connor said abruptly to his brother, without putting Caitlyn down. Surprise crossed Cormac's face, to be followed by another expression that was difficult to decipher.

"Thank the lord. Maybe then things will get back to normal around here," Cormac said, then turned back to his room and closed the door. Connor and Caitlyn both stared at that closed door for a moment. Then Connor grinned and started walking again.

"Do you think he thinks my disposition will improve once I'm wed?"

"It could hardly get worse. You've been a bear lately."

"I've been fighting a battle with my conscience. 'Tis glad I am to report that my conscience lost."

"Oh, did it now?"

His teasing made her smile and press a kiss to the side of his face. His stubbled cheek felt rough beneath her lips. She discovered she quite liked the sensation, so she put out her tongue to test it further. At that provocation he stopped where he was, halfway up the narrow stairs to the attic, and kissed her so thoroughly that she thought she might suffocate if she didn't die of bliss first.

"A week," he said as he entered her room moments later and laid her down on the bed, deftly whisking the covers from beneath her and tucking them over her. "It shouldn't take more."

"What shouldn't take more?" Her mind was barely functioning after that dazzling kiss.

"To arrange the wedding. Of course, I'll have to explain to Father Patrick that, far from getting behind me, Satan climbed all over me before having her wicked way with me, but. . . ."

Caitlyn swatted him. He grinned, planted a lengthy kiss on her mouth, and turned to go. As he started for the door she remembered something.

"Connor."

"Hmm?" He looked back at her.

"What does 'cuilin' mean?"

"Mickeen told me you didn't know your Gaelic. Ah, well, that's something else you'll soon learn. It means you, my lass with the beautiful hair." With a crooked smile he took himself off.

Caitlyn was still smiling foolishly as she fell asleep.

XXX

Connor informed his brothers of his future plans before Caitlyn came downstairs the next morning. No doubt aware of his brothers' bawdy humor, he had hoped to spare her the full brunt of their comments, but her own excitement had gotten her up early. When she appeared, a buzz went up from the younger d'Arcys. Not having expected such a reception, she hesitated in the dining room door, eyes wide as they moved from one grinning male face to another. She had taken extra pains with her appearance that morning, brushing her hair out until it snapped with electricity and shone like Connor's best boots. Then she had secured the silky cloud at her nape with a blue velvet ribbon that exactly matched the shade of her favorite woolen gown. The dress was a trifle faded (she hadn't had a new one in some months, and washing was hard on clothes) but the color became her, and the sleeves of her shift were a pristine white. She had dressed with Connor in mind, but now, under his brothers' eyes, she feared the care she had taken must be painfully obvious. Blushing at their loudly vocal enthusiasm, she looked rather beseechingly at Connor. He rose and came to

344

meet her, looking a trifle self-conscious himself as he smiled into her eyes.

"That's enough from the lot of you," he said, taking Caitlyn's hand in his and surveying his brothers with half-amused, half-rueful eyes.

" 'Tisn't every day we stand to gain a sister, Conn. Especially such a one as Caitlyn," Rory pointed out, grinning.

"Should we rise at her entrance henceforth, do you think? Of course we should! Why, she's going to be a Countess!" Cormac nudged Rory and got to his feet, sweeping Caitlyn an elegant, if grossly exaggerated, bow. Rory rose and bowed too. Only Liam remained seated, looking faintly disgusted at his brothers' foolery.

"Let the lass eat in peace," Connor said, drawing her to the table and pulling out her chair for her. Caitlyn sat, put out of countenance almost as much by Connor's unprecedented courtesies as by the others' raillery but warmed by them too. The men sat when she did. A bowl of steaming porridge was slapped down before her by a stony-faced but mercifully silent Mrs. McFee. Caitlyn could only assume from the woman's unvoiced disapproval that Connor had paved the way for her there as well. Probably he had threatened Mrs. McFee with instant dismissal if she did not keep a still tongue in her head, whatever her feelings about her employer's betrothal.

"When's the wedding to be?" Cormac inquired as they all watched Caitlyn lift a spoonful of porridge to her mouth. They had finished their breakfast, and Caitlyn realized that she was the focus of their attention. She swallowed the porridge with an effort.

"As soon as can be arranged. I've sent Mickeen with a message for Father Patrick."

Liam frowned. "Is that wise?"

Connor shrugged. "Wise or not, we'll be wed in the Church. Secretly, of course, but no less binding for all that. The official ceremony will be performed by a magistrate in Dublin. We'll be spending a se'ennight there afterward."

"Oh, a honeymoon!" Cormac nodded wisely, while Caitlyn, in the act of swallowing another bite of porridge, looked at Connor in a considering way. He had not consulted her wishes in formulating any of these plans, but she was too happy to be betrothed to him to remind him that she might have her own ideas about how she wished to be wed. Thinking the matter over, she decided that as long as it was Connor she was marrying, she didn't care a fig about the details. After the wedding would be soon enough for her to remind him that she didn't mean to be an entirely conformable wife.

Liam cleared his throat. His blue eyes met Caitlyn's fleetingly before moving on to Connor. "That should give us sufficient time to remove ourselves to other quarters. By the time you're ready to set up housekeeping here, we'll be out of your way."

Four pairs of eyes riveted on Liam. Caitlyn put down her spoon, frowning.

"What are you blathering about, brother?" Connor echoed her unspoken sentiments as he stared at Liam with as much amazement as the rest of them.

"Now that you're to be married, you'll be wanting to be private with Caitlyn. We can easily find lodgings in the village, or —"

"Don't be daft, Liam," Connor interrupted. "We're a family. We stay together."

"You haven't thought. You'll be setting up your nursery —"

"Nursery or not, this is your home."

"We're grown men now, Connor. You don't have to feel yourself responsible for us any longer."

"Are you saying that you don't want to stay on here after the wedding?" An ominous note had crept into Connor's voice. His eyes were fixed on Liam.

"I want you to stay, Liam, please," Caitlyn intervened hastily. His brothers were close to Connor's heart. He would be deeply hurt if anything came between them. She didn't want it to be herself. "You — all of you — are the only family I've ever known. I love you all. If you feel you can't live here with me as Connor's wife, why — why, then I won't marry him at all."

The disparate sets of eyes that had been fixed on Liam swung to Caitlyn. She met them with a determined lift of her chin.

"And then Connor will be mad as hell and take it out on us, and our lives won't be worth living," Cormac summed up with a dawning grin. "Take a damper, Liam. Conn don't want us to leave, and Caitlyn don't either. If Conn can learn to dandle babies on his knee, then we can too. 'Twon't be so bad."

"Are you sure, Conn? We won't take it amiss if you want to be private with your bride, you know." Liam looked searchingly at his brother.

"I hope to have a fair amount of privacy with my bride with the three of you in residence. Unless you're planning to take up sleeping in my chamber sometime in the near future?"

Cormac and Rory grinned at this sally, and after a moment Liam did too. Caitlyn felt a blush suffuse her cheeks at their masculine amusement, which she somehow felt was at her expense.

"If he wants to kiss her he can always tell us to go to the devil, you know." Rory, seeing her blush, grinned wickedly at her. Caitlyn, feeling more at ease now that one of them was treating her with the same teasing affection that they had always shown her, wrinkled her nose at him and returned her attention to her porridge, which had gone cold. After a single taste, she put her spoon back in the bowl and pushed it aside. Mrs. McFee removed it with an audible sniff.

"She's done now, Conn. You can give it to her." Cormac had noticed Caitlyn's rejection of what was left of her breakfast.

Connor frowned at his youngest brother. "This is one of those occasions on which a small amount of privacy might be called for," he said, while his eyes found Caitlyn's, who was looking at him enquiringly. His lips never moved, but she had the impression that he was smiling into her eyes with great tenderness. Mesmerized, she couldn't look away.

"Lord, Conn, don't go all syrupy on us. 'Tis scary to see a strong man brought so low, it truly is." Cormac pushed his chair away from the table, sounding hugely entertained. Connor spared a quelling look for his brother. Rory and Liam grinned, but stood up too.

"Methinks he's already gotten the knack of telling us to go to the devil," Rory said. Liam nodded agreement, and the three of them withdrew.

Connor stood up. He was wearing the rough-textured brown riding coat he often wore about the farm, over a white collarless shirt and buff breeches. It occurred to Caitlyn, watching him as he reached into the pocket of his coat, that he looked younger and more carefree than she had ever seen him. The tiny lines about his eyes had eased and his mouth was relaxed, almost smiling even in repose. Broad-shouldered and lithe and overwhelmingly handsome, he came around the table toward her, holding something in his hand.

"Close your eyes and hold out your hand," he said gruffly as he reached her side. Caitlyn did as he asked. He took her hand in his and slid something over her finger. At the feel of cool metal sliding toward her knuckle, she could contain herself no longer. Her eyes popped open, then grew huge as she saw the ring he was pushing down her finger. It was an enormous golden topaz set in a sunburst of diamonds each as large as the nail on her little finger. Dazzled, she stared at it.

" 'Tis the betrothal ring of the Earls of Iveagh," he said. "My mother wore it last."

"Oh, Connor," she breathed. Then she came out of her chair to throw herself at him, her arms going around his neck. At the unexpected impact he staggered a pace backward, his hands closing on her waist to steady her. She pressed fervent kisses to his smooth-shaven jaw, hugging him fiercely. He smiled at her excitement and stroked the long tail of hair that fell down her back. Finally his arms slid around her waist to pull her close. She lifted her face for his kiss.

At the first touch of his lips she trembled, and rose up on tiptoe to press wantonly against the hard length of him. He kissed her long and thoroughly, tilting her back against his arm so that her head rested on his shoulder. When at last Connor put her from him, her knees were shaking and her breathing was uneven. A bright gleam came into his eyes as he looked down at her, and then he placed another quick kiss on her swollen lips. Held a little away from him, she gazed up into those light eyes and whispered, "I love you." His hands tightened on her arms, his head lowered, and she thought he was going to kiss her again.

The sound of clapping brought her head whipping around and made Connor lift his. At the sight of his three brothers applauding wildly from the doorway, Connor scowled, while she turned fiery red. Then Caitlyn had to smile at the grinning trio she had come to consider almost as much her brothers as his.

"Next time I'll make sure to shut the door," Connor growled, but his frown had quickly changed to an almost sheepish grin.

"We thought you might want witnesses at some later date, in case she decides to throw you over for a better prospect," Rory told him. Liam came forward to offer Connor his hand.

"We wish you happy, Conn," Liam said as Connor took his brother's hand, pumped it, grinned, and then enfolded him in a big bear hug. Rory and Cormac added their voices, hands, and hugs to Liam's. Then Caitlyn came in for her share of hugs and kisses from the brothers, who cast sly looks at Connor as they held her close and pressed their lips to her cheeks. Connor laughed and threatened, and by the time they let her go, Caitlyn was both rosy and teary-eyed with happiness.

Hours later, Caitlyn was still in a happy daze. As she performed the hated indoor chores that fell to her lot because the steadily falling rain precluded the work in the garden with which she had meant to occupy the day, she took every chance to admire her ring. It was so heavy that her hand felt as if it were weighted down, and it was a trifle loose. Her greatest fear was that it might fall off and she might lose it. The thought made her shudder, and she vowed to tell Connor to have it made smaller as soon as he could. Even Mrs. McFee's scowling silence could not pierce the fog of her happiness. With the solid proof of his ring on her finger, Caitlyn could really allow herself to believe in what had happened: Connor had asked her to be his wife.

Connor too was extraordinarily cheerful as he went about the myriad tasks that were necessary to the running of a sheep farm. When, later that afternoon, he discovered that Rory had inadvertently left the lid off a barrel of seed intended for spring planting and that a pair of hungry sheep had tipped it over, destroying what they did not eat, Connor's only response was a shrug and a philosophical "Well, now, these things will happen." Rory, slack-jawed with relief, called down blessings on the power of love. This did earn him a sharp look from his brother, but a wry grin followed on its heels.

"You should be thanking your lucky stars, halfling," Connor told him. "Were I in my right mind, I'd be taking the cost of that seed out of your hide."

" 'Tis Caitlyn I'm thanking, and not stars at all," Rory retorted, smiling back at his brother.

Cormac, who was dosing sheep and had witnessed the entire incident, shook his head. "When will it wear off, I wonder? Caitlyn is bound to put you out of temper sooner or later, and my guess would be sooner. She always does."

"Yes, but now that we're to be wed, I'm on my best behavior. I've already promised Connor that I'll make him a good wife." Caitlyn had come hurrying into the barn in time to respond. Though she'd left countless chores behind in the house, she'd decided to let Mrs. McFee and her women's work go hang. If truth were told, she'd been unable to stay away from Connor a moment longer and had been in search of him when she'd heard his voice. Shaking out the shawl she held over her head to protect it from the rain, she smiled saucily at Connor.

"An obedient wife," he corrected with mock sternness, tapping her nose as she came to stand beside him.

Rory and Cormac hooted in unison. Caitlyn, standing in the circle of Connor's arm, stuck out her tongue at them.

"Conn, if you can stomach that impudent minx to wife, you're a braver man than I."

"I don't think that's ever been in doubt." Connor's response was dry. Rory grinned at Cormac's comeuppance.

"Well, this blissfulness is all very well, my children, but I've four more sheep down with this bloody flux. Conn, do you suppose I could borrow your intended?"

"For what purpose?"

"To sit on their heads," Caitlyn answered for Cormac, sighing as she detached herself from Connor's side to join Cormac in the stall and demonstrate by straddling the head of one thrown, squalling beast. "I'm just the right weight, you understand. Though as a Countess-to-be, I fear I may be demeaning myself."

"Ah, but there are Countesses and there are Countesses," Rory said, leaning over the side of the stall and watching the proceedings. "And you are definitely going to be one of the other kind of Countesses."

"Well, you —" Caitlyn started to retort spiritedly, only to be interrupted by Mickeen's hailing of Connor.

"Yer lordship! Yer lordship, there you be! I . . ." Mickeen was panting, shaking raindrops from his grizzled head as he hurried toward where Connor leaned over the stall beside Rory.

"Did you bear my message to Father Patrick, Mickeen?"

"Aye, I did, and —"

"And I decided to come myself to see you, Connor." The deep voice of a stranger interrupted. Situated as she was, Caitlyn could not see him, but she guessed straightaway that this must be the much-discussed Father Patrick. From Mickeen's miserable expression, she surmised that the priest's presence was what had caused Mickeen to rush in search of Connor. He had wanted to sound a warning.

"Good day, Father." Rory's voice was deferential, even a trifle nervous. Caitlyn gathered that this priest had considerable influence with the d'Arcys.

"Good day to you, Rory. Connor, in light of

our recent conversations, I was a wee bit surprised at the message Mickeen brought me. He said you're desiring to be wed? Within the week?"

"Aye."

"To the lass we were discussing?"

Though Caitlyn could not see Father Patrick, she could see Connor. He grinned wickedly. "Oh, aye, Father."

"Before I can agree to officiate at such a ceremony, I must make as sure as I can that it is in the best interests of both parties. I would talk with the lass, if you've no objection."

At that precise moment, Caitlyn was sitting precariously astride the head of a struggling sheep. As she realized that she was about to meet the priest who had counseled Connor to rid himself of her at all cost, Caitlyn lost her concentration. As a result, the sheep with a mighty toss of its head managed to send her sailing over its ears. Her head banged into the side of the stall, and she saw stars as she fell backward to land smack on her backside in muddy straw. It was all she could do to bite back an oath. Cormac, who had spilled half the sticky medicine down his shirtfront because of her fall, was not as fortunate. He swore roundly, condemning the sheep for its obstinacy and Caitlyn for her clumsiness in the same breath. Then, remembering the presence of the priest, he colored to his ears.

"Sorry, Father," he muttered, shamefaced. Connor had opened the stall and crossed to

Caitlyn's side. Concern darkened his eyes as he crouched in front of her, brushing errant strands of hair out of her face with gentle hands.

"Are you hurt?" he asked low-voiced, his fingers touching the reddened spot on her forehead where she had made contact with the wall.

"N-not really." Caitlyn shook her head, then smiled at him. "Just my dignity."

"In future find someone else to sit on the blasted sheep," Connor said over his shoulder to Cormac as he helped Caitlyn to her feet. Though she was recovering by the second, she was content to lean against Connor's side, supported by his arm. At least she was until she looked up to meet the grave gray eyes of the portly, balding priest, who was regarding them steadily through the stall's open door.

"I've no doubt at all that you are Caitlyn. Hello, child. I hope your head does not ache too badly. I am Father Patrick."

"Hello, Father. Connor . . . has spoken of you more than once." Caitlyn pulled away from Connor's side, self-conscious with the priest's weighing eyes upon her. She smoothed back her hair with both hands, wishing that she had tied it up with more of an eye to security than beauty that morning. Even before her disastrous encounter with the sheep, it had been escaping from its ribbon. Now it was entirely loose, flowing freely over her shoulders and down her back. Her ribbon, she surmised, was somewhere in the stall with Cormac and the sheep. Her dress was a mess too, stained with earth and straw where she had fallen. Her hands were not entirely clean either, since they had broken her fall. But there was nothing she could do about her appearance, so she straightened her spine and walked toward the priest with the dignity of a Duchess. Connor was close behind her.

"Would you care to come and talk with me a little, child? I must confess to some misgivings about this start of Connor's, but perhaps you could set them at ease. And I could use a spot of tea."

"If you'll come into the house, Father, I'll be happy to talk with you and get your tea too." Caitlyn looked steadily back at the priest, chin high. Whether he approved or not, she was going to marry Connor. She would climb over the carcass of the devil himself to get to Connor if she had to. But she sensed that Connor valued the priest's opinion, so she very much wanted him to approve.

Father Patrick smiled and tucked her hand in his arm. At closer range, Caitlyn saw he was a homely man, with a round red face and undistinguished features not aided by the fringe of gray hair that ringed his head just above his ears. His height rivaled Connor's, but his girth was such that in the flowing black robe he appeared immense.

"We'd be pleased if you'd stay to supper, Father, and then perhaps afterward —" Connor had fallen into step at Caitlyn's other side. The priest's nod interrupted him.

"Aye, Connor, and I thank you for the invitation. But for now, we've no need of you, have we, lassie? We'll do far better on our own."

Connor frowned and glanced at Caitlyn, who was dwarfed between him and the oversize priest. "Caitlyn . . . ?"

" 'Tis all right, Connor. I'll be perfectly fine with Father Patrick, I'm sure."

"Sure, and the lass has more sense than you. I'm beginning to think that you led me a mite astray in this instance." Father Patrick gave Connor a mildly censorious look over Caitlyn's head.

Connor met Father Patrick's look with wry comprehension. "Perhaps I did, Father, perhaps I did. Whenever I came to you, it was because I had been sorely tried."

This exchange made absolutely no sense to Caitlyn, but as she looked from one to the other she could tell that Connor and the priest understood each other perfectly.

"Go on about your business now and let me talk to the lassie in peace. We'll have a quiet tea and get to know one another."

Still Connor hesitated, looking at Caitlyn.

"I'll be fine," she said again. "Truly."

He nodded, then turned on his heel, heading back toward where Rory was helping Cormac dose the shrilly bleating sheep.

"So tell me, child," Father Patrick began as they walked through the drizzle toward the house, "are you of the Church?"

By the time they had taken tea together and the family had finished supper, Father Patrick knew most of what there was to know about Caitlyn (though some things she had edited, for after all, there was no reason to paint herself blacker than was strictly necessary). At the conclusion of the meal, as the men rose to leave the table and Caitlyn started to help Mrs. McFee clear away, Father Patrick motioned her over to where he stood with Connor and placed a beefy hand on her shoulder.

"I'll tell you both that I set out this morning thinking to save you, Connor, from a disastrous marriage. I've since changed my mind entirely. From what I've seen, it may be the making of you. 'Tis time your thoughts turned toward the future instead of the past. This is as sweet and loving a lassie as you'll find across the breadth of Ireland, and 'tis obvious you have a care for her. She'll make you a fine wife, give you bonny sons. You have my blessing, the pair of you."

"Thank you, Father," Caitlyn said, pleased and surprised at the praise, which she privately considered to be largely undeserved.

"You're a man of rare discernment, Father," Connor said with a grin, slipping his arm around Caitlyn and pulling her close against his side. "How soon can we be wed?"

"A month," Father Patrick said firmly and cocked an admonishing eye at Connor. "And by the bye I would have a private word with you, if I may, my son."

Connor winced. "The last time you called me your son, the penance made my knees ache for a week."

"I've a feeling they'll ache for rather longer this time. Come, I haven't much time."

Connor, looking resigned, took Father Patrick upstairs to the office. Not long afterward, the pair emerged on seemingly excellent terms, though Connor appeared a bit rueful. Caitlyn had left Mrs. McFee to finish the dishes and joined the younger d'Arcys in the parlor, where she passed the time by playing spinnikins with Cormac. Connor entered the room with the priest and crossed to stand behind her chair.

"Did you have to tell him about last night?" he bent to whisper with pained humor in her ear. She turned pink and cast an apologetic look up at him.

"I could not lie to a priest," she whispered back, then shushed him with a look.

Moments later, Mickeen appeared in the doorway. Connor left her side to join the little man in the hall.

"All's in readiness, yer lordship," she heard him say. She frowned in puzzlement. Before she could get up to join them, Connor was back, talking to Father Patrick in low tones.

"Is something wrong?" she whispered to Rory, who was standing nearby.

Rory shook his head. "Father Patrick will be holding a hedge mass for the people of Donoughmore. They've gathered together in the woods

360

behind the sheep barn. That way, if word of it gets out, blame will be harder to attach to any here."

"A hedge mass?" Connor was beside her then, draping a shawl around her shoulders before taking her arm. In almost total silence, they left the house in a group behind Father Patrick. Mrs. McFee joined them, and Mickeen, as they stepped out into the darkness. The rain had stopped sometime during the evening. The grass was wet beneath their feet, and the air was cool in the aftermath of the rain. About them the night was alive with people moving, converging on the thick grove of trees that flourished in a little hollow behind the barn. More people awaited them. As they recognized the priest's black robes and Connor, the peasants parted to let them through.

Someone had rolled a large tree stump with a flat top into the middle of the hollow. Someone else had placed a length of white lace and two tiny, barely flickering candles on it. A silver chalice that Caitlyn recognized as coming from the house sat between the candles, and next to it was the flat white circle of the Host. Father Patrick moved behind the makeshift altar. The crowd gathered around, grew silent. Someone sneezed, and there was a steady rustle of clothing as people shifted where they stood. The nearby stream gurgled; a night bird called. But it seemed as if a hush had fallen over the night.

"God's blessing on all here," the priest intoned quietly.

"And on you, Father," came the reply from many throats.

"Dear friends, we have not much time. Let us begin."

The chalice was passed, the Host shared. Forty or so people sank to their knees on the wet ground. Caitlyn, with Connor on one side and Rory on the other, knelt with the rest. The prayers were less loud than the gurglings of the stream. There was a palpable tension in the air. The saying of mass was forbidden by law; to be caught at their worship would result in dire punishment for all.

Though born and baptized into the Church, Caitlyn could not remember ever having participated in a mass, but she thought she must have when she was small, before her mother had died. Her free-roaming life on the streets of Dublin had precluded any formal religious observance, although Catholicism pervaded the very air of the city's slums. She watched and listened intently. Gnarled old men knelt in prayer next to their sons and grandsons. Women with tears streaking their cheeks bowed shawled heads. Beside her, Connor's head was bowed like the rest. His hands were clasped before him, his lips moving as he intoned the prayers. Caitlyn, glancing sideways at him as he made the sign of the cross, felt her heart swell with love, for him and for Ireland and for the Church and for everyone present. In that moment, it seemed to her that they were all part of one another, part of a living whole.

Then the last prayer was over, and they muttered, "Amen," in unison. The crowd stood up, melted away like the mist. Mickeen had brought Father Patrick's horse to the hollow; he stood with the d'Arcys and Caitlyn to bid the priest Godspeed before he rode off into the night.

Connor held her hand tightly in his as they returned to the house. She felt happier and more at peace than she had ever been in her life.

XXXI

❀ ❀ ❀ ❀ ❀ ❀ ❀ ❀ ❀ ❀ ❀ ❀ ❀ ❀ ❀

The next few days passed in a blur of blinding joy for Caitlyn. Though in fact it rained almost without ceasing, she felt as if the sun shone down upon her all the time. The only fly in her ointment was that Connor, prompted by conscience and Father Patrick, refused to continue his lessons in lovemaking until she was legally made his wife. Despite this prohibition and its ensuing frustration, Connor, too, was unprecedentedly jovial. His brothers observed him with wary amazement as he took even the most maddening happenstance with calm good humor.

Wherever Connor was, Caitlyn was usually nearby. She followed him about the farm, assisting him when she could or more often just admiring as he went about doing whatever was necessary for the running of the farm. He was strong and skilled, a far better sheep farmer than any of his brothers, and she watched with unalloyed pleasure when, stripped to the waist, he would single-handedly throw and tie a sheep or lift one to the cart for market. The play of muscles beneath his bronzed skin could hold her transfixed for hours. Her adoration of him was apparent to all, and the object of much good-natured ribbing from his brothers whenever Connor himself was not about to take umbrage on her behalf. Caitlyn took their jesting in good measure. She did adore Connor, and now that they were to be wed, she didn't care who knew it.

For the first time in her life she developed an interest in her wardrobe. Connor insisted that she be married in a proper wedding dress, and she discovered to her surprise that there was distinct pleasure to be gained from poring over patterns. With not quite three weeks until her wedding day, she selected a simple design with a high neck and long, tight sleeves to be made up in shimmery white silk. From a trunk in the attic she unearthed a fine lace veil, and that along with a white rosary that had belonged to Connor's mother completed her outfit. Connor rode with her to the village, where Mrs. Bannion, the local seamstress, took all her measurements and promised to have the dress ready for a fitting in a week. While in the village, which she had visited frequently since she had come to live with the d'Arcys, Caitlyn learned that she had become the focus of all attention. Mrs. McFee had trumpeted the news of his lordship's shocking engagement to the world, and the world turned out to stare.

"I feel like a two-headed calf," she said with some ruefulness to Connor as he reached up to lift her from the saddle on their return to the stable at Donoughmore. She could dismount perfectly well herself, of course, but Connor was increasingly solicitous of her as their wedding day approached, and she was not about to object to anything that gave him an excuse to put his hands on her. It had been nigh on ten days now since he had introduced her to the sins of the flesh, and she was growing increasingly impatient to experience them again.

"You don't look like one," Connor said with a smile as he set her on her feet. Caitlyn allowed her hands to linger on his hard shoulders, which were damp from the drizzle they had ridden through. Though she had worn a cloak, he had disdained one, and moisture gleamed on his buff coat and black hair. His shirt and breeches were splotched from the wet, and his boots had flecks of mud all the way up to their high tops. They stood so close their bodies brushed, her hands on his shoulders, his on her waist beneath the cloak. She had thrown back her hood before he reached up for her, and her long hair, secured only by a blue ribbon at the nape, tumbled in a soft mass down her back.

"I wish we were wed already," she said, her eyes and voice wistful. His hands tightened on her waist, and he pulled her a step closer. Her breasts in their prim bodice were pressed against his chest. His eyes slid down to her mouth, to where her breasts swelled against him, then back up to her eyes.

His smile widened, then crooked. "Ah, now that's quite an admission. Did I not tell you that you'd like lovemaking?"

She let go of one shoulder to give him a soft, playful smack on the cheek. Her hand lingered, enjoying the just slightly abrasive feel of his jaw. Although he had shaved that morn, bristles were already making their presence known again.

"Aye, you did, you conceited creature."

"Was I wrong, then?"

She eyed him. There was a glint in those aqua eyes that excited her. Her hand slid sideways across that bristly-skinned jaw so that her thumb just touched the edge of his mouth.

"No, you weren't wrong," she assured him, dropping her eyes and then flicking a veiled look up at him. The glint in his eyes brightened while the centers went dark. Caitlyn felt her heartbeat quicken. His skin beneath her hand seemed to heat. Her thumb moved, stroked the line where his lips joined.

His lips parted, drew her thumb into his mouth. Gently his teeth bit down on the edge of her thumb. Caitlyn's breath caught on a little gasp. She watched him nibble on her thumb and felt her knees weaken. Then she pulled her thumb away, going up on tiptoe to press her lips to his mouth. It was firm and warm beneath her lips, faintly moist from where he had nibbled on her thumb. His hands on her waist tightened, and she could feel the tension in him. Still he made no move to do what she wished.

"Just a kiss, Connor," she coaxed against that unyielding mouth. His lips parted slightly as he drew an unsteady breath.

"Oh, aye. Just a kiss. 'Tis easy for you to say," he muttered, but he was unable to resist her blandishments any longer. He pulled her so close against him that she could feel every muscle and sinew of his hard body. She could feel the man part of him huge and insistent against her, feel the racing of his heart, the faint tremors that shook the arms that held her. Her arms went around his neck, her hands in his hair, and she kissed him again with hungry passion, reveling in the taste and feel of his mouth. With quick, unsteady indrawing of breath, he slanted his mouth across hers, his lips and tongue hard and greedy as they took her mouth with an urgency that left her gasping. Caitlyn felt as if her bones would melt from the heat of his mouth.

"Enough of that, now." He put her away from him so suddenly that she had to clutch at his shoulders for balance. His voice was hoarse, his eyes afire with need, but the hands that held her from him were hard and steady.

"Connor!" she moaned.

"We'll wait till we're wed."

"Three weeks!"

" 'Tis not an eternity. You're to be my wife, and I'll not treat you like a doxy in the meantime."

"But I want you to treat me like a doxy! As long as 'tis you, I don't mind at all!" They'd had this argument before, and his insistence on being noble made her want to stamp her foot with frustration.

He frowned down at her. "You're not helping, you know."

"If we're to be wed, I don't see what difference it makes whether or not we wait for the actual official ceremony. In the eyes of God, I consider us already husband and wife. Do you not, Connor?" This argument, which had occurred to her on the spur of the moment, was so perfect that she had to restrain a triumphant smile. Let him get around that, if he could!

"I . . ."

"Yer lordship! Are ye about? I've news! There's — Oh. Sorry." Mickeen burst into the stable, looking excited about something, then stopped dead as he saw Caitlyn in Connor's arms. He frowned, discomfort and disapproval plain on his face. Like Mrs. McFee, Mickeen felt that Caitlyn was no fit wife for the Lord Earl of Iveagh.

" 'Tis all right, Mickeen. We're through here. Why don't you go on up to the house, puss, and change out of those wet shoes, and let me get some business conducted for a change?" This last was addressed with mock gruffness to Caitlyn as he released his hold on her waist and, with his hand on her rear, gave her a little shove toward the stable door. Caitlyn, charmed at this bit of impudent familiarity, smiled saucily at him over her shoulder as she obediently started to take herself off.

" 'Tis gold, yer lordship! Gold!"

These words, uttered in a fervent tone by Mickeen, assailed Caitlyn's ears before she was well outside the stable. Her attention caught, she stopped to listen, stepping to the side just beyond the open door so that she was out of Connor's view, should he chance to look. Even standing as she was beneath the protecting eaves, fine particles of moisture showered her, but she pulled her hood over her head, wrapped her cloak around herself, and ignored the rain as she listened shamelessly.

"What are you talking about, Mickeen?"

" 'Tis a payment to the treasury from the Blaskets! 'Tis coming overland to Dublin, and it should pass through Naas this very night! 'Tis a great secret, but I know a lad who knows a lad whose brother ferried a Sassenach gent and his supposed family from the islands to the mainland in his curragh before dawn three moons ago. He was not supposed to look inside the party's bags, but he did because the bloody things were so unaccountable heavy they nigh swamped him. 'Twas not a lady's wardrobe as he had thought that was weighing him down so! 'Twas trunks of gold — a fortune, he said! 'Tis said that the government hopes to avoid the possibility of robbery by moving the shipment in great secret, without any fanfare, you know, as if 'twere just a gent and his wife going on a little trip! There are to be no outriders at all, says the lad I know."

"They left the Blaskets at dawn three days ago?" Connor was frowning, deep in thought.

"Aye. And the lad I know says he understood that they would be putting up at an inn in Naas tonight. The way I figure it, they should be coming into Naas just after midnight, or there-abouts."

"Naas is a good bit away from here."

"Aye."

Connor was silent for a moment, thinking, while Mickeen watched him eagerly. A grin began to play about the corners of Connor's mouth. "How very interesting, to be sure!"

Mickeen grinned back at him. "Aye, I thought you'd think so."

Caitlyn could stay silent no longer. Shaking her hood back, she emerged from her hiding place to stand with hands on hips as she eyed Connor sternly. "And just what do you think you're about?"

He looked at her, his eyes narrowing. Mickeen gave her a disgusted glare.

"You were sent to the house." The charming man who had patted her rear had disappeared. She knew this Connor too. He was formidable, but she did not fear him. Not in the least!

"Aye, but I did not go. Pray tell me just what is so interesting about a shipment of gold?"

" 'Tis nothing to do with you. Go change your shoes."

She frowned at him. "I won't be sent away like a child, Connor. You mean to ride after that gold, don't you?"

"Hush, now!" This was Mickeen, looking around in alarm. Fortunately, except for the three of them, the stable and yard were deserted.

"And if I do?"

"Then I want to go too!"

"Don't be daft." His brusque response halted her in her tracks. She glared at him, arms crossing over her chest.

"If we're to be wed, then we're to be partners. I go where you go."

"The hell you do!"

"I want to go, Connor!"

"No! And there's an end to it! I'll not discuss it further." He came toward her as he spoke, catching her arm and turning her about. "Now go up to the house and change your shoes. I'll see you at supper. Surely you can find something to keep yourself occupied until then!"

"Women's work?" Caitlyn sneered at him over her shoulder. "You'll not fob me off with that! I can help you —"

"Damn it to hell and back!" Connor roared in a voice that made Caitlyn jump. "I'll have none of your talk of helping! Whatever I choose to do or not to do, you'll stay at home where you belong! Is that quite clear?" His hand on her arm tightened angrily before releasing its grip.

"No, it is not!" Caitlyn said, turning on him so swiftly that her skirts belled out around her. "If you think that just because we're to be wed I'll dance to your tune, think again, Connor d'Arcy!"

"You'll do as I bid you!"

"I'll not!"

"You will!"

"Not! And you can't make me!"

372

"Oh, can't I, now? We'll see about that, my lass!"

"What are you going to do, beat me?" It was an effective taunt, because she knew he'd never harm her. They were standing nose to nose now, shouting, just inside the stable. The drizzle blew in to shower Caitlyn with every gust of wind. Their noise attracted Cormac and Rory, who had been busy in the sheep barn. The two younger d'Arcys saw what was happening and came slogging across the muddy yard, grinning as they watched the battling pair.

"So much for wedded bliss," Cormac muttered to Rory, but Connor heard and turned on him.

"You keep your tongue between your teeth! And you" — he turned back to Caitlyn — "will do as you're bid! I'll not have a headstrong, hoydenish lass to wife!"

"Oh, will you not? Then perhaps you'll not have me to wife!"

"Perhaps I won't!"

"Take your bloody ring back then and be damned to you!" Angered past the point of reason, Caitlyn yanked the ring from her finger and hurled it at him. He caught it before it could hit his face, dark angry blood rising in his cheekbones as he glared at her. She turned on her heel and stalked from the stable, jerking the hood of her cloak over her head to keep out the worst of the rain as she went.

"Now that we're no longer affianced, I'll do as I bloody well please!" she hissed over her shoulder in parting. Then she stomped off toward the house.

"You'll watch your mouth, is what you'll do! I'll not have any wife of mine swearing like a bloody dragoon!" Connor came after her, unmindful of the rain, rage blazing in his eyes. Catching a glimpse of him over her shoulder, Caitlyn began to run, lifting her skirts with a muttered oath to keep them out of the slippery mud. He ran after her, reaching her before she made it halfway to the house and scooping her up in his arms.

"Let me go!" she screeched, beating at him with her fists.

"Not in this life," he said through his teeth and carried her into the house.

Left behind in the shelter of the stable, Cormac and Rory exchanged knowing glances. Then Mickeen came up to them, and the three lowered their heads as he told them about the gold.

XXXII

❈ ❈ ❈ ❈ ❈ ❈ ❈ ❈ ❈ ❈ ❈ ❈ ❈ ❈ ❈

"Don't you ever throw your ring at me again, or I'll blister your backside until you can't sit down!"

He had carried her into the house, past a scandalized Mrs. McFee, who was just on her way out the door, and up the stairs into Caitlyn's chamber, where he sat her on the edge of the bed. Leaning over her, he kept a hard grip on each of her arms as he growled the words into her face.

"Don't you dare threaten me!"

"I'll do more than threaten if you don't behave yourself!"

"You can't make me stay home while you go off adventuring! I want to come with you!"

Connor made a hissing sound through his teeth. He leaned over her until his face was scant inches from hers. "Listen, you little idiot, there's no 'adventuring' to what I do! There's danger! You could get killed! Faith, any of us could get killed! Remember when Rory was shot? Another couple of inches in either direction and he would have died. I don't like being shot at, I don't like my brothers being shot at, and I'm damned well not going to have you being shot at! Understand?"

"If there's that much danger, then you have

no business riding about the countryside robbing people! I don't want you to be killed either!"

"There are people depending upon me. I can't just quit, I've been doing it too long, I have obligations. I —"

"Then you can simply take me with you!"

"I'll tie you and leave you in the barn first!"

"You wouldn't dare!"

"Try me!"

She glared at him. He glared back at her just as fiercely. Neither gave an inch. After a moment his eyes narrowed and his grip on her arms eased. When he spoke again, his tone was almost coaxing: " 'Twould please me greatly if you would give up this idea of riding with the Dark Horseman, puss. The thought of you dodging bullets or swinging from a noose scares the hell out of me. If I'm scared, I'm not concentrating, and if I'm not concentrating, I could get killed. Do you want to be responsible for that?"

Caitlyn's eyes widened. He looked perfectly serious, but there was something . . .

"Oh, no, you'll not get around me that way, Connor d'Arcy! You've no more need to worry about me than about Rory or Cormac or Liam. I can help you, I tell you! Mine would be another pair of eyes to watch, another horse to carry things —"

"Another body to hang or shoot!" he finished for her grimly. "I've said my last word on the subject, Caitlyn. I'm perfectly willing to be an indulgent husband — indeed, you'll probably be twisting me around your little finger before a twelve-month has passed — but I mean to be obeyed on this: when we ride out, you will stay at home. Is that understood?"

"No," she muttered, still rebellious but suddenly tired of fighting with him. Arguing with Connor was basically a waste of breath, she had learned. He would shout and growl and threaten, and she would shout back just as furiously, and neither one of them would budge an inch. They would end up exhausted, and exactly of the same mind they had been when the argument started. It was better, far better, to skirt the issue rather than battle over it with him, she decided. With her decision came a measure of calm.

"Could I have my ring back now, please?" she asked meekly. He straightened, scowling down at her as she looked limpidly up at him.

"What plot are you hatching to plague me with now?" he asked, crossing his arms over his chest as he regarded her with suspicion.

"I simply want my ring back. Unless you meant it when you said you wouldn't have a headstrong, hoydenish lass to wife?"

"I meant it." He eyed her grimly. "I mean to break you of both traits if it kills the pair of us!"

"Oh, do you, now?" Nettled, she found herself in danger of forgetting her newfound resolve not to argue with him. Biting her tongue to keep from saying more, she eyed him in turn. He smiled at her sardonically and turned on his heel.

"Where are you going?" She jumped up and

tried to follow him as he walked through the door of her room to the hall outside, only to find her door being pulled shut in her face. Taken by surprise, she blinked at the closing door for the instant he took to close and lock it. When she saw that the key was missing from her side of the door, and heard the ominous click of a lock shooting home, she felt fury rise like a red fog before her eyes.

"You open this door! Don't you dare lock me in my room like a child!" She pounded on the door with her fist for emphasis.

His voice came from the other side of the wooden panel. From the sound of it, she could tell he was grinning.

"There's more than one way to skin a cat, my own. Do you think I can't tell when you're plotting mischief? You'll stay locked in your room, safe and sound and cozy, until I get back. If I were you, I'd go to bed."

"Connor d'Arcy, if you dare to do this, I'll never forgive you! I'll hate you for the rest of my life! I'll . . ." She faltered as she heard him walk away and start down the steps.

"Damn it, you let me out of here this moment!" she shrieked, pounding on the door. "Connor, if you don't let me out, I'll make you sorry! I'll . . . I'll . . ." She couldn't think of anything dire enough. Glaring at the closed panel, she clenched her fists and gritted her teeth. She would kill him for this! How dared he treat her in such a high-handed fashion! She would show him that she was not so easily dealt with!

The problem was, there was no way out of her chamber except through the door, and the door was securely locked. The small room had an equally small window that not even she could get through. Screaming for help would be useless; with Mrs. McFee gone home, the only ones to hear would be Mickeen and the d'Arcys. And they would probably split their sides with laughter listening to her cries.

She stalked over to the bed and sank down upon the edge of it. There had to be some way to free herself from her prison. There had to be. Quite aside from the fact that she wanted to ride with Connor, he could not be allowed to treat her so cavalierly and get away with it. It did not bode well for their married life.

After ruminating for a few minutes, Caitlyn came to the inescapable conclusion that the door was indeed the only way out of her chamber: It was locked, and Connor, the swine, had the key tucked safely in his pocket. In order to escape, she was going to have to get through that door. Frowning, she crossed to the panel, tested it. It was solid oak. A grown man couldn't break through that portal, much less her slender self. Growling under her breath, she kicked it. The faint tinkle of metal on metal came to her ears.

Eyes widening, she dropped to her knees to press her eye to the keyhole. What she saw there brought a grin to her face. Connor d'Arcy, the swine, was going to get his comeuppance yet!

He'd left the key in the lock.

It was on the wrong side, true, but that shouldn't present an insurmountable difficulty if she was careful. Sinking back on her heels, she pondered the best way to accomplish her objective. It could be done, she was sure — if she was careful.

She got up and crossed to the bed, removing the slip from her pillow. Then she went back to the door, knelt, and slid the slip under the door until just a corner remained on her side. Carefully she positioned it so that it was directly under the doorknob.

Next she needed something that would fit through the keyhole. Something hard, which would neither bend nor break. There was an ivory scratching stick on her dressing table that she had found in the attic and liked for its intricate carving. Connor had told her that it had probably belonged to his mother, who had worn elaborate powdered coiffures in the days before her marriage, when she had been at Court. If it was narrow enough to fit through the opening, and if the ivory was not too brittle, the stick just might work.

Fetching it, she knelt before the door again and carefully inserted the stick in the hole. It took considerable maneuvering, but at last she managed to dislodge the key. It teetered for a moment, then fell to the floor on the other side of the door with a muffled plop. From the sound of it, Caitlyn was sure it had landed on the pillow slip. Grinning widely at her success and the thought of Connor's face when he should set eyes on her and realize that she had managed to defeat him, she pulled the slip toward her. For a moment she feared that the key might be too thick to slide easily under the door and held her breath, but it came through with no mishaps. Snatching it up, she inserted it in the lock. A satisfying click was her reward. She pulled open the door, looked toward the stairs. All told, she couldn't have been in her room more than three quarters of an hour.

Moving cautiously, she stood at the head of the stairs and listened. The house was quiet below. Mickeen had said the gold was going through Naas, and from Donoughmore, Naas was a good day's ride. Or a hard night's ride, as the case may be. Mickeen had said the shipment would be passing through around midnight. If they hoped to make it in time, Connor and the others would have already left.

Hurrying, she grabbed the black hooded cloak and mask she had secreted in the back of her wardrobe and headed for Cormac's room. It took her only a few minutes to transform herself into a likely looking lad. Then she ran for the stables. As she had expected, Fharannain and the other horses were out of their stalls; saddling Finnbarr as quickly as she could, she realized that if she hoped to catch the d'Arcys she would have to be both lucky and fast. They had close to an hour's start on her. But they had left through the tunnel, she was sure, for whatever his hurry, Connor was a careful man. And she — she would ride across the land like the wind.

Swinging onto Finnbarr's back, she set the horse across the fields at a gallop. She knew the way to Naas, knew how the post road approached the town. Connor would be somewhere along that road. . . .

As Finnbarr flew over the rolling hills, taking walls and hedges in his stride, Caitlyn saw that a faint silvery glow breathed ghostly life into the dark landscape. When she had ridden out in pursuit of Connor before, the night had been so black she could scarcely see her own shoes. Glancing up at the dark wisps of clouds scudding across the wind-tossed sky, she found the answer: a tiny pale sliver of moon. This time, with the lure of gold drawing him out, the Dark Horseman had not waited for the full waning of the moon.

Finnbarr could not gallop for hours without respite, and after a while Caitlyn pulled him back to a canter. Impatient to catch up with Connor, she nevertheless had no wish to wind her horse. Or worse. Wet from the week-long rains, the ground was slippery beneath Finnbarr's hooves, and she did not want to chance an accident. Her only comfort was that Connor and the rest would be as slowed as she. Perhaps they would miss the gold entirely, and they could all ride back together.

Of course, Connor would be furious with her, which might take some of the pleasure out of this night's aftermath. But then, he'd been furious with her before and she'd survived unscathed. She looked on her escapade as an object lesson. He had to learn that, although she loved him, she did not mean to obey his every command. In fact, she meant to obey only those commands that suited her. Being a good wife, in her view, did not mean relinquishing to him absolute control over her every breath. He would treat her like a bairn all the days of her life if he could. Connor was protective of those he loved. But she meant to be his wife, his partner, not some plaything to be cosseted and relegated to the background while he got on with the serious business of life. Connor would find that taking her to wife would be more of a surprise than he was expecting.

Time passed, and at last she was nearing Naas. The sickle moon sailed high overhead. From its position she guessed that the hour must be just past midnight. She feared she was too late. . . .

To find Connor, she had taken to riding along the post road as she approached Naas. Now, coming around a bend, she saw that despite her misgivings she had timed it exactly right. At that very moment a light coach was under attack on the road not a hundred feet ahead of her. The horses reared, neighing, as the shouting driver tried to keep them under control. A guard in the seat beside the driver fired off shots at dark, menacing shadows on horseback that were flying at the coach from a copse of trees on the crest of a small embankment running alongside the road. The attackers fired back, the shots exploding through the cold, still night. One shot must have sailed just over the guard's head, because he abruptly threw down his weapon even as one of the attackers caught the lead horse's reins, effectively putting an end to the fight.

"Stand and deliver!" came the cry. Grinning in appreciation, Caitlyn slipped on her mask, yanked her hood up over her head, and spurred Finnbarr toward the fray.

The victims were descending from the coach as she slowed Finnbarr down to a jogging trot. Caitlyn saw to her surprise that they were not a family group at all, but two well-dressed men. The coachman sat still as death on his seat. The guard was motionless beside him.

Connor was dismounting, pistol in hand, black cloak swirling around him, totally unrecognizable in his mask to anyone who did not know him as well as she did. Liam was swinging down at his brother's side. Caitlyn's eyes were on Connor's tall frame as she rode up to join Mickeen and Cormac, who were still mounted and waiting with pistols drawn at the edge of the road, acting as both lookouts and guards. At the sound of Finnbarr's hooves, every eye slued in her direction. It was impossible to read anyone's expression through the masks, but she saw Connor stiffen, saw the sudden grim tightening of his mouth. He'd recognized her immediately, of course. From one of his brothers came a muffled guffaw. Caitlyn thought it might have come from

Rory, who was still astride Balladeer as he held the reins of the coach's frightened horses.

"You're a lass in a million, Caitlyn. Even if Connor does make you rue the day you were born," Cormac whispered out of the corner of his mouth.

"Pooh, I'm not afraid of Connor," she whispered back airily, though what little she could see of Connor's face warned her that she faced an uncomfortable time of it once he got her back home again.

"More fool you, then," Mickeen muttered and spat. Cormac, grinning, passed his spare pistol to Caitlyn, who looked at it in some surprise as she closed her hand awkwardly around the wooden grip. She was not very familiar with guns. Connor had absolutely refused to teach her anything but the fundamentals, saying that she would blow her own or someone else's head off for certain sure.

"You stand watch with Mickeen while I help Liam load the horses. Conn's being extra careful tonight and doesn't want anyone to dismount who needn't. But 'tis a good thing you came; gold's uncommon heavy, you know, and the more horses we have to carry it the more we can bring away with us."

Caitlyn nodded, gripping the pistol firmly in her hand as Cormac rode over to the coach and dismounted. There would be no trouble now, of course, the dangerous part was over and done, but if there was, all she had to do was pull the trigger. Nothing to it at all, so why did she suddenly feel so nervous?

"You," Connor was saying to the guard, "get up there on top and throw the baggage down. Be quick about it." The guard, moving with nerve-racking slowness, clambered onto the top of the coach, where three steamer trunks and assorted bandboxes and valises were lashed to the roof with leather strips. He fumbled with the lashings for what seemed an interminable length of time before Connor, impatient, tossed him up the knife in his boot and ordered him to cut them. The guard complied at the same pace as before.

"You." With his pistol Connor motioned to the driver, who had twisted around in his seat to watch the guard's progress. "Get back there and help him. If we have to stand around much longer, my trigger finger's liable to start twitching."

Thus encouraged, the guard hefted a steamer trunk, carried it to the edge of the roof, and dropped it. As it fell to the road with a muffled thud, Caitlyn frowned. A trunk full of gold should have been far, far heavier — so heavy that it required two men to lift it. So heavy that it threatened to burst on impact. And the guard was a scrawny little man, not any larger than Mickeen.

Connor must have been thinking the same thing, because he too was frowning as he called up to the driver, who was now on the roof as well. "Throw down the rest. Quickly."

The man complied, with as little effort as his predecessor had shown. Something was wrong. Either they had stopped the wrong coach, or . . . To her growing unease, she saw that the passengers, who stood under Rory's guard, did not appear frightened. Instead, smug little smiles played around their mouths. As she noticed that, she noticed something else as well: a faint drumming sound, as if countless horses were thundering toward them. The sound came from farther down the road, in the direction of Naas. . . .

"Nothing but clothes!" Liam straightened up from where he had been rifling through the contents of the first trunk. Apparently hearing the same drumming that puzzled Caitlyn, he stared in the direction from where it came. Connor looked the same way. Cormac, rummaging through a bandbox just beyond Connor, lifted his head as well. A horrid thought occurred to Caitlyn: could it be a trap?

"Mount up!" Connor yelled urgently to Liam and Cormac, who besides himself were the only ones unhorsed. Cormac turned, stared at his brother for a split second, and ran for Kildare, who was trailing rein nearby. At the same moment Liam jumped for Thunderer's back.

"Ride!" The hoarse cry came as Connor vaulted into the saddle and whirled Fharannain about. Rory on Balladeer was already streaking up the rise down which they had come and through the woods that had hidden them, with

Cormac and Mickeen in hot pursuit. Liam snapped off a delaying shot before spurring Thunderer after them. Connor's pistol echoed Liam's. Trying to hold rein on a lunging Finnbarr, Caitlyn also shot off her pistol. The resulting recoil sent it spinning from her hand. Her palm was numb, her fingers tingling from the shock of the aftercharge as she clapped her heels to Finnbarr's sides. A fusillade of bullets barked an answer.

Caitlyn looked back over her shoulder to make sure Connor was unhit. He was; Fharannain was streaking toward her with Connor, cloak flapping behind him like a raven's enormous wing, bent low over his neck. Behind him, just beyond the stopped coach, she saw a sight that struck terror into her heart: roughly two dozen dragoons charging after them. Bending low over Finnbarr's neck, clinging like a burr as he cleared a fallen tree with inches to spare, Caitlyn listened for Fharannain's thundering hooves closing the distance behind her and kept her eyes trained on the streaking figures of the others just ahead. She was more frightened than she had ever been in her life, but the danger of it was strangely exhilarating too. In front of her, the others galloped wildly across a flat, open field. Emerging from the woods, Finnbarr put his head down and streaked after his stablemates. From the corner of her eye, Caitlyn could see Connor on Fharannain coming up beside her. Through the slits in his mask she saw his eyes glinting at her. His mouth was set in a grim line. The speed at which they were moving precluded conversation. Caitlyn knew as clearly as if he had spoken that if they came through this disaster unscathed, he meant to kill her himself when they were safe at home.

Racing side by side, they came to a stone wall and cleared it in almost perfect unison. Behind them, bullets roared applause. Connor's mouth tightened still further, and he checked Fharannain's surging speed so that he was just slightly behind Finnbarr. Caitlyn realized suddenly that Connor was placing himself and Fharannain between her and the guns. Her stomach clenched, and her mouth went dry. What had been scarcely more than an exciting game to her suddenly took on a whole new dimension. For the first time she truly realized that they were running for their lives.

To attempt to circumvent Connor's intent to protect her with his own body would only endanger him further, she knew. The best thing she could do for him was to ride as she had never ridden before. And if they survived this night, if she and Connor got home to Donoughmore in one piece, she would meekly accept any punishment he chose to mete out to her. In the safety of her bedchamber, she had thought that he had merely sought to play on her emotions. Now she understood that he had been telling the exact truth: her presence tonight was endangering his life.

Fharannain was only a stride or two behind her when the bullets spat again. One sang through the air close to her ear; terrified, she ducked. Behind her, Connor cried out. As the import of that sound became clear to her, she sat up, twisting sideways in the saddle. Connor was slumped over Fharannain's neck, one hand pressed to his thigh. From his posture she could tell that he had been hit.

"Connor!" The wind bore away his name. Fharannain continued to run beside Finnbarr, his speed not slackening. Despite his wound, Connor was still conscious, still riding. There was no way she could help him. All she could do was ride. And pray that Connor could keep himself in the saddle.

With Fharannain beside her, she cleared a narrow gully to find herself on the heels of the others. Stealing a glance at Connor, she was relieved to see he was still alert, riding like a centaur while he kept a hand pressed to his thigh. She tried not to think that he might be bleeding to death. Kicking Finnbarr savagely in the ribs, she rode to overtake Liam. They had to get Connor in the middle in case he should start to lose consciousness and fall from the saddle; alone, she couldn't begin to help him. She didn't think the others even knew that he had been hit.

Bullets sang again. To her utter amazement, she went sailing head over heels through the air as Finnbarr crumpled beneath her. Even as she hit the wet turf hard on her back, she realized what had happened. Her horse had been shot from beneath her, but she was not injured — yet. Though it would be only a matter of a few minutes before the dragoons behind them closed around her. If she wasn't shot out of hand, she'd be hanged. . . .

Almost as soon as she hit the ground, she scrambled to her feet, crouching behind Finnbarr's body as bullets bit into the ground around her. His hooves were twitching faintly, but his eyes were already beginning to glaze over, and she knew he was dead. There was no time to feel more than a single stab of grief for the horse she had loved. There was no time for anything except frantic thoughts of survival. Fharannain had streaked by her when Finnbarr had gone down. Connor was wounded; he could not save her. She was on her own.

Fearfully she looked behind her. The dragoons were no more than a field away; they had only to clear a low stone wall and they would be upon her. Despairing, she looked after the others — and found that Connor had wheeled Fharannain about and was galloping back for her.

She ran crouching to meet him. He was upon her in a brace of seconds. Without ever slackening Fharannain's pace, he leaned down from the saddle, an arm extended toward her.

"Grab hold," he yelled, and as Fharannain rushed by, she was swept from her feet to hang twisting and scrabbling for purchase from Connor's arm as he fought to swing her up behind him. They were riding straight at their hallooing pursuers with her bumping against Fharannain's side. Connor's grip was like iron on her upper arm; his wound must have weakened him, she knew, but she also knew that he would never let her go. Frantically she kicked upward, trying to hook her heel over the saddle. Connor yanked with superhuman strength at the same time. Her heel caught, and her leg slid behind it over the saddle skirt. She was on Fharannain's back, righting herself and then clamping her arms around Connor's waist. As he released his death-grip on her arm, she clung for dear life to her precarious position on Fharannain's heaving rump. Sawing the reins, Connor wheeled Fharannain about again to send him streaking after the others. The dragoons were clearing the stone wall less than half a field away. Bullets peppered the air around them.

Connor was crouched low over Fharannain's neck, spurring him as she knew he never did as he fought to get every last bit of speed from the big animal. She released her grip on his waist to grab the roll at the back of the saddle, her knees gripping Fharannain's sides so that she would be as little drain on Connor's strength as possible. Her eyes fastened with horror on the bloody mess that was his thigh. He was hurt badly; she could see that at a glance. Blood gushed from an enormous hole; his breeches were black with it. She suspected that they were leaving a trail of his blood in their wake.

They were closing on the others, pulling slightly away from the squad of riders behind them. Just as they approached another wall, higher than the first with a ditch beyond it that made the jump doubly difficult, Liam looked back over his shoulder at them. From the sudden change in his posture, Caitlyn guessed that only at that moment did he realize what had happened. He reined in, slackening Thunderer's pace slightly to allow Fharannain to catch up. Mickeen, apparently seeing Liam fall back out of the corner of his eye, swung around in the saddle too. Like Liam, he immediately began to slow Aristedes' headlong flight, and shouted to Cormac and Rory up ahead. They would put Fharannain in the middle, protect their injured with their lives. If necessary, they would shoot it out with their pursuers. But Caitlyn prayed that it wouldn't be necessary. With so many to their few, and with their pursuers well armed and well trained, their chances were not good. Some of them would almost certainly be killed. The rest, captured, would hang. Terror tasted bitter on Caitlyn's tongue. But there was nothing she could do to save herself or any of them. All she could do was pray, and cling to Fharannain for her life.

In front, Cormac and Rory raced side by side, their horses sailing over the wall and the ditch without faltering. Caitlyn thought with an odd burst of pride that if they survived that night, any of them, they would owe much of the miracle to the great hearts of Donoughmore's horses. Then Mickeen was up and over, Aristedes' hoof catching slightly on the top of the wall but not going down. Liam went over without a hitch. Half a length behind and closing fast, Fharannain sailed into the air. He was going to clear that wall and the ditch beyond it as if he had wings.

At the height of their trajectory, something hit Caitlyn between the shoulder blades with tremendous force. She gasped as agonizing pain seared through her. Then she was losing her balance, falling down, down. . . .

Even before she hit the ground her world had gone black.

XXXIII

❋ ❋ ❋ ❋ ❋ ❋ ❋ ❋ ❋ ❋ ❋ ❋ ❋ ❋ ❋

The pain in his thigh was excruciating, but he could bear it. He had borne worse and lived to tell about it. But the loss of so much blood was affecting his concentration. He was getting dizzy, and he knew that if the wound was allowed to bleed unchecked much longer, he would pass out. Only grim determination had kept him conscious this long. To lose consciousness would be to sentence both himself and Caitlyn to death, and probably the others as well. He doubted that they would leave him without a fight.

He was concentrating so hard on staying in the saddle that it was a few seconds before he became aware that Caitlyn was not behind him. Slowly, as if the information was filtered through dense fog, it came to him that he had heard her gasp.

Sluing his head around, he saw that he was alone on Fharannain. Behind him, perhaps a furlong or so back, the dragoons were coming over the wall that Fharannain had cleared with ease moments earlier. A slight figure almost covered by a black cape lay crumpled on the ground just beyond the ditch. Though it was not much more than a darker shadow amidst all the other shadows that the night had made of rain-wet ground and ditch and wall, Connor knew it was

Caitlyn. His heart lurched. She lay without moving, her posture so awkward that he felt a sudden, driving fear that she was already dead. The pursuit was clustering around her. If she was not dead, she was taken.

"No!" he screamed, though the cry emerged as a hoarse whisper. He was growing dangerously weak. But he had to hold on, he had to! He had to go back for her. Hauling savagely on Fharannain's reins, he tried to turn the big animal about. A wave of dizziness engulfed him. Fharannain reared, confused and frightened by the unaccustomed pain in his mouth. It was all Connor could do to stay in the saddle. He slumped over the horse's neck as the animal came down again on all fours. Liam appeared beside him, snatching Fharannain's reins out of his weakened hand, pulling them over the horse's head as he spurred Thunderer away from the shadowy riders clustering about Caitlyn's fallen form. Cormac, coming up on his other side, made a daring leap from Kildare's saddle to Fharannain's rump, wrapping his arms around Connor's waist as he grabbed his brother's pommel. Cormac's arms served as a barrier to keep him in the saddle. Rory was leading the riderless Kildare, just as Liam was leading Fharannain. With Mickeen in the lead, they galloped frantically for safety.

"Caitlyn. . . ." Connor managed to groan through the blackness that was threatening to claim him. The pain in his leg was white-hot agony cutting through the descending darkness;

the pain in his heart was worse.

"We can't help her now, Conn," Cormac said in his ear, his voice rough with grief. "There aren't enough of us. You're shot, maybe bleeding to death. 'Tis going to take all of us to get you home safe. We can't go back for her. If we do, we'll all be taken, or worse. Maybe we can rescue her later, help her escape from wherever she's taken. But now we've got to get you home."

"I'll not leave her," Connor muttered, but he could hold the darkness at bay no longer. It descended on him like a rung-down curtain, sheltering him from physical pain and heartbreak alike. He slumped over Fharannain's neck, his arms dangling limply along the animal's sleek black sides. Cormac's arms were the only things that kept him in the saddle.

With their pursuers distracted and appeased by Caitlyn's fall, the rest of them made it home to Donoughmore without further mishap. As soon as they emerged safely from the tunnel into the stable, Cormac eased Connor's limp body down to Rory and Liam, who between them just managed to carry him into the house and up to his room. The hole in his leg was hideous, the blood loss immense. But they all knew that when their brother awoke, what would hurt him most would be the pain in his heart.

Grim-faced, they worked frantically for a quarter of an hour trying to stanch the blood. At last the flow slowed to a sluggish trickle, then stopped altogether. As Liam tied the bandage in place,

Cormac spoke, his voice loud in the tense stillness.

"I'm going to go find out what I can about
Caitlyn."

Liam looked at him, his hands pausing for an
instant in the act of knotting the bandage around
Connor's leg. "Is that wise?"

Mickeen made as if to spit, remembered where
he was, and swallowed it. " 'Twill be no help to
the lassie if you go getting yourself taken too."

"I'll be careful. There's a pub in Naas — they'll
know something there."

"I'll come with you," Rory said, and without
further objections from the others, the two left
the room.

When they returned hours later as dawn broke
over the sky, Mickeen was waiting for them in
the stable. He was sitting on an overturned
bucket, his hands clasped between his knees, his
head lowered. As they entered he looked up, his
face as colorless as theirs.

"Is aught amiss with Connor?" Rory asked
sharply, swinging down from Balladeer.

Mickeen stood up and took the reins from
Rory. When he was upset, they knew he liked to
calm himself by caring for horses. He'd started
life as a groom, and in times of stress he reverted
to his earliest habits.

"His lordship's awake and asking for her. He
don't — he don't remember what happened, exactly. He's burning up with the fever. Liam's had
to tie him to the bed to keep him from getting

up to look for her. He knows something's amiss, but he don't know quite what. He's fashing himself something awful."

"Oh, Jesus." Dismounting wearily, Cormac said the words as much as a prayer as a sigh. He tied Kildare to a ring, knowing that in his present mood Mickeen would see to him as well as Balladeer and be glad of the work.

"What of the lass?" Mickeen asked.

Cormac's eyes were bright with unshed tears. "She's dead," he said unevenly, then drew a deep breath. "Killed outright, they said. And how we're to tell Connor, I don't know."

But tell him they did, later that day when they thought he could bear it. Liam gave him the news. Connor refused at first to believe. At last, when he did, the cry of grief that rose from his throat was as piercing and mournful as a wolf's howl at the moon.

And thus, for Connor, began the period that forever afterward he was to think of as the black night of his soul.

XXXIV

✿ ✿ ✿ ✿ ✿ ✿ ✿ ✿ ✿ ✿ ✿ ✿ ✿ ✿ ✿

It was going to be a harsh winter. Though it was only late October, the night was cold, and the nip in the air threatened snow within the next few days. Even the crackling fires in the vast fireplaces of this English country home could not warm him as he stood on the landing, looking down on the merrymakers in the ballroom below.

The house belonged to the Marquis of Standon, a notorious rake who had recently buried his third wife. The guests were a motley mix of what among the Sassenach passed for gentlemen and their fashionable impures, and the merrymaking was very merry indeed. In fact, Connor had just been treated to the edifying sight of one slightly inebriated young woman stripping to the altogether while dancing on a marble-topped table to the tune of raucous cheers. His lip curled as he sought out the young woman, who was now being ushered, naked and giggling, from the ballroom by the gentleman who would enjoy her favors that night. It was the last night of a week-long house party, and Connor ventured to guess that, over its duration, the young woman had enjoyed at least as many partners as there were days in the week. It was not what even English society would term a select gathering.

The women — he could not term them ladies — who remained were outlandishly clad. It was a masquerade ball, and the costumes of most of the females were remarkable for what they were not hiding. Some of them had necklines cut so low and skirts hiked so high that there wasn't much to imagine between them. Others wore diaphanous gowns that clung to them faithfully. In their hair, some sported towering headdresses, others bobbing ostrich plumes, while still others had opted for wigs. A few were merely powdered and patched in the prevailing fashion. The gentlemen were more sedate, for the most part contenting themselves with enveloping dominoes in various jewel tones and black in lieu of costumes. Here and there a dandy sported something more elaborate, like the giggling Julius Caesar in the corner, but their rarity made them stand out. All wore masks.

Which was why Connor had chosen this particular house on this particular night. Entry had been ridiculously easy. In his domino and mask, he looked no different from any of the other male guests. He had been in the house for nearly an hour, and he ventured to suppose that he had made intimate acquaintance with the jewelry of nearly every female present, to say nothing of the lovely set of rubies his unwitting host had inherited from the estate of his wealthy, recently departed wife, which had been carelessly left in her jewel case that still sat out on her dressing table. Those rubies had been his object, the rest mere gravy. The purloined jewels were waiting in a small bag he had dropped from an upper window moments earlier. He was now on his way to retrieve them, before quitting the premises. A small smile lurked at the corners of his mouth as he considered the approximate value of his haul. All in all, when one weighed return versus risk, robbing houses certainly beat robbing coaches.

He was turning away, ready to descend the stairs, when his eye was caught by a young woman below. What it was about her that attracted his attention he did not know. Unlike most of the other females, she was clad in a black domino much like the one he was wearing. The towering plumed headdress she wore was black as well, and dangled beads of jet. Her elaborate cat's-eye mask was of gold satin. She was unsmiling, dancing with a tall, thin gentleman also successfully disguised. Then he realized that it was something in her carriage that had caught his eye. Her lithe gracefulness reminded him of Caitlyn. His eyes followed her even as his lips tightened. One hand went automatically to massage his damaged thigh. An arrow of pain lodged in his heart.

It had been a year now, almost to the day, since he'd lost her. He still caught himself doing double takes at black-haired young women, thinking that this one or that one was, miraculously, her. Which would be more of a miracle than even God could provide: Caitlyn was dead, shot from the saddle that nightmarish night. As befitted a highwayman, she'd been buried in lime within the week without benefit of word or prayer, so he had not even a grave to grieve over. Though that did not stop him from grieving.

He had not told her he loved her, and that was part of the poison that ate at his heart. He had not even known it himself until Liam had told him that she was dead. He'd been disbelieving at first, shouting and arguing with his brother. When he'd finally been convinced, for the first and only time in his life he'd wept in his brother's arms. As his leg healed as much as it was going to and his physical pain lessened, he'd thought the pain in his heart and soul would lessen as well. He'd been wrong. Even after nearly a year, any reminder of Caitlyn was more hurtful than his leg had ever been. Her loss was an open wound that refused to heal.

After he was up and about again, he'd tried to drown his grief in drink. That hadn't worked. When he was drunk her shade took on substance and form so real that it made the ache that remained when he was sober just that much more painful, as if he had lost her all over again. Finally he had realized that the most potent Irish whiskey in the world would not bring her back, and he had stopped drinking altogether. Instead he had packed up his brothers and Mickeen, left a care-taker behind at Donoughmore, and taken himself and his family out of Ireland. If he'd thought that would lessen the constant reminders he'd had of her, he'd been right. But the move had not eased his pain.

He'd lost Caitlyn. He did not want to lose any of the remaining members of his family. He'd discovered that he did not deal well with loss, and supposed that it came from the deaths of both his parents when he was very young. He'd felt very small and alone when they'd come to tell him about his mother, and when Mickeen had broken the news of his father's death, he'd felt just as lost, just as frightened. That was how he'd felt after Caitlyn's death as well, how he still felt now whenever he fell into a melancholy that he could not shake: like a child abandoned in the dark. He, Connor d'Arcy, Lord Earl of Iveagh, also known as the Dark Horseman, un-faltering paterfamilias, respected master of Donoughmore, had sometimes, in those first dark days after her death, cried in the wee hours of the night like a bairn. It was a secret that shamed him, and that along with fear for his brothers had driven him out of Donoughmore.

The Dark Horseman had died with Caitlyn. He no longer had the heart to ride, and a very real fear for his brothers' lives made it imperative that they not be allowed to take his place. He'd brought them with him to England, settling Cormac and Rory in at Oxford to get a long-delayed education, much to their disgust, although in deference to what they perceived as his grief-stricken state they had not protested overmuch. Liam had obstinately refused to leave him and was now ensconced in the London town house they shared. A faint shadow of a smile touched Connor's mouth as he thought about Liam. Quite the man about town had Liam become, though he and Mickeen, who had remained with him as well, acting as his valet of all things, watched over Connor like hens with one chick between them. As months had passed, and to outward appearances his grief had lessened, they had ceased to fret over him every time they set eyes on him, and now confined their searching looks to once or twice a week.

Three months ago, Father Patrick had sent word to him of tenants, a family of nine with a father dying of the lung sickness, on the verge of being evicted from Ballymara because they had no money for rent. There were many such, and Connor knew that their plight was more desperate than ever because the Dark Horseman rode no more. So he had taken up his present form of supplying them and himself with funds, and found that, when he was working at least, the sharp edge of his grief was temporarily dulled. Unless, like tonight, he came across something or someone that reminded him of Caitlyn. Then the aching pain would take up residence in his heart again.

Watching the young woman twirl about the dance floor below, Connor's hands tightened over the polished walnut railing until his knuckles turned white. She was dancing; Caitlyn had never learned to dance. In the brief glimpses he was afforded of her gown as the domino parted, he saw that it was of lace-trimmed silk, very costly. Caitlyn had never possessed a gown like that, never expressed any interest in possessing one. But the color of the skirt was the exact kerry blue of her eyes.

Of course, from this distance he could not see the young woman's eyes. They would be brown, or hazel, or maybe even, if she was a ravishing beauty, green. Up close, they would not be kerry blue, set beneath slanting black brows and fringed with lashes so thick they could be used as brooms. Her nose would not be slender and elegant; her lips would not part to show small, dazzlingly white teeth when she smiled. Her hair would not be a silky black cloud that fell past her waist, and her waist would not be small enough so that he could span it with his hands. In short, if he got closer he would see at once that she could not be Caitlyn.

But beneath her mask he could see her mouth, and it was full and red as Caitlyn's had been. Her jaw was fragile yet strong. And her skin was as white as smooth new cream.

Turning, he saw a footman passing behind him. Crooking a finger, he summoned the man to his side.

"Who is that?" he croaked, pointing. He knew it was folly, knew he was being foolish past permission, but he could not help himself. He had to know who she was — and was not.

"The lady in the domino? I don't know, sir.

She came with one of the guests."

Connor's eyes closed for just an instant as the footman started to move away. Then he stopped him with a hand on his arm.

"Do you know who she's with? What room she's been given?"

"No, sir. But if you wish, I'll find out."

"Please do."

The footman bowed and disappeared. Connor was left to watch the young woman below. She was still dancing, though with a different partner, and she held herself stiffly as if she did not like his touch. Her lips were curved up in a small, polite smile. That smile riveted him. It recalled Caitlyn so vividly that his heart shook. It was all he could do not to race down the stairs, shoulder his way through the cavorting crowd, and rip that mask from her face. To do so would call too much attention to himself, of course. It might even lead to his arrest.

But his heart urged him to it.

"Pardon, sir, but none of the staff is acquainted with the lady's name. However, I can show you where her chamber is located, if you wish."

"Yes. I do wish it."

Feeling dazed, Connor followed the footman, who led him to a door along a long corridor on the second floor of the east wing.

"Would you like to get inside, sir?" From the footman's smirk, Connor realized that the man thought he was enamored with the mystery lady and wished to try his luck with her when she returned to her chamber. Of course, he had to remind himself that the females below were all Cyprians, up for sale to the highest bidder. The high-flyer who bore such a heart-stopping resemblance to Caitlyn was naught but a common whore.

Connor inclined his head. With a flourish, the footman produced a key and unlocked the door. Connor pressed a note into the man's hand and entered, pocketing the key. Then, bethinking himself of something, he turned back.

"Say naught of this," he warned in a voice that was far from his normal one. The footman inclined his head and took himself off. Connor closed and locked the door, pulled off his mask, then prowled the room. There was nothing in it of Caitlyn. The clothes in the wardrobe were of the finest material and most fashionable cut. The brush and comb on the dressing table were of chased silver. There were boxes of powder, a tin of rouge. There was even a crystal flacon of scent. Caitlyn had never worn scent.

This young woman was not Caitlyn. He knew she was not. She could not be. He had to learn to accept the unalterable fact that Caitlyn was dead. He should take himself off now, before the thefts were discovered, before his bag of jewels was found in the shrubbery beneath the window, before he himself was exposed. He knew he should, but still he stayed. He was in the grip of an obsession so strong there was no fighting it.

Connor waited for what seemed like hours. Occasionally he heard high-pitched laughter accompanied by lower-pitched murmurs in the hall outside as the female guests retired to their rooms with bed partners in tow. It occurred to him to wonder what he would do if the object of his inquiry was accompanied by a male. Kill him, came the immediate savage thought, and again he had to remind himself that this female was not Caitlyn. If she was accompanied, he would merely ascertain her identity by whatever ruse was necessary and take himself off.

In any event, when she returned to her room she was alone. It was nearer dawn than midnight, and she unlocked the door and stole inside as if she feared being observed. Once inside, she turned the key in the lock and leaned against the panel in a silent posture of relief. She still wore her costume. At close range, the black silk domino topped by that outrageous plumed and beaded headdress and the cat's-eye mask made her look like some rare exotic bird. Beneath the disguise, her human identity was still impossible to determine. Connor stared, his hands tightening over the arms of his chair.

The bedchamber was lit only by the fire in the hearth, and it had burned low. It cast but a small amount of light, so he was deep in shadow as he sat in the room's only small chair. She carried with her a candle, which she used to light the taper on her dressing table before she blew out the one in her hand and laid it aside. Then, without becoming aware of his presence, she began to undress.

She stood by the bed with its sumptuous gold satin coverlet, her back to him, not more than six feet from where he sat. First she took off her domino, revealing the expensive dress in all its glory. Then she lifted off her headdress, shaking her head so that a mass of black hair tumbled down her back in a silken tangle that reached past her waist. Connor swallowed, watching with growing shock. He leaned forward, ceasing to breathe. As she removed her mask and placed it on the bed, he was sure the very blood had stopped coursing through his veins.

He still could not see her face. Her back was to him as she twisted both hands behind her and tried to work the hooks on the back of her dress. She managed one, then the next. The third one eluded her. Finally, out of patience, she yanked at it, tearing the delicate material. The soft curse that followed the faint ripping sound stilled his heart.

"By the blessed virgin," he breathed, staring transfixed at her slender back.

She must have heard him, though he spoke scarcely louder than a breath, because she whirled about. To his stupefaction, Connor found himself staring into the delicately powdered and painted face of his lost love.

XXXV

❈ ❈ ❈ ❈ ❈ ❈ ❈ ❈ ❈ ❈ ❈ ❈ ❈ ❈ ❈

"C-C-C-Connor!" Hands to her mouth, eyes wide with shock, she was staring at him with as much horror as if he were the ghost and not she. Despite his own shock, Connor's mind nevertheless managed to function. Immediately it recognized that his first prayerful hypothesis of what her presence, alive and unharmed and here, might mean — that she had totally lost her memory in the fall from Fharannain and would have no idea who she was or where she belonged — could not be the explanation. Because clearly she knew who *he* was, and from her expression was frightened out of her wits.

He could not talk. Eyes never leaving her face, he got to his feet like a man in a dream and took the few steps needed to bring him to her. She looked up at him as he stood in front of her, and there was no mistaking the terror in her eyes. She looked desperate — and desperately scared. Of him? It would seem so. Frowning, he raised his hand to catch her chin, tilt her face up to his for inspection. She shrank away from his touch, but he did as he intended nonetheless.

It occurred to him that maybe he was asleep and dreaming. But her jaw felt real enough beneath his hand, her skin as silky smooth as he

411

remembered. He could sense the tension that emanated from her body. She sank into a sitting position on the edge of the bed as if her knees had suddenly given out. Those kerry blue eyes that had been haunting him for nigh on a year remained fixed on his face. The next possibility — that he was losing his mind, that his subconscious was somehow projecting her features on an unknown young woman — was rejected too. She had called his name, and he had seen the shocked recognition in her eyes.

"C-Connor," she croaked again. She seemed almost as stunned as he. But not quite, he told himself with rising grimness. After all, he had believed her dead, while she had known that he was alive. Or maybe not, he thought as another possibility occurred to him. Maybe she had believed him dead from the terrible wound in his thigh, and maybe that belief had left her too grief-stricken to face Donoughmore again, just as he had been unable to stay on at Donoughmore with memories of her haunting him at every turn. Maybe the whole nightmarish year just past had been the result of nothing more than a horrible misunderstanding. . . .

"Caitlyn." He spoke her name as if his voice had rusted, his hand still under her jaw, his eyes moving over her face as if he had been blind and now could see. The small pink tip of her tongue came out to wet her lips. His stomach clenched. He would know that gesture anywhere. In happier days it had troubled his sleep more times than he could count. Finally he allowed himself to believe.

"Caitlyn," he said again, deeply, his hands moving to close over her upper arms. Then he pulled her off the bed into his embrace, hugging her so tightly against his body that the contact hurt. Her arms went around his waist beneath the enveloping black domino that he still wore, beneath the sober blue wool of his frock coat. He could feel the warmth of them even through his shirt, feel the softness of her breasts against his chest, feel the pounding of her heart. His own heart drummed in violent answer. For just a moment she clutched him as fiercely as he was holding her. His head bent, rested against the silky black hair that he had thought never to see again in this life. His eyes closed. Holding her as if he would never let her go, he breathed a silent prayer of thanks.

"By the miraculous grace of God, it is you! Ach, I have missed you, cuilin."

He felt her shudder against him even as his world slowly began to right itself on its axis. For once in his life, what was lost was regained. It had all been a hideous misunderstanding, a fiendish trick played by an evil Shedu, the details of which she would now explain. Not that the why or the how of it mattered. Not in the face of this wondrous blessing. She was alive, alive! God in His wisdom had given him his miracle, after all.

"C-Connor." She did not seem able to say his name without a catch in it. His eyes opened, and he blinked once to rid them of the burning that threatened to unman him. Offering another thanks to God, he pressed his lips against that shining ebony hair, dropped brief hard kisses on her eyes, her nose, her mouth, and her chin before burying his head in the hollow of her neck.

As if his fierce kisses were some sort of catalyst, her arms dropped from around his waist and she pushed against his rib cage, wanting to be let go. He could not bring himself to do so. Beneath the unfamiliar scent of a sweet perfume, he drew in the clean aroma of her skin and hair. He felt as if he had been frozen from the time she had left him and he was only now just starting to melt. The pain was excruciating, but it felt wonderful to be coming alive again.

"Let me go, Connor." The words were spoken quietly, but it was obvious from them that at least she had regained her composure. There was also a note in her voice that did not quite fit with his notion of a rapturous reunion. He drew a deep, shaky breath and lifted his head to look down at her questioningly. Still he held her close. Some part of him feared that she was naught but an apparition and that if he lost touch with her, she would vanish into the shadows of the night.

"We have to talk, Connor. Please let me go."

There was sense in what she said, he knew. They had to talk, to expose the circumstances that had caused him so much pain. Once the hows and the whys were out of the way, he'd be free to sweep her up in his arms again. To carry her back to Donoughmore, with everything the same as before. To marry her, and keep her beside him all the days of his life. To love her forever. He smiled with great sweetness down into her eyes, feeling as if shackles and chains and iron weights had suddenly been lifted from his heart. Unbelievably, miraculously, everything was going to be all right. Caitlyn was restored to him. Her death had been nothing more than a year-long bad dream, and now he had awakened at last.

"This is no place for explanations, my own," he told her, smiling though his voice was not quite his own yet. "What was lost is found, and for the moment that's miracle enough. Grab your cloak or whatever garment you need to make that pretty dress passably warm, and we'll be away. Mickeen's waiting at an inn up the road, and by now he's probably grown old with worry over me. I've been here far too long. What a surprise he'll have when he sees you! And my brothers! What a celebration we'll have! 'Tis a miracle, and no mistake! Caitlyn alive! God in all His glory be thanked and praised."

"I'll not be going with you," she said quietly, and succeeded in pulling herself out of his arms. He frowned. Something was very wrong, but the euphoria of finding her alive overshadowed all else.

"What do you mean, you'll not be going with me? Of course you will. You belong with me, my own, so get your cloak." He felt an unwelcome premonition even as he spoke. His eyes were seeing what his mind had refused to register. She was his Caitlyn, yet, hideously, not his Caitlyn. Her lovely face was whitened as much by rice powder as by shock, though the artificial rosiness of rouge was readily apparent on her cheekbones. Her lips were very red too, and he suspected she had used paint there as well. For the first time since he had made sure of her identity, his eyes left her face to run over her body. The gown she wore was just this side of indecent, like the gowns the tarts had worn in the ballroom. It was of fine blue silk trimmed with silver lace, caught up around the hem with big silver bows to reveal a silver lace petticoat beneath. The neckline bared neck and shoulders and more than half her lovely bosom. She must have been tightly laced beneath the dress, because her creamy-skinned breasts thrust provocatively upward, lushly available to eyes and touch, and her waist was even more impossibly slender than he remembered. Frowning, he looked her over again. She was tricked out like an expensive whore.

" 'Tis glad I am to see you, Connor, truly, and please give my love to your brothers, but I wish you'd leave now. Please."

Connor had the sense of falling again into a nightmare. His frown deepened into a scowl, but he was more bewildered than angry. He reached for her. She took a quick step back from him, and he let his hand fall to his side. "Suppose you explain yourself, lass. We've thought you dead, all of us, and now, when I by the sheer grace of God find you alive, you tell me to go away. We are affianced, Caitlyn. Your home is with me, at Donoughmore. Have you problems with your memory?"

She looked at him steadily as she took another step away from him. He allowed her to put what distance she wished between them, his eyes never leaving her face. That tantalizing tongue came out to wet her lips again, and he wanted to groan. She was his own beloved Caitlyn . . . and yet she was not. He began to question his sanity once more.

"You are entitled to an explanation, 'tis true. I've been remiss, I know, in not letting you know that I was alive, but I've been so . . . so happy this past year. I'm . . . I'm in love, Connor."

He felt as if he had walked into landscape that was familiar at first glance, but as he moved further into it, it became grotesque and hideously distorted.

"I thought you were in love with me." The words were very quiet, almost puzzled. Her eyes were huge as they met his, then dropped.

"Faith, this is hard for me to say! I had hoped to spare you this, 'tis one reason I didn't contact you after I . . . was able to. You were right, all those months ago at Donoughmore: I was naught but a child then. I loved you, and I still do, but not in the way I thought. What I felt then was nothing more than infatuation. You are a very handsome man, Connor! And now — why, now 'tis truly a woman grown I am, and I find I love you like a brother. Just a brother, Connor, and nothing more."

"A brother." He repeated her words stupidly, feeling as if he were fighting his way through a fog. She flicked a quick look up at him and spoke more rapidly.

"There's someone else now, the man who saved my life. He was with the dragoons who pursued us that night. When I was shot — oh, aye, I was shot — the wound was grave. I was hit in the back, it was very bloody he told me later, and the rest of that pack of jackals thought I was dead. But he . . . he found that there was some faint spark of life remaining in me, and that I was a woman. He said naught to the others but volunteered to take charge of the body. There was a reward, you know, which he paid himself out of his own pocket later so no one would realize the highwayman they'd shot had not truly died. But that night he took me to his l-lodgings, and over the next few weeks he nursed me back to health. He was kind, Connor. And . . . and I found that I liked him very much. I had no money, nothing to give him, so I . . . I paid back his kindness in the only way I could. Then, later still, I discovered I loved him. And he loves me. He is a gentleman, an English gentleman. When he returned to his home, he brought me with him. I truly thought it would be kinder if you just never saw me again."

Connor watched her as she spoke, disbelieving.

The Caitlyn he knew could not have done the things she said. She could not have bedded a man out of gratitude and pity, not when she was betrothed to another. She could not have fallen in love with someone else.

"For a twelve-month I have believed you dead." His voice was hoarse. "You are telling me that you were alive and aware all the while, bedding another man even, and had not the first thought of letting me know? Have you any idea of the grief we have suffered, not just me but my brothers, who loved you too? Have you lost your heart as well as your mind?"

"I'm very sorry, Connor. 'Twas thoughtless, I know."

"Thoughtless." He thought of the agony he had gone through, the heartrending pain that had stabbed him as recently as this very night, and fought an urge to wrap his hands around her soft neck and squeeze the life out of her in truth this time. "Aye, I'd say you were a trifle thoughtless in this matter."

His sarcasm did not seem to move her, and her very indifference enraged him at last. He caught her arm, pulling her toward the wardrobe that rested against one wall. Holding her despite her struggling protests, he flung open the door with his other hand and began to rifle through the contents. All the clothes were expensively lavish, and most were totally unsuitable for the midnight ride through a near-winter night that he had in mind. He threw several dresses on the floor before he yanked out an emerald-green wool walking costume. It had a decent neckline and long sleeves, and the material would be insulating. It would do.

"Put that on." He thrust it at her. She took it, stopping her useless struggles to stand glaring at him. "Until I sort this tangle through to the bottom, I'll not have you freezing to death."

"I told you, I'm not coming with you, Connor!"

"Oh, are you not, then? We'll see about that." With barely restrained ferocity he closed a hand in the shocking neckline of her gown and jerked downward. The thin silk gave with a satisfying rip. She gasped and tried to free herself from his hold, but to no avail. He stripped the gown from her, then his eyes narrowed on her underclothes. They were very pretty, white and lacy and trimmed with satin bows. The underclothes of a woman who meant for them to be seen. A pulse began to pound in his head. She'd said she had a lover.

"Stop it, Connor! You can't make me go with you! I'll not! Do you hear me? I'll not!"

He ignored her, whirling her around and yanking at the strings of her stays.

"What are you doing?" She tried to pull away as he untied the bow and loosened the strings, but he jerked her back into place by the very strings he was loosening.

"You can't ride in this." The stays fell away, and her bosom and waist returned to their natural configuration inside the shift and petticoat she still wore. Instinctively she clutched the green walking costume protectively to her breast as she whirled to face him.

"What do I have to say to convince you? I'm not going with you! I'm sorry if you've been hurt, but I don't love you any more! I love someone else now!"

"And what is your lover's name?"

She laughed. "Think you that I would be fool enough to tell you that? I know you! 'Tis crazy jealous you are, and have always been! You'd kill him in a heartbeat!"

"Aye, if you've bedded him."

"There, you see? You see? That's why I never told you I survived! Go away, Connor! I'm happy now, far happier than I was with you, so just go away!"

"I don't believe you."

"Oh, don't you now?" Her eyes narrowed, and an edge of fine Irish temper entered her voice. "You always were a conceited creature! You're a handsome man, 'tis true, but you've a temper like the devil and a damned highhanded way with you that I mislike! The man I love is gentle with me, and kind, and lets me do just as I choose! At Donoughmore, I worked from morn to midnight on your bloody sheep farm! And, had I wed you, I no doubt would have continued to do so until I died, and single-handedly raised a houseful of your squally brats besides! The man I love has presented me with my own house in

London, and I have servants to fill my every need. I sleep till noon anytime I like, and then do nothing more strenuous than shop! Remember the rags I wore at Donoughmore? The man I love has given me fine clothes, lovely clothes! Fashioned in the latest styles of silks and satins and velvets! See this dress?" She thrust the walking costume under his nose. "I had not a single gown that was half so fine when I lived with you! Now I have a wardrobe full, each more grand than the last! And you say you don't believe me when I tell you I prefer him to you?" She laughed derisively. Her eyes blazed at him. The scene was so familiar that he wanted to kiss her and smack her bottom at the same time — until he considered her words. Then he wanted to wring her neck. He felt his own temper, held in abeyance to some degree by confusion and shock, start to simmer. Whatever else might have changed about Caitlyn, she had not lost the knack of making him wild with anger.

"You little whore." He said the words coldly, deliberately, and had the satisfaction of seeing her face whiten.

"Call me what you like. It makes no difference, as long as you leave."

"Leave? Aye, I'll leave! Think you that I want a whore to wife? I should have guessed that one day you'd follow in the footsteps of your whore of a mother! Don't they say that the apple never falls far from the tree?"

"Don't you dare call my mother a whore!"

He'd known that would enrage her. In any other circumstances, he would have felt that using the knowledge she had given him of her mother's fate against her would have been a low blow. But at the moment he was too angered to care. He watched her eyes flame at him and used his own growing fury as balm for the hideous hurt beneath.

"You've no objection to the term for yourself, then?"

"Bastard!"

"A whore would swear like a bloody dragoon," he observed, and she launched herself at him, clawing at his face. He knocked her hands aside, but she was beside herself, kicking him and ripping at his shirtfront so that she could use those claws on his skin. He heard his shirt rip and caught her hands, squeezing her wrists until she winced.

"I hate you!" she hissed, tears starting to her eyes.

"Not near so much as I hate you." The words, at that moment, were heartfelt. They glared at each other, and then her eyes dropped to his chest, widened. Connor frowned, looking down at himself to see what had caused that shocked expression. If the little bitch had made him bleed, he would . . .

Nestled in the the dark hair on his chest, bared by his torn shirt, lay the betrothal ring he had given her long ago. Since her loss he had worn it night and day, suspended from a thin gold chain around his neck. Looking down at the amber beauty of the stone, seeing her look at it too, knowing what it revealed about his emotions, he felt a rage rise up in him that was so black and uncontrollable that he feared he might do her actual physical harm. With a curse he flung her away from him and, without a backward glance, turned on his heel and left.

XXXVI

He had been left with a limp. Catching herself on the edge of the bed, Caitlyn felt her heart turn over as he stalked out the door. Her magnificent Connor had been left with a souvenir of that terrible night, just as she had been. With only the slightest hesitation in his furious stride, he favored his left leg. As vividly as if she were seeing it again, she could picture the blood gushing from the enormous hole the bullet had torn in his thigh. Her fury melted away like butter over fire, leaving behind hurt. How she longed to run after him, to tell him that it was all a terrible mistake, to run away with him as he had been hell-bent on making her do! How she longed to wrap her arms around him, press her lips to his.

Caitlyn buried her face in her hands. Tears rose to her eyes, only to be forced sternly back. Over the past twelve months, she had borne too much to find comfort any longer in tears. There was no ease she could offer her aching heart. Pain of every variety had become an inescapable fact of her life. She had learned to bear it dry-eyed.

She had hoped never to see him again, and that was the price she'd been willing to pay for his life. Still, she had faced the possibility that one day he might find her, and had rehearsed her story until it was as convincing as she could make it. But she hadn't been prepared for what the mere sight of him would do to her. Finding him in her room unexpectedly had unnerved her, terrified her, stunned her so that she had ceased to think. For one brief, glorious moment, she had been in his arms again, hugging him close, being hugged in return. She had been home — and then her shocked brain had begun to function. Connor could not be found in her room, could no longer be a part of her life. He would pay with his life if he were. She had a secret, a terrible secret that he could not discover. Though it broke her heart to do so, she had to send him away. Drive him away. Because she knew that was the only way he would go.

The door to her chamber clicked open without warning.

Caitlyn lifted her head from her hands and looked up, both hoping and dreading to see Connor standing there glaring at her. She almost wished he would force her to go with him — that would take the terrible choice out of her hands. But she did not really wish it. Whatever she had to endure, whatever pain Connor might be suffering now because of her, was preferable to seeing him and his brothers hang.

The man who strolled so confidently into her chamber was not Connor. He shut the door behind him gently, then turned to smile at her.

Staring up at him, Caitlyn felt her knees begin to shake. She knew that smile. She had first seen it just before he had slapped her on that day when she had still been an innocent, that day when Connor had avenged her by beating him to a pulp. Though she had not known it or cared to know it then, that smile had portended a sickening depravity, as she had since learned to her misery. Sir Edward Dunne, who held her imprisoned as neatly and invisibly as a butterfly in a glass, derived pleasure from other people's pain.

"Well, my dear, I feared I had lost you after the party. I should have known better than that, should I not have? I will never lose you, will I, my pet?"

"No, Edward," she intoned woodenly. Though she was not aware of it, her hands were clenched into fists as they pressed into the mattress. He saw the impotent gesture, however, and his smile broadened.

"What a pretty thing you are, to be sure." He moved toward her. Caitlyn felt her stomach clench in revulsion. No matter how many times she had had to endure his touch, she still felt physically ill whenever he came near her. She had thought, at the beginning of this hellish bargain, that time might lessen her aversion. How naive she had been! She had thought she had known much of men, and she had known nothing.

"Why, what's this?" He stopped, frowning as

he looked down at the torn gown beside the wardrobe. The other dresses that Connor had pulled out lay crumpled on the floor nearby. The green walking dress was half on, half off the bed. Most damning of all, the black mask that Connor must have been wearing when he gained entrance to her chamber lay on the small chair. Alarm shot through her. Whatever happened, Sir Edward must not be allowed to suspect that Connor had found her. She did not know what her captor's reaction would be, but she was sure it would be terrible. And she had not suffered so much for so long to now endanger Connor's life.

"I . . . I was trying on dresses, trying to find the perfect outfit to wear tomorrow. I . . . I must have forgotten to lock the door. A gentleman — one of the guests — came in and . . . and tried to — he tore my dress." She knew that she was babbling, but she could not help herself.

"One of our fellow guests tried to bed you, eh? Well, as I said, you're a pretty package. I don't blame the fellow. I trust you discouraged him?"

"Y-yes."

"And how did you do that?" He smiled again. Caitlyn blanched.

"I scratched his face."

Sir Edward chuckled. Caitlyn watched him, hating him so desperately that she was sick with it, wanting to hurt him, to kill him but not daring to, since he held the ultimate weapon that kept him safe from her. Deliberately she called to mind the images of Connor beating him, of Sir

428

Edward cringing and bloodied and whining for mercy. It was the one thing that had the power to make her feel better. If she could tell Connor, if she could just tell Connor, he would kill this man for what he had done to her. But she could not.

When she had first woken up in the lodge on the grounds of Ballymara and learned that Sir Edward was the leader of the group that had so cleverly set a trap for the Dark Horseman and his band, and had refrained from exposing her identity for his own evil purposes, she had comforted herself with the notion that she had only, somehow, to get word to Connor and she would be free. Connor would kill her tormentor as easily as he would swat a fly, and she would be set free of the prison into which her own foolishness had led her. But Sir Edward had foreseen the possibility that he might one day face Connor's wrath for what he had done, so he had devised a scheme that made it impossible for her to ever tell Connor anything. Unless she wanted to see him hang by the neck until he was dead.

"You should not have left your door unlocked. One might almost think you were hoping to have company. Am I not man enough for you, my dear? I shudder to think that that might be so."

"No. No, of course not. It . . . it was merely an oversight on my part."

He nodded judiciously. "This is certainly possible, of course. But still, I trust I made it clear that you're to be my exclusive property until such time as I tire of you. I do not wish to take the chance of such an oversight occurring again. Accordingly, you must be punished."

Caitlyn clenched her teeth. Her stomach roiled with nausea. She had seen this coming, had known that he would find some pretext or another for it from the moment he had walked into the room. That smile had told her. He was a beast, a monster — and she had no choice but to submit. Just as she had submitted for the better part of a year, ever since her wound had healed enough to permit him to practice his particular form of gratification on her. She had submitted to every painful and degrading act he had demanded, though she was sickened in body and soul. Because if she refused, he would tell the authorities of the truth he had guessed as soon as he had recognized her on that dark night when she was wounded. Sir Edward had been the first to dismount and crow over the fallen highwayman that they had thought her to be. But as soon as he had gotten a close look at her, lying crumpled and senseless in her highwayman's guise, his devious mind had immediately seen that a prize of inestimable worth had fallen into his lap. He could have her body to use as he wished and gain his revenge on Connor at the same time. If she did not stay with him, did not do exactly as he told her at all times, he would announce to the world that Connor d'Arcy was the Dark Horseman and that she and his brothers were members of his gang. Connor would be hanged.

They all would be hanged. Though for herself she might almost prefer death to the hell that her existence had become, she could not bear the thought of Connor hanging because of her, or Cormac or Rory or Liam or even Mickeen. Sir Edward had her neatly and horribly as a butterfly fluttering on an impaling pin.

If Connor found out how she suffered, he would strike back at Sir Edward no matter what the consequences might be. And the consequences lay in identical sealed letters that Sir Edward had left with his solicitor, his man of affairs, his majordomo, and a host of others whose identity she didn't even know, along with instructions that they be opened in case of his death. Letters that named Connor d'Arcy of Donoughmore as the Dark Horseman, and the probable murderer of Sir Edward Dunne.

"Disrobe, if you please."

Caitlyn knew better than to try to reason or plead with him. It only excited him more, made him hurt her more. She had learned to withdraw to a place that existed only inside herself, to leave only the shell of her body for him to abuse. It was a trick that she had mastered long ago, when she had had to live by her wits on the streets of Dublin, and it was a trick that over the past horrifying year had stood her in good stead, enabled her to survive with her sanity and a semblance of pride intact.

Though her hands shook and her knees trembled so that they would barely support her, she got to her feet and began to untie the ties of her petticoats. There was no escaping what he had planned. She could only endure, and pray for a day of glorious reckoning. One day, though she knew not when or how, vengeance would be hers.

He walked to the wardrobe and reached inside for the riding crop he forced her to always keep on hand. Looking at its slender length, Caitlyn thought she would throw up.

"Tut, tut, Caitlyn, am I to wait all night?" His mildly reproving voice told her that he was anxious to find an excuse to get even angrier with her. Anger excited him, made him more vicious than usual. Swallowing nervously, she caught the hem of her shift and pulled it up over her head. His eyes went over her, gleaming with excitement as he examined her naked body with minute attention. Standing before him, helpless to resist him in any way, she felt shame so hot and deep that she wished she might die of it. She also felt hatred, and healthy, healing anger.

"You are truly an exquisite creature," he said, his voice thickening as his eyes touched her everywhere. "What a shame that you're so wicked, that I must restore you to righteousness with the whip. Will you never learn that you must be pure for me, that you must obey without question? It angers me that you force me to mar your lovely skin."

She said nothing, because there was nothing she could say that would stop his awful tirade. He launched into a variation of it every time he

432

came to her bed. It excited him, she knew, just as anger excited him, and fear. Her fear. Which she felt despite all her exhortations to herself to have courage. By blaming her for the livid marks that were never long absent from her buttocks and thighs, he found another reason for his anger. Her knees quivered. Tonight was going to be bad.

She lifted her chin at him in the only gesture of defiance she was allowed. If she could not save herself from what was coming, at least she could face it with courage. Or at least the face of courage, which in the end was much the same. Caitlyn O'Malley asked for no quarter, ever. Not that it would do any good if she did.

"Lie down and take your punishment, you wicked chit." The rough edge to his voice told her that his excitement was progressing to the point where he would soon not be rational. Biting back a whimper of fear, she climbed onto the bed and lay facedown on the cool, slick satin of the coverlet. The terrified trembling of her limbs was out of her control. She only hoped he would not see. Despite all the degradations he had made her suffer, she had done her best to keep him from knowing how deep were her fear and shame.

"Lift your hair off your back." His voice was guttural. Caitlyn felt a sob rise in her throat. She suppressed it, breathing deeply as she reached to pull her hair up over her head as he had ordered. Wrapping her arms around her head to protect it from the blows she knew were coming, she tried to project herself to that place where her mind hid. She had not quite made it there when the first blow fell with a whistle and a crack, searing agony into the soft flesh of her buttocks that was still bruised from the last time. A small cry escaped her. At first she had tried to take the beatings in silence, but she had learned that this only made him hurt her more. He needed the evidence of her pain to find his release.

He beat her savagely about the buttocks and thighs, striping her flesh again and again while she flinched and trembled and moaned beneath the whip. Finally he threw it down and came up on the bed behind her, catching hold of her thighs and yanking them apart to kneel between them. He never came inside her, but took his pleasure by spilling his seed on her abused flesh. When she felt the warm wetness spurting onto her buttocks, she went limp, knowing the horror was over for the night.

After a moment or two, he got off the bed and buttoned his breeches. Though she kept her face pressed against the coverlet, she knew that he was looking at her with a greedy intensity. This, too, was part of the ritual. He would look at her, naked and bruised and marked with his seed, as if to imprint the sight of her humiliation upon his mind. Then he would go away. Until the next time.

She heard the door open and close and knew she was alone. Her muscles relaxed, and the stinging, burning pain in her flesh increased a thousandfold. Gulping in great mouthfuls of air, she tried to hold back the tears. But this night, for the first time in months, she was unsuccessful. She clapped her hands over her mouth to stifle her sobs and then cried as though her heart would break.

But as she had known since she was a bairn, crying changed naught. When at last her tears were spent, her buttocks and thighs still throbbed and burned, she was still naked and defiled, and she was still Sir Edward's captive plaything. And Connor was still forever beyond her reach.

The thought made her want to cry again. Instead, she swung her aching limbs off the bed and limped to the washstand to do what she could to clean and soothe her abused body.

As she looked at herself in the long cheval mirror, Caitlyn felt that it was a stranger looking back at her. She didn't know this lass with the paint still clinging to her face, with the red-rimmed eyes and swollen mouth. Her nakedness was obscene. The marks on her buttocks and legs were livid purple welts overlying greenish bruises from the last beating. She felt like a stranger in her own skin and, not for the first time, wondered if she was on the brink of losing a grip on sanity. Then she gritted her teeth. She would not be cowed and defeated, she would not.

One day she would get her revenge.

XXXVII

❋ ❋ ❋ ❋ ❋ ❋ ❋ ❋ ❋ ❋ ❋ ❋ ❋ ❋ ❋

London was a large city, and finding one hell-born brat within its environs was no easy task. Connor went about the job methodically, reasoning that since Caitlyn's protector had set her up in her own house and had been a guest at the Marquis of Standon's house party, he must be a man of some means. English gentlemen of means were creatures of habit for the most part, and there were certain sections of London where such gentlemen kept their mistresses. Covent Garden was the centerpiece around which most of those areas revolved, and it was there that he focused his search.

He had told no one of his soul-shaking discovery. Not Mickeen, who had been on the verge of saddling his horse and coming in search of him when he had finally appeared at the inn that night. Not Liam, who had nonetheless guessed that something had occurred to overset him but, despite many subtle and not so subtle inquiries, could not determine what. Not Cormac nor Rory, to whom he wrote the obligatory letter once a week. No one. He could not admit that he'd found Caitlyn only to lose her again, not when he didn't understand it himself. He'd been too hurt, too heartsore and confused to question her

436

as he should have when she'd blurted her amazing story to him. His judgment had been clouded by the two things that appeared to be indisputable fact: she was alive, and she was living as the mistress of another man.

She'd refused to tell him her lover's identity, but he had little doubt that he would shortly discover it. As soon as he learned her location, he would set a man to watch her house night and day. When a gentleman entered, Connor would be notified. He meant to see Caitlyn's lover for himself. What happened after that would depend on many things.

It was nothing short of amazing, he reflected wryly, how well he had come to know the theater district in the three weeks since he had discovered that Caitlyn was not lost to him through death but only through her own incomprehensible will. Though he had many times cursed himself for a blind, stubborn fool, he could not bring himself to just let her be, even though she had said that was what she wanted. The more he considered the matter, the more he found it impossible to believe that his Caitlyn, with her fiery spirit and loyal heart, could have grown so callous and mercenary during the course of a single year. To have allowed him to believe her dead was a hideous act of which the lass he had known was simply not capable; to take such pleasure in material things was another facet of her character that did not agree with all that he knew of her. But his senses had not deceived him: he had found his Caitlyn all right, miraculously delivered from the dead. She had seen him, known him, remembered everything — and had sent him away, saying that she loved another man. Though everything he remembered of her screamed that this was not so, it was always possible that she was telling the truth. The question that ate at him was: what reason could she have to lie?

Searching for her, he wandered the twisting streets of the theater district, sometimes on foot though it still pained him to walk far distances, sometimes in his own hired curricle, sometimes in a hackney. The weather was for the most part foul. Though it did not deter him from his purpose, it did make his leg ache and worsened his temper, which was not oversweet to begin with. He hoped to see her on the street, then follow her home, but he caught nary a glimpse of her. Instinct warned him to move cautiously until he was sure of exactly what she was about, or he would have stood boldly in the center of every damned street in the area, bellowing her name until she showed herself.

Finally, when all his subtle strategies failed him, he was forced to employ more direct measures. Knocking discreetly on the door of several dozen residences, inquiring for a Miss O'Malley and describing her in case she should be residing there under some other name, he struck paydirt at last in the fourth week of his search. A plump maidservant answered the door of one of the neat row houses on Lisle Street. In response to his inquiry, the giggling creature allowed as how she didn't know no Miss O'Malley, but she did know that a young woman answering the description Connor had given her lived along the street a ways at Number 21, though she rarely left her residence. Connor thanked her for the information and walked away. His first thought was to go immediately and discover if he had, indeed, found his quarry. His second was cooler: it behooved him to go home and think this through first.

Like the house where Caitlyn was presently residing, this residence on Curzon Street was not a fashionable address, though it had been one before the street had been allowed to run down. Certainly no English gentleman of the first stare would live thereon, unless his pockets were severely to let. But Connor was not an English gentleman; he had no use for extravagance, and the neat town house suited him just fine. With Mrs. Dabney, a housekeeper-cook hired from an agency, to do the cooking and oversee the running of the house, two maids on whom Mrs. Dabney had insisted for doing most of the cleaning, and Mickeen to act as butler-cum-valet, Connor considered that he and Liam were positively pampered.

Liam, to his oft-expressed surprise, had found much in London to his liking. Connor did not doubt that the freedom of the English wenches (who, unlike the majority of Irish lasses Liam had known, did not consider themselves damned for eternity to Hellfire if they lifted their skirts outside of marriage) had much to do with Liam's reconciliation to their exile. Still, Connor suspected that, like himself, Liam sometimes longed to be back in the fresh air and green fields of Donoughmore. But if he did, Liam didn't say so. Like Rory and Cormac, who in agreeing to look to their long-neglected education to please Connor were making a real sacrifice on his behalf, Liam was determined to do all he could to help his brother cope with grief. Had he hated London, he would have stayed as long as he felt Connor needed him. That he did not hate it was a nice bonus.

"There you are, Conn! I've a notion to visit Cribb's Parlor tonight with some cronies. Would you care to join us? 'Twould do you good to get out, you know." Liam, resplendent in a yellow coat and dark green breeches that were only a small part of his new London wardrobe, was just descending into the entry hall as Connor let himself in through the front door. (Mickeen was not the most efficient butler, but then Connor wouldn't have known what to do with a true butler if he had had one; the fellow would have driven him right insane.)

"What? Oh, no, I've things to do tonight, thanks." Connor was deep in thought and barely emerged from his abstraction long enough to answer Liam, who was frowning at him with some concern. Since Caitlyn's supposed death, Liam had taken upon himself the role of his older

brother's keeper. Before Connor had redis-
covered Caitlyn, Liam had begun to relax his
vigilance, as Connor had seemed to be coping
better with his grief. But Connor knew that his
behavior of late was bewildering in the extreme.
Once or twice he had nearly told Liam all, but
he could not bring himself to do so, not yet. He
felt that in some vague way it would be disloyal
to Caitlyn. His brothers would hate her if they
knew she had been alive the entire time he had
been half mad with grief over her death. Though
his head told him he was being foolish, his heart
was not quite ready to give up on her.

Connor was moving down the hallway toward
the room he had commandeered as his office
when he bethought himself of something. "Mind
you don't play too deep, now. My pocket is not
bottomless," he cautioned, looking back over his
shoulder at Liam with a warning frown.

This typical statement wiped some of the worry
off Liam's face. He grinned, promised not to
bankrupt the family, and with a relatively light
heart left his brother to himself.

In the office, Connor sat and brooded. He
roused himself for supper, then retired to the
front parlor, where he stared into the fire without
seeing it and sipped at an excellent cognac. After
a while, deciding that cognac was not to his taste,
he made a decision: he would go for a walk. The
cold night air would clear his head, if anything
could.

Rejecting Mickeen's plea — almost a demand

— that he be allowed to accompany him, Connor donned hat and cloak and set off down the street. He walked for nearly an hour, thinking hard all the while, before finding himself on Lisle Street. Even as he realized where his wandering feet had taken him, he knew that this had been his object all along. From the moment when the maidservant had told him where Caitlyn lived, he had known he had to see her. For good or ill, the lass had a hold on him that was nothing short of an obsession.

No matter what she had said, or done, or felt or didn't feel for him, he could not leave it at that. Though she had told him in plain words that she wished it, he could not just pluck her from his life now that he knew she lived. She had woven herself too deeply into the tapestry of his heart. For love or hatred, there was a connection between them that would not be denied. He had to see her again. It was not a choice but a need. Whether she would or no, his heart cried out that she was his. If somehow she had forgotten what they had once been to each other, then he would remind her. But he would not let her go. Not without one hell of a fight.

Connor walked around the house, ignoring the aching in his leg that warned him that he had walked too far, and eyed it with the thoroughness of a professional. It was near eleven o'clock, too late to go banging on doors. Besides, he had no wish to have whatever servants might be inside attending to his very private meeting with

Caitlyn. What he had to say was for her ears alone.

It was always possible that the man she professed to love might be in the house with her, but that was a chance he would have to take. Connor smiled grimly, thinking of it. If the man happened to be disporting himself in Caitlyn's boudoir, that might solve the problem forevermore. Confronted with his rival in a compromising position with his love, Connor knew that he would likely kill the bastard on the spot.

The faintest glow lighted the curtains of the upstairs front room. Connor guessed it was her bedroom, and saw at once how he might enter unobserved. An elegant stoop extended along the front of the house. If he could get on top of it, he would have access to her window.

Getting up there proved no problem. He jumped, caught the parapet, and heaved himself up and over. His only fear was that he would be observed by someone from a neighboring house who would summon the watch. But, glancing around, he didn't think that was likely. It was a very dark, moonless night, the kind of night the Dark Horseman had been wont to favor for his rides. The top of the stoop; on which he crouched behind an ornamental railing, was deep in shadows. Occupants of the occasional carriage rattling along the street below would not be able to see him. Not all the houses nearby were dark, but most were. The ones that still showed lights showed them in the bedrooms. The residents of those houses would probably not be looking out their windows while they did whatever they did to get ready for sleep, and therefore were not likely to see him, if he was even visible at all except as a shadow amidst other shadows.

The curtains were drawn. Though his face was pressed against the glass, Connor could see nothing inside the room. He would have to take the risk that the chamber was Caitlyn's and that she was alone. Extracting the knife from his boot, he slid it along the window frame until it caught on the latch. Carefully he worked the knife, and was rewarded by the sound of the latch falling against the window jamb. Then, with utmost stealth, he edged open the window. The curtains still blocked his view. He parted them just a sliver. The sight that immediately filled his eyes almost caused him to fall off the roof.

Caitlyn stood not ten feet from where he peered through the curtains. She was naked, facing him, and she was just stepping into a steaming porcelain bath.

Before she sank into the water he got a good, long look at the whole luscious front of her. Staring, he felt his blood heat and his loins tighten. He had forgotten how achingly beautiful she was.

Perhaps a saint would not have crouched and stared, but Connor had fallen so far short of sainthood in the past year and a half that he no longer had to worry about what a saint might do. He watched her with frank enjoyment, admiring every lovely curve and hollow. Her masses of hair were twisted into a soft pile on top of her head and secured with an elegant gold pick. Her silky black brows were as delicate as brushstrokes against the petal-smoothness of her brow. She was looking down at her hands as she busily lathered a cloth, so he caught just glimpses of the fathoms-deep blue of her eyes. But her lashes were long and black and feathery as they cast faint shadows over her cheeks, and her lips looked as soft and pink as the lushest rose. He admired the elegant lines of her face, the daintiness of her features, the graceful movements of her hands when she lifted them to splash herself with water. The tub stopped his view at her waist, but not above. Like a man too long denied water who finds himself unexpectedly confronted with a stream that is, torturously, just beyond his reach, he stared. The wind blew around him, and small flakes of snow floated down to melt on his skin and clothes, but he never noticed.

He stared at her breasts, remembering how they had felt in his hands, how they had tasted. His body hardened to the point that he was physically uncomfortable in a matter of seconds. No other woman had ever affected him so much so quickly, not even his first. But then, he had never since that first wench gone so long without availing himself of a woman's comforts. Connor reminded himself savagely that he had not had a woman since that night with Caitlyn. As the thought and all that went with it registered, he cursed himself again for being a bloody fool. Here he had been mourning her like a monk, while all the time she had been playing the harlot as if she'd been born to the role.

He stood up to relieve the discomfort she had caused, adjusting the tight black breeches with a gathering scowl. Whatever rhyme or reason had motivated her, Miss Caitlyn O'Malley had much to answer to him for. And he was here to ask the questions that his shock and hurt had saved her from the last time they had met.

Crouching again, he raised the window inch by inch until the opening was large enough for him to pass through. With knife in hand, he slid one leg over the sill, then his body, then pulled the other leg through. When he was safely inside, he paused, still sheltered by the cascading curtains, and looked carefully around the room. It was elegantly decorated in shades of pink, with a carved fourposter bed spread with a rose satin coverlet. The mirrored dressing table in the corner was of fine mahogany; its top was littered with the miscellany that fashionable women considered necessary to their lives, though in her previous incarnation Caitlyn never had. A tall wardrobe rested against the opposite wall, its doors partially ajar. In front of it was an open valise half filled with dresses and other items of feminine apparel, and a pair of bandboxes. Either she had not yet finished unpacking from the last trip, or she was soon to be leaving on one. He reminded himself to ask her, then turned his

446

attention to other things. Like the dressing table, the wardrobe was also of fine mahogany. Whoever he was, her protector did not stint her materially. Heart clenching like an angry fist, Connor wished the man were there before him now. He would slay him with the greatest pleasure on earth.

Narrowed, his eyes returned to Caitlyn. The bath had been placed before the fire, which, besides the candle on the bedside table, was the only illumination in the room. The firelight bathed her in a soft orange glow, while flickering shadows shifted in the corners of the room. A quick glance followed by a second, thorough one confirmed his original impression that she was alone. Reassured on that head, he allowed his attention to revert to Caitlyn. She was in the process of washing her face. Her eyes were closed tight as she worked soft white lather into her skin. It was clear that she was still completely unaware of his presence. The soap she used must have been scented with lilacs, because the soft fragrance filled the room. For a moment the lovely sight of her bathing naked, accompanied by the beguiling scent, threatened to make him forget just why he had come. But only for a moment.

Moving quietly, he stepped before the tub so that she would see him when she opened her eyes again. As he waited, his arms crossed over his chest, his frown was replaced by a savage half-smile. He'd wager double every groat that

Liam was in all likelihood losing at that very moment in Cribb's Parlor that looking up to find him there would give Caitlyn the surprise of her life.

XXXVIII

❊ ❊ ❊ ❊ ❊ ❊ ❊ ❊ ❊ ❊ ❊ ❊ ❊ ❊ ❊ ❊

Caitlyn rubbed the soft cloth across her face, concentrating on the feel of its gentle abrasiveness so that she would not feel the burning pain in her buttocks and thighs. The hot soapy water caused the marks left by Sir Edward's latest beating — delivered the night before — to sting unmercifully. But she was becoming almost accustomed to bathing (indeed, living) with pain and had found that if she concentrated on something other than her discomfort, the discomfort actually seemed to lessen, if not disappear.

Splashing her face to rid it of the soap, she groped for the towel. Minna, the bracket-faced maid Sir Edward had provided for her use along with the house, had set the towel out on the small table by the tub before Caitlyn had dismissed her for the night. As it always did, pride had forbidden her to allow Minna to remain. She could not bear the idea of anyone seeing the shameful marks that bore silent witness to the beatings she endured. Minna was in Sir Edward's employ, hired as much to guard as to serve, Caitlyn suspected. Minna and the hulking butler, Fromer, followed her orders insofar as she gave them. Since she had never requested them to do aught but the most mundane servants' duties, she had never tested their loyalty to the point that they were openly insubordinate. But she had no doubt that that point could be reached: the servants were Sir Edward's minions, not her own. If the two should conflict, she knew that Sir Edward's interests would be served.

Her groping hand found the smooth wood of the tabletop, moved across it. An extra bar of the same lilac-scented soap in which she had bathed skittered to the floor. It landed on the carpet beneath the bath with a muffled thud. The towel must have fallen to the floor too, because she could not find it.

"Devil take it," she muttered crossly and opened one eye to search for the towel. The sight that met her bleary gaze caused both eyes to pop open, along with her mouth.

"I give you good-evening, Caitlyn," Connor said suavely. There was a glint in his eyes that told her he had been watching her for some time. Caitlyn gave a momentary prayer of thanksgiving that he had not chosen to call on her in such a manner the night before, when Sir Edward had, at just about this time, been practicing his beastly ritual on her. The thought of Connor's reaction had he witnessed that made her shudder.

"Cold?" He misinterpreted her shudder and held out the towel, which he had apparently appropriated. She accepted it, closed her mouth, and patted her face dry with great deliberation while she willed herself into her role. When at last she again met his eyes, her own were guarded, cool.

"What are you doing here?"

"Paying you a call. Did you think I would not find you?"

"I hoped you would not."

His eyes narrowed at the calm statement. "Then 'tis sorry I am that your hope was misplaced. If I were you, I'd step out of that water. You'll be chilled to the bone before long."

"If you'll turn your back, I will."

He laughed then, the sound unamused. "Turn my back? Come, come, Caitlyn! Over the course of the past several months, you've surely lost all claims to feminine modesty. You are, after all, no matter how much you profess to love your gentleman friend or how much he may profess to love you, naught but his whore. Just as you were mine. So why bother to pretend to a modesty you cannot feel? Physically, at least, I know you well, from the scar on your thumb to the little black mole on the left cheek of your luscious behind."

"Will you turn your back?" There was an edge to her voice. His comments were both insulting and unsettling, but beyond that they reminded her of the telltale marks on her flesh. She knew that if he saw them, the fat would be in the fire indeed. Because she loved him, and because he was in mortal danger though he did not know it, she had to be strong. She had to drive him away this time for good and all — before the whole

451

situation blew up hideously in her face.

"No." The one-word reply bordered on brutality. Caitlyn eyed him for a moment, then made up her mind. She would play the role of whore that he had assigned her, and hoped to give him such a disgust of her that he would never want to see her again. It was the only way she could think of to keep him safe.

"Very well, then. As you say, 'tis useless to be modest with you. I had quite forgotten how well we once knew one another. 'Twas very long ago, after all."

"A year." His reply was toneless as she stood up, stepping from the tub, careful to keep her abused backside turned away from him. Thus she presented him with what looked like a deliberately wanton view of her full frontal nudity as she patted her body dry with carefully assumed languor. His eyes took on a dangerous gleam that she thought was a combination of anger and desire. Still damp, she abandoned her self-ministrations without the least appearance of haste and reached for the white silk wrapper Minna had left lying over the back of a nearby chair. Pulling it around herself, tying the belt, she felt marginally safer. At least the incendiary evidence of the abuse she had suffered was hidden from him. The servants were retired for the night, and Sir Edward, his lust slaked for a few days from their hellish encounter of the night before, was unlikely to make a late-hour appearance. She would have no better opportunity to convince

Connor of her unsuitability for him once and for all.

His eyes were fixed on her body, the shape of which was clearly visible through the thin silk that clung closely to every damp curve. So for just a moment she allowed herself the luxury of looking at him. The last time she had seen him, she had been too shocked to notice much in the way of detail. Now she saw that he looked older, with lines of suffering in his face that had not been there in those days at Donoughmore. Here and there a silver thread glittered against the night-black waves of his hair. He was altogether taller, bigger, more formidable-looking than she remembered. His clothes were new and very fine, the work of a fashionable English tailor, she imagined. The cloak he wore was of fine black wool, fastened at the neck with an elegant frog. Beneath it his frock coat was a sober fawn over snug black breeches. His high-topped boots were black and spotted with water from the dampness outside. His linen was faintly crumpled, his neckcloth looking as though he had retied it in a hurry. She wondered if, beneath it, he still wore her betrothal ring on a chain around his neck. The thought made her heart contract. He was still her impossibly handsome Connor, lean, dark, and dangerous. Though she had gone a whole year without seeing him, she had not forgotten the smallest detail of his appearance, from the blue-black sheen of his jaw as night waxed into morning to the heart-stopping impact of those aqua eyes.

His eyes lifted from their avid contemplation of her curves to find her studying him just as hungrily.

"You've not changed," he muttered, and the flames that leaped to life in those devil's eyes nearly unnerved her.

"You have," she said and laughed, a carefully calculated little trill. One of the ladybirds whom she had met at the latest demimonde party to which the gentlemen had brought their mistresses instead of their wives had laughed like that. At the time, she had thought it was the most wanton sound she had ever heard. Its effect on every gentleman within earshot had been immediate and apparent. Emerging from her own throat, its effect on Connor was immediate and apparent too. He looked both furious and disgusted.

"I had forgotten just how . . . very handsome you are," she breathed, deliberately fanning the flames, and reached up to pull the gold pick from her hair. As the silky black cloud tumbled around her face and shoulders, fell down her back, she smiled at him with conscious provocation. As she had expected, his face tightened. What she hadn't expected was his next reaction. He was in front of her in two strides, his hands gripping her upper arms hard through the flimsy silk.

"Now stop that," he said, glaring down at her, fingers digging punishingly into her soft flesh. "I'll not tolerate your acting the whore in my presence, at least."

"I'll act any way I please, in your presence or

454

out of it," she snapped back, startled out of her careful pose. His brows lifted, and he looked briefly struck. The expression vanished almost instantly, to be replaced by a black frown.

"You'll do as I tell you, my lass. And I'm telling you that I'll have no more of your whorish tricks, unless you're wishful to feel my hand on your backside."

"Lay a hand on my backside, Connor d'Arcy, and you'll draw back a bloody nub! You forget that I'm no longer subject to your hell-born temper!"

"I'll have no more of your swearing, either!"

"Bastard! Son of a bastard! Hell-born son of a bastard! Bloody —" This deliberate litany of curses, uttered in furious defiance of his edict, earned her a little shake.

"You watch your mouth!"

"I'll swear if I want to! What I do is no concern of yours any more! Who asked you to come sniffing after me, anyway?"

Caitlyn suddenly stopped her tirade and took a deep breath. She was horrified to discover that she had been arguing with him in precisely the same vein as she always had. Taking a grip on herself, reminding herself of her object, which was to save Connor at whatever cost to herself, she deliberately put a lid on her wrath and softened her voice to a tone of mild exasperation.

"What will it take to convince you, I wonder? I don't want you any more, Connor. I don't need you any more. 'Tis grateful I am that you rescued me from the back streets of Dublin, and doubly grateful that you taught me not to fear men. But I'm not a bairn for you to raise any longer. I'm all grown up, and I've chosen my own path in life. One that does not include you. So go home and mother your brothers, and leave me be!"

By the end of this neat speech, Connor was glaring at her so fiercely that his eyes were mere glittering slits in his dark face.

"So you're grateful to me, eh? Aye, you should be! I saved your life, you hell-born whelp, took you home and fed you and turned you from a grimy, thieving lad into a lovely little lass! As you grew up, I turned myself inside out trying to save you from my brothers and myself, and from so many others that I've lost count! Had I known that whoring was in your blood, I'd not have bothered! Doubtless if we'd passed you around the family, you'd have thanked the lot of us for the compliment!"

Caitlyn, unable to stop herself, scowled at him. Staring down at her through those glittering slits of eyes, he continued softly. " 'Tis a second miraculous escape I've had, no doubt. For had you not possessed a clearer head than I during our recent touching reunion, I doubtless would have fetched you back to Donoughmore with me. And then the fat would have been in the fire, indeed."

"And just what does that mean, pray?"

He smiled then, a slight, taunting smile that lit her temper again despite her best efforts to control it. "Why, it means that, no matter how willing you might be, I could not see you bed my brothers, my little soiled dove."

Before she thought, on a blinding blaze of temper, she slapped him. His head jerked back, his eyes widened, though for just a moment she thought she saw the merest hint of satisfaction in them. Before she could think further, he was jerking her against him, bending his head to find her lips. He kissed her, grinding his mouth against hers as if he wanted to hurt her, to punish her. She fought him, tried to pull away, but he was too strong, forcing her lips apart with hurtful insistence. Despite her anger, despite the warning voice inside her that bleated doom if she failed to keep herself under control, she could not stop the tiny spurt of passion that flared to life under his mouth. He must have felt the beginnings of a response she could not control, because he released her, pulling back to study her with unnerving intensity.

Appalled and frightened at her own response and his apparent knowledge of it, she managed to jerk her arm free of his hold and slap him again. The openhanded blow was vicious, motivated by panic as much as by anger, and it rocked his head to one side. Before he could recover she slapped him a third time. This time he caught her wrist, imprisoning it. The mark of her hand was plainly visible on his dark cheek, the whitened imprints quickly filling with red. His hair had come loose from its ribbon, framing his face in night-black waves. A muscle twitched at the corner of his hard mouth, and his jaw with its near a day's growth of beard was set and grim. He towered above her, his shoulders in the black cloak wide enough to block her view of the rest of the room. She had forgotten how tall he was, how strong and muscular. Always, to her, he was simply Connor. Her Connor, who would never harm her. But now, looking up at him, she bethought herself of something: he was no longer her Connor. By her own words and actions she had stripped herself of that protection. Now she was vulnerable to the devil in him. And "devil" was exactly the right word to describe how he appeared to her in that moment.

With a kind of dreadful fascination she met that glittering aqua gaze. And she remembered how, when she had first laid eyes on him, she'd thought that he had devil's eyes. Now she was seeing those eyes again, and as she stared up into them she realized that she had managed to awaken the sleeping devil, and no mistake.

XXXIX

❋ ❋ ❋ ❋ ❋ ❋ ❋ ❋ ❋ ❋ ❋ ❋ ❋ ❋ ❋ ❋

He didn't say a word. He didn't have to. His eyes were eloquent enough. Caitlyn stared into them, felt his hand tighten on her wrist. He jerked her against him, and she had no thought of resisting. If she had, she would not have been able to. He was too strong, too angry, too determined. He pulled her against him, imprisoning her arms with his, and bent his head to her mouth. The kiss he forced on her was insulting. Never before in her life had Connor kissed her in such a way. She would not have believed him capable of inflicting such deliberate cruelty, even on a female he despised. Connor was essentially a kind man. In that moment Caitlyn realized just how much pain he must have suffered because of her.

Somewhere she had heard that hatred was love's twin. The bond that tied her to Connor and Connor to her was far too strong to be destroyed even by the cataclysmic assault that this tangle of events had wreaked on their relationship. What he thought was her betrayal of him had made his love for her turn to hate. But down deep somewhere, under the hurt, under the hate, Connor's love for her still existed. Despite the grinding punishment of his kiss, knowing that made her mouth go soft beneath his.

He felt the change in her, felt her go limp and pliable in his hold, and lifted his head to look down at her. Caitlyn met his eyes. The bright glittering aqua was molten now, glazed with need, with wanting her. Although her mind screamed she shouldn't, her heart overruled. This was Connor, her Connor, whom she had hurt badly and who must love her more than she'd ever guessed for him to want to hurt her so. Her heart swelled with an aching need for him, with an almost uncontrollable desire to console and love and make up to him for all he had endured because of her. In that instant, she imagined how she would have felt if she had thought him dead, and the resulting clenching of her heart almost made her cry out. That was how he had suffered, was still suffering from what he thought was her betrayal. But she could not tell him the truth, the one thing that would mend his wounded heart. All she could do was offer him the sweet solace of her body.

She reached up to twine her arms around his neck, going on tiptoe to press her lips to his mouth. His eyes closed, and his arms clamped around her so tightly that his hold hampered her breathing. She felt him shudder against her as his mouth came down on hers again, not hurting this time but kissing her as if he would steal her very soul.

She felt him move, felt his arms shift position until one was behind her back and the other was behind her knees. With a single lithe movement he swung her up off her feet, his mouth never leaving hers, and carried her the three strides to the bed. Then he was laying her down, leaning over her, pulling her robe apart with quick jerky movements. Keeping her eyes shut tight, as though not to see would be to close out the world, she held him tighter and moaned his name into his mouth. For just a little while she would let the hurt and shame and pain go. For just a little while she would allow herself to pretend that things were as they had been between them before she had sought to join the Dark Horseman on that hell-born night. For just a little while he would be hers again, and she his. For just a little while. . . .

He cursed, his breath warm in her mouth, and tore at his clothes, as frantic for her as she was for him. She heard the ripping of cloth, the popping of buttons, but still she kept her eyes closed. Not to see was not to acknowledge the danger of what she was doing. For just once more, only once more, she would allow herself to love him, permit him to love her. What harm could come of just one more night?

He was naked now. She felt the heat of his skin, the rough abrasion of his body hair as he wrapped his arms around her, coming down on top of her so that her swelling breasts were crushed by the weight of his broad chest. His thigh, hard and urgent, was parting hers. She caught her breath, quivering at the feel of it, and spread her legs for him, still without opening her eyes. Then he came inside her, hard and hot and enormous and wonderful. She gasped, and clasped him close, her nails digging into the back of his neck. She had forgotten that a man could feel like this. That she could feel like this.

He drove deep, shuddering with need, and she cried out, her legs shifting of their own accord to wrap around his waist. His mouth left hers to trace hot kisses along her neck before he buried his face in the space between her shoulder and neck. She kissed his cheek, his ear. His skin was rough with the beginnings of a beard and tasted salty beneath her mouth. He was driving into her relentlessly, his movements hard and urgent, his body convulsing over hers as if he was no longer in control of what it did. She clasped him to her, and as she felt the near-forgotten tightening in her loins she cried out his name.

"Oh, dear God, Caitlyn, Caitlyn. My own, my love," he growled in anguished answer. Then he was coming into her so hard and fast and relentlessly that she was sent spinning away by the force of his strokes, rendered deaf and dumb and blind to everything but Connor and the way he was making her feel. She found that wonderful place again, that magical place that he had introduced her to so long ago, and entered it with a gasping moan as the whole world dropped away. She heard him cry out too, felt him tremble and shudder and stiffen. Then he collapsed on top of her, still holding her close, his breath warm on her neck, his sweat-damp body clinging to hers as if they were truly of one flesh.

The world came back slowly, but it did come back. Reluctant to acknowledge what she had done, she tried to hold the realization at bay. She stroked her hand over his thick hair, stroked the warm, damp skin of his shoulder and down his spine. She never opened her eyes, and retained just enough presence of mind to stay flat on her back. Even in this last bittersweet moment, she knew that she must not let him see the marks on her skin.

"Caitlyn." She felt him lift his head from its berth in the hollow of her neck and knew that he was looking down at her. Still she kept her eyes shut. To open them would be to confront reality, to do what she knew had to be done for his sake.

"Look at me, Caitlyn." His voice was quietly insistent. Caitlyn felt his weight shift until he was no longer lying on top of her but was stretched out alongside her, one leg thrown possessively over her thighs as she lay flat on her back. She knew that she would not be able to hold him off much longer, but still she tried, lifting her face with involuntary need to strengthen her contact with his finger, which was ruffling the lashes that rested so stubbornly against her cheeks.

"Open your eyes, cuilin," he said in a near whisper. The sound of that Gaelic endearment on his tongue was almost her undoing. With searing intensity she remembered when he had first called her that. Tears threatened to overwhelm her, and only with great difficulty did she manage to fight them back. She could not soften in her resolve, not now. For his own sake, she must play the part she had to play. Later, when he was safely out of her life, she could cry over the pieces of her broken heart.

Taking a deep breath, she opened her eyes. As she had thought, he was leaning over her. He was so handsome and so dear and she loved him so much that she could almost hear the cracking of her heart. But for his sake, she had to drive the tenderness from his face and touch.

A nerve twitched at the corner of his mouth as he looked hard and long into her eyes.

"Now tell me you don't love me," he said finally, his eyes never leaving hers.

Deep in the nearly depleted well of strength that had sustained her through every adversity, Caitlyn found a tiny remaining reservoir that was untapped. Drawing on it, she forced herself to meet those eyes with derision dawning in her own.

"Oh, Connor, don't be such a romantic fool! 'Twas not love that prompted me to this. 'Twas merely the need of a woman for a man! Any man." She emphasized this last with that wanton, trill-noted laugh she had employed earlier. He stiffened, stared at her grimly.

"You lie."

"Do I? Methinks all your conquests have gone to your head. Not every female you bed is dying for love of you, you know."

She could see the telltale jumping of a tiny muscle in his temple. His eyes iced over as his expression hardened.

"You little bitch of a whore."

"There's no need to be insulting. After all, you certainly managed to pleasure yourself."

"As did you." His face was very grim; rage leapt from his eyes as they moved over her face, her body. As casually as she could, she tugged free the wrapper, which their passion had left twisted and tangled beneath her, and pulled the folds of crumpled silk around herself.

"Oh, aye, I've learned to take my pleasure where I can," she purred, all the while screaming inwardly at the agony she was inflicting on him. But there was nothing for it but to continue her charade. She had to drive him away. Hellfire blazed at her suddenly from those strange light eyes. For a moment she almost cringed, so sure was she that he was going to strike her.

"May your soul roast in hell, along with your cheating little body," he growled instead, rolling away from her and off the bed. As he began to pull on his clothes with savage motion, she saw that the ring and chain were absent from around his neck. For a moment she wondered what he could have done with the ring that she still thought of as hers. Then his nakedness distracted her from all thoughts that were not directly of him. She watched him, heart swelling with pain as for the first time she saw his damaged thigh. The scar that twisted halfway to his knee was obscene in the face of so much masculine beauty. She had to tear her eyes away from it or be overcome. . . .

"I wish your lover joy of you, and all those who will no doubt come after him. May they be as deceived by the angel face of you as I was; and may they come to know the devil that lurks inside."

"Why, Connor, that sounds almost like an Irish curse!" she said on a note of amused delight, and had the painful satisfaction of seeing him go pale with anger before he turned on her.

XL

"Hold your tongue! 'Tis enough and more I've had of your blather." He glared at her for a moment, draping his neckcloth around his neck without bothering to tie it, so that the ends trailed down his shirtfront. He pulled on his boots, shrugged into his coat, then cocked a thumb at her. "Get up and get dressed. You're coming home with me."

Caitlyn gaped at him. She had not been expecting that; the idea had been to infuriate him enough so that he would wash his hands of her for good and all. She had succeeded in infuriating him, clearly — he looked angry enough to chew nails. But she had not foreseen that he would still be intent on carrying her off. One look at that dark, set face told her that she had a problem. She had seen Connor look like that before, and when he did he invariably got what he wanted.

"Don't be daft. I'm not going anywhere. Though I wish you'd leave and not bother me again."

"Oh, I'm leaving, all right. And so are you."

"I'm not! You can't make me!"

"What a child you are," he said contemptuously, and came over to the bed and yanked her to her feet. Caitlyn pulled her hand out of his and backed away, glaring at him.

"Damn it, Connor, you can't come in here like this and start bullying me! You don't own me! You have no rights to me at all! I don't want to come with you! I don't even want to see you again! Can't you get it through your head that what was once between us is over?"

"The hell it is," he said and came after her. Alarmed at the look in his eyes, Caitlyn backed away until she had reached the wall and could go no further. Still he kept coming, until he was a scant handbreadth away from her.

"Are you going to get dressed?" he asked, his voice ominous as he crowded her against the wall. Those aqua eyes glittered down at her like twin daggers. Looking up at him, Caitlyn wanted to scream with frustration, and cry and laugh at the same time. She knew this Connor well. He would take her with him, would she or wouldn't she, by force if need be. And oh, how she wanted to be taken! But she couldn't permit him to sweep her up and carry her off. Because as soon as Sir Edward discovered that she had disappeared, the tale would be told. She didn't know if he would search for her first or go straight to the authorities. She did know that there would be hell to pay for the man she loved.

"I am not going to get dressed," she said, meeting him glare for glare and trying to sound calmly determined. "Because I am not going anywhere. I have a new life now, and it is here. You are making things very difficult for me, Connor. Please, please, just go away and leave me be!"

"In a pig's eye," he said through his teeth. Before she could guess what he meant to do, he threw his cloak around her shoulders, wrapping her in it. Then he bent and hoisted her onto his shoulder. She hung facedown for a surprised instant while he turned toward the window. Then she began to fight, kicking and squirming until her hands were finally free of the enveloping cloak and could pound his back with her fists.

"Damn you, Connor d'Arcy, put me down!"

He continued to walk toward the window. She punched him in the small of his back with all her strength. He did not even flinch.

"Put me down, do you hear? I'm not alone in the house, you know! I'll scream for help!"

"Scream away," he invited, steadying her with a hand on her backside. His other arm was wrapped securely around her legs to keep her from falling and/or kicking him as he maneuvered the pair of them through the window. The freezing cold of the night struck Caitlyn like a blow. It was dark as pitch, the wind was blowing, and a few fat flakes of snow drifted down. Even with the haphazard protection of his cloak, the wind found its way up her legs. The silk wrapper she wore beneath was totally inadequate as a decent cover for her nakedness, let alone as protection from the weather.

"You can't just kidnap me, damn you! I'm not even dressed!" Despite her furiously hissed protest, she clung to the back of his coat with both hands. Upside down as she was, the distance to the street below was terrifying. He walked the length of the stoop as surefootedly as a cat, despite his limp, but she did not want to chance an ill-timed bite or pinch that would make him drop her on her head on the cobblestones.

"I thought you were going to scream," he taunted. Reaching the edge of the stoop, he bent to catch hold of the decorative railing with one hand. "Hold tight," he advised her and swung himself over the side, so that the pair of them were dangling over the muddy side yard while he hung from the railing with one hand. Caitlyn gasped as the ground spun perhaps ten feet below her reeling head. She shut her eyes and clutched him for dear life. He let go, and she had the brief, terrifying sensation of falling until with a thump he landed on the balls of his feet without ever relaxing his grip on her.

"You swine," she said, opening her eyes when it occurred to her that they were safe on terra firma.

"Bite me and I'll make you wish you were dead," he threatened by way of answer, apparently remembering her previous reaction to being carried off in such a high-handed fashion. Caitlyn knew better than to bite. His retaliation would be swift and more painful than he could imagine, given her battered backside. She contented herself with hissing curses at him as he strode off with her down the street.

"You watch your mouth or I'll wash it out with soap for you when I get you home," he warned her, sounding grim.

"Damn you, I'm not a child! Quit treating me like one! You can't wash my mouth out — and you can't carry me off like this either! I have a right to my own life! I want to go back! Damn you, Connor d'Arcy, do you hear me?"

They had reached the end of the street. A hackney rattled past. Connor let out a shrill whistle, and the driver pulled up. Caitlyn could not see the man's face, but her own burned as she considered the picture she must present: barefoot, next door to naked, and being carried like contraband over Connor's shoulder.

"Giving ye trouble, is she, mate?" the man asked with a jovial chuckle. Caitlyn clenched her fists in the soft, damp wool of Connor's coat. Just wait until she was on her feet again! She would rock his head for him!

"A mite," Connor allowed. Though Caitlyn could not see it, she guessed that the two exchanged purely masculine grins before he stepped up into the cab with her and the driver shut the door on them.

"You are the most . . . !" she sputtered as he bent to deposit her on the seat. Upright, she clutched his cloak closer and glared at him while he settled himself opposite her. Two small, nearly burned-out candles guttered in sconces set high in the hackney's shabby sides.

"The most what?" he questioned with a lifted

eyebrow. The candlelight caught those aqua eyes and gave them a startling life of their own. He was too arrogant by half.

"The most despicable, loathsome, high-handed bastard it has ever been my displeasure to encounter!" she snapped, huddling inside the cloak to ward off the chill wind that seemed to blow right through the coach. "How dare you carry me off this way! What are you going to do, lock me up somewhere? I warn you, 'tis what you'll have to do to keep me!"

"Whatever it takes until one of us has come to her senses," he said, lounging back in the seat. Now that he had the upper hand, much of his fury seemed to have dissipated. He was watching her like a hawk, but there was a kind of weighing in his eyes as well that Caitlyn was too furious to ponder.

"Until one of us has come to her senses?" she repeated with a disbelieving laugh. "Are you implying that you think I've lost my senses by preferring another man to you? You are an arrogant bastard!"

"And you'll be eating soap as soon as we get home," he responded almost amiably. The coach lurched to a stop. Caitlyn felt panic begin to build. She knew Connor, and he would have not the slightest compunction about locking her in an attic somewhere until she, as he put it, "came to her senses." The only problem was that as soon as Minna missed her in the morning, she was bound to send word to Sir Edward. Caitlyn had to get back inside that house on Lisle Street before Sir Edward discovered she was missing and carried out his threat. She had to!

"Are you going to walk, or do I carry you?" His eyes gleamed at her as the driver swung open the door. Defiance was useless, she knew. One way or another, she would descend from the hackney. But pride refused to let her give in to Connor without a show of protest. She regarded him stonily. Her only answer was a lift of her chin.

"Very well, then." Despite her outraged hiss, Connor hoisted her to his shoulder as he had done before. Prudent or not, this time Caitlyn sank her teeth into his back just as he was stepping down from the hackney. He yelped and almost fell, the cabby chuckled, and Caitlyn braced for the hand she expected to fall on her backside. But it didn't.

"You'll pay for that, you hell-born brat," he muttered instead and shifted her so that she could not bite him again, though he could not wholly guard himself from her furious kicks and blows. He did not stop to pay the driver but climbed the steps to the front door, which opened before he touched it.

"Me — me lord," Caitlyn heard a shocked gasp and knew that it was Mickeen. She was too angry to care. Cursing like the street urchin she had once been, she squirmed and fought against Connor's iron hold.

"Pay the man, would you?" Connor grunted

to Mickeen by way of a reply and strode into the house. He did not stop in the vestibule but went straight up the stairs and down a corridor to a door which he kicked open. Caitlyn got a hazy impression of a comfortable if shabby room warmed by a blazing fire before he kicked the door shut behind him and deposited her on the bed, yanking his cloak from her in the process.

"Damn you, Connor d'Arcy!" she sputtered as she bounced helplessly on the soft feather mattress.

He threw the cloak down over a chair back, crossed to the washstand, and turned back to her with a grim expression and a cake of wet white soap in his hand.

"You'd not dare!"

"I did warn you," he said, and before she could scramble off the bed, he was bearing down on her with the soap. She fought, but to no avail. He pinned her against his chest, wrapped a hand in her hair, tugged her head back, and washed her mouth out thoroughly. She gagged and thrashed wildly, and when he finally let her go she collapsed back on the bed, crawled to the side, and retched miserably.

"I hate you, you . . ." she muttered with real loathing through the horrible-tasting bubbles that still coated her tongue and teeth and lips. A rap on the door interrupted her before she could expand on her theme.

"Go away," Connor responded irritably, never taking his eyes off her as she spat at him.

"Conn, Mickeen says . . ." It was Liam on the other side. Before he could finish speaking, Connor crossed to the door and pulled it open, holding it wide so that Liam and Mickeen behind him had a full view of the bed. Caitlyn, disheveled, half naked, and still spitting soap, glared at the pair of them as she clutched at the wrapper that had threatened to part from its moorings in the melee with Connor.

"St. Patrick and the Blessed Virgin!" Liam gasped, his mouth dropping open. Behind him, Mickeen crossed himself.

"Behold our latter-day Lazarus," Connor said dryly. "Before you start thinking about exorcisms, let me tell you that she is not and has never been a ghost. She merely neglected to let us know that she survived the little incident that upset the rest of us so much. Though she's apologized for being so thoughtless, of course."

Caitlyn spat out more bubbles and transferred her glare to Connor. An errant strand of her hair, which was tumbling wildly around her barely clad form, got in her face and she pushed it back with an angry movement of her hand. Liam and Mickeen watched her with as much horrified fascination as if she were in truth risen from the dead.

"You swine, Connor d'Arcy," she said with loathing. Liam blinked.

"That's Caitlyn," he said, as if he had not been convinced until that moment. Then he turned his stunned gaze on Connor. "But how — ?"

"I'll explain the whole thing in the morning," Connor interrupted, and swung the door shut in Liam's and Mickeen's wondering faces. "As for you . . ." He turned his attention back to Caitlyn. "We have some talking to do."

"I've nothing to say to you," Caitlyn stated, crossing her arms over her breasts and hitching herself up so that she was sitting against the pillow.

"That's just as well, for I've a great deal to say to you. First of all, I want the name of your lover."

"Hah!" Caitlyn said scornfully, pulling her legs beneath her and jerking the topmost quilt over her lap. Though an oath trembled on the tip of her tongue, she managed to swallow it. Connor would not think twice about assaulting her with the soap again. "What kind of fool do you take me for? Shall I make you a present of his name so that you can go and kill him for me?"

" 'Twill be easy enough to find out, do you not tell me."

"Find out, then. For I'll tell you nothing, except that I dislike being dragged from my home by brute force and held against my will. To say nothing of being subjected to your barbaric punishments!"

"Drastic situations call for drastic measures," Connor said with a shrug, coming to sit on the edge of the bed and look intently at her. The unwavering stare made Caitlyn uncomfortable. She had the uncanny sensation that he could see into her soul.

"Does your protector bed you, then?"

Caitlyn gaped at him, unable to believe that she had heard him correctly. The look on his face assured her that she had. A hot blush suffused her skin from her collarbone to her hairline. Connor, she remembered, had ever been one for plain speaking.

"How dare you ask me such a question!"

"That act of outraged modesty cuts no ice with me," he said grimly. "We've discussed — and more than discussed — matters far more delicate, if you will cast your mind back. I want an answer: does he bed you?"

"What do you think he does, feed me a handful of hay from time to time like a blood— ah, great horse?" she hissed in reply.

"The soap is near at hand," he warned, watching her.

"Try that again and I'll . . . I'll . . ."

"Rend me limb from limb," he finished for her with a quirk of his lips. "I remember. I'm quaking in my boots."

She eyed him. He was watching her like a cat at a mousehole, and she was suddenly assailed by the notion that she'd said something, done something, to make him doubt her tale. Connor had too much pride to shanghai a reluctant woman — unless he had some reason to believe that she was not so reluctant as she pretended. Perhaps because of the ardor with which she had responded to his lovemaking? Remembering her impassioned reaction to his touch, she blushed again.

"You would have me believe that you have been his mistress for the better part of the past year, is that correct?" He looked at her as if for a response. When she gave him nothing but a stony glare, he went on as if she'd nodded. "Then tell me something, if you will: why are you not with child?"

Caitlyn's eyes widened. Though she had not thought about it before, she knew that what she and Connor did together was how people got babies. With Connor, before this nightmare had begun, she hadn't cared. In fact, she would have loved carrying his child. But with Sir Edward. . . . She barely managed to restrain a shudder. It seemed she had something to be thankful for, after all. If Sir Edward had been a normal man instead of a depraved monster, the chances were excellent that she would even now be expecting his bairn. The idea sickened her; she tried not to let her face show how she felt.

"How do you know I am not?" she challenged when she could speak.

His jaw hardened, and his mouth tightened. Real rage flared for a moment in his eyes. Observing him, Caitlyn thought he looked on the verge of violence for just a moment before the sudden flare of rage faded, to be replaced by that expression of watchful attention again.

"Are you hoping to convince me that you're

with child?" His voice was carefully guarded. Caitlyn realized that he too was working hard to keep his true emotions from showing.

"No." The confession was sudden and abrupt. Not even if it would make him let her go — which she didn't think it would — could she pretend to be carrying Sir Edward's child. The thought made her want to throw up.

"Why are you not, then? Have you been doing something to prevent it?"

"Certainly." Her reply was haughty. His mouth curved slightly in a derisive smile.

"Pray enlighten me as to what."

Since Caitlyn had not even known there was a means of preventing conception, she was all at sea. She suspected that he was laying a trap for her, but she was too canny a bird to fall for that!

"Use your imagination. 'Tis grand enough," she snapped. He actually smiled that time, though the smile was a trifle grim about the edges.

"You forget I know you well. You're lying in your pretty little teeth, my own, and I want the truth. When I made love to you tonight, you were as tight and untried as a maid again. Now, I know full well you're no maid, but you're no woman of experience either. As you should be by now, if all that you tell me is true. And you should not have gone up in flames at my touch either."

"Your imagination is exceeded only by your conceit," Caitlyn said through her teeth.

"You did not respond like a woman betraying a man she loves," Connor continued softly, his eyes never straying from her face. "In fact, though I hesitate to lay myself open to another charge of conceit, you responded as if you were in love with me."

Caitlyn said nothing, merely eyed him with growing unease. Connor was not going to desist in his questions. She was afraid that, sooner or later, knowing her as well as he did, he would divine something alarmingly close to the truth, which would be disastrous. He would go into a rage that would not ease until Sir Edward was dead by his hand. The catastrophe that she had suffered so much to avoid would occur, and all her sacrifice would have been in vain.

From the moment that Connor had discovered that she still lived, the situation had spiraled down into utter chaos. In her present unsettled state, she could see no clear way to save it. But she knew that the first step involved getting herself away from Connor and back to the house on Lisle Street. She had to be in her own bed when Minna came in with chocolate in the morning, or the elaborate tapestry she had woven for Connor's protection would unravel with alarming speed. Her presence in that house would not hold the crisis at bay forever, she knew, but like a finger in the dike, she figured that it would do until she could think of something else. Besides, she was going out of town on the morrow, summoned by Sir Edward to an intimate gathering of his particular cronies at his hunting box in Kent. Connor would be unable to locate her for nigh on a se'ennight, which would give her time to think of a more permanent solution to the problem.

"I want to go home, Connor. To my own home, I mean. On Lisle Street. Tonight. You had no right to bring me here against my will." Her voice was weary as she tried to reason with him. His mouth twisted.

"Did you never hear of the right of might, my own?" he asked. She set her lips and refused to respond. Alter a moment, he came to the conclusion that he had gotten all he would from her for the time being at least. Getting off the bed, he pulled off his neckcloth and shrugged out of his coat. Caitlyn watched him with astonishment mixed with growing indignation.

"And just what do you think you are doing?" He was working on the buttons of his shirt.

"Going to bed. I expect an interesting day tomorrow, and I need my rest."

"I sincerely trust that you are not planning to sleep with me!"

"Then you sincerely trust wrong. I don't mean to let you out of my sight until I've got to the bottom of this. If you want to go home, as you call it, you'd be well advised to tell me the truth. The whole truth. For I don't buy what you're trying to sell me."

"You don't want to buy it, you mean," she muttered sullenly. "Because you're naught but a stubborn jack-donkey." In the firelight, his skin was paler than she remembered, and she realized that it must be because he had done no outdoor work this past summer. Nevertheless, his chest and arms were as muscular as she recalled, his shoulders as broad and his waist as narrow. His abdomen above the buff breeches was flat and ridged with muscle. The curling wedge of black hair on his chest narrowed down into a trail that bisected that flat abdomen before disappearing beneath his breeches. Looking at him without his shirt, Caitlyn felt her breath catch. He had always had that effect on her, from the very beginning. She glanced up suddenly to find his eyes glinting at her. He had seen and recognized her response, she knew.

"So you're in love with someone else," he taunted softly, sitting down on the edge of the bed to pull off his boots. His back was turned to her, and for just a moment she caught herself admiring the satiny skin, the workings of his muscles as he tugged at his boots, the deep line of his spine. The urge to run her fingers along that line was so strong that she had to bite her lip to keep from giving in. Instead she realized that he had presented her with the perfect opportunity, if she had the strength of mind to use it. His back was to her, his attention on his boots. And a hefty silver candelabra was within reach on the table beside the bed.

If she wanted to get back to that house on Lisle Street before she was missed, knocking Connor unconscious and escaping was the only way. He slept lightly, and he would be expecting her to attempt escape. She would not get away from him while he slept. Besides, she wouldn't put it past the wily swine to tie her up in some way. If she wanted to make sure of escape, this was likely to be her best chance. The question was: did she have the strength of mind and purpose to take it? For Connor's sake?

She stole another glance at him, then reached over to pick up the candelabra. He nearly had his second boot off. . . . Wincing, she rose up on her knees and brought the heavy piece of silver crashing down on the back of his head. It landed with a terrible thud. He grunted, wavered, then slowly collapsed, sliding to the floor as if his bones and muscles had turned to liquid, and lay there still as death.

Horrified, Caitlyn dropped the candelabra and scrambled down to kneel beside him. She was assailed by the sudden dreadful conviction that she had killed him.

But his chest rose and fell with reassuring evenness. Her exploring fingers found no blood, only a swelling lump on the back of his head. She smoothed the disordered waves of hair over that lump as if to make amends for her recent act of violence.

"I'm so sorry, Connor," she whispered, though she knew he could not hear. Giving in to overwhelming temptation, she bent and pressed a quick, soft kiss on his barely parted lips. Then she got to her feet and looked wildly about the room. There was a window facing the street. Catching up Connor's cloak, and in the process dumping the rest of the clothes he had discarded onto the floor, she was over to the window and opening it in a flash. It was a goodly drop to the ground, but his house, like hers, was embellished with a stoop running its entire front length. From the window to the top of the stoop was not such a great distance.

Hesitating on the sill, she looked back at where he was sprawled on the floor. The bed partially blocked her view, but she could see his head and shoulders and one outflung hand. Her heart ached at leaving him so, but there was nothing else to be done. For his sake, she had to go.

"I love you, Connor," she whispered because she had to, and then she was lowering herself from the window.

XLI

When Connor came around he knew immediately what had happened. Groaning, gingerly touching the throbbing back of his head, he levered himself into a sitting position. Why he had been so careless as to turn his back on the little bitch he couldn't fathom. He knew the cut of her cloth as well as he knew his own. He should have been expecting . . .

A rush of icy air from the window she'd left open behind her helped to clear his head. He couldn't have been out more than a quarter of an hour, if that. She'd hardly had time to get back to Lisle Street, which he was fairly certain was her immediate goal. He had to go after her, now, or he feared he would have the devil of a time finding her again.

He staggered to the door, threw it open, and bellowed for Mickeen. The little man must have been closeted with Liam nearby, for the pair of them appeared on the instant. They saw him swaying and scowling in the doorway, clad in naught but a pair of breeches as he felt his sore head, and they exchanged a single speaking look.

"The little bitch blind-sided me," Connor growled by way of explanation before they could find the words to ask. "I'm going after her.

Mickeen, I'll be needing the curricle."

"I'm coming with you, Conn," Liam asserted, and Mickeen visibly bristled.

" 'Twill be a fine old time you'll have of it leaving me behind, yer lordship. I wanted to go with you the last time. I told you how 'twould be."

"Have done, Mickeen — my head is pounding all to hell." Connor winced as he found the lump on the back of his head. The thing was as big as an egg and painful as a boil. "You both may come if you wish. I'll probably even be glad of the escort. I've a notion there may be trouble. There's something about the situation she's got herself into that I mislike."

"What — ?"

"I'll explain later, Liam. Arm yourselves. It will take me a moment only to dress." He turned back to his room and staggered, going down on one knee.

"Conn!"

"Yer lordship!"

Both Liam and Mickeen were beside him immediately. Connor permitted them to help him to his feet and ease him onto the bed. He lay back for a moment, closing his eyes and gritting his teeth. From the feel of it, Caitlyn's blow had come close to splitting his skull.

"What did she hit you with?" Liam sounded faintly awed.

"The candlestick, the little besom. She's not changed a particle. I should have known not to turn my back on a she-devil."

"Conn, the suspense is killing me! You need to lie there for a bit before you try to go anywhere, and I have to know: how is it that Caitlyn lives? Where has she been? How did you find her? And for God's sake, why did she hit you over the head with a candlestick?"

Connor felt strangely reluctant to tell his brother the truth about the exact circumstances she had been in when he found her, just as he felt inclined after all to decline their escort to Lisle Street. It both stung his pride and boded ill for their opinion of Caitlyn's moral character that they should know she had been living for the past year as another man's mistress. Whatever she had or hadn't done, he could not bring himself to expose her as the piece of Haymarket ware her own words made her out to be. Deep in his bones he felt there was far more to the story than she would have him believe. However, Liam had a right to know some part of what had happened, though Connor would edit the most shocking bits as best he could. And Liam was right: he needed to lie still for just a minute. Just until his head stopped swimming. . . . But then there was Caitlyn, half naked and alone on foot in the streets of London. The telling of stories would have to wait until he had her safe again.

"Later," he said, sitting up despite the ringing pain in his head. The room seemed to swim around him. Amazed, Connor realized that Caitlyn must have struck him a mansize blow: he was going to pass out.

487

He muttered a curse as nausea overcame him. Then his eyes rolled up in his head and he slumped sideways on the bed.

When at last he made it to Lisle Street, it was past daylight. No one responded to his frenzied knocking. Finally he entered the house the same way he had before. As he had suspected, it was empty. The bird had flown the nest.

XLII

A se'ennight and two days later, Caitlyn reluctantly returned from Sir Edward's hunting box. Sir Edward himself had left Kent two days before with his guests, but, hoping to postpone the inevitable confrontation with Connor, Caitlyn had lingered, pleading illness, until she could linger no longer. Sir Edward wanted to show her off that evening at a public ball to be held at London's Pantheon. A group of his friends and their current ladybirds would round out the party, to which she looked forward to with about as much enthusiasm as she would to having a tooth drawn. Should she not be ready when his carriage came for her, he would be angry, and possibly even suspicious of her motives. Lingering in one of the houses to which he sometimes took her was not like her; she usually couldn't wait to get away, to get back to London, where, if she were fortunate, she would see him no more than twice a week.

As she dressed for the ball, Caitlyn was near despair. Every time there was a sound anywhere in the house she jumped like a scalded cat. She fully expected Connor to come bursting in at any moment. Her nerves were stretched to the breaking point. She was exhausted, in pain from the beatings that had occurred almost nightly at the

489

hunting box since Sir Edward had had her in such proximity, and frightened half to death. She had still not arrived at any solution to the problem of Connor, though she had racked her brain during the entire time she was away, and the moment of reckoning was, she feared, near at hand.

"The carriage is here, miss." Fromer's rap on the door startled her out of her thoughts. Minna, whom she had admitted to do up her buttons and style her hair, stood back from where her mistress sat on a stool before the dressing table, brush in hand as she surveyed her handiwork with a critical eye.

"Sir Edward will be pleased, miss," she intoned expressionlessly. Except for the fact that Sir Edward would be angry if she did not look as glitteringly lovely as he liked to see her, Caitlyn would be just as pleased if her captor did not admire her looks. Though whether she was in looks or not, he was hardly likely to come to her tonight after the ball. He had surely had a surfeit after that entire monstrous week — though it had been two days since he had practiced his particular form of gratification upon her. Her stomach churned at the thought.

"Thank you, Minna," Caitlyn said, standing up. Though they both knew it was a fiction, she and Minna continued to behave as if she were in truth the mistress and Minna nothing more than her maid. As long as Sir Edward was pleased with her, that was how it would be, though she was forbidden to leave the house without either Minna or Fromer in attendance.

"Will you wear your new cloak? It is quite cold out." Minna's voice was so impersonal that it was almost as if a piece of furniture spoke. Caitlyn nodded, and as the woman turned to fetch the cloak, she studied herself for a moment in the cheval glass. The young woman who looked back at her was tall and wand-slender, her black hair worn piled high with only a single curl coaxed down over one white shoulder. Her face was delicately painted, porcelain perfect, with enormous eyes like jewels and a rose-red mouth accented by a strategically placed patch at its corner. Lush creamy-skinned breasts were more than half visible above the tantalizing neckline of a breathtaking gown of emerald-green silk generously trimmed with black lace. Emeralds set in gold sparkled in her ears and around her neck. She looked beautiful, expensive, remote — and she was a total stranger. This lavishly turned out woman had nothing to do with the person Caitlyn knew herself to be.

"Don't wait up," Caitlyn said as Minna draped a luxurious velvet evening cloak around her shoulders. It was sumptuous, as were her dress and her jewels and the furnishings with which she lived and even the carriage Sir Edward had sent to fetch her without bothering to come himself. In her lean days in Dublin, her eyes would have popped if she had known that one day she would live in such splendor. She would have thought life could hold no greater happiness than to have so many lovely things, to say nothing of a warm home and plenty of food and servants to do her bidding. Settling herself back into the fine upholstery of the carriage seat, Caitlyn didn't know whether to laugh or cry. She had every material thing of which she had ever dreamed, and she was more miserable than she had ever imagined possible. She would trade every dress, every jewel, every feather to be home again at Donoughmore with Connor.

Had Sir Edward been an ordinary man of moderate means, the situation would perhaps not have been so hopeless. But his friends included many peers of the realm, and his influence was vast, far greater than Connor's, who, she rather thought, had none. Connor was not wealthy; to her certain knowledge he gave away most of what he managed to acquire. She had no way of knowing the full extent of Sir Edward's wealth, but from every indication he was a rich man indeed.

Sir Edward's hunting box, occupied perhaps four weeks out of the year, was far larger than the manor house at Donoughmore, where the four d'Arcys and she had lived year-round. Sir Edward owned four other residences that she knew of: Ballymara, where he spent the summer and early fall, though he had not been back since leaving Ireland with her; his fashionable town house in Grosvenor Square, where his sister, Sarah, presently lived with him as his hostess in complete ignorance of Caitlyn's presence in quite another part of town; his principal seat, Dunne Hall, in Sussex; and her own snug house on Lisle Street. Each dwelling was elaborately furnished and maintained without interruption by a staff appropriate to its size and function. He dressed impeccably, ran the finest horses and carriages, and at every meal at which he was host his table groaned with more food than the entire gang of lads she used to run with in Dublin could consume at a sitting. He dressed her well, ordering outrageously expensive outfits for her by the dozen from London's finest modistes. Boxes were delivered weekly. The cloches were all designed to show off her charms and beauty to the utmost, at the expense of both decency and good taste.

He enjoyed exercising absolute power over her. That power was one reason he had kept her so long as his mistress. He also enjoyed making his friends envious of his possession of her — and envy him they did. Gloating, he told her that they called her a diamond of the first water and offered him tremendous sums to secure her services for themselves, which offers, thankfully, he declined. To share her would cause her to lose some of her value.

Caitlyn knew that as long as she had such value for him, he would never willingly release her. Not even his death would free her, not as long as Connor lived. Sir Edward's death would bring Connor's with it. Whether Connor caused it or no, the letters would be opened, and Connor would be exposed, arrested, tried, and ultimately hanged. For just a moment Caitlyn tried to imagine what would happen if she, Liam, Rory, Cormac, and Mickeen all swore to Connor's innocence. Her lip curled. Would any magistrate anywhere believe them against the dying statement of a man as wealthy and powerful as Sir Edward Dunne? She rather thought not.

The carriage pulled into the line of vehicles jamming Oxford Street as they waited to discharge their passengers at the glittering doors of the assembly rooms. Linkboys and lackeys carrying lanterns ran along the street, lighting the way for those who chose to abandon their vehicles to the confusion and walk the rest of the way. Caitlyn stayed where she was, in no hurry to join Sir Edward and his party, but in no time it seemed she was at the entrance. The Pantheon itself was magnificent, Caitlyn saw as a footman helped her to alight. Gargoyles and Gothic arches were everywhere, and every embellishment that conceivably could be was gilded. Enormous crystal chandeliers blazed from domed frescoed ceilings. Marble steps led up to a huge rectangular ballroom with numerous saloons and boxes and alcoves leading off from it. A group of musicians played vigorously from a raised platform at the far end of the room. The rooms were crowded, though the hour was relatively early, lacking nearly an hour and a half to midnight. The motley crowd was dressed in everything from elaborate evening clothes such as Sir Edward had instructed that she wear, to dominoes, to various costumes. Nearly half the company was masked. Caitlyn knew that it was considered a daring thing for members of the *ton*, carefully disguised beneath dominoes and masks, to attend a Pantheon assembly, where they would rub shoulders with everyone from country rubes just come to town to the most vulgar members of the muslin company to the sharps who hoped to lure unwary young men to their gambling establishments.

Another footman had apparently been watching for her arrival. He led her to the box where Sir Edward waited with his party. For a moment after setting eyes on Sir Edward she hung back, struck by a wave of hatred and revulsion so strong that it was all she could do to make herself overcome it. Had she ever thought him not unattractive, with his tall, thin frame, thinning fair hair, and light gray eyes? It seemed inconceivable to her, as though that assessment belonged to another person in another life. But then, of course, she had had no notion of the true evil that dwelled beneath the bland exterior.

Sir Edward turned and saw her. She put one foot on the marble step leading up to the box and walked across the wooden floor to join him. He watched her as she came, his eyes moving over her critically. His evening clothes were of dull gold satin, and she knew that he had ordered her to wear the emerald silk with an eye to the picture the pair of them would present. And she had to admit it: had she not known him as she did, she would have thought him an arresting-looking man. But she did know the cruelty and depravity that were the cornerstones of his character, and as he reached out a hand to pull her close to his side, she had to repress a shudder. His eyes met hers, and she thought that he guessed something of what she felt and was enjoying the idea of her hating him while being helpless to do anything about it. Still holding her eyes, he bent his head to press a lusty kiss on her mouth. It was done for the benefit of his envious friends, she knew, but she had to steel herself not to pull away.

"You're late," he said under his breath. Though his tone was mild, she knew that he intended for her to worry over his displeasure. Her pupils dilated slightly, but she tried not to let her instinctive fear show. Surely he wouldn't come to her again tonight! Please God he wouldn't!

"I'm sorry," she managed, and was relieved when he nodded and turned to present her to those of the party she didn't know. There were three couples besides herself and Sir Edward. The men were all of the *ton*, though they were dissolutes who for the most part flitted around its edges. The females were of the Covent Garden variety. Like herself, they were dressed to appeal to the men who provided their daily bread. Their coiffures were elaborate, and two were thick with powder in the prevailing fashion; their faces were painted and patched, and they were clad in slightly vulgar ballgowns that left most of their charms on view. Their names were Yvette and Suzanne and Mimi, and if they had a drop of French blood in their veins, Caitlyn was an Englishwoman born and bred. She sat down with them to partake of supper, and though she tried to join in with their spirit-fueled hilarity for fear of Sir Edward's later displeasure, she had to make more of an effort than usual. When supper was over and couples began taking to the floor, she was relieved. Out of Sir Edward's immediate vicinity, she could concentrate on the problem at hand: how to get Connor safely out of her life again.

One of Sir Edward's friends solicited her hand for the quadrille that was just at that moment striking up. She accepted with alacrity. The dancing master whom Sir Edward had employed to teach her had drilled the steps into her head so that she could dance without thinking about her feet. Her partner was not so fortunate. While he counted out the steps under his breath, her mind was free to turn itself to coming up with possible solutions.

No matter what tale she thought up to tell him, Connor was not likely to just go away. She had known him too long and too well to believe that for more than a hopeful instant. The idea of telling him all, and asking his advice as to how Sir Edward could be circumvented, was tempting. Perhaps they could simply run away together, his brothers and Mickeen as well. . . .

No, it would never work. Connor's character and Connor's temper coupled with his hatred of Sir Edward, which had been born long before she had ever come on the scene, and his rage would know no bounds if he were to discover how Sir Edward had compelled her to go away with him. Once that was out, there was little likelihood that she could keep the secret of Sir Edward's physical abuse. Contemplating Connor's reaction to that, Caitlyn actually shuddered, causing the arms of the man holding her rather closer than the movements of the dance called for, to tighten.

"You're so beautiful tonight, just like a glowing emerald. Why don't we take a stroll around the saloons together? There is much — oh, much! — I would show you." The Honorable Winthrop Cunningham actually giggled in her ear at what he doubtless considered the witticism of this last. He was well on his way to inebriation and was not quite steady on his feet as he moved with her in the elaborate figures of the dance. Caitlyn barely managed to mask the distaste on her face. Sir Edward, she knew from experience, would be furious were she to be openly rude to his friends.

The Honorable Winthrop dared more than he ever had and placed his hand on her breast. Sir Edward or no, she kicked him in the shin, her reaction instinctive. The thought that he might complain to Sir Edward and she might suffer for it crossed her mind, yet she could not be sorry. She felt much of her old spirit beginning to return, ousting the hopeless despair that had been her companion for most of the past year. Though it was senseless, just knowing that Connor was nearby was bringing her back to life. She was less able to tolerate insults and pain, more likely to rebel. Only the thought that to do so would endanger Connor himself ultimately kept her in line.

"Oh! Ah! Why, you kicked me!" The Honorable Winthrop jumped back and nearly fell on his amply padded rear. No one else on the crowded dance floor seemed to notice. They were too busy pursuing their own intrigues. Trading partners for the night or longer was one of the objects of those who visited the Pantheon. It was an ideal place for gentlemen to meet ladies who were less careful of their virtue than they should be, and for ladies to meet gentlemen wishful of getting to know them better. Of the three couples who had rounded out their party at supper, two, Caitlyn saw, gave every evidence of having already changed partners for the night.

The third gentleman was the Honorable Winthrop, whose friend Suzanne had disappeared with Sir Edward, for which Caitlyn was thankful. Not that there was a hope that Sir Edward would replace her as his established mistress. He could not perform as he preferred with the others. There was always the fear that they would scream, and cry, and tattle.

"I'm so sorry, my foot must have slipped," Caitlyn answered, speaking carefully to keep as much of the Irish as she could out of her speech. Sir Edward did not like her to appear too provincial before his friends. It was something else that might lessen her value in their eyes. She smiled with patently false contrition at her partner. "It does that, you know, when gentlemen allow their hands to slip."

"You're a saucy wench," the Honorable Winthrop told her with a hiccup, reaching for her to resume their dance. There was really no harm in this portly gentleman, so Caitlyn allowed him to pull her back into the quadrille. Some others of Sir Edward's friends genuinely frightened her. She took good care never to be alone with any of them if she could help it, and locked her door whenever she was forced to attend one of their house parties. The Honorable Winthrop was a fat fool, but she could handle him without much difficulty.

"Where did Neddie find you, anyway?" her partner muttered as the movements of the dance brought them close again. "You are truly exquisite! A pearl beyond price!"

"You must ask him." Caitlyn responded as she had painfully learned to do to any too-intimate inquiry into her history. Sir Edward had made his views plain the time or two, when she had first appeared in public as his mistress, that she had given out too much information. Caitlyn rather suspected that, despite all his safeguards, Sir Edward feared the news of her whereabouts might somehow find its way to Connor. Sir Edward feared Connor almost as much as he hated him, and with good reason.

"I'd reward you handsomely should you like to visit one of the antechambers with me, you know. We'd be gone no more than a half hour, you have my word. If Neddie wouldn't like it, why, don't tell him. You may be sure I will not."

Caitlyn barely bothered to repress a sigh. She wished her amorous partner would hush so that she could think. Time was running out. Connor might even be waiting for her when she returned to Lisle Street that very night.

The dance came to a swirling conclusion, and Caitlyn curtsied to her partner. Already the musicians were striking up again. The Honorable Winthrop mopped his brow. The room was warm despite its size, and he was a full-figured man whose portliness was not one whit disguised by the creaky corset he wore beneath his elaborately embroidered waistcoat. So much exertion caused him to perspire profusely. Streaks of perspiration marred the exquisite maquillage which in any event did little to whiten his florid face.

"Should you care to dance again?" he inquired, delicately patting his cheeks with a perfumed handkerchief. Caitlyn was on the verge of taking pity on him and shaking her head when her attention was caught by a tall man in a black domino and mask making his way across the dance floor. Though he was some distance away, his progress impeded by both the other dancers who were now assuming their poses and the slight limp that was just barely noticeable as he threaded his way among the posturing crowd, she felt her heart begin to pound. The hood of the domino was pulled well over his head, his face was masked, and none of his features were visible. But she knew. She would have known Connor anywhere in the world, in any guise. A glad little thrill ran through her, followed immediately by a cold wash of dread. Her time for reflection was at an end.

"No," she answered, her first instinct being flight. Then she realized that if Connor were to find her, the dance floor was the safest place to be discovered. She could not let him come across her in the box with Sir Edward at her side.

"I mean yes, I should very much like to dance," she amended quickly and, clutching the Honorable Winthrop's plump hand, urged the surprised gentleman into the twirling movements of the dance. She was not certain that Connor had seen her yet, though it was too much to hope that his presence at the Pantheon was merely a coincidence. Somehow he had found out where she was and had come after her. What was she to do?

Connor had changed direction and was coming directly toward them as they pirouetted around the floor. Caitlyn's heart began to beat so loudly that she could hardly hear the music over the frantic pounding. As she had with him, he had an uncanny sixth sense where she was concerned. As unobtrusively as possible, she looked around for Sir Edward. He was nowhere in sight. She could only hope that he had retired to a private room with Suzanne. If she could somehow get rid of Connor without Sir Edward seeing him, all might not yet be lost.

"Is something the matter, lovely one?" Even the Honorable Winthrop had noticed her agitation. Caitlyn wrenched her eyes back from their desperate survey of the huge ballroom to smile with forced unconcern at her partner.

"Oh, no, not really. I've just seen an old friend. I — it's rather tiresome, but I must speak to him, I suppose. He's — he's brought news of home."

The Honorable Winthrop looked both surprised and interested. "I had no notion you still had ties to your home. Neddie gave me to understand that you had no one. In fact, he's been dashed mysterious about you, now I come to think of it."

"Sir Edward is a — somewhat possessive man," Caitlyn said, her mind working rapidly. Connor was nearly upon them. "Uh — Winthrop" — it was the first time she had ever said his name — "if you could please fail to mention to Sir Edward that I've — I've encountered my friend, I would be most grateful."

The Honorable Winthrop almost stopped dancing as he looked at her speculatively. "How grateful?"

"Extremely grateful," Caitlyn said through her teeth. Connor was only a few feet away. As the Honorable Winthrop gave her to understand that nothing would ever induce him to betray her as long as she was sufficiently grateful, Connor came up behind him and put a hard hand on his shoulder. Though he was still masked and hooded, Caitlyn could see enough of his expression to guess what he was thinking. His jaw was grim, and his mouth was set in a hard, straight line.

"No, no, it isn't he," she squeaked, while the Honorable Winthrop turned toward Connor with an indignant protest that died to a sputter as he took in the size and style of his adversary.

"Dance with me," Caitlyn said desperately, sliding between Connor and the Honorable Winthrop before any attention-attracting altercation could occur. From the set of Connor's jaw, he was ripe for murder. "Please!"

"I expect you to be very, very grateful," the Honorable Winthrop said to her in a sullen undertone as she caught Connor's arm and tugged frantically. Connor stood eyeing her for a moment, his eyes glittering at her through his mask, and the Honorable Winthrop, still muttering, melted away.

"Not carrying any candlesticks up your skirt, are you?" Connor inquired nastily, ignoring her efforts to get him to move.

"Please dance," she said again, disregarding his remark. "I don't want to attract attention."

"Don't you, now?" Connor said in a voice that warned her of trouble to come. "Why is that, pray?"

They were standing stock-still in the middle of the ballroom while all around them brightly clad dancers turned and swayed. Connor's grim demeanor, coupled with his height and size, which were emphasized by the starkness of the black domino, was already beginning to cause a buzz.

"Dance!" Caitlyn hissed, aware of speculative eyes turning toward them from all sides and praying that none of them belonged to Sir Edward. She curtsied and turned in her part of the dance, and after an instant Connor followed her lead. He was amazingly adept despite his injured leg. It occurred to her that she had never before danced with him, never even imagined dancing with him. Dancing in this formal, correct fashion had been as foreign to her as the French tongue when she had lived at Donoughmore. Now she thought that, under other circumstances, dancing with Connor would be pure pleasure. His hand was warm and firm as he guided her in the movements, his body strong when she brushed against it. The domino parted as he moved, and she saw that he was wearing an evening coat of silver brocade over a matching waistcoat and black inexpressibles. He looked every inch a gentleman of the *ton*. Caitlyn felt a heady influx of pride in him, which was immediately erased by fear. She had to get him out of the ballroom, away from the Pantheon, at once. For Sir Edward's later delectation, she would make up some story of having suddenly become ill. Though he would be furious and take out his fury on her flesh, he would not know the truth. And Connor would be safe for a little while longer.

She danced with him down the length of the room, keeping a wary eye out for Sir Edward, who could come looking for her at any minute. She had only to keep the two men from meeting. Even if he saw Connor from a distance, he would not recognize him. Not with Connor in domino and mask. And not with the limp, about which Sir Edward knew nothing.

"Is your lover here? Is that why you're as nervy as a canary with a cat in the room?" That hard voice made Caitlyn jump, started out of her thoughts. Looking up at that well-loved chin, which at the moment was set more aggressively than she had ever seen it, Caitlyn felt her heart sink. Connor was spoiling for a fight.

"How did you know I was here?" She tried to control the quick, nervous looks she had been casting around her as they danced, knowing that it would be fatal to let him see the panic that suffused her. They were near the edge of the dance floor. Sir Edward could be in any of the little saloons.

Connor smiled grimly down at her as she twirled beneath his hand.

"I've had a man watching your house since you disappeared. He saw you arrive this afternoon and came to tell me. I was away from home, but when I returned I got his message. I immediately paid a call in Lisle Street, only to discover that you were out for the evening. At the Pantheon. So here I am. You won't get away from me this time, my lass, so you needn't bother trying to bash in my skull again."

"Connor, won't you leave me be? Even if I tell you that I'm happy, I don't want you, and you're spoiling things for me?" Real despair colored her voice. Through the slits in his mask she could see that his eyes had narrowed.

"You belong to me, my own. I'll never leave you be. You know that as well as I do."

So be it, then. That was the answer she had expected, the one she'd both longed for and dreaded to hear. Suddenly she knew, as well as if some higher being had whispered in her ear, what they had to do.

"Then let's get away from this place now, together. Quickly." Her words were urgent. He frowned as he looked down at her. Around her, the other ladies pirouetted and curtsied, but Caitlyn quite forgot to perform her part. Instead she stood clutching his hand, kerry blue eyes wide and frightened in the whiteness of her face.

"Let's get off the dance floor, at any rate," Connor said, studying her from behind the protection of his mask as he tucked her hand beneath his arm and led her to the side. Behind them, the dancing continued unabated. Laughter and music and the lighthearted banter of countless flirtations washed over them from all sides. It was a merry scene, no place for fear or desperate flight. Yet Caitlyn was both fearful and anxious to flee.

"Hurry," she said, trying to tug him along at a faster pace as she made for the nearest exit. Like the dance floor itself, the edges of the ballroom were packed. Dodging the loitering throngs was no easy task, especially without Connor's cooperation. He resisted her efforts to hurry him, strolling along as though he had all the time in the world.

" 'Tis very eager you are to go away with me all of a sudden." There was a thoughtful note in Connor's voice. "What of your gentleman friend? The one you were so in love with?"

" 'Twas naught but a lie," Caitlyn said, tugging at him. "I'll explain it all to you, if you'll just hurry."

"Caitlyn!" The call behind her made her gasp and glance around in terror. Connor stopped dead, his head swinging around in the direction from which the call had come.

"Where have you been? I've been looking for you. It is most reprehensible of you to desert our friends. And who is this gentleman?" Sir Edward's icy voice sent a chill down Caitlyn's spine. From the look of him as he approached her, eyes as cold as his voice and hardly sparing her tall companion a glance, he had no inkling as to Connor's identity. His fury was all for her. As Connor turned to face the man, menace suddenly stiffened his entire body at the sight of Sir Edward. He was incredulous, and the confrontation Caitlyn had most feared was on the verge of happening.

"Please go! Please. You can come for me later, to Lisle Street," she whispered frantically to Connor, though she knew it was a waste of her breath. Even as she beseeched him, he was reaching up to untie his mask.

"At last I begin — just faintly — to see the light," Connor said, releasing her hand at the same time as he removed his mask. Sir Edward stopped as if turned to stone. His face shook once as if the muscles beneath had suddenly been afflicted with a palsy, and his skin turned pasty white.

"D'Arcy," he croaked. Connor pushed back the hood of his domino and stood regarding Sir Edward with a frighteningly grim smile.

Frozen with horror, Caitlyn looked on helplessly. The situation was beyond fixing. Connor's hair gleamed black as a raven's wing in the light of the hundreds of candles illuminating the room. His aqua eyes glinted dangerously at Sir Edward. Inches taller and more muscular than his opponent, in any fair fight Connor would be the winner by a rout. But Sir Edward, still pasty-pale but regaining his composure, would not fight fair.

"I give you good evening, Sir Edward," Connor said with the most awful affability she had ever heard. Then those glittering light eyes shifted to her face. "Tell me something, my own: by what means did this English cur compel you to become his mistress?" His tone of voice was almost conversational. Only Caitlyn, who knew him so well, could detect the violence of the rage that was building inside him. Looking from Connor's face to Sir Edward, she saw that the latter had nearly recovered from his shock. There was precious little time left for Connor to escape. Yet she knew he would never leave without her. Not in this life.

"He did not compel me. I went to him of my own free will. I — I knew you would be angry. 'Tis why I didn't tell you. Oh, please, won't you go away and leave us alone? For my sake?" Her words were frantic as she pushed at Connor's arm. Her eyes gave him a desperate warning, but he was as unmoving as a stone. His eyes traveled with leisurely interest over her face before fixing on Sir Edward again. An interested crowd, sensing a scene in the making, was forming around them. None of the three principals had a glance to spare for the spectators. All were focused upon themselves, upon the drama that was being played out among them.

"Indeed, d'Arcy, she chose me over you," Sir Edward said with a glint in his eyes. "Do you find that so hard to believe? I have much more to offer, you know. Let her choose, and see if she does not come to me. Witness for yourself that it is of her own free will."

Sir Edward was indeed recovering his aplomb. Caitlyn saw a chance, just a chance, of getting Connor out of this with a whole skin. If she could only convince Connor that she had willingly gone with Sir Edward, he might stalk off in a rage and leave her to lie in the bed she had made. Sir Edward would be delighted to triumph over Connor — though she would be made to pay for it later. What did that matter, when the cost of her freedom was Connor's life?

"Would you truly go to him, my own?" Caitlyn met Connor's steady gaze and nodded jerkily.

" 'Tis a pity I let you talk me out of killing him the last time. We would all have been spared much," Connor observed, still without apparent heat. Then he looked at Sir Edward again. Caitlyn saw pure murder flash from those devil's eyes. Sir Edward must have registered the same message, because he stepped back a pace. Connor smiled and pushed Caitlyn gently to one side. Then with a lightning movement he reached out and caught Sir Edward by his coat front, jerking him up so that he dangled from Connor's hold.

"As God is my witness, I'll not make the same mistake twice," Connor said through his teeth. Caitlyn caught at his free arm.

"You don't understand — you can't kill him — listen to me, please!" she cried.

Connor twisted his hold on Sir Edward's coat front so that the collar tightened around the man's neck, making him gasp for breath. "I listened to you the last time, my own, and look where it brought us. Now I mean to kill him."

"You'd best listen to her, d'Arcy!" Sir Edward choked. His face was turning blue from lack of air. His feet barely brushed the floor. Caitlyn realized that Connor was hanging Sir Edward right there before her eyes.

"Someone send for the Watch!" she heard a voice in the crowd scream. She grabbed Connor's arm again, dragging on it, making him look down at her.

"You must go! I'll come with you, but we have to leave before the Watch comes! They'll hang you! Sir Edward knows. . . ."

"What does the bastard know?" Connor was smiling, a terrifying smile with his eyes fixed on Sir Edward's face. He was wheezing for breath, clawing at Connor's hand. Until that moment, Caitlyn had never realized just how extremely strong Connor was. Sir Edward was as helpless in Connor's hold as she herself would be.

"For God's sake, don't kill him! We must get away! Please, Connor, please!" She was frantic, near tears as she tugged at his arm.

Connor glanced down at her, frowning. Something in her urgency seemed to get through to him, making him recall where he was and take note of the audience that was agog around them. His jaw clenched. Then some of the rage died from his eyes, to leave him no less angry than before but rational with it. If he murdered Sir Edward before so many witnesses, he would likely pay for the privilege with his life. With a final twist of his hand so that Sir Edward's mouth gaped open like that of a landed fish, he released his hold. Sir Edward collapsed like a suit of clothes with no one in them and knelt gasping on the floor, his hands lifted to his throat.

Connor leaned over him and spoke in a low, menacing growl that Caitlyn alone of the bystanders was close enough to hear.

"I'll kill you, you Sassenach scum, but it won't be murder when I do. 'Twill be a fair fight. You'll have a chance, which is more than you gave my father, or Caitlyn. And I warn you, if you try to run from me, I'll find you if it takes all the days of my life."

"Connor, please, please . . . let us go!"

"Pistols or swords, the choice is yours. At dawn, on Hounslow Heath. Be there, or spend the rest of your miserable life looking over your shoulder. You'll never know when I'll catch up with you, but be assured that I will." Connor straightened, sent a piercing look around the crowd, which backed away as one, then caught Caitlyn's hand. She nearly fainted with relief. At least he would not be taken here and now.

"What's this now? What's this?" A quartet of burly constables was shouldering through the crowd.

"Run! We must run!" Caitlyn was frantic as she pulled on Connor's hand, but her warning was too late. Even as Connor's hand tightened over hers, Sir Edward was struggling to his feet and launching himself at Connor's back. Connor staggered forward under the unexpected assault. Caitlyn screamed.

"Hurry, officers!" Sir Edward yelled even as

Connor grabbed a fistful of hair, bent, and sent him catapulting head over heels. "Arrest this man! There's a price on his head in Ireland — he's the one they call the Dark Horseman!"

XLIII

"Really, my dear, you've been very naughty. Very, very naughty. You must be punished most severely."

" 'Tis a monster you are, not a man! I warn you, lay so much as a finger on me and I will see you in hell!"

"What an ungrateful chit you are! I could have turned you over to the authorities along with d'Arcy, you know. Instead, I'm prepared to keep you, though you've betrayed me with that Irish gallows' bait. Why, if you behave yourself, I might even let you watch his hanging."

"They'll never hang him!"

"Indeed they will. He will kick and scream and twist while the rope cuts off his air — and then he will die."

"In that case, pray tell me what is stopping me from slitting your throat one fine night?"

Sir Edward smiled at her. She had turned on him like a small wildcat when Connor, under guard by four large horse pistols, had been taken from the assembly rooms. He had required the help of his coachman and a footman to drag her, thrashing and screaming, to his carriage, where he had ordered her bound with her own torn cloak. Three footman had done the dirty work, and the coachman had carried her, trussed like a Christmas goose, inside when they had reached the house on Lisle Street. Sir Edward had followed her up to her chamber and told Fromer to keep watch below. After his surprise at finding Caitlyn with Connor earlier, he was taking no further chances.

"You are forgetting the brothers, are you not? At a word from me, they could easily swing beside d'Arcy, you know. As could you."

Caitlyn glared up at him from her prone position on the bed. Bound at wrists and ankles, with more strips of cloth securing her arms and legs for good measure, she was effectively helpless. Sir Edward was gloating over her, his eyes alight. Connor's arrest and her impotent fury and despair delighted him. He loved others' misery and pain.

"So you think to keep me by holding Liam and Rory and Cormac over my head, do you?"

"And your own life, my dear. It is no small thing."

Caitlyn seethed with rage and hatred. He smiled at her and slowly removed his gold satin coat while she watched, knowing what would come next. But fear for Connor obliterated all concern for herself. Sir Edward could terrify her no longer. His shirt was blindingly white in the candlelight as he crossed to her wardrobe and took out the riding crop that was kept there. Though the worst had come to pass and Connor was taken, he thought to use her as though nothing had changed.

"What will you do if Connor escapes?" Her voice taunted him as he came to stand beside the bed, his tall form casting a dark shadow over the torn skirt of her once-magnificent emerald ballgown.

That made him pause for a moment. Nervously he flexed the whip.

"He will not. No one has ever escaped from Newgate."

"Connor is quite extraordinary."

"Do you know, I am tired of hearing you talk of your lover. You are a sinful wench. Sinful. You have been fornicating with him, I know it."

"Indeed I have," Caitlyn said with vindictive pleasure. He stared at her for a moment, not having expected her to admit to any such thing. His eyes took on a hot, hungry gleam. In the past that glitter would have reduced her to trembling jelly. Now she was strong again, fueled by a hatred more virulent than anything she had ever known.

"You are shameless," Sir Edward muttered and, reaching down, ripped at her clothes until she was naked. Still bound, she barely managed to roll onto her face before he brought the whip whistling down across her shoulders. At first, she did not scream, did not cry out. Eventually, though, as he continued to beat her unmercifully, she could not hold back. He did not confine himself to her buttocks and legs this time, but beat her about the head and shoulders and back as well. With her hands bound, she could not protect herself at all, though she kept her eyes shut and her face averted. One lash caught her full on the cheek, splitting it open. She could feel the welling of blood even as she screamed. . . .

At last his strength was spent. He mounted the bed, used her as he always did, then left the room. As soon as he had closed the door, Minna entered. She made no move to ease Caitlyn's pain or aid her in any way, but merely sat in the chair in the corner of the room and took up her tatting. Caitlyn turned her head despite the excruciating pain and looked at the other woman. There was no pity for her in those cold black eyes.

Caitlyn bit her lower lip until she tasted her own blood in her mouth. Naked, bound, grievously hurt and humiliated, stabbed clear to the heart with hideous fear for Connor, she nevertheless felt stronger than she had since the night she was shot. Her hatred welled inside her like a living, breathing entity. Soon now, soon, she would have her revenge. . . .

As Caitlyn suspected, Fromer and Minna were far more efficient jailers than servants. Over the next two days she was kept tied to the bed, except for certain necessary times which were tended to by Minna with Fromer within call. The erstwhile servants took grim pleasure in keeping her informed of the hoopla that surrounded the taking of the Irish brigand whose downfall, they told her gleefully, was the talk of Londontown. The trial itself would be held in Dublin, as that location was more convenient for witnesses. The outcome was in little doubt. Bets were being taken on how speedily the hanging would follow the verdict. Fromer had put ten quid on the following day.

On the third day after Connor's arrest, Sir Edward came again to visit her. It was late at night, as his visits usually were. Minna had untied her so that she could attend to nature's call before sleeping. Sir Edward entered the room without knocking. Caitlyn straightened with a grim smile as he immediately dismissed the other woman, who had even been sleeping in her chamber; Sir Edward had given orders that she was not to be left alone at any time. Apparently he feared she might somehow manage to escape him. But escape without vengeance had never been her plan.

He looked her over, his eyes lingering on her body in the diaphanous nightrail.

"I marked your lovely face. It is healing well, I see. I have often remarked to myself how quickly your skin heals. I hope your heart is as resilient, because I heard today that your Irish lover will swing within the month."

Caitlyn said nothing, though the news hit her like a blow. But she would not let him see. Hatred burned from her eyes. He saw it, and frowned at her for a moment before chuckling.

"Why, I believe you really loved that Irish rogue. Put him from your mind, my dear. He is as good as dead already."

"I would not count him out so fast, were I you."

Sir Edward chuckled again, removing his coat and laying it carefully over the chair near the bed.

"And are you reconciled to your fate, or must I continue to have Minna and Fromer guard you like dogs with a bone? Though d'Arcy will die, you may still save his brothers and yourself, you know. If you but will be sensible."

"I am very sensible."

He looked at her, his eyebrows lifting. She returned his look steadily. "Whether you believe it or not, I am not quite a fool. I value my own life, and even the lives of Connor's brothers. I will do naught to endanger them."

"Why, I do believe you are sensible!" he marveled delightedly. Then his expression changed. "But still, you must be punished. You have made me angry, made me mark your face when it was never my intention to do so, embarrassed me in front of my friends when you had to be carried screaming like a fishwife from the Pantheon. You will admit that you deserve yet another punishment for that, my dear. Disrobe, if you please."

Caitlyn's hands clenched at her sides. He was already turning away from her, walking to the wardrobe where the whip was kept. Quick as a cat, she took a step to the side and knelt beside the chair in the corner. Beneath it was the basket in which Minna kept her tatting. In the basket was a pair of embroidery scissors. His back was still to her as she found them, clasped them tightly in her cold hand, straightened.

"What, why are you not undressed?" He flexed the whip in his hands as he turned around to face her.

"My arms are too sore from the beating you gave me last. I cannot lift them," she replied with deceptive meekness, keeping her hand with the scissors hidden in the folds of her nightrail. "If you would but call Minna to assist me, I would undress with all speed. Pray do not be angry. I cannot help it."

He scowled at her. "I will help you myself," he said abruptly. Laying the whip down on the bed, he walked toward her. Even as he reached for her, Caitlyn struck with lightning speed. She jumped for him, aiming for his neck, burying the scissors deep in the soft flesh where his neck joined his shoulder. He let out a cry, jerked back. His eyes went wide as they gaped at her. The scissors were embedded in his neck, the twin silver circles of the handle gleaming in the candlelight. Blood welled up around them, stained his white shirt. His shoulder and chest were scarlet within seconds. He opened his mouth, tried to speak. Nothing came out except a hoarse croak. He lifted a hand to the scissors, fumbled at them, staring at her all the while. Horror rose like bile in Caitlyn's throat. She clapped her hands to her mouth to hold back the scream that hovered there. Then, when she thought he would stand there forever, he swayed and sank to his knees. For just a moment he knelt, reached for the scissors again, then pitched facedown on the floor.

For just an instant longer she stared down at him. Then she remembered Minna and Fromer and crossed the room to put her ear to the door. She heard nothing in the hall outside. Apparently Sir Edward's cry had not sounded out of the ordinary to Minna or Fromer, if indeed they had heard it at all. They were well used to screams and moans emerging from this chamber. But it behooved her to make all speed if she were to make good her escape.

Quickly she dressed in the warmest gown she possessed, and caught up her hooded woolen cloak. Then for just a moment she stood looking down at Sir Edward's prone form. Blood had puddled under his neck, staining the rug. His face was gray. The fingers of one outflung hand twitched. Was he not dead, then, or was that merely a muscular contraction? Should she stab him again, to be sure? But if he was not dead he was surely very near it, and Caitlyn found to her surprise that she had no stomach for removing the scissors from his neck to strike another, probably unnecessary blow. The taste of vengeance was not at all sweet, as she had supposed, not since it meant having had to lose Connor in order to gain freedom.

"I hope your soul screams in Purgatory for eternity," she said to the man at her feet, then spat on him before climbing out the window into the freezing night.

XLIV

Hell itself could not be much more miserable than Kilmainham Gaol, Connor thought as he leaned his head back against the slimy stone wall and contemplated the progress of a roach as it made its way across the mildewed granite of the ceiling.

The harsh January winds howled outside and whistled along the dark, dank rabbit warren of passageways that led to the cells. Kilmainham was as bone-chillingly cold as Hell was reputed to be hot. Soon he would be able to compare the two at first hand. His trial had concluded a se'ennight ago. He was to be hanged at dawn tomorrow, publicly, on a gallows even now being constructed at the edge of Phoenix Park. Enormous crowds were expected to attend. Any hanging was the occasion for a public holiday, but the execution of the notorious Dark Horseman promised to be something special.

He would be taken to the site chained in the back of an open cart so that all might witness his downfall. The guards, who were reasonably affable on account of his notoriety, informed him that people were already setting up camp on the best spots along the route and close to the gallows in order to have the choicest views of the next day's entertainment. Disembowelment, a high treat for the crowd, which involved cutting out the hanged man's entrails and burning them, would follow the hanging. To Connor, that was a mere bagatelle. They could do what they wished with his body once he was dead.

Shivering, he pulled what remained of his silver brocade coat closer around his neck. He had not been warm in the near six weeks since he'd been taken. The air in his small cell was so cold that every time he breathed, a tiny cloud of vapor formed in front of his face. Were he not to be hanged, he'd doubtless die of pneumonia before long. Many like him did, if Liffey fever did not claim them.

They'd taken him from Newgate across England in irons in a prison cart, then put him in a cage like an animal for the ferry ride across the channel to Dublin. Within a fortnight after his arrest he'd been locked up in Kilmainham Gaol, and he had not left the grounds since. He would not until he was taken forth to be hanged.

He was hungry. Sweet Jesus, was he hungry! He'd had no more than moldy bread and scummy water during the entire time he'd been imprisoned. Oh, no, there had been a bit of briny cod's head included with the meal on Christmas Day. No one could say the bloody British were not hospitable to their prisoners.

But hunger, like disembowelment, was something that he would soon not have to worry about.

He should be thinking of the state of his soul,

worrying about making his peace with God. He should not be envisioning a juicy mutton stew, or wishing for a pint of ale or a roaring fire to warm himself at. Although such physical needs did keep him from thinking of other, less palatable things.

He did not want to die, and there was the plain truth of it. He was not yet thirty years old; he had a lot of living yet to do. He did not want to die, and he especially did not want to die in the way they had planned for him. To be dropped through a trapdoor with a rope tight around his neck and his hands tied behind him was a horror he would rather not contemplate. He would face it when he must, with courage, he hoped. Until then, he would not allow himself to dwell on his fate.

The trial had been held in the prison itself; it had been short and to the point, his guilt a foregone conclusion. The bloody Sassenach magistrate had practically rubbed his hands with glee as he had passed sentence on the Dark Horseman. His execution would be a sign to the Irish that their English masters were firmly in place and in control.

He had been allowed no visitors since his arrest. Not that it mattered. The only people he cared to see were the ones who would face mortal danger if they came. His brothers had ridden with him and faced the same fate he did if taken. His prayer was that they would have the common sense to lie low until all was over. And Caitlyn . . . Caitlyn. It was torture imagining what was happening to her. He prayed that she had not fallen again into Sir Edward's hands. His only regret was that he had not managed to kill him before he had been taken. It galled him to think of quitting the earth while Sir Edward still breathed. Had he it all to do over again, he would have broken the man's neck while he had the chance. But, of course, he could do nothing over again. No one ever could.

One of the guards, taking pity on him because he was to die on the morrow, had provided him with quills, ink, and parchment. Connor shivered, tugged at his coat again, and bent himself once more to the task of writing farewell messages to those he loved. If all fell out as it was supposed to, he would not see them again on this earth.

XLV

"But there must be something more we can do!" Caitlyn looked beseechingly up at Father Patrick. Though it was still daylight outside, the tunnels beneath Donoughmore were as black as the blackest night. Only a single lantern illuminated the spot where the six of them huddled. Beyond that small circle of light, all was echoing darkness.

"The seeds are planted and should, God willing, bear fruit. All that is left is to wait for the dawn and pray."

"We could attempt a gaol break." Like the rest of them who had spent most of the daylight hours of the past month in the dark tunnels, Cormac was pale. He was thinner too, as were Liam and Rory and Caitlyn herself. Mickeen was down to a bone. The only one who was much the same as he had always been was Father Patrick, who had been working tirelessly on Connor's behalf since he had heard the news of his arrest.

"Kilmainham is impregnable," Father Patrick answered with the weary air of one who had said as much before. " 'Tis no sense in throwing your lives away on such foolishness. Sure, and Connor would not thank the lot of you for getting yourselves killed as well as him, and well you know it."

"But, Father, do you think 'twill work?" Liam chewed on a fingernail as he looked across at the priest. They were sitting on saddles and other makeshift seats, the remains of a meal of bread and cheese that Father Patrick had brought littering the makeshift table on which guttered the lantern.

"To tell you true, Liam, I do not know. I can only pray to God. But to my way of thinking, 'tis the only chance your brother has."

"We cannot and will not let him hang!" Rory jumped to his feet and paced about in agitation.

"Believe me, there are many who feel as you do, and in that we must place our hope. Come, are you ready?"

The rest of them got to their feet. The time had come for them to travel to Dublin. It would be a risky journey, as dragoons still combed the countryside with an eye out for the Dark Horseman's band. Only by remaining safely beneath the surface of the earth had they avoided capture so far. But they would ride singly and in pairs so as to attract less attention, meeting at a prearranged spot in the part of Dublin's slums known as Botany Bay. The arrangements for the morrow were all made. Now came the most difficult part: the waiting.

"Father, have you any means to give Conn word of what we would attempt? He must be . . ." Liam's voice trailed off, and he finished the sentence with an expressive gesture. Caitlyn imagined how tortured must be Connor's thoughts on this, possibly the last evening of his life, and felt sick. She longed to go to him, to comfort him. It might be the last time she would see him in life.

"Be at ease, my children. I have made such plans. Connor has a part to play on the morrow as well." Father Patrick's eyes ran over the five faces that regarded him so anxiously. His tired face was somber. "Even the bloody English would not deny a condemned man access to a priest on the night before he is to hang."

"You'll see him, Father?"

"Will they let you, do you think?"

"Tell his lordship — tell him — ah, tell him what you will." Mickeen, unable to put into words his message of loyalty and affection, scowled and spat.

"They'll let me see him, have no fear. I will do what I can to ease his way unto death — or whatever." A long-absent twinkle appeared in Father Patrick's eyes. "Though it took quite a hefty bribe to arrange. Fortunately, the Sassenach are quite venal."

"Then if all the arrangements are made, why are we standing around here? Let's be away!"

"Not so fast, young Cormac! I'll have your word — all of your words — that you'll not be doing anything daft! Your role is tomorrow at dawn, not before."

"You have our word, Father." Liam spoke for them all. Father Patrick nodded. The group then headed toward the entrance to the tunnel that was hidden just above the Boyne. The horses were kept there, fed and watered and exercised at night and well hidden during the day. They saddled up in silence; Mickeen saddled Fharannain as well. His inclusion, riderless, in the journey was a testament to their hope. If all went well, Connor would be riding Fharannain when they fled Dublin on the morrow.

"If I may, I'll ride with you, Father," Caitlyn said, stopping beside the priest as he tightened the saddle on his well-fleshed bay. He looked down at her, compassion in his eyes. Then he nodded.

"Aye, my child, you may. I'll be glad of your company, in truth."

Caitlyn, in breeches and coat for the occasion, swung aboard the pretty piebald mare that Cormac had procured for her during one of his nightly forays into the world above. Caitlyn called her Meg, and tried not to envision the disaster that would occur should she, through some terrible mischance, come face to face with Meg's former owner. But Cormac assured her there was small risk of that, as he had taken the mare from the stable of an inn on the far side of Crumcondra.

Mickeen rolled aside the huge rock that blocked the entrance to the fissure. In a moment they were out in the freezing rain, pulling their hoods tightly around their faces as they split up. They would meet again just before dawn.

"I'll ride with you as well, if you've no objections, Father," Cormac said, bringing Kildare up beside Meg. "I'm loath to let Caitlyn here out of my sight. Conn would be wroth with us should we get him away and lose Caitlyn again in the process."

Father Patrick expressed no objection, and the three of them rode in silence toward Dublin. There was a considerable amount of traffic on the road, all bound for the hanging on the morrow. The whole countryside was astir with news of the Dark Horseman's fate.

They were some hours on the road, and the darkness and freezing rain made the ground underfoot treacherous. Riding single file, sandwiched between Father Patrick's comfortable bulk ahead of her and Cormac behind, Caitlyn was so anxious to arrive and get on with it that she could scarcely restrain herself from setting Meg to a gallop. But she had to be patient, she reminded herself. For Connor's sake. For weeks now she and the younger d'Arcys had been going insane trying to dream up ways to save him. Father Patrick had come up with the only plan that had the remotest chance of succeeding. It hinged on so many factors that the possibility of something going wrong was immense. But everything that could be done had been done. The only thing that could make a bit of difference now was prayer. And pray she did, fervently, even as her thoughts wandered over the weeks just past. . . .

After dealing with Sir Edward, she had fled at

once to Connor's house on Curzon Street, only to find it deserted. She learned later that, immediately upon receiving word that Connor was taken, Liam had quitted the house and ridden for Oxford to collect Rory and Cormac. Sure that the authorities would soon be looking for them as well, the three of them and Mickeen had prudently taken lodgings in a seedy rooming house near the quay while they awaited word of Connor's fate. Their fears were well grounded. Even while he was using them to threaten Caitlyn, Sir Edward had already revealed the younger d'Arcys' involvement in Connor's crimes. Caitlyn was uncertain whether he had mentioned her, though she rather thought not. He had still had use for her at the time, after all. But it was not wise to take chances when one might pay with one's life.

Alone and penniless on the streets of London, afraid she was being hunted as a highwayman and murderer, Caitlyn had reverted quickly to as close a persona of what she had once been as she could manage. Stealing clothes hung out to dry, she had garbed herself as a boy and for the next week had haunted the streets surrounding Newgate Prison, where street talk had it they had taken Connor immediately after his arrest. She had not thought to take Sir Edward's purse from his pocket before she fled, but she managed to sell to a whore the clothes she had been wearing when she left Lisle Street. The few coins that brought her kept food in her stomach, and she slept on the streets. It was amazing how easily the survival skills she had learned when she was O'Malley the thief came back to her.

After nigh on a se'ennight had passed, she'd heard that the Dark Horseman would be moved that very day to Ireland for trial. Joining the small crowd gathered in front of the prison, she had seen no more of Connor than the outside of a curtained prison wagon as it pulled through the gates. But in the crowd she had spied Mickeen also trying to catch a glimpse of Connor at his brothers' behest. Though she stood right beside him, he did not recognize her until she grabbed his sleeve and, in a hiss, made herself known. For the first time since she had known him, he had seemed glad to see her.

"Because his lordship would be wishful for us to look after you," he said, and took her back to the seedy inn with him. Her reunion with Cormac and Rory had been tearful, while practical Liam had sworn eternal vengeance in his brother's name when she told them some part of how she had been used. The three of them would have charged in pursuit of Sir Edward and murdered him on the spot had she not been able to assure them that she had taken care of it herself.

They then had set out for Ireland, where they had gone first to Father Patrick at St. Albans. He had counseled them to hide while he did what he could for Connor. None of them had really thought Connor would be hanged. Irrationally, they had expected a miracle, but no miracle had as yet occurred. Connor would die on the morrow unless their last desperate gamble paid off. Caitlyn could not bear the thought. If Connor died, she would want to die too.

When they rode into Dublin it was past midnight. Revelers packed the streets despite the freezing rain. The town had a carnival air about it. A public hanging was an event even if only the lowliest pickpocket was to forfeit his life. When the condemned was as well loved and well hated (depending upon whether one was Irish or Anglo) as the Dark Horseman, the entertainment promised to be of the highest order. Everyone who could manage to travel to Dublin was there.

Outside St. Catherine's their ways split. Kilmainham Gaol was to the east, Botany Bay to the north. Father Patrick reined in and turned in his saddle to bid them farewell.

"Till dawn, my children," he said, lifting a hand. Caitlyn pushed Meg closer to his mount. She had an urgent request to make of the priest, though she hated to tell him what she feared she must to secure it. He would think her wanton, indeed. But if it was the price she must pay, pay it she would, and gladly.

"Can you find no way to take me with you, Father? I would see Connor, if I could. He — I — we have much that is unfinished between us."

"I would go too, if 'tis possible." Cormac spoke up from the darkness behind her. Father Patrick shook his head.

"You, Cormac, are a man grown now and

should recognize folly before you suggest it. Do not forget that they are looking for you, and for Rory and Liam as well. You look too much like your brother, so you are impossible to mistake. As for you, lass . . ."

"We've had no word that I'm being sought." Seeing Father Patrick's hesitation, she shamelessly appealed to the soft spot he had developed for her. "Please, Father. Should Connor die and I . . . not have speech with him, I — I —" Her voice broke. "If there is any way, I beg you."

Father Patrick frowned. " 'Tis too dangerous. I cannot permit it. 'Tis sorry I am, lass, but —"

"Please, Father!" Caitlyn broke in. " 'Tis more important than you know. There is something I must tell him." Haltingly, she explained the urgency of her mission. By the time she was done, her entire face was bright crimson, and Father Patrick was staring at her from beneath lowered brows. Cormac looked like he had been poleaxed.

"Dear sweet Jesus," Cormac muttered, his eyes running over Caitlyn. She silenced him with a look.

"That does make a difference," Father Patrick agreed after a long silence. "Very well, you may come with me. I will get you in somehow. But there is one condition."

When he told her what it was, she threw her arms around his neck and kissed his cheek, nearly unseating him from his horse.

XLVI

❋ ❋ ❋ ❋ ❋ ❋ ❋ ❋ ❋ ❋ ❋ ❋ ❋ ❋ ❋ ❋ ❋

Left alone with his thoughts in the cold, damp darkness that imprisoned him on the final night of his life, Connor had nearly fallen asleep when the scraping of the key in the lock of his cell told him he had company. For an awful moment, he thought that it was dawn already and they had come for him. Then he saw the black-robed figure that filled the doorway behind the guard. As light from the candle the guard held illuminated the homely round face, he recognized his visitor.

"Father Patrick!" He would have surged to his feet, but surging was difficult, hampered as he was by a game leg and iron chains. His bed was naught but a single blanket on the cold stone floor, and the relentless chill had caused his leg to stiffen. The chains that linked his ankles and secured him to the wall rattled as he got painfully to his feet.

"I have come to give you what comfort I can in your last hours on this earth, my son," Father Patrick intoned piously, walking forward to embrace Connor. Another priest entered the cell behind Father Patrick, head bowed and hands tucked into his robe. Connor spared hardly a glance for the second priest. He was so glad to see Father Patrick that a lump rose in his throat.

536

For a moment he feared he would be unable to speak.

"God bless you, Father."

"And you, Connor," Father Patrick responded, stepping back and making the sign of the cross over him.

"Heathen Papists," the guard muttered with an expression of distaste, settling the candle into the iron sconce near the barred door. Then, with a nervous look along the corridor behind him, he added more loudly, "Not too long now, Father."

"No longer than it needs, you may be sure," Father Patrick answered calmly, his eyes never leaving Connor, who, with six weeks' worth of black beard covering his jaw and his hair grown overlong and untidy, looked every inch a brigand. The guard sniffed and went out, locking the door behind him with a great grating of iron against iron. Connor, recovering his composure, dropped the priest's hand.

"If you would, cover the peephole," Father Patrick said to the second priest. Connor barely noticed as the man obeyed; his attention was all on Father Patrick.

" 'Twas good of you to come, Father. But perhaps a trifle unwise."

"I would have come sooner if I could. Be assured, no difficulties will befall me for this. But come, we have much to do and not much time to do it. I have a surprise for you. I hope 'tis to your liking."

"Did you not come to give me Supreme Unction, then? I confess I hesitate to meet my maker without it." Connor smiled a little, his expression wry. Father Patrick laid his hand on his shoulder.

" 'Tis my fervent hope that you'll long outlive me, my son. But just in case, I will give you absolution before I leave you. Are you not curious as to my surprise?"

"You are surprise enough for me, Father. But aye, I would see what you've brought. I warn you, I'm hoping for a nice bit of mutton and maybe some turnips. . . ."

"I did not think of food," Father Patrick muttered, sounding put out with himself. "But then, I wager you'll not think of it in a moment either." He turned and beckoned to the second priest, who stepped forward. Connor watched with casual interest until something about this unknown priest's movements held his eyes. Even before she lifted a hand to pull back the cowled hood, he knew.

"Caitlyn," he groaned as she ran into his arms. They closed around her, holding her tight. "Oh, Caitlyn." His voice broke, and he buried his face in the mass of her shining hair. She clung to him, murmuring love words that he could not make out, so soft and warm and alive in his arms that she banished the specter of the grave that yawned before him. He held her for what seemed like an eternity. Then, finally remembering his interested audience, he lifted his head from her hair and smiled rather unsteadily at the priest.

"A fine surprise, indeed, Father."

"I thought you would like it." Father Patrick's voice was dry, but the candlelight caught just the faintest suspicion of moisture in his eyes.

"Connor, you do love me?" Caitlyn lifted her head from his chest at last, a touch of uncertainty in her eyes. He looked down at her, remembered that he had never told her, and smiled tenderly.

"More than my life, my own."

"Enough to wed me?"

"Aye, willingly. But . . ."

"The lass tells me she thinks she is with child. I would not like her to be left in such a state, unwed, should you die on the morrow." Father Patrick looked at Connor with as much sternness as he could muster under the circumstances.

"With child!" Connor looked stunned. His face whitened, tightened as he gazed into the kerry blue eyes that stared at him so apprehensively. For a moment the reason for her nervousness eluded him. Surely she knew that he would never deny her — The thought that it might not be of his seed popped full-blown into his brain. The brat might be the spawn of his deadliest enemy, and Caitlyn's rapist. . . . He looked down at the beautiful face he loved more than anything else in this world or out of it, and knew it did not matter. If Caitlyn was with child, he would wed her. Of whatever issue, he would give her and the bairn the protection of his name. That was all he had left to give them.

"Are you pleased?" she asked, low-voiced. His

mind boggled. He could not by the greatest stretch of good will on earth term himself pleased.

"Pleased?" he equivocated, and felt her stiffen before she pulled out of his arms. Both she and Father Patrick fixed him with chilling glares.

"Aye, pleased!" Though her voice was low, her anger was unmistakable. "As a man should be when told he's to be a father!"

" 'Tis disappointed in you I am, Connor." Father Patrick was no less disapproving than Caitlyn.

Connor stared at the two of them, then gave it up. "All right. Aye, I'm pleased. I'll certainly wed you, my own, with the greatest happiness on earth. And I'll give a name to your child, whether it be mine or no. I —"

"Whether it be yours or no!" Caitlyn's horrified interjection was echoed in Father Patrick's expression. Connor, realizing that the shame of what she had no doubt suffered at Sir Edward's hands had made her wish to block all the reasons that the bairn might well not be his from her mind, could have kicked himself for a clumsy-tongued fool.

"I didn't mean that. 'Twas a slip of the tongue, a — a misstatement, if you will." He desperately tried to retrieve the situation. Caitlyn and Father Patrick glared at him.

"It is yours! Whose else would it be?"

"Sir Edward . . ." As soon as he said the name, he could have bitten off his tongue. Caitlyn's eyes got huge. Father Patrick looked scandalized, and Connor guessed that there were large parts of her life over the past year and a half that Caitlyn had not confided to the priest.

"Could you excuse us a moment, Father? We — I think we have the need for some private speech here." Connor looked over Caitlyn's blushing head at the priest. He nodded and took himself to the door of the cell, where with an imperious kick he demanded that he be let out.

"Forgot my rosary," they heard him grumble to the guard when the door was opened and he stepped outside. "Have to have a rosary, you know. Father Simeon can hear his confession, but have to have a rosary. Do you suppose . . . ?"

The door clanged shut again, locked. Connor turned his attention back to Caitlyn, who had recovered the presence of mind to pull her cowl back over her head before the guard looked into the room. He would have put his arms around her, but he could not reach her, chained to the wall as he was. She looked up at him, wet her lip.

"I never did — that — with Sir Edward," Caitlyn said quietly, the wrath dying from her eyes. "I forgot you did not know. Sir Edward was not — he did not — he was not a normal man. He took his pleasure from — from hurting me. . . ." Her voice was very low, and at the end trailed away entirely. Her lower lip quivered, and she looked down at the rough stones beneath her feet. At the sight of her face, pale and shamed,

Connor felt his heart twist with love. He reached for her again, but the damned chain tethered him to the wall so that he could not quite get his hands on her.

"No," she said, shaking her head and stepping back. Then to his astonishment she was loosening the rope that tied the priest's robe about her waist, sliding it from her shoulders. Beneath it she wore a shirt and breeches. As Connor stared, she began to unbutton her shirt.

"What — ?" he started to ask, amazed. She shook her head again, turning her back as she pulled off her shirt. His mouth went dry at the sight of her standing there clad in nothing but a man's breeches and boots, her shining mass of hair the only thing covering the nakedness of her back. He cast a quick glance at the door. The peephole was covered by a cloth, and Father Patrick was sure to give a loud warning of his return. He turned his attention back to Caitlyn. She had dropped her breeches. The gray wool lay in a puddle around her feet. Her back was to him still. His heartbeat speeded up at his knowing that she was naked, though her hair effectively concealed most of her flesh from his eyes.

"I want you to see for yourself so you'll know that what I'm telling you is the truth. I'll not have any doubts lingering in your head about whether or not this babe is yours." Even as she spoke she swept the fall of her hair aside. Connor felt as though a fist had slammed into his stomach as he stared at the mass of scars crisscrossing her lower back and buttocks and thighs. They were nearly healed, but the faint purple marks of a whip were still clearly visible against the translucent ivory satin of her skin.

"Oh, my God," he said, the words both prayer and curse. Then curse got the better of him. He swore loud and long, rage a red mist before his eyes, condemning Sir Edward to fiery torment in a hundred different ways before it occurred to him that she was facing him now, breeches in place, already pulling on her shirt and buttoning it. The look on her face shocked him back to sanity. He could not get his hands on Sir Edward at the moment. He could, however, get his hands on Caitlyn.

"Come here, cuilin," he said low, opening his arms to her. She looked up, saw the expression in his eyes, and with a little sob ran into his arms. They closed around her, held her tight against his heart. He bent his head over hers, enfolding her in his embrace as she gasped out disjointed pieces of what she had suffered at Sir Edward's hands. By the time she had told of how she waited for the chance to kill him, she was sobbing. Connor's face was white, his eyes glinting murder as he listened. With far more passion than before, he regretted he had not killed the swine himself, when he had had the chance.

"Cry it out. 'Tis all right, I have you safe now," he whispered into her hair, and she did, weeping against the tattered front of the shirt he had worn for more than a month, clutching him as if she would never let him go. At last, little by little, her sobs lessened. Finally she gasped, and gulped, and sniffed, and lifted her head to look up at him.

"Oh, Connor, I do love you so," she whispered, a pathetic little catch in her voice.

"And I love you, my own," he answered, his own voice hoarse. Teary-eyed and pale, she was the most beautiful thing he had ever beheld in his life. His arms tightened around her. "I'll love you always, forever. If I die on the morrow, then be sure that I'll love you long after my body is cold in its grave. I'll love you through the joys of Heaven, or the torments of Hell."

"You must not talk of dying! 'Tis bad luck," she moaned, and when fresh tears came to her eyes he bent his head and kissed her. It was a long, long time before he let her go, and then only because they heard Father Patrick loudly condemning the guard because he had not found a rosary anywhere on the premises. By the time the key had turned in the lock again, Caitlyn was dressed once more as a priest, her back to the door and Connor on his knees before her as she pretended to hear his confession.

"Ahem — children. We've not much time," Father Patrick said as the door shut behind him, leaving the three of them alone. "I assume you have the matter, er, resolved to your satisfaction?"

Connor nodded. " 'Twas my mistake, Father.

The babe is mine. It could not be otherwise."

He caught Caitlyn's hand, pulled her close. She rested her head against his chest like a tired child. He kissed the cowl, then pulled it back and kissed the top of her head.

"I take it you are prepared to wed us? Here and now?"

Father Patrick nodded. "I am, my son."

"Then please do so, but first —" Connor looked at Caitlyn, his eyes tender, his voice gentle. "Will you do me the honor of becoming my wife?" he asked.

"Aye, I will," she answered with love shining in her eyes.

In moments Father Patrick was reciting the words that would unite them, while she leaned against Connor and clutched his hand. They were wed like that, in the middle of the night in a freezing cell in Kilmainham Gaol, with the soft murmurings of a priest washing over them and their hearts filled with love and the fear of imminent loss. When Connor lifted his head from the traditional kiss with which he claimed her as his wife, Caitlyn clung to him and burst into tears again. It seemed she had cried more in the past hour than she ever had before in her life.

"Caitlyn, lassie, 'tis sorry I am to remind you, but I must have a word or two with Connor before . . . We've not much time remaining."

Caitlyn trembled, clutching Connor closer. Father Patrick's words struck terror clear to her heart. Soon she would have to leave him, possibly never to see him again. . . .

"Don't weep, my own; it might harm the babe," Connor said in her ear. When she looked up, startled at the proprietary tone in which he spoke of what was no more than a tiny bud of life curled deep inside her, he kissed her, brief and hard. Then he put her away from him. Swaying slightly, she nevertheless stood on her own two feet as she drew her hands over her cheeks, wiping away the wetness left by her tears.

"You'll see her safe away, Father? I'd not have her watch . . ." He could not put the thought of his grisly end into words, not with Caitlyn standing right there beside him, heart in her eyes as she listened to his every word.

"Should it come to that, you may be sure I'll get her away. But it may not come to that. 'Tis what else I have to tell you. There's a chance . . ." And Father Patrick went on to detail what he hoped would come to pass on the morrow. When he had finished, Connor's eyes were bright with hope, and his hand was wrapped tightly around Caitlyn's.

"Father, if this works, I will personally travel to Rome and petition the Holy See for your canonization." A crooked smile at Father Patrick was so familiar that it near stopped Caitlyn's heart. The scheme had to work. She could not live in this world without Connor.

"Remember the signal; 'twill be the cannon."

"Aye, I have it. I'll be ready."

"In that case, my son, we'd best be on to other

things. Caitlyn, forgive me for the suggestion, but should things not fall as they should tomorrow, you will want Connor to be prepared. 'Tis a precaution, you understand, no more."

Though Caitlyn looked blank, Connor nodded, his hand tightening on hers before he released her. "I must admit 'twould comfort me to mount the scaffold knowing myself at peace with God."

"Then let us begin, my son."

Caitlyn, understanding at last, moved to a corner of the cell to give them privacy. Connor knelt and made his confession. Then Father Patrick recited the service for the dying over him. The familiar sound of the last rites struck deep into Caitlyn's soul. Closing her eyes tightly, she prayed with all her might that Connor would be spared. She knew just how chancy were the plans for his rescue, but surely God could work a miracle one more time.

It was done quickly, the words a soft patter against the muted background of prison noises. When it was over, Connor got to his feet.

"Thank you, Father."

"I've something for you, my son. 'Tis yours, I think, and your father's and grandfather's before you."

Caitlyn crossed to Connor's side and was enfolded against him by a hard arm as Father Patrick reached beneath his robe and pulled out an intricately wrought Irish Cross that dangled from a silver chain. Connor stared at it, then held out his hand. Father Patrick laid the medallion in his palm. Connor's fist closed slowly around it. For a moment he held the cross tightly, looking down at his clenched fist. Then he opened his hand, brought the cross to his lips, kissed it, and slipped the chain around his neck. The medallion gleamed brightly in the candlelight, its magnificence at odds with his tattered finery and unshaven jaw.

"You shall live or die as the Dark Horseman, beloved by all true Irishmen, and in your true faith," Father Patrick said, as if in benediction. "Whatever comes to you tomorrow, take comfort from that."

"Whatever happens, I am grateful for all you've done. Now, what of my brothers? And Mickeen?"

"All fine." Father Patrick shook his head. "Though they are wild with worry for you, of course. Still, I have them convinced of the need for caution, I think."

"Give them my love. Tell them — if aught goes wrong tomorrow and I in truth pass from this life — tell them that my last request of them was that they care for Caitlyn and the babe."

"Connor . . ." Caitlyn pressed closer against him, shuddering as her arms slipped around his waist. He bent his head to touch his lips to her hair even as the sound of a key sliding into the lock galvanized them all.

"Take care of yourself, wife, and our babe," Connor whispered in her ear as he put her from him.

She just had time to mouth "I love you" before the guard was opening the door. It was Connor who had the presence of mind to pull the cowl back over her head. When the guard got the door open, he saw nothing but two priests comforting a condemned man.

"Time," he said sourly, reaching for the candle. Caitlyn looked at Connor, tears brimming in her eyes. He smiled at her. Father Patrick made the sign of the cross again, said, "Be of stout heart, my son," and, putting his hand on Caitlyn's shoulder, half pushed and half led her from the cell.

XLVII

Outside the prison, Caitlyn was half blinded by tears. She clutched Father Patrick's arm as the priest hurried her along toward where their horses had been stabled at a nearby inn. The night was dark and moonless, and Caitlyn reckoned it lacked two hours yet of dawn. Drunken revels were taking place in the street around the prison even at this wee hour of the morn.

With so much activity going on, she paid no attention as a closed carriage rumbled down the street toward them. Only when it stopped did she look up. Two men leaped from the inside, brandishing clubs. Father Patrick stopped short, thrusting Caitlyn behind him.

"In the name of God, begone!" he thundered. "We've naught for you, naught worth robbing!"

" 'Tis not your valuables we're after, ye bloody idolator! We've come for the wench. Hand her over, or we'll split your skull for ye, priest or no!"

"Ye may try!" Father Patrick roared, and lunged at one of the men as he bellowed at Caitlyn to run. But there was no time. The second of the men brought his club down on Father Patrick's head with a sound like a melon splitting. Father Patrick dropped to the street like a fallen tree. Caitlyn, on the verge of flying to his defense, looked up at the men advancing on her and turned to run. She got about two feet before one of them caught her by the flapping tail of the too-big priest's robe and jerked her off her feet.

"Hold her, now! Ouch, watch out, she bites! Get her in the bloody carriage, mate, and quick!"

Caitlyn screamed and fought, but they were big, burly men and she had to have a care for the babe inside her. The drunken revelers camped in front of the prison barely paused in their merrymaking to watch. Such scenes were all too common in Dublin. Until one of them noticed that the man lying unconscious on the ground was a priest. . . .

"Eh, look there, they've bashed a Holy Father, bloody Protestant dogs!"

"A priest? They've harmed a priest? Let's be at them!" The clumsy charge of rescuers came too late. Caitlyn was bundled inside the coach as the drunken gladiators rushed across the road. She heard an outcry, and the sounds of battle, and assumed the two men who had attacked her were themselves under attack. For whatever reason, they were left behind as the coach lurched forward. She fell heavily, hitting her head against the floor. Someone caught her, held her arms. Someone else leaned over her, pressing a foul-smelling rag over her face. Even as she fought for her life, she looked up and saw the face of the man who would suffocate her. She recoiled with horror. It was Sir Edward Dunne!

And then she lost all consciousness.

XLVIII

The streets were lined with armed Volunteers. Behind them, ragged peasants craned their necks and jostled for position with better-dressed shopkeepers and lawyers and doctors. Above street level, the windows were packed with spectators. Ladies waved handkerchiefs, serving maids their feather dusters and bare hands. Grenadiers carrying Irish battle-axes marched behind the open cart in which Connor rode. Drummers pounding out a deafening rhythm on their huge kettledrums strode ahead. Here and there Straw Boys with green scarves tied around the ends of their shillelaghs broke through the ranks of the stolid Volunteers to yell Gaelic words of encouragement and wave their embellished staffs. More often than not, the outraged Volunteers rewarded their efforts with a split head.

Heavy artillery had been broken out for the occasion. It rolled with an escort of mounted dragoons behind the Grenadiers, the guns decked out incongruously in multicolored ribbons. Farther back came a band of Calvinists, who marched under a banner stating: "Open Thou our mouths, O Lord, and our lips shall sing forth Thy praise." A line of flutists was followed by a quartet of bagpipers. Their music trilled and swirled through the chill of the morning, competing with the booming of the drums, the thud of marching feet, the rattle of wheels, and shouts, catcalls, and raucous singing from the crowds. Last of all came an army of ragtag marchers who fell in behind the procession willy-nilly, fighting and carousing as they followed the condemned to the gallows.

The crowds along the pavement cheered as he passed, for all the world as if they were spectators at a sporting match. With a wry smile, Connor acknowledged the huzzahs. If he had had a hand free to wave, he would have. But the guards who stood tensely on either side of him had already tied his hands behind his back. Iron shackles linked by a length of stout chain encircled his ankles. They were taking no chances on a possible escape.

The noise was deafening, the spectacle as colorful as a circus. If he himself had not been the centerpiece of all the hoopla, he might even have been enjoying himself as were the rest of those who had turned out. But for him, the bright dawn might well have a very different ending. They would go back to their lives, to their small concerns and prejudices, to their families and homes. He could hang.

As the cart rolled up the hill leading to Phoenix Park, Connor had all he could do to stand upright against its lopsided pitching. He would not fall, if he could help it, to be dragged ignominiously to his feet again by the men who stood guard over him. If he was to die, then he would do it like a man. He would not shame his country, his family, or himself. Though he hoped, nay, prayed, that Father Patrick's scheme would come to fruition in time to prevent such a gruesome end.

Spectators stood on the gray walls lining Phoenix Park, except in those parts where the stones had already tumbled to earth. It had been built by a swindler not so many years before, and from the day the last stone had been put in place, it was constantly falling down. The deer that customarily roamed the park had been put into an enclosure for the occasion. Their human replacements occupied every bit of the vast, ordinarily empty green fields.

The gallows had been built hastily for Connor's exclusive use. After his corpse was duly disemboweled, his head would be cut off and placed on a pike to serve as a signal warning to those who might emulate his deeds. What remained of his body would be wrapped in a sheet and placed in a proper coffin in a hearse that waited beneath the gallows at that very moment, to be borne in some state to Arbour Hill. There, without benefit of word or prayer, his remains would be thrown into the pit that had long been the receiving ground for Irish martyrs: it was popularly known as the Croppies' Hole. The gallows would be torn down, and Phoenix Park would be just as it was before, with the addition of one more ghost to scare the superstitious.

At the moment, however, the gibbet stood on a small rise just inside the park, its raw lumber clumsy-looking against the graceful willows and blue pond slightly beyond.

A cheer rose up as the cart jolted to a halt in front of the gallows. The crowd surged forward, to be held back by the extended rifles of the Volunteers. A dead cat sailed out of the crowd to land on the head of one of the nearby guards. He let out a startled oath, but to no avail. More dead cats pelted the cringing Volunteers.

"Come along, now." The guards who helped Connor from the cart were not unfriendly. They were brusque men, merely doing their job. Connor stepped down, took the few steps that would bring him to the foot of the gallows, and began to climb, awkward because of the chain linking his feet. On the platform above, the black-hooded hangman waited. Connor scanned the crowd, looking, vainly, for a familiar face. All within his view were strangers. He could only hope that his brothers were where they should be. There was no sign of them either. Had everything gone awry already?

There was no time to ponder. He would carry through the plan as best he could. He closed his eyes briefly, muttering a prayer that the complicated interweaving of elements would come together as they must for his salvation. Despite the cold, he could feel himself begin to sweat. Caitlyn's face rose up in his mind's eye. Father Patrick had promised that she would be kept away today, just in case. . . . He loved her more than he had ever imagined he could love a woman — and she was carrying his child. Dear God in heaven, he was not yet ready to die!

As he set foot on the platform from which he was shortly supposed to fall to his death, another cheer went up. Rotten apples and other fruit pelted the gallows, landing indiscriminately on him as well as on the guards and the hangman. There was no priest present to give him comfort, the practicing of the Catholic religion having been outlawed years before. Though if aught went wrong, and he ended this day in Hell instead of safe away, it comforted him to reflect that Father Patrick had already given him Final Absolution.

Once he gained the platform, one of the guards stopped him with a hand on his arm and the other bent to unlock his shackles. His hands they kept bound behind him.

They flanked him across the platform to the hangman's side. The black-hooded executioner stepped forward to ask his pardon, as was traditional. Connor nodded, said, "I give it freely," and prayed there would be nothing to pardon the man for. Then the guards and the hangman alike stepped back, and Connor turned to face the crowd. Every condemned man, before he died, was permitted to make a statement. Though frequently, if what he said was unpopular with his audience, the prisoner would be jerked to his doom without being permitted to finish his (sometimes very long) speech.

Clad in the tattered silver coat, black breeches, and boots, but without a neckcloth though he had managed, in the last few minutes before they had led him from the gaol, to beg a razor and water for shaving, he was a lean, impressive figure as he strode to the edge of the gallows, looked down at the crowd that was thousands strong. A raw egg slapped into the wood just inches from where he stood. He ignored it, gazing out at the spectators as they subsided into muttering silence. The rising sun sent bright rays through the scattered cumulus clouds above that touched on the black waves of his hair and the gleaming silver medallion on his chest. He was a figure out of legend, a myth. Every man, woman, and child in that crowd had heard more than one tale of the Dark Horseman.

When at the last the crowd was silent enough to suit him, Connor took a deep breath and stood for a moment more looking out across the shifting sea of humanity. Then, with a quick inner plea that God would inspire his words, he began, his voice echoing across the fields, gaining strength as he went.

"My friends, I stand before you today condemned to die, accused and convicted of crimes against God and man. Those against God I deny. And of those I am held to have committed against man, I say to you that I committed them in the service of mankind, inspired by God against the very men who would have my blood — and yours. Aye, your blood, and the lifeblood of Ireland! Ireland, my country — and yours. An Irishman I was born, and as an Irishman I will die, and proudly too. Long after my body lies rotting in the Croppies' Hole, my soul will cleave to her green velvet meadows and floating mists, to her rivers and valleys and hills. Long after carrion crows have picked the flesh clean from my bones, I wish for you, my Ireland, and for you, my Irishmen, *slante geal*."

During that brief, passionate speech, many a tear rolled down the cheeks of many a man and many a maid. At the forbidden Gaelic of his farewell, a roar went up. Irish Catholics beyond the ring of Volunteers rushed forward. The heavy artillery that had been stationed for show at the perimeter of the park was suddenly shifted, aimed at the Volunteers. From the distance came the sound of running feet. A battalion of armed Straw Boys appeared, and scuffled with the Volunteers. Rifles fired. Women screamed. Men swore and stormed the gallows. In the distance, a cannon boomed.

"It's a Rising! A Rising!" came the cry from somewhere in the crowd. Connor waited for no more. As the guards grabbed for him, he kicked aside the plank on which he would have stood for hanging and jumped down into the blackness below as Father Patrick had instructed him to do. He tumbled into an open hearse, felt hands grab and steady him as the hearse shot forward. Then they were away with a jolt and a jerk, plowing through the battling crowds that nevertheless parted for this symbol of death.

"Whip 'em up, Mickeen, for the Lord's sake! And ours!" a familiar voice shouted, adding the last as an urgent afterthought. Connor, shifting to his side after landing flat on his face in what he rather suspected was his own coffin, looked up. Cormac, garbed all in black as befitted a pseudo-undertaker, grinned at him. Rory clapped his shoulder. Liam, on the seat with Mickeen, looked around.

"By damn, 'tis good to see you, Conn!" he yelled over his shoulder, even as Cormac and Rory sawed at the ropes binding his hands.

"Aye, we've got you safe away, yer lordship, by God we have, though it took a bloody revolution to do it!" Mickeen sounded exultant as he whipped up the horses and sent them galloping away from Phoenix Park.

"Let's go retrieve Caitlyn and get the hell out of here!" Connor grinned and wrapped an arm around Cormac's shoulders as his brother helped him climb out of his would-be coffin.

XLIX

There was fighting along the road as the coach in which Sir Edward held her captive tried to get through. Bands of Volunteers clashed with gangs of Straw Boys; peasants marching on their landlords with burning torches and scythes for weapons filled the road at several points. In some places, passing dragoons had engaged the warring peasants in battle, leaving scores dead. Corpses lay where they had fallen, Protestant and Catholic alike. Blood and death and rebellion were in the air. The proposed hanging of the Dark Horseman had touched a chord in the hearts of Irishmen everywhere. He was their own, universally beloved. It was on this love, this sense of the Dark Horseman as a symbol of a conquered nation, that Father Patrick had banked when he had sown the seeds of Uprising in the most productive ears. The peasants were in revolt, the Catholics bent on avenging themselves on their Anglo oppressors. That the Dark Horseman, whom a downtrodden people had taken to their collective hearts, had not died on the gallows after all was a matter for fervent pride among those he called his own as the tale spread from mouth to mouth.

Still groggy from whatever had been on the rag that Sir Edward had held over her mouth, Caitlyn nonetheless was aware of the turmoil raging in the countryside. Cursing, Sir Edward had called on his coachman to get them to a place of safety. But there was no place of safety on this day, and the coachman could only continue along the road and pray that they would be allowed to pass unmolested.

It was near noon, according to Caitlyn's somewhat fuzzy-headed calculations. Though the coachman had stopped several times to let one or the other warring group pass, and had exchanged comments with many, still she knew nothing of Connor's fate. From several gloating comments Sir Edward had made, she knew that he was assuming Connor had been hanged as scheduled. She hoped against hope that he had escaped.

They were headed north in the general direction of Donoughmore and Ballymara. She guessed that he was taking her to the lodge on Ballymara land where he had kept her while she was recovering from her wound. Given its proximity to Donoughmore, she did not think that it was a wise hideaway, from his point of view. But then, he was basing his plans on the assumption that Connor was dead and the younger d'Arcys on the run. And for all she knew, he could be right.

The motion of the carriage was making her nauseous, and she lay back on the seat with her eyes closed. Sir Edward had bound her hands behind her back, and her ankles, too, with ropes he had brought for that purpose. She had been unconscious for quite a while, and had been faking unconsciousness for sometime more. She and Sir Edward were alone in the coach, the man who had originally been inside with them apparently having climbed up on the box with the driver. She was reluctant to open her eyes and face Sir Edward. He would have harsh plans for her, she knew. But she also knew that, whatever happened, she could no longer allow herself to be abused. She had the child to think of. Somehow, she must find a way to escape.

The carriage jolted through a huge rut, and Caitlyn's teeth came down hard on her tongue. Taken by surprise, she cried out and opened her eyes. Sir Edward was looking at her narrow-eyed.

"I rather thought you were awake, my dear. The dose I gave you was not strong enough to induce such a sleep as you have been pretending to these last miles."

Caitlyn said nothing, merely looked at him, her expression stony.

"I expect you are mourning d'Arcy. What a pity you missed his hanging."

Still not quite sure that Connor had not indeed been hanged, Caitlyn was stung into retorting:

" 'Tis a pity I did not strike a second blow with the scissors!"

Sir Edward smiled at her, that cruel smile she had come to know and dread. She stiffened her spine and glared at him. Now that his hold on her was at an end, he would find that he was dealing with a very different lass.

"Ah, yes, from your point of view it must be. But we are never permitted second chances in this life, you know. The fact remains that you merely wounded me. I am quite recovered now — and you will soon be punished for what you tried to do. Severely punished." He drew this last out as if he enjoyed the sound of the words.

"One day I will kill you." It was a statement, not a threat. His smile faded momentarily, only to slowly renew.

"Do you know, I think I like you defiant? It will add spice as I bring you to heel."

He reached out and put a hand on her breast with casual familiarity. Though she knew he did it merely to demonstrate his mastery over her, Caitlyn could not bear his touch. But, bound as she was, she could not strike his hand away. So instead she spat full in his face.

"You bitch!" He jumped back, glaring at her as he slowly wiped the spittle from his cheek. Then, smiling, he drew back his hand and slapped her with brutal force across the face.

Caitlyn cried out as her head snapped back. She tasted blood in her mouth from a split lip. She straightened, cheek numb and burning, and saw that he was drawing back his hand to do it again.

"Whoa, there! Whoa!" The driver's startled oath, coupled with the reining in of the horses, distracted him.

"What's to do?" Sir Edward called out the

window. Caitlyn sank back with relief.

"Men in the road — brigands from the look of 'em, yer worship. They've got it blocked."

"Drive through!" Sir Edward ordered as Caitlyn heard the familiar command.

"Stand and deliver!"

"Connor!" she cried, scooting across the seat toward the window. "Connor, I'm here!"

"Get back, you bitch!" Sir Edward hissed, his slap sending her reeling as the door was jerked open before the carriage had come to a complete stop. Connor stood there, still clad in the tattered clothes in which he had faced the gallows. A murderous scowl marred his face. Caitlyn knew without a word being said that he had witnessed the slap. Behind him, she could see Cormac astride Kildare holding the rest of the horses. She knew that Liam, Rory, and Mickeen must be at hand as well.

Even as his eyes found her, assured himself that she was safe, Connor was reaching into the coach and dragging Sir Edward out.

"He's wearing a sword, watch out!"

Connor reached out, closed his hand over the one Sir Edward was using to draw his sword, and applied pressure. Sir Edward cried out, his hand falling away from the hilt. The sword rattled to the floor of the coach.

"That slap will cost you dear," Connor said through his teeth, his hand wrapped in Sir Edward's coat front. Then he dragged Sir Edward the rest of the way out of the coach and flung the man from him. "Watch him," he said briefly to someone Caitlyn could not see but knew must be either Rory or Liam. Sir Edward stood very still. She guessed that a pistol was pointed at his heart.

"Oh, Connor!" She collapsed back against the seat, smiling foolishly as he came inside the coach and sat beside her, reaching for the sword on the floor and using it to saw through her bindings.

"You gave me quite a fright, my own! When we came to the place where we were to collect you, only to be greeted by Father Patrick with the news that you'd been taken. . . . Well, I hope never to endure another morning like it, is all I can say."

"How did you find me?" Her hands were free, and she rubbed them together as he worked on her ankles.

"Some public-spirited bystanders caught one of the thugs who grabbed you. Father Patrick — ah — persuaded him to tell who had taken you, and where. We rode like the devil to overtake you. I was sore afraid that he might do you harm — the bastard. Did he harm you? Besides the slap that I saw."

"Only another one like it. Nothing more. I am so glad to see you! I was worried you hadn't gotten away."

He straightened up from freeing her feet, and Caitlyn threw herself against him, hugging him fiercely. He wrapped his arms around her, kissed the uninjured side of her mouth.

"I have you safe now, my own, and I don't mean to ever let you go again. Let me just deal with this vermin outside, and we'll be away."

"They'll be looking for you. He doesn't matter. Not any more. There's no time — you must flee!"

He shook his head, put her away from him. "I have too many scores to settle with him. Not until they're discharged will I be free."

Looking at him, she realized that to argue would be a waste of breath and time. "Be careful," she said in a husky voice, but he was already stepping down from the carriage, Sir Edward's sword in his hand. He helped her down, then turned, her hand in his, to face Sir Edward.

"When you abused my wife, you sealed your death warrant, you stinking excuse for a man," he said. "However, I will give you the choice I promised you once before: you can be shot where you stand like the dog you are, or you can perish in a fair fight."

Sir Edward, who was held at bay not only by Rory's pistol but by Liam's as well, looked wildly around. The driver and the other man were under guard by Mickeen. They showed no signs of wishing to come to his aid. The carriage had just rounded a bend in the road when it was stopped. Another bend lay ahead. A small rise blocked the view of the countryside to the east. Far to the west, across a meadow and a stream, could be seen a group of peasants, scythes in hand as they marched in what Caitlyn assumed was the direction of their landlord's house. Sir Edward's face paled as he realized that there was no help at hand. He faced death, and he knew it.

Then, slowly, his spine stiffened and his shoulders squared. He turned to face Connor, who was regarding him with steely intent.

"Very well, I'll fight you, d'Arcy. And kill you too, just as I killed your father before you. Do you know what he whispered before I pushed him over the edge of that window? He wept, 'Have mercy!' like the coward he was. As will you, just before I sink my sword into your heart."

"You lie, you whoreson bastard!" Cormac's head came up, and so did the hand holding the pistol. For a moment Caitlyn thought that Sir Edward would be shot out of hand.

"No!" Connor said sharply, holding up his hand to stop his brother before he could fire. " 'Tis a long time I've waited for this, Cormac. Do not cheat me of it."

"He lies, Conn!"

"Aye, like the lying worm he is. 'Twas said to enrage me merely. Pay no heed to it."

"Conn!" Connor looked around to where Liam had dismounted and untied one of the bundles from the pack horse they led. He was holding out a sword with a jeweled hilt to his brother. Connor crossed to him, taking Caitlyn with him, and accepted the sword.

"Watch her, brother," he said briefly to Liam and let go of her hand. Liam moved to stand beside her as Connor tested the blade by flexing it.

"Sir Edward!" Connor tossed Sir Edward's sword to him. He caught it, flexed it. Then he looked at Connor, his eyes filled with hate.

"Do I win, your brothers will kill me out of hand. Not quite a fair fight, after all, is it?" he sneered.

"You'll not win," Connor said with confidence and laid his sword aside to take off his coat. Sir Edward, scowling, followed suit. That done, they picked up their weapons and faced each other.

"To the death," said Connor; his aqua eyes glinting as coldly bright as his sword.

"To your death," Sir Edward amended, his face just as intent. The swords came together, rang in salute. Caitlyn drew in her breath. She was sore afraid. Liam put his arm around her, his hand tight on her shoulder.

"Do nothing to distract him," he warned in an undertone. Caitlyn could feel the tension in Liam, and this frightened her as nothing else could. If Liam was afraid for Connor, then she had every reason to be. Liam knew his brother's ability with a sword — and Sir Edward's.

The onlookers held their collective breath, their attention all on the two men as the fight was joined in earnest. It was silent except for the deadly clash of steel on steel, and the grunts as each combatant fought for breath and advantage. The men feinted, parried, lunged. Sir Edward was a master swordsman, Caitlyn discovered to her horror, light on his feet with superb moves. Connor, while not quite his technical equal and hampered by his lame leg, brought a strength and stamina to the fight that, as they moved over the uneven terrain without either gaining the advantage, gradually began to tell. Sweat popped out on Sir Edward's face, ran down his brow. Connor, seeing that telltale sign, smiled. Sir Edward rallied, lunged. His sword flashed along Connor's arm before Connor could jump back out of the way. Caitlyn saw a long line of red slowly appear through the tear in the white shirt, and gasped. Liam's hand tightened on her shoulder again, reminding her to keep still. She saw that Rory and Mickeen were pale and intent on the fight, while Cormac kept fingering his pistol. Caitlyn guessed that only the thought of Connor's wrath should he be cheated of his long-sought prize stayed Cormac's hand.

The wound merely seemed to increase Connor's ferocity. Disregarding the blood that dripped from his arm, he pressed his attack, driving Sir Edward slowly backward. Finally Sir Edward was gasping, his eyes desperate as he fought to turn away the savage parries that were beating him to his knees. A flick of the sword, a lunge, and Sir Edward's sword went flying through the air. A collective sigh of relief went up from the watchers. Connor paid them no heed. He advanced on Sir Edward, held his sword to the man's throat. To Sir Edward's credit, he never flinched.

"Do it and be damned to you, d'Arcy," he snapped.

Connor slowly shook his head. "I want you to

tell me how you killed my father. Every little detail of how you murdered a brave man."

Sir Edward swallowed. The point of the sword pricked his throat, drawing a bead of blood. Then, his nerve breaking, Sir Edward began to talk, describing the events of that long-ago night. When it was over, with himself branded the old Earl's murderer, Liam, Cormac, and Rory all looked ripe for murder. Connor, his sword withdrawn just a little from Sir Edward's throat, was pale but calm.

"Now I believe you owe my wife an apology."

Sir Edward looked toward Caitlyn. She could see hope gleaming in his eyes. She herself could not believe that Connor would let him live, no matter how much talking he did. But Connor had ever been a strangely moral man. . . .

"I apologize, Caitlyn." Sir Edward's voice was little more than a croak. Caitlyn, from where she stood some short distance away, could almost smell his fear. Yet she felt no pity for him. His crimes against her, against those she loved, were too great. Were she holding the sword, Sir Edward would have stood not a chance.

"I mislike your addressing my wife so familiarly. She is Lady Iveagh, to you." Connor's voice was as cold as the steel he held.

"I apologize, Lady Iveagh."

"Mount up, Liam, and take Caitlyn up the road a way."

"No!" Caitlyn shook off Liam's arm.

"Think of the child," Connor said without

looking at her. Sir Edward, realizing that his end was near, began to pant. His breathing sounded obscene in the sudden silence. Liam took her arm, and this time Caitlyn did not fight him. She mounted Meg docilely enough. To argue with Connor would be useless, and would only slow him down. But before they had gone fifty paces up the road, she turned the mare around.

"You heard what Conn said." Liam came back beside her, trying to catch Meg's reins. "Think of the babe."

"Oh, pshaw!" Caitlyn snorted, snatching the reins out of his reach. "I want to watch. Don't be a dolt, Liam. Neither the babe nor I will come to harm from just watching. Don't forget, I almost killed the bastard myself. This time I want to make sure he is dead."

Silenced, Liam watched as Connor put the point of the sword to Sir Edward's throat.

"If you know aught of prayers, now is the time to say them." Connor's voice was barely audible at that distance.

Sir Edward began to babble. Connor smiled into his eyes and thrust the point of the sword clear through his throat, so that a foot of steel showed on the other side. Blood gushed forth, stained the ground. Connor withdrew the sword with a quick pull. Sir Edward fell forward and died.

L

The following dawn found them at Inver, a small fishing village just west of Donegal. The six of them had dismounted on a promontory overlooking the Eany River, resting their horses and themselves before they rode down into the village where a curragh was waiting to take them across Inver Bay. At the farthermost sliver of land, a ship bound for the Colonies would stop that morn to pick them up and carry them across the sea to a new life. The Colonies had recently won their independence from bloody England. It seemed a fitting destination. Father Patrick had made the arrangements, knowing that there would never again be safety for any of them in strife-torn Ireland. Across the land, rioting still raged. Talk had it that troops were being called up from Connaught to quell the fighting. Caitlyn did not doubt they would succeed. Of the Dark Horseman, much was said. His legend had already grown bigger by far than the man who had given birth to it. Or maybe not.

The gentleman in question was, at that moment, wrapping his one good arm around his wife and resting his lips against her hair. His other arm was too sore to move and was secured by a sling. Her back was turned to him, but at his caress she smiled and reached up to lay her hands on the forearm that encircled her shoulders.

" 'Twill be a long journey. Are you sure you're up to it? We could mayhap go to France instead."

Caitlyn shook her head. "Don't worry so, Connor. I'm with child, not afflicted with a fatal illness. America is the place for us. Why, I'll hardly be showing by the time we get there. I'll take no harm from the crossing, nor will the babe."

"I hope not." Connor still sounded worried, so Caitlyn turned in his hold to plant a kiss on his lips. Casting a quick eye over to his brothers and Mickeen, who had taken advantage of the stop to stretch out on the ground and catch a little sleep, he bent his head and kissed her so thoroughly that her knees went weak. When at last he lifted his head, she stared, dazzled, into his eyes. They gleamed down at her as brightly as the morning sun.

"I love you," she said.

"And I love you, my own. Forever." His words were as solemn as a vow. She smiled at him, then looked down at the topaz ring that was back on her finger, where it would stay forever.

"You'll miss this," she said. "Ireland, and your land. Your family's land, for generations back."

Connor shook his head. "Believe me, my own, I can survive nicely without Donoughmore, or even Ireland. What I cannot survive without is you."

Her eyes moved over him, touched on the black waves of his hair, the lean, hard features, the firm mouth, the aqua eyes. This was her Connor, her wonderful, handsome Connor. Her husband, the father of the child she carried. Her heart swelled, and she knew exactly what he meant. As long as she had Connor, the rest of the world faded into shadow.

She smiled up at him and lifted her head for his kiss.

The employees of G.K. Hall hope you have enjoyed this Large Print book. All our Large Print titles are designed for easy reading, and all our books are made to last. Other G.K. Hall books are available at your library, through selected bookstores, or directly from us.

For information about titles, please call:

(800) 257-5157

To share your comments, please write:

Publisher
G.K. Hall & Co.
P.O. Box 159
Thorndike, ME 04986